PROMISE *and* Punishment

MINE TO KEEP SERIES
BOOK 2

VIVIAN MAE

MIDTOWN PUBLISHING LLC

Standalone:

Burning Little Secrets

Merry Little Mishap

FREAK

Mine to Keep Series:

Lawsuit and Leather

Promise and Punishment

This novel in its entirety is a work of fiction, which means all names, characters, and incidents portrayed in this production are fictitious. If there is any resemblance to a person, living or dead, it is coincidental.

Copyright © 2023 by Vivian Mae; Midtown Publishing LLC

www.VivianMae.com

Editor: The Romantic Editorial Services
Cover Design: Midtown Publishing LLC
Image @ Shutterstock
First Edition: March 2023
Midtown Publishing ISBN: 978-1-7367965-8-0

Dedication

To those who are often the other half of a story that never gets
told... I see you, I hear you.
Your story matters.

Disclaimer

* * *

This book contains content that some may find sensitive, including mental health disorders, domestic abuse, drug abuse, childhood trauma, and death. It is filled with explicit mature sexual content which is recommended for readers who are at least eighteen years old.

Important Note

* * *

Promise and Punishment is book 2 in a continuing series and MUST BE READ in order. If you've picked this book up first, you MUST READ Lawsuit and Leather by Vivian Mae, book 1 prior to starting book 2. Otherwise, it will not make any sense as it is a trilogy to be read in order.

Thank you, please enjoy!

CONTENTS

Playlist   13

Prologue   17
Chapter 1   34
Chapter 2   47
Chapter 3   58
Chapter 4   67
Chapter 5   84
Chapter 6   95
Chapter 7   102
Chapter 8   118
Chapter 9   127
Chapter 10   137
Chapter 11   143
Chapter 12   151
Chapter 13   160
Chapter 14   166
Chapter 15   177
Chapter 16   186
Chapter 17   195
Chapter 18   206
Chapter 19   215
Chapter 20   225
Chapter 21   236
Chapter 22   250
Chapter 23   262
Chapter 24   268
Chapter 25   280
Chapter 26   295
Chapter 27   310

Chapter 28   322
Chapter 29   338
Chapter 30   353
Chapter 31   365
Chapter 32   370
Chapter 33   376
Chapter 34   381
Chapter 35   388
Chapter 36   402
Chapter 37   409
Chapter 38   421
Chapter 39   434
Chapter 40   447
Chapter 41   460
Chapter 42   473
Chapter 43   483

Epilogue   501
Up Next   511
Review   513
Bonus Content   515
Acknowledgments   517
About the Author   519

Playlist

Adele - "Easy On Me"
Palace - "Never Said It Was Easy"
Sabrina Claudio - "Holding the Gun"
Harry Styles - "Adore You"
Kali Uchis & Rico Nasty - "!aquí yo mando!"
Demi Lovato - "Cool for the Summer"
Dua Lipa - "Hallucinate"
Maggie Rogers - "Light On"
Coldplay - "Warning Sign"
The Weeknd - "Call Out My Name"
H.E.R. - "Let Me In"
Sabrina Claudio - "Protect Her"

— HAMPTONS —

Alton Ellis - "Breaking Up is Hard to Do"
Bobby Pickett & The Crypt-Kickers - "Monster Mash"
Hailee Steinfeld - "Coast"
Marvin Gaye and Tammi Terrell - "Good Lovin' Ain't Easy to Come By"
Majid Jordan - "Waves of Blue"
David Cook - The Time of My Life
Mazzy Star - "Fade Into You"

ASTN - "Tidal Wave"

— Manhattan —

Xavier Omär - "Afraid"
Billie Eilish & ROSALíA - "Lo Vas A Olvidar"
Alina Baraz - "The One"
LEISURE - "Til the End of Time"
Cyn - "I'll Still Have Me"
Adele - "Love You in the Dark"

Prologue
PARKER

14 years earlier - 2008

On the corner of Palmetto Street and Wilson Avenue was the equivalent to what I always thought was a deli. I learned quickly that it wasn't.

"A *tortaria* is much better than a deli," Mateo Gomez, who owned La Parrilla—the *non-deli* on said corner—would always remind me. "Delis are cold, you smell nothing when you walk inside one. But here, you smell the chorizo before you even get to the door. I should charge for that alone, not just for my *tortas*," he overexaggerated the word chorizo, pinching his fingers in the air.

He wasn't wrong, but any time I tried to say torta, let alone tortaria, my pronunciation made him laugh, so I avoided it all together. "Why can't I just call them sandwiches?" I'd ask, knowing damn well the question made him sigh.

"Because these are better. They're hot, filled with potatoes, salsa, crema, and pork. It's not just a sandwich, it's a meal."

"A meal between two slices of bread…" I maintained.

"Wrong! Not bread, a *telera*! It's flat but sweet, *como las nalgas de mi esposa.*" Mateo always said this, but I never knew what it meant. Gloria, his wife—who spent more time cooking than eating—would smack Mateo with a dish towel whenever he'd repeat himself.

I tried not to argue with him, and honestly it was more playful banter than anything else. Mateo was the only man who'd hire me, a twelve-year-old kid, who didn't know a lick of Spanish on this side of Brooklyn.

"I'll give you ten bucks to run the route and deliver all the papers with my coupons. If anyone mentions your name while ordering food, I'll give you an extra ten cents per order. You bring in one hundred customers, and I'll add you to the *Wall of Fuego.*" That was Mateo, he was all about the recognition, and for some reason he thought he could entice me the same way. "You could be up there with Oscar De La Hoya. Think about it, *güero*!" He'd demonstrate, pointing to his collection of autographed portraits that hung adjacent to the cash register.

Güero… that was his nickname for me, which was better than *gringo*, the name some kids tried to call me at school, but I'd never let them. Mateo was different though, more endearing, like a buddy, not a bully. I just wish I knew how to say the word right.

"Wet... toe," I attempted, repeating the nickname as I rode my bike down the street, tucking Andy, the stuffed giraffe, back into the blue Ikea bag I carried the newspapers in.

I knew Mateo wanted to ask about the plush animal, and why it said *Kings County Pride* on its little green shirt, but I didn't want to explain it. How could I admit that the toy wasn't mine, or that I wasn't actually going on the paper route first, but instead, riding to Gemma's house to drop it off?

That'd be a lot to explain. If I told him about the giraffe, then I'd have to tell him how I got it, about how much work it took to win him at the county fair, a prize that wasn't for me, but rather a girl. No, not just any girl, but Gemma, my best friend, the very person who left Andy at my house during a sleepover two nights ago.

And if I told Mateo that, then I'd have to explain why it was so important to drop this off first; admitting that Gemma was more of a priority than his potential lunch crowd. He thought I was working to get onto the *Wall of Fuego,* but in reality, it was because of Gemma.

It was for her… just like how Andy was for her. Anything and everything typically was, though this in particular was special. I was saving money to buy Gemma a birthday gift in the coming months, and that was huge. What would Mateo think if I confessed that I was getting her a ring, one with a small, silver butterfly at its center? I think I'd die from the admission.

He'd surely ask if I had a crush on her, and I'd have to tell him no, but that'd be a lie, and I didn't like lying. It made me feel sick. But even if I said no, it technically wasn't a lie, because what I felt was far more than just a *crush.* I wouldn't know how to explain it to him, because maybe I wasn't sure exactly what *it* was I felt.

Like… at any moment I could explode.

Perhaps, I'd explain how my stomach always felt full, and how food always tasted dull when I wasn't with her.

Or, I could tell him how I didn't even have space in my head to think about *how* Gemma made me feel, because all I felt and thought of… was her.

What a big feeling in itself, and the most confusing jigsaw of emotions I'd ever confronted.

With her, my insides felt as though they were made of marble, but also of boiled water. I was melting and stiffening all at once, and at times I thought I was going crazy. What if I told her that myself? *"Gemma, you make me crazy."* How would that sound? Or, *"Gemma, I think I'm failing seventh-grade math because you sit in front of me, and all I do is stare at the back of your braided, auburn hair."*

I'd sound like a psycho, but considering how much we loved horror movies, it may not have been such a bad label to give myself. Honestly, I wasn't sure what I'd say to Gemma, but I'd tell her everything after surprising her for her thirteenth birthday.

Pulling up to Gemma's apartment, I made my way through the old steel door that creaked as it opened. It wasn't safe to leave my bike outdoors, so I carried it up four flights of stairs—bike on one shoulder, bag of papers on the other. I didn't mind it, considering each arduous step allowed me an opportunity to think. I had plenty of time to know what I'd say to Gemma on her birthday, but I wasn't even sure what I'd say to her now. *Hi? What's up?*

Hello sounded too simple, but everything else felt equally lame in my head. The thought of even seeing her face made me nervous, especially as I approached her door, regretting my stupid outfit. What was I thinking, wearing a grey shirt with a comic book cover on it? *Amazing Fantasy,* issue fifteen? The first appearance of Spider-Man swung across my small chest, and it made me feel like an asshole.

I blocked the thought out, knocking three times before placing my hand right back at my waist. I decided to play it cool, delivering the perfect greeting as the door opened.

"Wha'd up?" My voice cracked, shifting from squeaky to deep. I sounded silly but was saved by the fact that it wasn't Gemma who answered the door.

"Parker?" Mrs. Harrison looked down at me, but not before poking her head out. She peeked from side to side, checking for anyone else in the hall, looking both nervous and hopeful. When her eyes came back to me, they appeared more sunken in than I remembered. They were dark, but not as much as the living room behind her.

"I'm sorry to bother you, Mrs. Harrison." I couldn't tell if she had just woken up, or if she hadn't slept at all, and the way she clutched onto her robe seemed as though she could tear it apart at any moment. "I'm here for Gemma…"

"*For*, Gemma?" she asked. "Where are you taking her?"

"Nowhere ma'am," I clarified, unsure of her interpretation. "I only meant that I'm here to *see* Gemma. Not take her."

She seemed confused. "Did she call you?"

"No…"

"So, you don't know where she is then?"

"I didn't know she was gone," I stated, uneasy by the

way she asked me. She was stern, and the newly formed lines around her lips made me guess that they were born from years of frowning. I had only seen her a few times before, but not once had we ever really talked. This was by far the longest time we'd spent together alone, and I could truly see the color of her hair now, its auburn hue less vibrant than Gemma's, held in a pink scrunchy that matched her robe. She was pretty, but faded like an old photograph, her steely eyes scaring me with an intensity that made me want to leave.

"She's probably out looking for him…" she muttered.

"For who?" I asked.

Mrs. Harrison considered her answer, staring at me, then down at my bag of papers. "Never mind…" She opened the door wider. "You can come in and wait for her, *if* you want."

I looked past her again and into the house, the place where the light of day seemed lost. In the hall where I stood, it felt like early morning, but behind Mrs. Harrison, it seemed like dusk.

"Ok…" I reluctantly stared back at the stairs hoping Gemma would appear at any moment. I wanted to wait for her, considering she would be desperate to have Andy back. I pulled my bike to bring it inside, but Mrs. Harrison stopped me.

"No bikes in the house," she quickly instructed. "Leave that and the bag outside. I don't know where it's been."

I didn't respond. I only did as I was told, leaning it against the wall outside. I pulled Andy out, keeping my attention on the scuffed white tips of my converse as Mrs. Harrison stepped aside. Right when I passed, she shut the door behind me, magnifying the darkness that surrounded us.

"Do you know when Gemma will be back?" I asked, taking a seat on the brown tufted couch in the living room. It was corduroy and scratchy, but once I sat, I didn't move. The T.V. was on, playing *Terminator 2*, and in it, Arnold Schwarzenegger pulled a shotgun out of a box of roses, shooting Robert Patrick in the chest. The sound was low, but the static in the room felt deafening. Mrs. Harrison didn't answer me, she was in the kitchen for a moment before bringing me a glass of water.

"She'll be here soon enough, I'm sure," she finally responded, sitting by my side, placing the glass on an old whicker coffee table. I picked it up, noticing it was a recycled jelly jar with Tom and Jerry on it.

I took a small sip. "I hope so. I'm kinda on a schedule." The water was warm, and Robert Patrick was now shooting back at Arnold.

"And what are you doing today?"

"I'm out delivering papers for Mr. Gomez. Would you like one?"

"Not particularly," she sighed, "but thanks." She reached for my water and took a sip herself. "Why are you out delivering papers?"

"Just for… some extra money."

"Money?" Mrs. Harrison laughed, and for the first time actually smiled. "Don't your parents have enough of that?"

"Yes," I answered. "But that's their money, not

mine." I didn't like when people assumed I was made of money. Mom didn't raise me like that, and in fact, I never wanted anything that I didn't earn myself. "I'm trying to save as much as I can."

"Really?" She cocked her head, no longer looking at the screen, but directly at me. "And what could you possibly be saving for? More trading cards?"

I wasn't sure if I wanted to answer, but it felt like a good idea to do so. This was Gemma's mom after all, and that meant she was important, and if she knew how I felt, then maybe she could explain it to me, or at least, say it in a way that would make everything less confusing.

"It's for Gemma," I blurted out. "I'm saving to get her a birthday gift."

"A birthday gift?" she grinned. "You are a sweet boy, aren't you?" She combed a piece of hair away from my forehead and studied me for a minute. I was thirsty again, but the water felt far, and I wasn't sure if it was considered mine anymore after her sip. "Wait here," she lowered her voice, lifting herself off the couch to enter the kitchen. She clattered around, grabbing a few items as I watched more of the *Terminator*. The kid that played John Connor was running in a garage, kickstarting a dirt bike to get away from the killer robots. I wanted to do the same, but thought it'd be rude. What would Gemma think if her mother told her I ran away? That I was scared? Or, as my shirt painfully demonstrated, that I was some small, child?

I forced myself not to move an inch, as Mrs. Harrison returned with a small purse, resting her knee on the cushion near my lap. "Have you ever smoked a cigarette before?" she unzipped the bag.

"No," I shook my head.

"Good. It's a bad habit. It'll kill you, you know?" I nodded as she dug into her purse, pulling out a red and white packet of opened Marlboros. "But then again, some of the best things in life will kill you." She tapped on the pack, removing a cigarette and sticking it between her lips. She reached back into her purse, pulling out a small book of bar matches, placing them into my hand.

"What are these for?"

"You want to earn money, right?"

"Yes."

"Well, I'm going to pay you to light my cigarette for me," she gestured with her chin. "You can do that, right?"

"I could figure it out," I said half-confidently.

She puckered her lips. "Then strike it. And hold it for me until I'm done."

I looked away and back at the matches, flipping open the thin white lip of its cover. The matches inside were smaller than I expected, their stems almost papery with a white tip. I grabbed one, peeling it off from the rest. Mrs. Harrison leaned forward as I placed the tip near the striker, swiping it once. The match nearly bent in half, it felt so flimsily. I tried again, this time, sandwiching the match between the striker and the front cover. I pulled it through, igniting a small blue flame that lit the space between our faces.

"Good job, sweetie," she bent closer, meeting the tip of her cigarette to the match. "Now hold still."

She took a few drags, the flame in my hand contouring the swollen, red puffs under her eyes. If I had to guess, I'd assume she'd been crying, not only from the way she looked, but from how the energy itself was built into the walls around me. Just like how her smoke filled the air, so did something else. I felt it as soon as I entered, as if the static from the T.V. floated across the room and raised the hair along my arms. This home was scary, and I didn't like it.

The flame on the match inched closer to my finger, its heat drawing nearer to my skin. I wanted to shake it away, but did as I was told, keeping it in place until it reached the tip of my thumb.

"Shit!" I finally pulled away, dropping the match in the process. Immediately, I pulled my thumb into my mouth, sucking it.

Mrs. Harrison said nothing; she simply scooped up the match and dropped it into the jelly jar.

"You hurt?" she finally asked, resting her elbow on the back of the sofa.

I knitted my brows. "I think I'm ok…"

"Good. Now why are you really here?" She took a long moment to look at me, then down towards Andy.

"Gemma forgot this." I lifted Andy while my thumb continued to throb. I tried to hide the pain, not wanting to worry her, but even if I showed it, I wasn't sure if she'd even react.

"This ol' thing?"

"It's her favorite," I pulled him back to my chest.

"Oh, I know it is. I know all about how you won it for her. How you spent hours and hours at the county fair. You're not wrong, poor girl can't sleep without it."

"Yes," I laughed nervously, fighting the smoke that entered my nose.

"You did all that for her. Isn't that right, Parker?"

"Yes, ma'am."

"And you're here now, delivering papers to buy Gemma a gift?"

I nodded again, "I want to do something special."

"And you can." She kneaded her chest, nervously twisting her robe. "You can do something for her that she'll never forget." My ears perked at the idea as I looked back up.

"Really?"

"Of course… but it's really serious, and I don't know how serious you can be."

"I can be serious. I'm almost thirteen." I said, flaunting some desperate credential.

Mrs. Harrison looked disgusted. "Almost thirteen? You say that as if you'll be someone different than who you are now, and that's not what Gemma needs."

"And who would that be?"

"Everything you already are, and nothing more," she said breathlessly, exhausted from an idea that caused her hand to rest on my knee. "You're a sweet boy, Parker Jones," she stammered, her eyes more feverish and red.

"I try my best."

"No. You are, and that's why I adore you, that's why I trust you… for now anyway." The ash grew longer on the tip of her cigarette, hoisted like a dirty stick of incense that filled the room. "Do you like Gemma?"

"Of course. She's my best friend."

"And do you care for her?"

"Yes…" I lowered my voice.

The heat of her mouth felt so close, and her questions were met with a gluey, wet gloss over her eyes. I felt like I could see myself looking back, unsettled by the noise of gunshots from the T.V.

"I know you do. I knew it the moment I saw you. It was the same look my husband gave me."

"My look? What look?" I asked desperately, needing to know. Mrs. Harrison was an oracle of sorts, reading my eyes like she could tell the future. I wasn't sure if she was happy or sad, but her nails suddenly pinched into my leg.

"It's the look of love…" she choked, releasing a single, unthreatening tear. The way her lip quivered caught me off guard.

"Love?" I repeated cautiously, the word round like a big balloon in my mouth. I almost suffocated.

"Yes, and not just any kind, but the most incredible type. Love that can change a life in the most spectacular and powerful of ways. I can tell it scares you, and it should… there's so much potential there."

"Potential for Gemma?"

"Just for her," she guaranteed. "Something so precious that it could only come from answered prayers. But you care so much, and I know you'll do what's right, because this type of love is nuclear." She snatched my forearm, letting her cigarette fall onto the sofa.

"Nuclear, as in a bomb?" I worried as the ashy tip of her Marlboro rolled towards my thigh.

"As in the *biggest* bomb. And this kind of love takes everything. It explodes, and it's magnificent, and blinds you so much that you can't see anything, not even the damage it caused. It transforms the very being of your existence till all you are is the explosion itself." Her neck grew stiff, corded and strained, "Do you want to hurt, Gemma?"

Her thumb pulled at the corner of my eye, stretching it open, forcing me to absorb the entirety of my senses: every word, every scent, and every taste made me feel less like a person, and more like the wet ink to a manifesto.

She. Absolutely. Terrified. Me.

"No... never..." I finally stuttered, blinking slowly, incapable of missing a moment.

"If you love her, you'll save her from that. You'll spare her from what happened to me. And don't say no, don't say it won't happen because I see it in you, Parker. There is a love that has killed me, that has led me to who I am and the things I've done. When that bomb blows, it takes you far from home, and leaves you somewhere different than where you came from. And here, where I am, is dead." She curled her hand behind my neck, holding it still.

"I want to leave..." I whimpered, struggling to pull my arm away.

"Promise me that if you love her, you'll listen to me, because the older you get the worse it'll be."

"But you're older… don't you love Gemma, too? Can't I be like you?"

"You could never be like me. Someday you'll be a man. You'll become a problem. Now look at me, and tell me you'll be the friend she needs, never the bomb. That's how you'll hurt her."

"But… I could never hurt her."

"What you think and what you know are different. You didn't mean to burn your finger on a match, but the fire got too close, didn't it?" she asked, as my thumb continued to ache. "That's you, Parker; you're the flame, and the closer you get, the more likely it is that you'll burn Gemma. So I'll ask you again, do you want to hurt her?"

I wanted to shake myself free, but her cold insistence dug into me, haunting like a shackled ghost from the future. Could she really see that in me? She was right about everything else; about what I felt for Gemma, about what I struggled to say and describe. Every word, every sense she produced coiled itself to my core, pulling me closer to her lips and words. If she knew this already, then could she know my future too?

"I don't want to hurt my Butterfly," my lip shook, horrified by what she saw in me.

"Then, promise me, swear on your life that you'll never get close enough to love her, to be the man who ruins her life."

"I—" I barely trembled out.

"Promise you won't be like my husband, the man who left, who Gemma's out there looking for. Now, promise!" she shouted, causing me to flinch. She was broken in the most horrific of ways, burrowing into my mind like a dirty seed, and what she said made no sense, especially about where Gemma was. Her father left years ago, but Mrs. Harrison's panicked look made me feel as though it had just happened.

"I promise…" I inhaled, blinking as she finally let me loose, my arm stinging worse than my thumb. My own tears threatened to fall as she turned away.

Mrs. Harrison sniffed, her palm a rag to her tears as she reached back into her purse, pulling out a quarter, dropping it into my hand. "No one needs to know about this. No one needs to get hurt. If you keep her safe, you'll always be a sweet boy…" she squeezed my palm shut and leaned in to kiss my cheek, her lips wet with tears. "Thank you for holding the match."

I looked down at the quarter, terrorized by everything she said—about love, about Gemma's dad, and my role in her life. But I refused to believe it. I went to open my mouth—

"PARKER!" Gemma slammed the front door, shrilling. I turned around as she stood in a pink turtleneck, her hands clenching a tiny bag of cookies. She was home but not excited to see me; in fact, she seemed mad, if not frantic. "You need to go!" She shook her head, lifting me up without another word.

When I stood up the stuffed giraffe fell off my lap and onto the floor. "But I brought you, Andy!" I clutched the quarter in my hand as she stared at him, then scowled at her mother. "I figured you'd want him."

"Thank you. But leave!" She looked like she was about to cry as she twisted my arm, forcing me out.

Mrs. Harrison didn't blink once, instead mouthed the word *promise* as she stared into my eyes.

"Gemma, are you ok?" I asked, shoved out the door. "What's happening? Talk to me!"

For the first time ever, Gemma didn't look back at me, instead, focused on her mother as she slowly inched the door closer to her body. I knew it then and there, the things Mrs. Harrison said were true. Whatever happened, whatever Gemma's father or mother did, led her here. It was a bomb, and the tears that burst from her eyes made me want to die.

"Parker…" she whimpered. "I'm sorry."

Gemma slammed the door, locking me out with a quick click of the latch. I stood there, out from the dark and into the light of the hall.

Everything suddenly became so silent that I nearly forgot to breathe, lost in the realization of what I knew was true all along, of something I felt from the moment I first met her.

Before, I didn't know how Gemma made me feel, because all I felt was her. That wasn't the case anymore, and in place of that was the worst kind of truth…

I was completely in love with my best friend.

And I could never tell her.

Not on her birthday, not ever.

And as much as I wanted her to know, I knew I never wanted to see her face like that again; worried, filled with tears, and pain. Could I really do that to her? Could I be the person who ruins her life, a match to burn her finger? I wasn't sure, but knew I never wanted to find out.

Slowly, I looked to my side, seeing that my bike was now missing, along with Mateo's newspapers. Someone stole them.

For a moment I paused, unsure of what to do. I wanted to knock again, I wanted to get her out, but instead I walked away.

Gemma Rose Harrison was the love of my life, and I'd protect her from that, even at the cost of my own desires.

I knew now…

This was my promise.

This was my punishment.

Chapter 1

ALEJANDRO

Present Day

In my lifetime, I had already broken seven different bones. Four ribs, one toe, and two in my hand from a punch to the face of a man I hardly cared to talk about. The others were earned while shooting scenes in a movie, those where I'd jump off roofs or crash through windows.

It was quite possible that I was on the brink of breaking another. Removing handcuffs wasn't hard at Midtown Precinct South, a police station that was clearly under budgeted. They still had an old faulty brand that could be removed easily with the precise slam of its key post. Done incorrectly though, it could fracture my wrist.

The pain would probably be worth it, considering the promise of freedom was such a delectable idea. If anyone saw me do this, they'd know instantly that chaining me to the fixed steel table was just an illusion of control, a psychological tool I could use if needed. The next person to walk through that door would be prepared to ask me questions, ones I didn't want to answer. Honestly, it wasn't just their questions, it was their intent. They wanted to exploit my weaknesses, and it wouldn't be difficult if they started with Gemma…

I couldn't risk them bringing up her name, revealing the noticeable reaction my face would cause. I still wasn't sure where they put her or if she was even here. She was my weakness, because at this moment all I could think of was her; even the handcuffs were a reminder of Gemma. I thought of when she picked up the pair she found on my coffee table the first time she came to my penthouse. If only she knew I'd been watching her the whole time from upstairs, not lurking, but admiring. She had no idea how dangerous it was to hold those, how I wanted to click them around her wrists, to condemn her to the post of my bed. I'd pull her arms right over her head, just to hear her gasp, just for the assurance that air was filling her beautiful lungs with fuel to speak my name.

If only she could say it now, over and over again, convincing me that I was someone better than I felt, just as she did eight hours ago when we kissed on the roof.

Enough… Alejandro…

I couldn't think of her, not like that, not now. I had to fight back my eagerness, just as I did around her time and time again. With her I'd scowl so hard, suppressing how desperate I was for her affection, not wanting to look so utterly helpless.

"Hola." The lambent expression of a bald and broad-shouldered man made his way through a clanking steel door. That wasn't a greeting, that was a sardonic hello from Sergeant Dennis Fields, who undoubtedly didn't speak Spanish. "Not surprised to see you again, O-migo."

"Mr. Fields, I'm glad you could join me," I grinned, making him feel at home.

"It was only a matter of time; I just didn't expect it to be so soon." He carried a blue and white cup of coffee, its Greek letters begging to be read out loud.

"*We are happy to serve you.*" I recited its written sentiment, mocking Fields's enthusiasm. "Is that what the New York Police have been doing recently?"

"Not well enough," he took a seat, passing me the coffee. "Especially with people like you out there."

"It's not your fault. I just have better lawyers than you have officers." I provoked, remembering from previous interactions how easy he was to antagonize. I had already talked to him in this room before. The night after the party at The Pierre, he locked me up to this very table, but unfortunately, unlike that night, today I was absent of legal assistance.

"And where is that pretty lawyer of yours?"

"She landed an hour ago…" I took a moment to look up at the pale white clock on the concrete wall, "which gives you maybe thirty more minutes until I'm gone." When I called for Lina, my lead attorney, her secretary told me she had already left LAX late last night. She'd been out in California, handling another troubling task.

"Does she fly a broom?" Sergeant Fields laughed at his own joke.

I didn't reply, opting to study him with the same

calculated stare I gave anyone who entered my sight. I knew immediately that poor humor was a way to deflect his fragile, little ego.

A bead of sweat dripped along his forehead as he patted the sides of his unorganized papers. I tried not to gloat. Fields wasn't a man, just an intimidated boy. I knew so much just by the details he'd thought I'd miss.

At first, his lateness was something I took as a spiteful tactic to waste my time, but now I knew it wasn't. Sergeant Fields had missed a button along his salmon-colored shirt, leaving a gaping hole that revealed his pink, sweaty belly. He must have been rushed and skipped it by accident, his eagerness to appear in this room further evident by the dark splotch of coffee that fell beside his tie. He had probably sipped it before it was cool, burnt his tongue, and spit it back into the cup, the very cup he pushed my way now.

His boorish chuckle puttered out as he realized how closely I paid attention to him. I couldn't even bring myself to smile at his little fucking joke, searing my eyes so deep into his, daring him to blink. The look we exchanged, though brief, was rewarding as his lip began to twitch.

"You smoke still?" He had the audacity to pull out my own pack of cigarettes, placing them out of reach.

"Only when I'm stressed," I feigned interest.

The truth was, I did want a smoke, but I'd been trying to stop despite my urges. I considered it a practice of self-control, something I lacked around Gemma. Though she didn't mind the smell of my smoke, I knew it bothered her, and I especially knew that the flick of a lighter sent her into a troubled stare. It was enough to make me quit the habit all together, though, without their aid, I wasn't sure how else to quench my needy hands.

Shit.

I was thinking of her again, wishing my thumb could brush her plump, bottom lip, and for a moment my face dropped.

"You're scared of what I got for you, aren't ya?" Sergeant Fields noticed, sifting the papers like a deck of cards. He licked his finger and removed a sheet out from the pile. "One violation of trespassing, one count of concealment of a deadly weapon…"

"Deadly weapon?" I raised a brow.

"A switchblade…"

"Hardly…"

"It's illegal."

"By that standard, are toothpicks illegal as well?"

"Don't be a smart ass." He continued to flip the pages, searching for what he could. So far he only caught me on the roof of an abandoned building with a switchblade in my pocket. He grinned before letting out a long whistle. "This one's my favorite," he muttered, clicking a pen in his hand. "One count of reckless endangerment… oh that's a big one, buddy, but I'm sure it's familiar."

"No one was in danger."

He chuckled, "Sure. I've heard that before."

Having Gemma on the roof was far from dangerous. True danger? I'd never allow it. Keeping her close to the edge was not the same as risking her falling. I was there, I could stop it; and for once I felt like I had control, like I could prevent the bad things from happening, things like in the past. *That* moment with her gave me purpose… *that* gave me life.

Could she tell that my kiss was more? Not just an affirmation of all the things I ever felt, but a desperate thank you?

I knew now I was capable of being more, of being someone just like her—patient, kind, worthy of love. If she could see that in herself, then maybe she could see it in me too, making me less scared to open up, to show her who I was and who she was meant to be; my redemption for those who I should've been there for, but couldn't, people like my brother… people like Natalie.

"Gemma's safe," I replied, less for Sergeant Fields and more for myself.

"Just like that poor girl at The Pierre?" He brought up the topic to crawl under my skin. "You can't be trusted with anyone, Rivers… First, the girl at the hotel, now this bitch on the roof of an abandoned building? You have a knack for getting girls killed, don't you?"

I slammed my wrist along the table, freeing myself from the cheap cuffs with a loud bang. Sergeant Fields scooted back, screeching his chair as he placed his hand on the holster of his gun. His eyes popped, as if air filled them from the other end of their beady existence.

Carefully I leaned forward, testing the limits of how courageous—or rather—foolish he'd be. I lifted the pack of cigarettes, pulling one out, unable to deny at least the butt of its cherry taste to touch my lips.

"Don't ever threaten me with a gun…" I bit through the muffled guard of my cigarette. "You ever pull that shit on me, and I'll shove it down your fucking throat. And as for Gemma… you say her name again, and I'll kill you."

Whatever cat and mouse game we played seemed far too real for even Sergeant Fields, who was smart enough to decipher a good actor from an actual pissed off man. What did he see to make him believe the words I just said? Confidence? Desperation? Everything that Gemma bore in me was like the thirst evoked by a Jalisco sun. I'd do anything to capture that feeling, to savor it, because now with Gemma, I had a purpose, rather than a distraction. I wouldn't sink or fall… I'd float.

"Threatening an officer?" He finally spoke, almost as if he forgot the authority he held. "Believe whatever you want, but don't think for a second that you're anything but a horrible person. That girl out there, she doesn't know you, she doesn't care for you. How could she? Tell her who you are, then you'll really know what she thinks of you." Sergeant Fields's cheeks rose with gratification, finally succeeding in making me avert my eyes. I looked down at my hand, at the black rose and ink that reminded me how scared I was about admitting my past.

"That's enough." A sturdy female voice appeared casually by the steel door. "My client has already requested a lawyer, you know better than to be here, Mr. Fields." Sergeant Fields sighed as Lina Castillo entered the room. Her normally black, wavy hair was pinned back, probably to tame the unkempt frizz of an overnight flight; yet somehow, her dark eyes and red lips seemed fresh, as if she got the best sleep of her life. She was, in fact, a greater actor than I could ever be.

"You have your fucking work cut out for you," Fields snipped.

"Your charges won't hold up." She diverted her attention to her phone, "I already read the police report, and we can agree on one thing. There's certainly some reckless endangerment here."

"Good, you can join him at the arraignment. The judge is ready to notify him on the charges."

"Careful," she smirked. "You're in over your head."

"Hardly. I'm good at my job, just as good as you are at bullshitting." Fields began to pull his paperwork out, but Lina raised a finger.

"The reckless endangerment is not with my client, it's with the city of New York. I drove by the abandoned building: the one being demolished to make way for a state-funded institution. There's just one problem… it's in direct violation of local law."

"Bullshit." Fields crossed his arms.

"Bullshit is right, just like these charges. All construction zones must be in compliance of local safety regulations, which requires a fence of eight feet minimum in height to be placed on the inside edge of a walkway." She glanced over at me, before looking back at Fields, giving a shit-eating grin that cost me over eight-hundred dollars an hour. "You could imagine my disappointment at the city when I drove by and no such fence existed." She frowned, "So unsafe…"

"You're a bitch," Fields sneered, slamming his folder shut.

"That's me alright, and unless you want the commissioner to know that their sergeant is the reason for a colossal fucking lawsuit, I suggest you drop the charges," she smiled again. "Now tuck your tail between your legs and go home and kiss your wife. Tell her how your career as an inadequate leader was saved by a *bitch.*"

Fields said nothing, and, in reality, what was there to say? He walked past her, slamming the door, his otherwise noticeable height almost minuscule compared to Lina's poise.

"He's afraid of you," I said, my first real greeting to her.

"He should be. Also, I should charge you double for how good I am," she unplugged the security camera, avoiding any recordings.

"It would be worth every penny," I replied as she made her way over, sitting in the chair where Sergeant Fields just sat, remaining unusually quiet. A silent Lina was a concerning Lina, and considering what I sent her back to California to do, it had me slightly on edge. "How was L.A.?"

She leaned forward, fiddling with the coffee cup on the table. "Challenging. But I think Miguel got the message."

I *hated* that she even said his name.

"Suing him isn't enough… the man has nothing," I sat back into my chair as Lina pulled a lighter out from her suit jacket. She didn't smoke but always carried one for me. I still held the cigarette in my lips, and thank god Gemma wasn't here, because the flint wheel sounded particularly sharp as I rolled my thumb for a flame.

"Suing is all we have. It's all I'm legally able to do."

"It may not be good enough, especially if he's eager to talk."

"All this attention from The Pierre Hotel has him motivated. He seemed pretty upset, but also very vague."

"What did he tell you?" I inhaled a full drag of my cigarette, enjoying it like it was my last, though I knew it wasn't.

"Nothing, which gave me little leverage. Alex, between you and him, I'm in the dark…" she shrugged.

Her mention of the *dark* was evoking. Again, I thought of Gemma, of our time at The Met, of her vulnerabilities. I'd pluck those insecurities out from her like dirty thorns, reminding her she wasn't some burdened rock, but instead, my *piedra preciosa*, my precious gemstone.

I once said it was in the dark where I found her, but sometimes I wondered if what happened was actually something far crueler. Did I find her, or did I drag her into it? I accepted her, but could she do the same for me? I wasn't sure if Gemma and I could survive the truth; both from The Pierre Hotel and the past I tried to hide in California.

"I'll have to make the message clearer to Miguel…" I decided out loud.

"I'm a good lawyer, so you know that I'm here to tell

you to be on your best *fucking* behavior," she advised sharply.

My impulsive track record had made her equal parts rich as it did stressed.

"I always play nice," I responded, hiding the need to snarl, to get on a plane and go to L.A. and get rid of Miguel myself. "Alex..." Lina said. "As your legal counsel, I'm here to remind you that anything you share with me is confidential. Attorney client privilege is something I don't take lightly. Now, I'm going to be straight with you. No bullshit. No fucking around." She hesitated, "Is there anything you want to tell me about your past? Anything I need to know or be prepared for?"

Yes. I wanted to say, but *no* was all anyone would ever get.

"My past is pretty." I grinned unconvincingly, but she accepted it with the roll of her eyes.

"If you say so. You're set to leave now," she motioned with her hand. "Just stay out of the way of the other attorney's business. Tonight was a fucking headache."

"What other attorney?" I blew out a final puff of smoke, dropping the cigarette into Sergeant Fields coffee cup.

"Please, save the act," she sighed. "The attorney defending the husband and family that is suing you because of The Pierre Hotel?"

I cocked my head, I wanted to laugh because of how alarmed she appeared to be. "Who exactly? I'm in the dark…" I repeated her words, lost to who she was talking about.

"Your friend out there? Gemma?" she asked, assuring her name. "She's roommates with our opposing counsel, and I don't say that lightly." At first I cared little about what she said, focused on the fact that Gemma was out there waiting for me. I couldn't imagine how she felt, how little sleep she had, or how much she worried. It made me sick; it made me think of the person who caused this to happen.

"The boy?" I asked to clarify. The supposed best friend that Gemma clung onto, the man who landed me in jail.

"He is definitely not a boy…" Lina shook her head, "He's a man, and a big fucking problem of one too. If there ever was a threat to this case, it's him and his reputation. The guy wins, Alex, probably charges more than I ever could." She propped open the door, allowing the morning sun to seep into the sterile blue light of the room where I was held. "That pretty girl out there is waiting for you, but she's probably about to go back home to the biggest lawyer that New York has ever seen."

"What's his name?" I massaged the knuckle of my hand, tracing the tattoo once more.

"Parker…" she stopped me from leaving, "Parker Ellis Jones…"

I repeated his name to myself, remembering every word Gemma ever said of him. I was in his house, I was in his closet with Gemma in my hands, twisting the band of her panties along my fingers unbeknownst to him.

I smiled and reconsidered a previous thought.

In my lifetime, I had already broken seven different types of bones. Four ribs, one toe, and two in my hand from a punch to the face of a man I hardly cared to talk about: Miguel out in L.A.

Now… I wondered what it would be like to break an eighth.

Chapter 2

GEMMA

As much as I wanted a hot green tea, the thought of displacing the sweet cherry taste I'd absorbed from Alejandro's lips was a discouraging idea. It was bold: masculine like tobacco tended to be, but light enough to lie across my tongue. He kissed me hours ago in a moment that felt so monumental it bordered on catastrophic. The feeling I earned, the feeling I'd been holding onto since I entered this building, wasn't caused by the staggering height from where we first kissed, but instead, from the fact that I'd allowed myself to be vulnerable.

Alejandro showed me what it was like to be him, to feel the contradicting and maddening sense that formed the man I still barely knew. He was both freed and shackled, floating and sinking, desperate to show me how badly I was needed, how I, the poor girl from Bushwick, gave him hope again.

Everything he did had purpose; therefore, he saw purpose within me. From the flowers on my dresses, to the way I crossed my legs, and stroked my neck. There was no hiding from his narrow attention, and if I had any chance of knowing this man, then I'd have to be as observant as him, because before Alejandro was arrested, before our night tumbled into a spiraling disaster, he requested, or rather demanded, a response to a non-question I was unprepared for: *tell me you belong to me.*

And while I briefly fell asleep in the lobby of this old police station, while I dreamed of him, I answered his request in a million different ways: *yes, of course, take me!* Each answer was better than the last, each more desperate and excited, but marked with an ugly asterisk of inevitable concerns. He wasn't from New York; he wasn't a clean-cut version of safety and predictability. He was possibly the very bad boy that my own mother would love to have, and that made me incredibly nervous.

"Here you go, hun." A receptionist who kept me company all night brought over the very same green tea I contemplated on even drinking. "It's very hot, so be careful. We have no more sugar, and I can't imagine creamer tasting nice for this type of tea."

"Thank you," I unintentionally croaked; my throat dry from the lack of sleep. The sun was already rising, reminding me how long I'd truly been waiting. "Do you have any idea when he'll be released?" I asked, possibly for the fortieth time.

"His lawyer arrived while you were asleep. I'm certain it won't be long now. Meanwhile, are you sure you don't want to make a call?" She asked again, even though she talked to Parker earlier on the phone to confirm I was safe. That was more information than he even deserved.

The nerve he had on reporting me as a missing person, of the absolute trouble he caused, drove me insane. I wanted to scream in his face, to actually push him. I felt humiliated, but also completely conflicted with the meaning of his intentions.

"I don't have anyone I want to call. Thank you for the tea, though." I politely refused, burning my tongue as I took a sip.

The taste was overwhelmingly bland, missing the honey Parker always remembered to add; four equal drops stirred in. And while a part of me did miss Parker, the other part felt less than thrilled to see him—actually more like completely and totally upset.

There was no doubt in my mind that he hated Alejandro, but how he felt about me was the most devastating mystery that circled my entire life.

I still didn't understand why he reported me missing and figured this could have been solved with a simple call, or so I thought. It wasn't till I arrived at the precinct that I realized I hadn't even brought my phone. It was most likely back at home, still on the couch from when Parker sat dangerously close, brushing his arm against mine. I wondered if he knew Alejandro broke into his house by now and hid in my closet. Or was that still my dirty secret?

I stretched my legs and made my way to a vending machine, my stomach aching as I looked over the small candy bars and prepackaged pastries that sat in coiled metal claws, unprepared for my own shocking reflection. My mascara was totally smeared at the edges from yawning, and my skirt was much shorter than I cared for it to be anymore. I certainly looked the part, as if I were a party girl, or more so, Alejandro's *girl.*

"Do you mind?" A bald and flustered man brushed me aside, grimacing as he made his way towards the vending machine. Every bit of him was pink but his knuckles, their blood drained as he dug his hand into his pocket, cupping a ball of loose change.

"It's all yours…" I stepped aside, watching as he fed the machine.

"That fucking prick…" he darted his eyes between a bag of M&M's and a Honey Bun, pouring his aggression into each punch of the keypad. "Why are you dressed like that?" He turned in my direction, side-eyeing his Honey Bun as it dispensed.

"Like what?" I tugged at my skirt, already feeling self-conscious.

"It's… just a lot."

"It was for a night out. Not that I need to explain that to you, but I'm sure you can imagine I wasn't expecting to be here."

"No one ever is. Still, the way you dress says a lot about you." He bent over for his breakfast, splitting open the pastry, taking a quick bite. "But the two don't match."

"Match?" I crossed my arms, tugging my leather jacket close to my chest.

"Your face and that skirt." He shook his head, "It's wrong, all wrong."

"It's not. There's nothing wrong with what I'm wearing."

"Of course there is. I'm not trying to be an asshole, I'm just making an observation. It's your face… it's too innocent, but that outfit… it's…" he shrugged, deciding a delicate choice of words. "I don't know, a little hectic. You don't seem like the wild type is what I'm saying."

"And what type do I seem like exactly?" I grew more irritated, exhausted, hungry, and mad at his declaration of my *innocent* face. Innocence felt like an agitating word, ever since Claire used it as a way to describe its absence in Parker's character, as if he couldn't be trusted around me. I hated acknowledging anything she said.

The man chewed through his mustache, eyeing my growling stomach. "Are you hungry?" he asked, not answering my question.

I didn't answer his.

He sighed, scooping out another handful of quarters, sticking them into the machine. "I didn't mean to insinuate anything. I'm a father. I just worry about girls like you around guys like him."

"Like who?" I snipped, watching as he pressed the buttons to free a package of white, powered donuts.

"Guys like Alex Rivers," he struggled, bending over once again, handing it to me, "he's just no good."

"You don't know him," I glanced down at the donuts, quietly opening them up.

"Honey, I've been on the force for over thirty years. I know the type."

"Maybe, but not from my perspective," I said rather confidently, drained from having my experiences belittled by others.

"And how long have you had to form that perspective?" he asked, causing me to go quiet. It had been almost two months since I'd met Alejandro, and was that enough time to be so sure?

"Long enough," I settled.

"I hope so for your sake. I got a daughter your age, and I can't imagine her around a guy like him. His scene, his lifestyle. It's not… safe, especially those parties…" he chewed.

"Parties?" I asked, but knew all too well what he meant.

The Pierre.

This was another warning just like Parker's. I still wasn't sure what I was missing; Alejandro was the pinnacle of protection; he saw me when others didn't and held me tighter than anyone had before. To hear this constant and repeated warning felt tiresome, or more so, deafening. I stared back at my reflection, and at my skirt, lingering on Claire's previous warnings about men like Alex. I refused to believe I was anything like her, misguided by a man who was attempting to steal my heart.

"Yes… parties. I can't see another girl like you, an angel from Belmont Hills, fall into trouble," he said, clearing his throat.

"Belmont Hills?" I frowned, unsure of what he meant, or who he was talking about. He got quiet as he realized the figures standing by his side.

All the exhaustion I felt, the crick in my neck and bones, the discomfort of a cold night in a stale, bright room instantly disappeared as I suddenly saw the darkest angel.

"Hey there, good girl…" The melodic and staggering charm of Alejandro rolled across the room, warming me hotter than the boiled tea in my hand. I blushed, reddened by his greeting, almost as if it were the first time all over again.

"Alejandro?" I whimpered with surprise, but was hushed by the comfort of his body as I threw myself into his arms. My god, the heady lure of cherries seeped out from his gold, glowing skin. All I saw was him, his dark ink tatted everywhere, darker than his brows or chocolate eyes. He wrapped himself around me, our position feeling permanent as if carved into stone. I buried my head in his chest, digging myself closer into his body as I fought the urge to cry, cherishing the moment, an embrace that was instantly met with the tilt of my chin. Before he said anything else, he kissed me. Hard. His lips pressed into mine so securely, so definitively, that I questioned if I was even awake.

"Sorry I kept you waiting. Are you ok?" He leaned his head against mine.

"Better…" I laughed more awake, but also eager to fall asleep in his arms.

"Better is good, but not good enough. I'm taking you back home with me," he dared, teasing the almost eternal rest of his bed. I imagined it was the size of a pool with soft sheets and cool pillows for our hot bodies.

"That'll have to wait." A woman in a sharp, black suit gazed at her phone, before shooting a tempered look at the man who bought me donuts. "Sergeant Fields…" she sighed, annoyed as if she just overhead the things he was saying. "I trust you're leaving my client alone? And more importantly, keeping your mouth shut?"

"Client?" I asked.

"Lina is my attorney, but now, she's also yours," Alejandro confirmed.

"It's my absolute pleasure to meet you, Miss Harrison." Lina greeted, shaking my hand with a level of professionalism that made my outfit feel even more inappropriate.

"Thank you… I don't know if I'm in trouble, but I can't possibly expect you to pay for a lawyer…" I shook my head.

"Don't be ridiculous," Alejandro grinned. "As if I would ever let anything happen to you. I told you I'd take care of you, and that involves securing only the best of attorneys at your disposal. Lina kept your name out of the papers, even after The Met."

"That was no easy task, but easy is never fun." She turned to the apparent Sergeant Fields who scowled with the Honey Bun still in his hands. "You can leave now," she declared, shooing him away with the wave of her hand.

He listened, but not before taking a moment to look me in the eyes. "Be careful…" he warned, garnering a sincerity I could only imagine coming from a father as he walked away.

Alejandro rubbed his large thumb on the back of my hand, returning my attention. I scanned his perfectly, clean face, unblemished from the awful night we had. Was he used to this, staying up late, being unfazed by the lack of sleep? Maybe it was a side-effect of his supposed wild parties, and how they possibly lasted into the late hours of the night.

"You're cold." Alejandro lifted the leather jacket he

held in his hand, placing it over my shoulders. Its weight was heavy, covering me in the stale prison musk that masked the summery scent of his faded cologne. I felt little within its wings, but even smaller within Alejandro's arms. "Shall we?"

"Not so fast," Lina chimed in. "I can't have you leave and rest the day away. We have business to attend to."

"It can wait."

"No. *This* can't." She waved her phone in the air, "Business in California needs your attention. I'll need you indefinitely."

"Is this about the case?" I blurted out, not realizing how nosey I sounded. The natural creases of Alejandro's face relaxed, amused by my question. Lina's did not. She raised an eyebrow, appearing more curious about what I may know versus the question itself.

"Other business…" Alejandro corrected. "But you can stay at my penthouse. Whatever you need I'll take care of it."

"Actually, I should probably go back home," I answered, pulling his jacket closer to my chest.

"Home?" He cocked his head, sounding unenthused.

"There are things I need to take care of. You'll be busy with Lina and work… I still have to finish your suit." I shrugged, reminding him how our relationship truly began.

"I can arrange for all of that to be sent to my place."

"I couldn't possibly do that. I need my space."

"Space… home…" he repeated my words. "All with

a Mr. Parker Jones?" My heart stopped, feeling as if I were entirely caught, my best friend now an unintentional secret. He said Parker's name for the first time to my face, something I never shared with him before.

"Yes. With Parker. I'll take care of that. He needs to hear from me."

"I'll come with you," he calmly caressed my hand.

"I'd advise against that, Alex," Lina shot a look, and I agreed.

"She's right. This is already complicated as it is. Let me take care of this. Let me spend time working on your suit, making it perfect. I want to do a good job for you."

He smirked to himself, unbothered by the idea. "That's not even a worry of mine. I know you'll do well. My good girl always does."

My good girl. In his mind I was already his, and as much as the idea thrilled me, the questions still unanswered made me nauseous. How could I be his when he still couldn't be mine? Our relationship was different, it hinged on all the secrets we wanted to share but couldn't; it wasn't the fantasy I had with Parker, who I still wasn't ready to face.

I didn't want to hear what others had to say about Alejandro anymore, because I knew what I felt in this moment: secure, happy, calm. But was that just an illusion? Was it a byproduct of my mother, who always trusted the wrong guys? I refused to believe it, to settle on the explosions to come, on the gradual but inevitable truth Alejandro would speak. Maybe I'd tell him about the night my father left, and maybe he would tell me about his family, the ones whose deaths he scolded me about before our night ended.

This could work, and maybe I could accept the possible truth, that just because Alex Rivers was a *bad boy*, didn't mean that Alejandro Rivera-Marquez, himself, wasn't a *good man*.

Chapter 3

GEMMA

"Parker!" I shouted, swooping the hair out from my face, slamming his apartment door shut. The living room was bright, annoying me with the early morning sun as I threw my keys on the counter, still clutching my paper cup of tea from the precinct.

Parker was near the hall, lifting his body on a pull-up bar, grunting, shirtless, pumping out a rep that flexed the hardness of his strong back. He ignored me as music blared in the background, and instead of competing with it, I yanked the speaker chord loose from the outlet.

"Parker Ellis Jones! What the hell did you do?" I scolded so loudly, it burned my throat. He finally let go of the bar, landing on his feet with an immeasurable thud. If I weren't so pissed, I'd probably be nervous, his astonishing height intimidating enough, but more so menacing now with the coiled veins on his large, brawny arms. He turned to me with a glare.

"What the fuck were you thinking?" he growled harshly, filling the room with a chest rattling rumble.

"You don't get to ask me that! You weren't the one waiting all night at some police station. How dare you?"

"Excuse me?" He stepped closer, taking the tea out of my hand, slamming it on the counter. I tried not to avert my eyes from his as every bead of sweat rolled down his body, seeping into the loose grey sweats that dipped below his pelvis. "Do you have any idea what you put me through? How worried sick I was?"

"You have no right to invade my life. Parker, you called the cops! You had Alejandro arrested! Do you realize what you've put him through?" I threw my hands in the air, still unable to fully wrap my head around the insanity of the situation. "I'm not some animal to be hunted or some child that needs to be rescued."

"No, don't even," he warned pointing his finger right in my direction. "Don't talk to me like some brat. I'm not your fucking daddy, but since you're sneaking out like a little girl, I'll treat you like one."

Parker gaveled his fist onto the table, his pupils narrowed into black dots and swirling green pools. I scoffed, taking notice of the unbelievable light that poured through my gaping doorway. I pushed myself past his body, getting closer towards it, covering my mouth. It was completely destroyed.

"What the hell, Parker?" I screeched. "What did you do to my door?" I marched back into the living room, watching as he wiped his sweaty face with a towel, tossing it across the table. "You and Camilla were hanging out. Everything was fine. How did we go from *that* to *this?*" I pointed back to the hall, demanding an explanation.

"Do you know what happens when someone undoes the latch to a fire escape here?" He twisted the drawstring of his pants, yanking it tight. "It's timed,

Gemma, it's not meant for coming and going as you please."

"Timed?" I asked, suddenly less confident.

"Yes! Timed as in sensitive to how it's used. You unhooked it, which caused the delayed alarm to sound. And why?" he asked, already angry at the answer, leaving me unsure of what to say. If I told him that Alejandro actually snuck in and took me away, he'd certainly lose his mind. I couldn't say that, not right now.

"I wanted to go out," I defended as if I were some victim.

"With *him*?" He scowled.

"Yes, with him, and why is that so wrong?"

"Cause the way you did it panicked the whole building, my-fucking-self included. And, of course, he had something to do with this. I'm not surprised." He threw his arms up.

"It's not his fault."

"It is. Everything he touches gets ruined, everything he does has consequences that you're not prepared for. Don't debate me on this, Gemma."

"That's not fair. I know him better than you, just like you claim to know Camilla better than me. Where's the boundary here?"

"You know him better?" he asked. "So I'm supposed to ignore all the case filings I've read about him, just because you *think* you know the actor who *pretends* for a living?"

"Real mature… So his profession is below being a lawyer, the job where sneaky men in suits free criminals who have enough money?"

"Oh, so I'm sneaky?"

"Yes!" I shouted. "You broke into my room. You called the cops."

Parker stepped forward, backing me into a corner, pinning me against the wall before slamming his hand above my head. It scared me, but not as much as his incredulous stare, as he suddenly leaned in so close, so tempered that I thought I'd scream from surprise.

"So now I'm the bad guy?" he asked, his abs catching rays of sunlight, glistening like his chest that heaved like pliable stone. I dropped my chin, caught by the unkempt curl of lose hair that fell over his face. "I am bad: bad at hiding the fact that I'd do anything for you, that I'm one fucking straw away from breaking through any misconceptions you *think* you have about what I'm willing to do to keep you safe. Gemma, they evacuated the building, everyone thought there was a fire. I shouted for you. I banged on your door so many times; and each fucking second got worse, worse because the idea that something—anything—terrible could ever happen to you kills me. So yes, I kicked that fucking door down, and I'd do it again, and again. They couldn't get me out of here without you, and I'd rather burn than not know you were safe." He fought himself from leaning further, as if the weight of his words were too much to carry, a unique position I'd never seen or felt in the twenty some years we'd known each other.

Who was he right now? Yes, he was Parker the protector, he always had been, but this was different. There was fear in his choking voice, and I didn't know anyone who treated a sister like this, let alone a close friend.

"But I was ok…" I whispered.

"I didn't know that. I saw your window open and thought the worst, because if I ever lost you, Gemma, I don't know if I could live with myself," he dipped his nose lower, brushing against the bridge of my own. My knees began to shake, realizing his stare had become focused on my lips. I didn't know if I wanted to cry, if I felt anger or remorse, or maybe both.

"Parker—" I calmed myself.

"Don't… don't say my name like that. You have no idea what it does to me… goddamn it, Gemma, I can't even think straight." He turned to rest his hands on the counter, his knuckles white. "All I see is you being taken, and I—" he stopped himself, reliving whatever he felt as he massaged his forehead. I was too nervous to move, to feel anything that could make me more vulnerable than I already was around him.

"What is it that you see? What are you afraid of?" I asserted, demanding an answer. "If something is happening then you need to tell me, because I'm done guessing. And yes, I'm sorry. Had I known this would happen, had I known…" *How you felt*, was what I wanted to say, but wasn't sure how. I was nervous about what my assumption would do, what it would cause, if not frustration within me. Parker reached up, his large hand nearing mine but stopping short of actually touching me.

"Don't apologize for *him*." He peeked up, stiffening his shoulders. "This isn't your fault. This is just who he is; a burden… a problem that has been in my way for too long now. I won't rest or stop until you're safe, till you're protected, Gemma, I… I don't know how else to say it. This is what I'm supposed to do. And that's it." Parker shook his head as he pushed himself away, seemingly annoyed at me or the situation as a whole. "I have no choice. No options or regards other than one. I need to meet him."

"Parker—"

"No," he warned me. "You'll arrange this, or I'll go find him myself, and it won't be good. Either way, I'll meet him face to face, and we'll see if he's half the man you think he his." Parker lifted the tea I brought, placing it back in my direction. "Gemma… I warned you if he did anything like this again, that I'd ruin him. And just like any other case, I'll win." Parker combed back his hair, then reached for my phone to swipe it open. "I'm expecting us to meet and have this settled. I won't accept no for an answer."

I scoffed, "Like another third wheel date?" The idea was priceless, almost inconceivable. I couldn't imagine the three of us in the same room, let alone at dinner or a bar. Why did he insist on this, if not to assert himself in my life? I felt embarrassed. I felt like a child.

"This *isn't* a date," he emphasized. "It's a meeting to set expectations and to draw the line between where he begins and where I say he ends."

"Then settle that in court, Park. That's where your relationship begins and ends with him. What I do, what I have, is mine and mine alone, and it doesn't concern you."

"You have no idea what this guy has even done… He'll never do right by you, he'll never sacrifice what I've sacrificed to keep you safe."

"Don't talk to me about sacrifice. I've been vulnerable, Park, I've taken chances when no one else would. Have you? Alejandro has, or at least he's trying."

"I've given everything!" he shouted. "You think he's someone great? Fine. Make this meeting happen, and we'll see if you can change my mind." He slid my phone across the table, "Tell him we're meeting."

"He's a busy man. He's finishing his movie, when do you expect this to happen?"

"He's got till the end of this month. That's his fucking deadline," he waved his hand, short and quick. No exception. I hesitated for a moment, lifting my phone from the table.

If there was anything I learned from Alejandro thus far, it was that the character of a person could be molded by the actions they took, or possibly the ones they didn't. I had to know, in my own way, the limits of this new Parker and as much as he wanted to push, I could push back too.

"We'll be there." I stood my ground, "And believe me, Parker, I do agree with you about expectations being made. Not just for Alejandro, but for you." This sparked his attention.

"In what capacity?"

"You breaking down my door, your interest in me and my life. On Alejandro. How does that make Camilla feel? What does she think of you and me?" Parker ignored me, his focus shifting away, passing me and out the window.

"If she doesn't know by now, then I'll remind her," he argued.

"Remind her about what? About how you feel for her? Or how you feel for me?" My words broke his stare from the buildings outside. He flinched, immediately reaching for his towel, tucking it behind his neck.

"Just make the call," he commanded, exiting the room. The tension was suffocating, returning like a wave as I felt him edging closer to who I knew he was all along, someone and something more. He slammed his door, leaving me alone, rattled, and shaking.

Mindlessly, I lifted my cup of tea, chucking it into the trash as some pathetic attempt to relinquish my rage. I hated that Parker wanted this, but I also hated that he was right. This meeting was a chance, as he said, to set an expectation. I could only live in the fantasy that Parker and I were meant to be together for so long, realizing its effect had been stemming much longer than I cared to admit. He needed to know that my decisions were my own, and that they concerned only the people I included them with.

I walked through my room, kicking a splintered piece of wood across the floor, while Alejandro's suit sat in the corner, perfectly untouched. I pulled out my phone and fell into bed. There were twenty missed calls from Parker's number, shaming me on the screen with its notifications. I swiped them away, pulling up a new message to make the most uncomfortable request ever.

Parker could ask us to meet, but he couldn't make

me choose who I wanted to be with. He of all people should know that choices come with consequences, a lesson I myself learned from both my college confession and from Claire. *Trust a man with your heart, and trust him with your disappointment.*

I punched the final words on my phone, my thumb hovering over the send button, until I had the courage to send it through. I texted Alejandro and hoped for the best, knowing already the worst was still to come.

GEMMA

Hey rebel, do you have plans in a few weeks?

"If you ever do that again, you're fired. I fucking mean it," I warned, unbuttoning the top notch of my tailored navy suit. I was already on edge, completely annoyed with myself, with this whole fucking situation. I couldn't believe the way I spoke to Gemma, the total loss of control I had. It was too much, too obvious to how I felt and how desperate I'd become. But how could I contain myself, when the thought of losing the only person I ever cared for was happening in real time? I didn't want to be here, I didn't want to be scolding my own subordinate, taking my anger out on him.

"I barely said anything." Tommy, my fraternity brother from Columbia, quickly responded. He was good at defending others in court but had little effect in defending himself. The moment his smile wasn't returned with my own, he pinched the bridge of his nose, knowing he was in trouble.

"You said *enough*, and I swear to god, Tommy, if anything from the Brower-Rivers case leaks out, I'll make you leave New York."

The ding of the elevator door opened. Tommy followed me out into the windowed lobby of the towering MelBrook Law Firm. People scurried across the luxurious marbled floors, their heels clicking like an orchestrated backdrop to the tune of hard-working elites. They parted in my presence, reserving their *good mornings* for when my firm expression eased. Everyone nodded, mirroring the nervousness that Tommy portrayed.

"It's not all my fault! What about your princess? Isn't she to blame?" He responded, reminding me that it was Mila who coaxed him into divulging about Alex's case.

I could've forgiven him, had he shared some minor detail. But no, he had to give away the single most sensitive aspect of the case itself. I inhaled deeply, sobering my thoughts with the smell of freshly brewed coffee and expensive leather decor.

"She was doing her job. She's a journalist. She'll say or do anything to get you to spill." I finally exhaled. Mila was good at exploiting others' weaknesses, and when she told me how Tommy confirmed that a girl was *found* in Alex's bed at The Pierre Hotel, I nearly shivered at the catastrophic possibilities. "Over six-hundred hours of non-disclosure agreement meetings were spent, resulting in a four-hundred-page document to be sent to witnesses and associates all across New York, and for what?" Tommy struggled to keep up with my pace, already loosening the black tie around his neck. "Because of you?"

"I fucked up."

"No shit. But why?" I already knew the answer, but I wanted to hear him say it.

"It was Mila's eyes…" he sighed. "She gave me *the* look. You know… the one where her chin drops, and her eyes go innocently big," he admitted, stopping at the front of my office door, scratching his chin.

I knew the look he referred to, and more so of its effect. She'd given it to me before, and had my mind not already been hopelessly devoted to Gemma, I might have fallen victim to it myself.

"Did you say her name? Did you tell Mila about Natalie Brower?" I asked cautiously, speaking a name out loud that felt almost illegal in itself, because it was. The girl, the victim, the rolling stone to the previously mentioned nondisclosures.

Tommy pouted, squinting as if I were the sun itself. "Jesus. No, Parker. I'm a fool, not an idiot." He looked disappointed in me for even asking.

I reached for his shoulder, giving a firm but assuring pat. I may have been more aggravated than he expected, because his childlike frown suddenly made me feel bad. He didn't know that I was up all night, feeling uncontrollably anxious about what would happen once Gemma got home. Everything was messy, not perfectly safe like it was supposed to be, and in fact, I believe I led her down a more complicated path. No one could even realize how sick I felt, how I was physically ill with the thought that Gemma could have feelings for another man, one who I feared could ruin her life, just as he had for the girl in our case. I wanted to save her from it, but instead I pushed her toward it. What the fuck was I doing?

"Look at me." I stuck my finger into his chest, jabbing it. "Look at my eyes. Are you looking?"

"Yes."

"Good. I want you to remember them. Absorb what they look like and describe them to me."

Tommy contemplated for a moment, guarded only by the whiff of his juniper aftershave.

"Fucking pissed," he admitted under his breath.

"You're god damn right. Now if Mila ever gives you *that* look again, I want you to think of me. If you see her eyes, you think of mine. Is that sexy to you?"

"No."

"Good. Now don't talk to her again." I nodded slowly, till he did the same. I looked past him to Scarlett, my latest paralegal. She carried both my coffee and my mail. Tommy looked at her, a small brunette with a top bun, white blouse, and a grey fitted pencil skirt. "Don't look at her either," I warned, redirecting him back to me. "She's a professional. We all are."

"Good morning, Mr. Jones," she greeted, shifting around Tommy as if he were a pillar of sharp glass. I waved him off as Scarlett followed me into my office.

"Scarlett," I returned kindly, lifting the coffee from her hand. "You know I can get this myself. You're the best paralegal we have at the moment, not a receptionist."

"I aim to please," she said quietly, almost nervously as I made my way to the dark, quartz desk at the center of my office. I took a quick sip of coffee, always being too preoccupied to ever fully appreciate my corner view of West Forty-second Street and Sixth Avenue. Bryant Park sat outside like a tiny oasis, a small patch of green heaven in a sea of steel beams and grey bricks.

"Well, you're doing great. I appreciate how

thoughtful you are," I assured, giving her my first true smile of the day.

"Hold your praise. The coffee is to wake you up."

"For what exactly?"

"Quinn from Tri-Tech moved your meeting up from twelve to ten."

"That's sudden, but I can manage."

"Well… that's not what the coffee's for," she hesitated. "Lina Castillo is here to see you," she gestured towards the hall.

"Lina?" I groaned, taking a longer sip of coffee, returning to the stack of mail.

I knew why she was here, arriving much sooner than the attorneys' meeting we had scheduled for later this afternoon. This was about last night, about her client's involvement with my Gemma, my best friend, my Butterfly. I was already shifting in moods. This was not the *good morning* that Scarlett greeted me with, this was an early chess match with a powerful legal savant.

"Strong enough?" Scarlett checked in, referring to the coffee, rather than my interpretation. I took it as a question to my preparedness for Lina, who was clearly desperate to either intimidate or smooth things over. I figured both would be attempted, neither of which interested me.

"Always," I replied confidently, unlike Scarlett's hands which wrung together. She was good at what she did, but was still young, still too inept in the skill of disguising the anxiety of inevitable conflict. She wasn't like Lina, whose overwhelming confidence always rivaled mine. At times it felt as though we were more like bucks than people, our horns locked in either a gaze or a verbal joust, exchanging cruel, and personal jabs that others found overtly competitive. All Lina and I ever wanted was to win. "Give me ten, then bring her in."

I sat down, sifting the mail, stopping at a particularly thick, cream-colored envelope. I peeled back its embossed enclosure, removing a matted brochure from *Belmont Hills*. I didn't expect it to arrive so quickly, having just requested Scarlett to retrieve it last night after ordering a pizza that Gemma and I never got to share. It was here now, reminding me of what I needed to do, of the promise I made as a child.

It was that promise to Claire that caused me to request this brochure in the first place. Above all else, who I was and what I was meant to do, was to keep Gemma safe.

But what did that even mean anymore?

I could feel my promise slipping, laboring like one sweaty hand grabbing onto another, struggling to keep myself from falling. The anticipation of losing her made everything feel so anxious, so urgent. I never felt more like a desperate fool, but *desperate* nonetheless. Even if I left right now and ran to Gemma, what would I say to her? How could I ever put into words all the things I wanted to say in a single breath?

Gemma, I'm so sorry it took me forever to say this out loud, but I couldn't help it. The boy you grew up with still lives in me, along with the fear he felt the day he came to see you, but instead found your mother. All I wanted was you, but all I got was the antithesis to what I wanted to say:

I love you.

I love you.

I love you.

And please let me say it again, because I could never get tired of saying it, and I could never get tired of the relief it gives my heart.

I want to run away, I want to find you and tell you how I feel, but I'm still there on that couch, waiting with Claire, my finger burning and my mind melting. I'm not sure if I could ever leave that place, especially now, since it's been imprinted in my mind like a script.

All I ever wanted to do was keep you safe, and all I know, all I was ever told, was that my love for you—my truest and deepest love—was completely, fucking, nuclear.

I wish I could say that. I wish it were easy. The truth was, and what I could admit to myself, was that my life was the cumulation of tiny fires, all of which I would accept responsibility for, because, in reality, they were all my fault. Every piece of shattered glass, of webbing, and stone that plagued my life was there because of me and my fear. I knew that, I recognized that, but maybe there was still hope for change. I could still protect her, and I could start with the woman who we both shared in common: Claire.

I promised Gemma I'd take care of her mother, not once giving her details, but assuring her that she'd never have to return to Claire's house again, or be bothered by her, so long as she wished; and that started with Claire's unknowing admittance to Belmont Hills.

A knock at my door caught my attention, redirecting it to the arched brow of an unimpressed Lina.

"Mr. Jones," she stuck her chin up, attempting to meet mine as I rose from my seat.

"Miss Castillo," I replied, concealing the fact that I was completely dismayed. "You're early."

"You know me, always keen to see you."

"A glutton for punishment?"

"That'd be an understatement." She took a moment to stare out the window, admiring my inescapable view. "I'm sure you're surprised to see me."

"No. I understand why you're here."

"Good. Then you can agree that a boundary should be made. We don't want things to get complicated."

"For whom, exactly?" I leaned back in my large, leather chair, raising my ankle over my knee.

I ran my thumb along the Montblanc pen in my hand, testing its strength like a sturdy stress ball. Lina took a seat on one of the twin tweed chairs before my desk.

"You know for who. I'm not in the mood to play games," she finally remarked.

"Neither am I, Lina. So if you have something to say, I suggest you speak up. And quickly." I cocked my head, taking a long breath, inhaling her black plum perfume. She must have just sprayed it before coming in, covering the undeniable airport smell she carried.

"Grouchy?" she asked firmly.

"Assertive."

"Maybe you're not getting enough sleep. How was your night last night?"

"That's personal."

"Burdensome seems more appropriate," she said

convincingly. "You haven't shaved. I like the stubble. Very refined. Can't say I've ever seen you with it, though. Were you rushed to get in?"

"I was a lot things, Lina, none of which were patient." I warned with a stern look.

"If it's not the stubble, then it's your eyes. They're tired."

"Wrinkled maybe? Much like your suit. Did you sleep in the car ride over?" I returned.

"I've had too many espressos for that."

"That explains the jitters." I pointed at her bobbing knee, but she immediately stopped as I called her out.

I smiled, but she didn't.

"You're getting dangerously close to harassing my client, Mr. Jones. Having the police scouring for Mr. Rivers is a perverse attempt to paint him negatively in the media."

"I care very little about *scouring* for that criminal. *Who* I care for and *who* I was looking for was my roommate." My attempted indifference in avoiding Gemma's name was purposeful. I needed to appear detached, covering the slightest bit of weakness, which Gemma certainly caused. "Of course, I was surprised that someone with such a clean record could be caught in a compromising position, that is, until I found out who she was with."

"Your roommate?" Lina paused, searching her head for a name she most likely knew. "Oh, you mean Gemma, correct?"

I bit my tongue, physically restraining the drop in my face. "Yes."

"Gemma is a direct employee to Mr. Rivers. Their relationship is understandable."

"*His* relationship is mixing with mine, and I fear it's with ill intent."

"Don't confuse their relationship with your own paranoia, Mr. Jones. To be frank, a missing persons report seems a little dramatic and not like something the judge would like to hear about."

"To be frank, you're finding yourself a little too comfortable in my office, and given the potential emergency that she could have been in, I'm glad I did so."

"How were the two of them together an emergency, exactly?" she asked, her fingers swiping back and forth, attempting to connect imaginary dots.

"Maybe not at that moment, but I prefer she stay away from the criminal who spends all his money in court. Don't get me wrong, it's for your client's safety too, because trust me, Lina, if what happened to Natalie Brower happened to Gemma, not even Christ himself could save Alex from me."

"*Easy…*" Lina lulled. "There are strict rules about that name, and about saying it out loud."

"Strict is my dedication to Gemma's safety. Don't think that a judge won't find it suspicious that your client is stalking by proxy." I knew Alex couldn't be using Gemma to get to me but spat it out regardless.

"I'm not convinced. If my client wants to file harassment charges, then I will be in full support of them doing so."

"Harassment? On what grounds?"

"On your misuse of a missing persons report on her, of course." Lina smiled wide, my face shifting into a scowl. A report on *her?* Gemma? What the fuck was she even saying?

Three timid knocks came at my door as Scarlett poked her head in. "Mr. Jones," she announced quietly. "Miss Camilla Martinez is here for you."

Fuck.

Of all the times for Mila to show up, it had to be now. Lina could easily find out who Mila was—hell, Mila herself was usually dying to tell others about what she did for a living. Dating the gossip columnist of New York's biggest social magazine certainly put me in a compromising position, especially with Alex on the case. I couldn't risk this.

"Please advise Miss Martinez that I'll be finished shortly." The look I gave Scarlett sent a message far clearer than my words. *Not fucking now.*

"Camilla Martinez?" Lina asked, lifting the single framed photo that sat on my desk.

Of course she had to look at it, the one image of me hugging Gemma at an arcade in Soho. We posed in front of a *Frankenstein* pinball machine; having finally placed third on the leader board for highest score. In it, my arm reached around her small shoulder, pulling her close to my chest as we both leaned towards our glowing initials.

We looked so happy in the photo, and in fact we were, but even then I was miserable at a distance, feeling like the potential bomb that could ruin her life. My thumb physically throbbed from the memory of Claire's words and scolding match.

"Is she your girlfriend?" Lina looked at the picture, but I assumed she was referring to Mila.

"What an odd question," I scoffed. "She's a client. Unlike what you just assumed Gemma was to you. She has no legal ties to your firm. She would never file a harassment suit."

Lina shook her head. "Actually, you're wrong. Mr. Rivers has me on retainer, and in turn I have been hired to do the same for Miss Harrison." She placed the photo back onto my desk. "And I take that very seriously. If she wishes to press harassment charges against you, I'd fully support that."

My eye twitched at the audacity; the blatant ownership she placed over Gemma. Alex was using my own profession against me, attempting to take my spot even as legal counsel to the woman I loved.

"I want you to be *very* careful with your next words." The deepness of my voice seemed to startle her, as her hand suddenly recoiled from her knee to her lap. I was Gemma's Rattlesnake for a reason. "Any cross moves will be met with serious legal ramifications."

"In the form of what, exactly?"

"Test me and find out," I growled.

"You don't have the resources or funds my client does." Her rebuttal was weak, almost laughable, as if she had any idea of what I was capable of.

"What I have is far more exceeding than *Alex Rivers*. And if you don't believe me, I challenge you to try. Because trust me, Lina, I'll gladly take you down with him. People will see you, and all they'll think of is me—the *big*, red, fucking *X* on your tepid legal career."

"Go ahead and try," her earlier confidence stammered itself, she was too eager to rebut.

"Oh, I will, in court. And once your head is spinning, once you realize how little it is you know about law, don't say I didn't warn you."

"All you do is talk."

"And soon, all you'll do is listen, which is what you should be doing right now. Threaten me again, and you'll have nothing…not even *that* yesterday's-laundry-of-a-suit you're wearing," I attacked, a more viscous critique than what she was prepared for.

Her competitive spark fizzled out, her otherwise dimpled cheeks smoothed by a quick but painful frown. She looked down at my desk again, observing the Belmont Hills brochure sitting by my side. She studied it, absorbing its connection to me, and to the case at large.

"Belmont?" she questioned quietly.

"It's not about Natalie Brower," I responded, assuring her that even though Belmont Hills and Natalie were related, they weren't in this particular instance.

"What else could it possibly be about?" she asked, not believing me, fearing any potential strategies I had in the case against Alex Rivers.

"It's personal. I promise," I assured, knowing the unfortunate truth that had shackled my life. When I made a promise, I didn't break it. We stared for a moment, unsure of what to say next, and if this was indeed a chess match, then it started to feel like a draw.

Another knock appeared at the door.

"Parker!" Mila came in, carrying what appeared to be a fresh cup of coffee in her hand. She seemed disappointed, immediately seeing that I already had one on my desk. Scarlett rushed to her side, giving a look of both panic and remorse. "If they kept me waiting any longer your drink would've gone cold," she winced, catching eyes with Lina before setting the coffee down. "Last night was just so crazy, and I figured you would need the pick me up." She looked to Lina with a smile, "Hi, I'm—" She reached out, but I was quick to halt any exchange of titles.

"Miss Martinez! As your legal counselor I'm going to advise you to refrain from talking. Now." I said sharply, not out of malice, but urgency. She seemed stunned, but Lina shook her head.

"It's ok… I was on my way out, anyways." Lina stood up, moving her focus between me and the Belmont Hills brochure. "I believe your warnings, Mr. Jones. I'm certain you know more about law than I do, but it doesn't take a freshmen from Yale to know that a breach of a non-disclosure can be catastrophic." She tapped her finger on the brochure, making her message clear about Natalie Brower.

The girl from Belmont Hills…

The girl who they found *dead* in Alex Rivers' bed…

This case was less about The Pierre Hotel, and more about the secret of Natalie—the very secret that Tommy almost told Mila. I hated Alex and the turmoil he caused, but in turn, respected the wishes of Natalie's husband to remain quiet through the mediation process.

My patience was teetering though, not once wanting to settle, but rather, to take Alex Rivers to court, to have him pay for his damages, both publicly and privately. This was what drove me mad, this was what I wanted to warn Gemma about, but never could.

"Just be careful what you do, Mr. Jones. You can't control everything… and the sooner you realize that… the better off you'll be."

Reluctantly, I agreed, giving her my silent approval as she left my office.

Mila sighed, lifting the coffee she brought for me and taking a sip of her own. "I didn't mean to intrude," she said somewhat shyly.

"You didn't. And thank you for being quick to listen. I hope I didn't catch you off guard." I welcomed her closer, guiding her to the chair where Lina just sat.

"That seemed so serious."

"Lawyers make everything feel serious. Even lunch is a debate."

"Hopefully not for us. Can I take you out later? I know last night was a little chaotic, and I didn't exactly make things easy." Her timid response was Mila's way of apologizing. To be honest, she didn't handle the fire alarm so well, though neither did I. I was in no position to judge her, and I certainly didn't want her to feel bad.

"It was a tense situation. The whole night was." I sighed, "But yeah, let's grab lunch." Time out of the office would be needed, and I was certain Gemma wouldn't consider eating with me, not after our morning together. I thought of her even now, of what she said and her perception of me. I knew I was losing control, physically slamming my hand over her head, leaning close to her face, tempted once and for all to kiss her—not just slowly—but fucking deeply. I only hoped that hadn't been lost, that I could make her see how dangerous Alex really was while maintaining what little professionalism I still had.

My phone buzzed on my desk, a response from Gemma, replying to my command to meet Alex face-to-face earlier this morning.

GEMMA

9:00 p.m. - last Friday of the month at Dante's, 60th floor at the bar. You, Me, Alejandro.

Mila read the text out loud, sounding surprised. "Alejandro?" She asked.

"Alex Rivers," I responded, pulling the phone away, placing it into my pocket. She chewed her lip, not even allowing a second to pass before asking the dreaded question.

"Can I come?"

"It's work-related."

"With Gemma too?" She pouted.

"It's a sensitive subject."

"Is it about last night? How you broke down her door? How you tried to rescue her from the non-fire?" She made it sound so pathetic, and maybe it was, or maybe, I was just that reckless now.

Tommy passed by my office, catching a glimpse of Mila, but immediately turned the other direction. What I feared and what I presumed I was, was a lot like

Tommy. I wasn't sure if I could be so careful around Gemma or keep the secrets I held. Maybe I would blurt them out, maybe I would ruin everything just like Claire said.

"If you come, you cannot ask questions," I sighed, knowing it was both a good and bad idea. If Mila was there, I could try and be on my best behavior, to remind myself not to say things I shouldn't out loud. But not even that was a guarantee. Mila smiled, wobbling her head like a bobble doll.

Immediately, her smile turned into a frown as she caught a glimpse of the Belmont Hills brochure.

"Wow," she read the subtext out loud, "Private Home and Women's Facility."

"A treatment center. For trauma and abuse victims," I buried my response, taking the pamphlet from her hand and placing it in my drawer.

"Is that for work?" she asked.

"Remember. No questions." I said, knowing that I'd call them today, and that soon, Claire would get the help she needed, and Gemma would get the relief she deserved.

Chapter 5

GEMMA

I wasn't ready to zip up the black garment bag that hung in my bedroom, taking one final look at Alejandro's suit, assessing the non-existent wrinkles and hand stitched details I crafted in his honor. In the weeks that passed, I only had time to focus on finishing this project, hardly leaving my room, avoiding interactions with Parker. This was an uncomfortable new territory for us, and I wasn't sure why we kept so quiet, but the longer we did, the bigger it all felt.

He'd come check on me, and I'd appreciate it, but maybe it was the fact that he hadn't apologized yet that had me feeling so upset. Either he couldn't acknowledge what he did was wrong, or worse, didn't feel it was wrong in the first place. Our blatant silent streak was chalked up to busy schedules, both of our work circling around Alejandro, both of our feelings on opposite ends of the spectrum.

I had hung a curtain over my empty door frame, using excess fabric from Alejandro's suit. I was certain it wasn't what Parker wanted, seeing the design of the man he hated used as a physical barrier between him and me.

But despite all he'd done, and all he'd failed to say,

there were still moments where *I* was the one who *felt* guilty.

Every night he'd knock on the doorframe, seeing if I'd answer or not. I never did. I'd only watch under the curtain, quietly waiting until his feet disappeared, removed like a considerate ghost down the hall. This was most nights, but on other occasions he'd wait longer, the wet separation of his lips almost audible, as if he wanted to say something, but decided against it. What did he want to say, and was it the same as me? *Sorry, but also, not sorry?*

I took one last look at the suit, imagining what Alejandro would say when he saw the hidden details I included. Would he tell me I did a *good job?* Would he call me his *good girl*, like he always had, brushing my lips, smearing their color with his promising thumb?

I sat on my bed, anxious for tonight, lifting Andy, the giraffe, into my hands. One look into his marbled, black eyes reminded me that Parker cared, but caring wasn't good enough anymore. I needed answers, a less patient distinction than what I had with Alejandro, because we were different; we were still *new*, still adjusting to who we were as people, devoid of a lifetime of memories like I had with Parker, a lifetime I wondered if I could ever walk away from.

I rushed to get ready, placing gold studs in my ear until I heard a knock at the door. Not having heard the buzzer, I was surprised to see who was waiting on the other end as I made my way over.

"Lina?" I opened the door, not expecting her just an hour before the most tension-filled gathering of my life.

"Evening, Miss Harrison," she held up a small cup in her hand. "Green tea?"

"Umm yeah, sure…" I stumbled, twisting the butterfly ring on my finger, taking the cup.

"I thought I remembered correctly. You drank one at the station when we met. I hope it was out of preference."

"Oh! Yes, of course," I felt obligated to take a sip, noting the missing honey. I couldn't imagine how I appeared, feeling somewhat frantic as she looked inside. "Thank you," I said, shaking my head. "Sorry, I'm just so surprised you're here."

"I flashed this to your doorman, I told him I was here to serve you court papers." She held up an envelope but smiled, "Works every time."

"Thanks for that," I laughed awkwardly. "Do you want to come in?" I stepped back, making way for Lina. "I think I know why you're here… but he isn't in yet."

"Who?"

"Parker. He's still at the office, but probably on his way home soon."

"Parker?" She shook her head. "No. I'm here to talk to you." She scanned the room, absorbing the territory of what I could only assume was her rivals.

"Me?" I asked, feeling like I was on the cusp of a business meeting with how Lina was dressed. She looked completely professional, her jacket removed, revealing only a fitted, white blouse that tucked into her sleek, bellowed slacks. "Can I get you anything?"

"Your stiffest drink would be great, but I'm afraid I won't be long."

"Sounds like you've had a long day."

"A long few weeks, Miss Harrison."

"Please. Call me, Gemma." I corrected, her formality too odd for how little of an age difference I felt we had. She took a seat in the living room, her shoulders finally dropping.

"I appreciate that. I'm afraid I start to sound like a fucking robot at times, copying the talk of boring old men."

"Sounds thrilling."

"Thrilling is that outfit," she wafted herself with the envelope, pretending she was hot as she motioned toward my yellow, silk dress with spotted white petunias. It was a fitting flower, given the occasion, though I doubted Lina knew that, or how their meaning represented both resentment and desire.

"Thank you! It's a vintage St. La Vie."

"Good taste. I can see why he likes you."

"Alejandro?"

"Yes, to you maybe, but to me, he's *Mr.* Alex Rivers."

"How's he been?" I asked curiously, considering our communication was as prevalent as mine and Parker's.

"I thought *I* was busy. Stealing him away between shoots has been nearly impossible. Especially with him being so far away from home."

"Home?"

"Los Angeles," she sighed as if she missed it.

It was just another reminder that Alejandro's stay was temporary. I tried to hide the drop in my face.

"Of course!" I pretended to be happy, enduring a

moment of awkward silence that fell between us. I looked at the envelope in Lina's hand, curious as to why she was here, especially because of what tonight entailed. "So, Lina… now that my doorman thinks I'm wanted in court, what should we talk about?"

She thumbed the corner of her envelope, shooting a courteous smile. "As you may know, I've been appointed to oversee any legal situations that may occur for you—"

"Actually, I'm glad you brought that up. I feel like that's a problem."

"Is it?"

"Well, of course. Parker is already my legal advisor. I'm not sure how he'd react if I told him about you."

"He already knows."

"He does?" I asked, immediately fidgeting with the gold studs in my ears, "Well, what did he say?"

"A *whole* lot. He's certainly protective."

I laughed nervously, unsure of how to respond or how that even looked. Parker didn't mention this to me, but then again, I'd been avoiding him.

"He's my best friend," I admitted. "He has always been protective."

"Well I'm protective too. Mr. Rivers is my top client, and that makes you my top client, as well. I have an obligation to keep both of you safe from the public eye."

"Makes sense," I said, watching as Lina slid the envelope in my direction.

"It does. And I'm sure it's no surprise that Mr. Rivers gets *a lot* of attention. Hence the need for *extra* protection." She signaled for me to open it up, which I did, unfolding a single sheet of paper. I read it to myself, quietly deciphering the legal jargon that seemed to escape me while picking up the overall clear idea.

"A non-disclosure?" I crinkled my face.

"A precaution. A small one, at that. Trust me, they can get much bigger." I had no idea that this would ever be needed, but then again, I never knew what was happening behind my back. Parker was already informed of my *new* attorney, and Lina was in talks with Alejandro for over the past two weeks.

"Is this about us all meeting tonight?"

"Meeting?" She pulled her head back. Clearly this was one thing she didn't know about. I tried to cover my tracks.

"I was meeting Alejandro to discuss the completion of his suit," I lied.

She laughed. "Well, no. This isn't about your meeting. This is about a number of things, and, honestly, I'm not sure how much you know."

"Like about what?"

"Like about Sergeant Fields's major misstep at the station. That morning when I went to release, Mr. Rivers, I heard him talking to you as I approached."

"And what did you hear?"

"The mention of Belmont Hills, of course. What did he say about that?" she asked flatly, reminding me of the place I'd almost forgotten about. Honestly, I figured he was just another man who couldn't mind his own business, but Lina made it feel different. He did compare me to someone else; not only to his daughter, but to a girl—any girl possibly—who was destined to fall for Alejandro.

"Belmont Hills? Nothing." I answered truthfully, still unable to remember what was really said. "Until now, I had almost forgotten about that. Things have been… hectic," I answered. Her face dropped, as if she regretted ever saying anything at all.

"Gemma…" she collected herself, "Can I ask you a personal question? What's the nature of you and Mr. Rivers's relationship?"

Our relationship? I certainly wasn't prepared for her to ask that. If only it were easier to know what *we* were together, or what we *should* be together—easy as in the assembly of a suit. If I could stitch the pieces of our unknowing future into a clearer, more idealized version, I'd probably have a proper answer to give her, but I didn't, because like Lina mentioned, he was from California, and unfortunately his life, whether I acknowledged it or not, was filled with uncertainty. But despite this, I reminded myself of a single guarantee: that Alejandro completely, and truly, cared for me. Couldn't that be enough?

"He's my boss," I crossed my arms.

"Are you sure about that? Gemma, it's my job to protect both you and Mr. Rivers. Part of that protection is making sure that any information shared with you stays in private."

"It would, I'd never say anything, I'd never betray his trust." I took it seriously, but Lina didn't seem convinced.

"As his lawyer I have to be preemptive in what

happens to him. It's my job to put out fires, but my fear with you, Gemma, is that you aren't something I can put out."

"I don't understand."

"You should, it's a good thing but also a burden. I'm not sure Mr. Rivers sees you only as his employee, and that makes him vulnerable—it puts cracks in the foundation that I work very hard to protect."

"And what exactly would you be protecting?" I asked.

She smiled and shook her head, "Honestly, not even I know sometimes. That man is built like a fucking wall. What I do know—what is circling his case—cannot be compromised. I'm sure you wouldn't want to hurt his image."

"Well, of course not. How could I even do that?"

"Lots of things can happen, Gemma. People come and go. I'm not sure what he's willing to share, probably more with you than ever with me. And if that time comes, I need to know his privacy is safe."

Lina's precautious attitude left me little room for comfort. Either she knew what happened at The Pierre Hotel was bad, or she knew better—that the things she wasn't yet told could possibly be worse. She was here to *represent* me, though it felt less about that and more about Alejandro.

"Does Alejandro know you're here?" I asked firmly.

Lina pivoted to a graduation photo of Parker, his charmed smile sandwiched in a kiss from me and Mama Meg. "Full disclosure. He doesn't. And I'd like to keep it that way."

"So, if I'm hearing you correctly, you want me to conceal his potential secrets by keeping this a secret in itself?" I scrunched my brow. "I'm not too sure how he'd feel about this."

"It could be mutual," she returned. "Gemma, is there anything that I should know? Discretion is my key objection, what you tell me will never leave this room. If there are any parts of your life that you wish for him to sign an NDA on, I'll be happy to do so…The truth is, I don't know you. But you know yourself, right?"

She asked an important question, and I wasn't sure if I could answer honestly. I only saw myself as one person: the lonely girl who was too scared to make a choice, to risk the chance of ever becoming someone like Claire. I never wanted to push myself to that limit.

"I like to think I do, but to answer your first question, no," I finally settled. "I have nothing to hide."

"And that's perfectly fine. My client, your *boss*, has a lot going on. His situation is unique, and I cannot let things slip by. And unfortunately, with you living with the prosecutor of his case, I can't help but be extra cautious. There is more to this than you probably will ever know, or even want to find out. As an indirect favor for Mr. Rivers, I'm going to ask you to sign this," she pulled out a pen, clicking it sharply and placing it on the table.

A favor for Alejandro seemed like the right thing to do, but in secrecy it felt wrong. I wanted Alejandro, and I wanted us to find our own path, and a part of me felt like that involved being trustworthy. Signing this behind his back wasn't just wrong, it was deceitful.

"I'll think about it," I said sternly, placing the pen back in her direction. Lina's strained eyes softened, briefly shutting as if to refrain from either begging or demanding.

"I'd appreciate that. And please be mindful of the things I said today and the things Sergeant Fields told you."

"Things you reminded me of," I added, "Belmont Hills?"

Her face dropped again, but this time from her vibrating phone. It lit up on the coffee table, reading a name that made her wince: *Miguel*. She physically snapped her jaw shut, testing its durability with a steady grind of her teeth. Whoever it was, whatever they wanted, didn't make her happy. "Busy, busy…" she sighed.

"Parker will be here soon. I'm sure he's already in a cab," I interjected, worried she would press me further to sign the document.

Lina silenced the call, allowing it to go to voicemail. "That's my queue. Keep the NDA, and here's my card," she handed me her information as she stood from her chair.

"Thank you," I palmed it in my hand, walking her to the door. "For the tea, as well. It was very thoughtful."

"Thoughtful? That'd be doing the right thing, even when it feels wrong to do." She winked, "Good luck at your meeting tonight."

She walked away, not once looking back. She was wrong though; I knew there was another way for Alejandro and me. We didn't need to conform to this life

—of fame, of gossip. What we needed was to be ourselves, or more so, who I hoped we were. I knew tonight was part of that, and maybe that's why I felt so nervous. Whatever answers Parker wanted, I hoped he'd get, because I was moving on, with or without his approval.

"He's late." Parker checked his watch, scowling, saying his first true words since sitting down by the fireplace. He took a slow sip of his scotch, not breaking his gaze from the front door where Alejandro would hopefully appear.

I tugged on my dress, its fabric taut above my knees, feeling slightly self-conscious, not unnerved by Parker's focus, but provoked by its unanticipated directness. He watched me for a moment, holding the longest stare we shared in weeks.

"He's not late," I corrected. "We're early and that's fine. He'll be here soon." I hoped, anyways, considering Alejandro had a serious reputation for being late. The two hadn't even met yet, and according to Parker's associates, Alejandro's tolerance for stress was minimum.

"I'd be surprised," Parker graveled, sitting confidently still, his shoulders back in a charcoal-grey suit.

"Don't act like you're above him. It's not a very good look," I scolded, watching as Camilla stood over by the bar awaiting her drink while Parker and I finally sat alone.

"Are you really that impressed by him?"

"Is that why we're here? A pissing contest? It's not about being impressed. It's about giving you what you want so you can leave me alone."

"Haven't I done that enough lately? What next? Just shut me out, like always?"

"I don't shut you out, Parker. I'm entitled to my privacy."

"Guess Alex is too... it seems like he knows you better than me these days."

"I hate that you just said that."

"Good, because I hate how it feels…" he mumbled, swirling the glass in his hand before taking another long sip.

I looked away, uncertain of what to do next. Parker was never an angry man, never with me at least; not even as children, like when I squirted mustard on his signed Derek Jeter jersey at a ball game. Anything I'd ever done to him personally never transpired into something as awkward as this. But then again, this wasn't about him, this was about me.

"I don't want to argue with you." I settled.

"I'm not trying to be an ass... it just feels like after everything we've been through, you've picked a side… and if you think I enjoy doing this, then you're wrong."

"Well, you're the one who wanted this. I don't know how else to explain it. It's like you want to control what happens to me, but this isn't you, Park."

This seemed to strike a chord, the crease of his brow deepening amongst the thunder outside. It all felt so daunting.

"I'm not controlling you. You're my best friend," he uttered.

"Best friend? Sister? Think of me however you want, just don't pretend that ever entitles you to anything."

Parker looked down at his drink, his thumb tracing its rim as his cheeks hollowed in silence. Why did every word feel like a misstep, like every exchange was a loose stone to an already brittle bridge? The concept of us ever being angry with each other was so foreign, making these past weeks impossible to navigate, considering we'd only ever been comfortable with each other.

"If it makes you feel better, I didn't ask Lina to be my lawyer," I said as Parker looked up, mildly relieved. "Not that I owe you that courtesy, but it feels like the right thing to say. You know, if I ever needed help, I'd only come to you, not her." I sighed, squinting towards the bar, "I'm trying to be considerate, and I wish you'd do the same… I just don't understand why you'd bring Camilla with you tonight."

"She's more of a convenience than I'm willing to admit." Parker's momentary relaxation quickly faded as he suddenly huffed. "And thank you for telling me about Lina, but that doesn't change how I feel. I won't apologize for trying to do what's right."

"What's right?" I laughed. "I admit I'd come to you if I ever needed help, and that's what you have to say? I don't even care about that anymore… what I really want, what I really *need* is my Parker back…" I folded my hands above my lap, un-soothed by the silk dress I originally reserved for something special, an impossible fantasy that Parker and I would ever go on a date someday. "I don't even know if that's possible anymore. I just want the real you, but maybe you don't want the real me."

"I know the real you, and this isn't her."

"I'm still the same person, Parker... the girl who hates oysters, who hums 'Monster Mash', who sleeps with the same stuffed giraffe you gave her forever ago. I've always been me. It's you who's different. You wanted to change, you wanted to try new things. So if this isn't the real me, then who am I?" I argued. "You don't care about me, or how this whole spectacle makes me feel."

For a moment, Parker's lip trembled, the fireplace by his side glistened in his eyes. They were wet, full, and undeniably hurt. Maybe it was true, maybe he didn't want this, but then why were we here?

"It kills me that you think so little about what I really want," he fought back a look that broke my heart.

"No," I warned. "I love you, Parker... and if you love me too—whatever spectrum that may be on—then you'd respect me enough to let me go."

"Love?" he asked, his voice rough, the kind of rough that could only occur when every exhausted word had already scathed your throat. "Was it love when you kicked me out of Claire's? I trusted that *you* knew best, because I didn't know what it was you were hiding. But I respected it. Love can be uncomfortable, Gemma. It's doing what's right, even when it hurts. And trust me, I'm always hurting."

I composed the burn in my throat, our candid moment instantly ruined as Camilla appeared by our side. I looked away, but Parker refused.

"Do you really know Alex Rivers?" Camilla sighed; her martini glass held delicately between her red painted nails. She looked like the devil herself, her shiny, black hair falling along the thin straps of her red dress.

"That's a silly thing to ask," I answered, checking my phone one last time.

"Silly is imagining that Hollywood's biggest star would even show up, especially for his stylist."

"I'm his designer."

"And he's your boss," she retorted. "Or is there more to this?"

"That's enough." Parker inhaled calmly, his low voice bristled with the burn of scotch. Either he was focused on the interaction to come or annoyed by Camilla's question. Regardless, he silenced the both of us, leaving me no room to answer.

Besides, what would I say anyways? Alejandro and I had no labels, we had nothing but the beginning of an idea, the possibility of some partnership, but I knew that nothing good could ever come from keeping secrets. Lina's nondisclosure sat folded inside my purse, and her approach from earlier was an alarm to the patterns I always had, the attempts I'd made to avoid tough topics.

"Good evening, Jones Party," a waiter greeted, interrupting with a silver tray in hand. He bent over, resting a bottle of crystalline liquor on the table. "Compliments of Mr. Rivers," he placed two accompanied glasses along its side: one for Parker, the other for Alejandro.

"*Don Jefe*?" Camilla laughed, reading the unfamiliar label of the newly set bottle. I examined the embossed *Jalisco* letters as Camilla reached into her clutch, pulling out a cigarette. "Shots for a ghost. How imaginative."

"I said enough, Camilla," Parker commanded, using her full name like a disappointed parent. Camilla's response was stifled, disguised with the flick of her lighter, its sharp wheel giving me the most unbearable chills.

She took a long drag, holding it loosely between her fingers. Between the anticipation of Alejandro arriving and the pungent cigarette smell, I began to feel anxious. I stroked my neck, just as I always had, but covered it by trailing my thumb along a gold necklace I wore.

"There's nothing here that needs your approval." I pointed Camilla to the exit, "This isn't some Great Pumpkin moment. You're welcome to leave."

"Don't get me wrong. I just never assumed Alex to be so underwhelming. The drinks, the waiting, the exaggerated sense of self-importance. Parker was right, he should be here by now. Feels… I don't know… not as courageous as I'd assume an action star to be."

Camilla always had a sense of superiority, an ability to make me feel like the discounted version of herself. I never appreciated that from her, but the look of disappointment she gave when I didn't react was pure ecstasy.

I assumed she wasn't expecting me to smile, but I couldn't help myself. It had been so long since I'd seen him, and now he was through the door and by her side; the man who crept his way from my fantasies and into my life.

I grinned.

"Maybe you should tell him yourself. It appears he's on time."

Chapter 7

PARKER

I imagined this meeting going a thousand different ways in my head. Each time there was a different introduction, a different setting. But not ever—and I mean ever—did I picture the greeting I heard from Alex's deep, provocative voice.

"Good evening, Gemma." He inhaled her name, allowing it to enter his mouth with such delicate intention.

I hated it.

It made me fucking sick.

And as much as I despised how it burned a pit into my stomach, the discomfort he caused was nothing compared to how Gemma responded.

"Hi…" she stumbled out, breaking into an uncontrolled shyness that pinned my back to the bottom of my chair.

Hi? Just like that? Sweet and in awe? It was nothing like how we'd spoken to each other for weeks now, her enthusiasm as candid as Mila's, whose wide eyes stilled on Alex as he lifted the cigarette from her fingers.

"Gemma doesn't like the smell of smoke," he growled, extinguishing her black Sobranie onto the linen tabletop.

Of course he knew that about Gemma, but then again, it wasn't a secret. Regardless, he was better than me in this moment, bold enough to correct Mila in something I should have but was too distracted to do so. All I could focus on was how Gemma stared at Alex. Her chin dropped, her eyes stitched from his shoulders up. I wanted her to stare at me the same way I did her, with complete amazement, because she looked so beautiful, and I wish I could say that out loud, not just to her, but to everyone, to be that annoying husband that points and boasts, *"See her? Isn't she perfect? That's my wife, the girl with flowers on her dress and in her heart."*

But all the lovely compliments I had for her began to compete with the anxiety of making a stern first impression with Alex, thinking and assessing all at once, determining his and Gemma's dynamic like an ill-prepared computer. I hated to admit it, but I felt overwhelmed.

"Alejandro, this is my best friend, Parker Jones, and this… is his girlfriend, Camilla." Gemma rose from her seat, making the uncomfortable introduction. God, hearing the word best friend killed me, each syllable like a thousand pounds on my chest, and despite having already described myself in the same way, I didn't want Alex to hear it.

I fixed my face as he made his way towards me, his dark, unreadable eyes meeting my own. He was fucking tall, wearing a black suit with even blacker tattoos, his confidence placing my insecurities back to the feeling I had when I was in front of Claire's awful green door.

"Mr. Jones." He reached out, his calloused hand meeting mine, his overall appearance as carefully crafted as his Omega watch.

"Mr. Rivers." I shook his hand, our unanimous strength fastened like the yank of a leather belt. "I'm happy you could join us. You're very hard to get ahold of."

"Still am."

"And yet here we are, finally meeting. This must be important to you," I said, giving him one final grip of our handshake before sitting back down.

"Perhaps. Mainly curiosity is what brought me here. That and appreciation…" He took a purposeful long look towards Gemma, scanning the entirety of her gorgeous, fitted dress. I stopped myself from snapping my finger, directing his attention like the pull of a leash.

I realized quickly that this wasn't just a meeting, this was the life cycle of a trial: one with opening statements, evidence, and closing arguments. It all focused on the mental deliberation of one judge, and one judge alone: my Gemma. I could be domineering in court, but place me next to her, and I was always on the cusp of crumbling.

Every move counted.

"Did you say appreciation?" I adjusted my hands into a steeple. "I like that answer, it's a little odd, but funny. Especially because of how awkward this could be."

"Is it?" he asked.

"I'd imagine so, given our relationship, or, the lack thereof."

"Don't take it personally. My attention is typically more narrowed, but I wouldn't miss this for the world, considering there's a lot to be grateful for."

"I'm sure that's not because of me." I laughed to myself.

"No. Not particularly, but it could be."

"Sounds complicated."

"That's the perfect way to describe us." Alex uncorked the tequila bottle by his side, commanding the attention of the room with the clank of crystal shot glasses. "I don't need another friend, but outside of business, there's no reason for us to dislike each other. Things can be both burdensome and rewarding… just like this," he tilted the bottle. "Did you know it could take twenty years to make a single batch of tequila? Eight of those just for the agave to mature," he asked Gemma, grinning only for her.

"That's not too long, given it takes people their entire lives sometimes." Gemma answered in my direction, her role in this immediately clear; she was acting as Alex's defense.

"Agave can be mature, but maturity by itself doesn't give you tequila." I said, watching Mila's studious gaze as she made meticulous, mental notes on everything we said. Being discreet was an absolute requirement.

"You're not wrong. You have to harvest it, cook it, shred it, ferment and distill it, but most importantly, and what really separates it from the rest, is its age." Alex seemed pleased, as if distinguishing us apart, inspecting the nauseating translucent liquid against the fireplace.

And did he really have to mention age? He had well

over a decade on Gemma and me, and I supposed he thought it meant something. Maybe that's why he seemed so confident, or perhaps maybe he was just a good actor. Gemma never showed an interest in older men before, and sure, she was old enough to date who she wanted, but the visual of Alex with her felt like complete robbery.

"Age is good. However, it's gross when someone wants it before it's ready. You know, younger than expected," I jabbed, fighting to keep my eyes from moving towards Gemma.

"It's old enough…" Alex added, "I'd know. I made it myself."

Gemma reached for his knee, leaning in with the widest smile. "Wait, is this the project you've been working on?" she asked impressed, her enthusiasm deflated me.

She obviously knew of some backstory, and my mind immediately pictured her and Alex together, exchanging pieces of their past, tucked away in his penthouse—or worse—his bed. The unstoppable image caused my heel to bounce.

"I'm proud to say, yes. It took years to perfect. It was completely frustrating and painful to work with, but the best rewards often are. You'd think I hate it by now… but in fact, I appreciate the hell it put me through."

"You must love me then." I said sardonically as he unfortunately poured me a drink.

"You've cost me a lot of money, but that's ok. I have more to spend than you know." He pushed the drink in my direction, "Taste it, and tell me what you think."

It was my first true move, akin to the beginning slide of a single chess piece; but I fucking hated tequila, ever since that New Year's Eve party when I got completely sick with Gemma. My throat cramped up with the anticipation of its taste.

Gemma watched, knowing damn well I could barely say the word tequila, let alone drink it, but she didn't even try to stop me, and in fact, said nothing, like she was secretly punishing me.

I lifted the shot to my mouth, pulling it to the back of my throat, attempting to ignore the fire building in my chest as Alex slowly swallowed his drink, actually enjoying it.

"Do you like it?" he asked.

"I could drink it all day." I lied, knowing I had to take back control of our conversation, physically feeling my watch tick along my wrist.

Tick.

Tok.

"Good. You're the first to try it." He poured me another. "Consider it a gift… for all that you've done so far."

I laughed at him, "You must be drunk already. I can't think of anything you should be thanking me for…"

"Don't act so sure. Despite what I think about you, you're important to Gemma… That single saving grace has allowed you the opportunity to look after her, and in a way, it feels like you've kept her safe till I could find her. So, thank you," he raised his glass. "But your job is done now. I'll take it from here."

Take it from here? I leaned against the armrest, my thumb settled under my chin to keep it from shaking. I hated his unwavering need to grin, and how he assumed that both him and Gemma were grateful for me, grateful as if I could now rest easy. My job wasn't just out of love, it was out of pain and discomfort, it was out of sacrifice. I'd never let it go to waste, not on someone like him.

"What exactly are you taking over?"

"That'd be up to Gemma, of course. I'm not replacing you. Aren't you her best friend?"

"Since first grade."

"Good. She can have as many as she'd like, me included… but I want more than what you two share. And I'm not shy about my intentions." We both shot our drinks back.

Gemma's lips formed into a perfect O-shape, pursed only to be opened for a sharp breath. No clarification, no objection. Mila stared at me, but I sought more from Gemma, her nervousness enveloping me. This burned more than the tequila.

"I'm certain you have many intentions. But do you really consider yourself friends with Gemma?" I snipped.

"We're friendly."

"No offense, but you don't seem friendly."

"I'm not here to convince you, I'm here to settle business."

"I don't settle, and that offer doesn't interest me. I'm focused on you right now, and since you're so keen on *taking over,* you wouldn't mind the work it takes to earn Gemma."

"You act like that's up to you."

"Thought you'd appreciate being put through hell?" I reminded, certainly not buying the act.

"Parker," Gemma hushed, "I'm doing this as a favor to you. I don't need you to pry." She gave me a clear warning of her patience. I wanted to respect it, but I also wanted her to see a glimpse of what Alex was hiding.

"I'm going to ask him a few more questions," I stated.

"Is this an interview or an interrogation?" Alex interjected, spearing my intentions.

"Aren't you used to both?" I asked.

"That's unfair," Gemma said.

"Of course it's not. He has a chance to prove me wrong, and I'm willing to listen. I'll keep the first one simple. Have you ever been arrested?" I asked, knowing the answer.

"I have," he said, relaxing into his own response.

"How many times?"

"Enough times."

"Don't be vague. That doesn't benefit Gemma. I'm asking specifics, and I need to know if you can be honest." I maintained, cornering him to be truthful. I needed any and every advantage I could get.

"I can be honest."

"You can also *not* be, then? Does that pertain to right now?"

"Everyone can be dishonest, but dishonesty isn't always wrong. Have you ever lied to protect someone?"

Relevance?

His question couldn't have been more eerily accurate to my life, but also, provided me with an opportunity to push back. This was evidence, this was my move.

"I have," I answered. "But protecting someone and protecting yourself are two different things. I think the latter may pertain to you more."

"Sounds like you're assuming something."

"I'm assuming Gemma knows very little about who you are, because if she did, she'd never look at you the same."

With shut lips, the impression of Alejandro's tongue rolled over his teeth. For a brief moment he looked at his watch, hiding his discomfort. He was recovering from some mental glitch, a trait that lawyers could sniff out like blood in water.

"He hasn't done anything wrong, Parker," Gemma stopped me. "Please… don't be rude."

"I'm not rude. The facts are simple. In the few months you've known each other, he's already pulled you into two separate illegal activities. He broke you into The Met and snuck you onto the roof of some dilapidated building. Neither should have happened, and both could've led to serious consequences."

"So, The Met story was true?" Mila muttered, taking a long sip of her dirty martini.

I shot Mila an indicative arch of my brow,

reminding her of the conditions that she agreed to. *No questions, no interjections.*

"The roof was my idea." Gemma ignored her, catching me by surprise, and maybe she didn't expect to say it, but the stiffness in her posture signaled she wasn't going to back down.

"So, you broke him into the building, and you took him upstairs?" I asked, struggling to pivot.

"Yes."

"In over the twenty-some years since we've known each other, you just decide to do something like that? You don't do that, Gemma."

"Well, I did, and I wanted to see how it felt. It was about making my own choice."

"But if you knew the truth about him, you wouldn't have done that. Trust me."

"What makes you say that?" she belittled it with a scoff, but I fired back.

"Because, you don't know why people are so scared of him," I argued.

Gemma stared off for a minute, unable to reply, fidgeting with her dress strap that didn't need to be fixed. I didn't want to use fear as a tactic, but fear was all I had. Alex was part of something horrific, and the blast of his presence was far more nuclear than anything Claire ever warned me about.

"No one is scared of me. Except maybe you." Alex poured another drink, skipping my glass. How petty. He wasn't completely angry, but the way his words needled out, let me know I was getting close.

"Gemma knows when I'm telling the truth. She just

has to ask me to promise. And if I do, that's enough. Am I wrong?" I asked her.

She seemed reluctant at first, but then agreed. "It's true. Parker never breaks a promise."

Alex disapproved with a sigh. "Promises mean nothing. People make them every day, only to break them. Have him *swear* it to you, then you'll know his word is true."

"Play semantics all you want. I doubt you could ever be honest, swear or no swear," I challenged.

This seemed to intrigue Alex as he drew himself closer to the table. Whatever game we were playing was now heating up. "I'll be honest with you. You're asking a lot of irrelevant questions to pin me in a certain light, when in fact, it's you who's in the wrong."

I ignored his quip, asking something more pressing of my own. "Does she know what you've been accused of? Have you asked how that makes her feel?"

"She's a big girl. She's managed just fine without you." Alex looked away, breaking our unofficial staring contest. "I knew you were protective, but fuck, you're overbearing."

"You're too scared to answer. Just admit it."

"If Gemma wants to entertain some idea you have of me, then she can find it in a magazine. You don't give her enough credit... and that's why you'll lose her."

"I'm not losing anyone," I gritted, spilling an accidental vulnerability.

Alex smiled. "Don't act like a child."

"Then don't lecture me on losing people."

Alex squeezed the empty glass in his hand, my last

remark causing him to glance at Gemma, then over his shoulder. Whether he admitted it or not, he wanted to run.

"Who are you looking for?" I asked, commenting on his vacant stare. "You need Lina to come help you?"

"I don't need Lina for this but keep talking, and I just might."

"There's no need to bring anyone else into this, Park." Gemma's interjection was more so considerate than harsh. "Lina was helpful, she kept my name out of the papers after The Met."

"That's the least she could have done, considering how reckless her client was."

Mila couldn't help herself, adjusting in her seat to get closer. "What else does she keep from the papers? And please, be specific."

"Gossip," Gemma responded for Alex. "There's always some vulture like you lurking for a story. I'm sure you could understand."

"I understand better when it comes from the person themselves, not from their attorneys, and certainly not from their little stylists. Parker's asking good questions." Mila redirected the conversation, playing a witness I didn't need, considering Gemma despised her.

"He's only asking questions because he's afraid of answering his own." Alex stretched his neck, "Ask Gemma, herself. She knows I'm good at reading people, and I've already read you, Parker… here's a truth, I neither like you nor trust you."

"Good." I leaned back. "You shouldn't trust me. In fact, you should be careful around me."

"Is that so?"

"Yes. I made this clear to your team of attorneys, but since you're never brave enough to attend our meetings, it's best if you know now… I'm not too fond of your juvenile reputation."

"And what would that be?"

"A bad boy," Mila chimed in, using me as a shield for her directness. "I read that you've settled in twelve different assault cases in the past eight years. Not to mention your history of disorderly conduct charges. Trespassing, vandalism, and public endangerment."

"There are two sides to every story," Gemma rebutted. "You don't get to sit there and point fingers. I can't think of anything dirtier than what you do."

Mila scoffed. "What? Tell the truth?"

"You couldn't be more delusional," Gemma rolled her eyes. "You capitalize on the misfortune of others and the truth for you is whatever gets a bigger paycheck."

"Haven't you heard? The world praises negative press. It's not my fault his poor choices make for good news."

"And it's not his fault that the world is a snake pit full of Camillas. Why are you even here?" Gemma asked the ceiling, shutting her eyes to reorient herself.

"To support Parker."

"Parker or your career?"

"This isn't about me, or Mila." I responded. Everyone felt involved, and I was losing control.

Adjusting the sleeve of my suit, I fought how tight it suddenly felt along my shoulders. Alex glared at me, and

Gemma seemed to be positively annoyed, her voice pitched higher than normal.

"Don't sit there and act like it isn't. You pretend to be honest, and worse, pretend this is for Gemma," Alex commanded silence. "This has been about you, and only you."

I clenched the arms of my chair.

About me?

How the fuck would you even know what this was about?

Did you carry Gemma home when she fell off a bike, or for that matter, teach her how to ride one afterwards, because her father never did? Or did you give her your dessert each day at school, picking Star Crunch at the store—even though you loved Twinkies —just so that she could actually enjoy something other than the sandwich you brought her?

I did, and not just as a boy, but as a man. Cause it was never just about giving up my jacket to keep her warm or waiting forty minutes in a cold Manhattan morning to pick up her favorite bagel. It's about her, not about me. It's four drops of honey, and everything else that I cherish about her…. Everything I do is to protect her, because I'm so fucking helplessly in love with her.

I bit my tongue from saying all of that. Now wasn't the time, and I owed her a hell of a lot more than bringing that shitstorm in front of everyone to judge, yet I couldn't help but feel entirely defensive.

"How could you ever truly know Gemma?" I shouted.

"How could I? How could you not by now?"

"Stop. I've always been there for her. How have you ever done that?"

Alex tsked his tongue, annoying me with his

disapproval. For a moment, there was nothing else, no crowds, no fireplace, no dark marble pillars or ground to stand on. Just us and the pulled hammer of our pistoled words.

"Please, where were you the night she waited for you at the play and you stood her up? You didn't see her all alone like I did. I was there, not you, asshole. So you can cut the shit on pretending to be reliable."

His brutal answer caused me to spit out, immediately coping with the pain in my chest. I shouldn't have shouted, but I did, unable to think of an adequate response. "Reliable like your police record?"

Alex laughed at me. "Is that all you have? This is supposed to be about Gemma and what is best for her. Do you think she enjoys this? I know damn well she isn't appreciative of your tone and that your yelling actually hurts her. Instead of telling her that you care, start listening… because that's what I do, and I won't stop till I know everything about her."

"I do listen to Gemma. And me being here doesn't take away the fact that she is free to do whatever she wants."

"Prove it." Alex turned to her, "Gemma, let's go." He stood up.

Immediately, all my goals and intentions collapsed into a single defining moment of Alex calling my bluff, testing me to the point where I knew I could never turn back. He reached for Gemma's hand, and before she could even react, I fucking panicked.

"No," I said through my teeth, snatching his wrist, yanking it into the air. My entire life with Gemma flashed before my eyes, abruptly and upsettingly, ending itself like an old movie whose film began to sputter into a hot, white mess. I couldn't believe it, unable to stop myself from growling, from bleeding out the most honest threat I'd ever made. "Touch her again," I said, "and I'll fucking kill you."

Chapter 8

GEMMA

"Parker… what the hell are you doing?" I scolded so viciously, stunned by the relentless hold he had on Alejandro's wrist. Camilla covered her mouth, her stare a frantic urge for me to step in. I couldn't, and the thought of moving made me feel fragile, as if one look from either man could obliterate me.

"You really doing this in front of Gemma? You're not fooling anyone. This isn't about protecting her," Alejandro said.

"Think whatever you want, but Gemma believes you're a good person, and I know that's not true. If you want to prove her right, then do it." Parker's hold on Alejandro tightened even harder, and I feared he was dangerously close to saying something I wasn't prepared to hear.

"Prove her right? How about you prove you're not just her friend. Look at you. You're a mess and all I see is fear—" Alejandro's bark caused an unintentional squirm in my belly, as he balled his fist.

"No." Parker blurted out. "I'm what I need to be, the fucking man who'll expose Gemma to the truth about what happened at The Pierre Hotel." He responded so abruptly I nearly missed the end of Alejandro's words.

The immediate mention of The Pierre Hotel made me feel ill, as if each word was laced with a contagious sense of uneasiness. I traced my hands down my neck, soothing the tightness I felt, stifled by the eyes of the entire bar.

I was slowly suffocating.

"You don't know what you're getting yourself into," Alejandro warned.

"No," Parker asserted. "It's Gemma who doesn't. And that's because you hide behind NDAs like a fucking coward."

"You better watch it."

"Or what? Who's scared now?" Parker taunted with all the confidence in the world, but each word he spat felt like stepping on broken glass: painful, impossibly transparent, and difficult to extract.

Alejandro ripped his hand away from Parker's. "You got a problem with me, take it up in court… but you leave Gemma out of this." He reached for me again, but Parker stood up.

"You don't fucking listen, do you?" His rumble lodged itself into my chest.

I stood up immediately, and Camilla followed, reaching for Parker's side. "Gentlemen…" I said quietly.

"I'm everything you're not, including appreciative for who and what Gemma really is. I won't stop until she's mine to keep. *Every piece of her.*"

"She. Is. Not. Yours," Parker hammered each word,

stepping closer to Alejandro, bracing his position for god knows what. "Fuck court, I've made my judgments."

Alejandro glared, silently contemplating his next words until he caught my pleading eyes. He knew I didn't want this, he always knew everything, just by looking at me. "You need to calm down. I'm not doing this in front of Gemma—"

"Parker, please," Camilla interjected, watching as the crowd began to whisper to each other, with no security to stop us. "People are staring."

I tried to remain calm, my thoughts disrupted by how close Parker was to Alejandro. I noticed everything, my own anxiousness and anger reflected in his eyes, the suspended uncertainty of what was to come. They were each watching the other, pensive and quiet, seeking any excuse to lose control.

But then, Parker stopped everything that he was doing.

Sniffing.

Furrowing.

"What the fuck is this?" He took a step back, uncertain of what he was fathoming, "Cherry smoke?" Parker turned to me with a fiery gaze as I covered my mouth.

The secret was out. Parker knew I lied about the perfume, the scent he smelt on the couch, as Alejandro hid in my bedroom. God, the whole thing made me feel so feverish.

"I like them sweet." Alejandro grinned, "I told you before, I won't stop till Gemma is mine... and that means going where I want, when I want, even through the window of your own fire escape."

Parker slammed his hand onto the table, reaching beneath it, flipping it over as if it were weightless. He removed all barriers blocking him from Alejandro, attacking him with all the rage he bottled inside. I barely processed the screams of others around us, as their drinks fell to the floor, shattering shards of tequila-scented glass along my heels.

He snatched Alejandro, dragging him by his lapel. "You broke into my house? You were in Gemma's room? I'm pressing charges!"

"Prove it." Alejandro replied, eerily calm.

"Gemma will attest to it… she'll always choose me."

"Parker, don't you dare!" I shouted, causing both men to stop and acknowledge me. This wasn't a legal battle, nor a disagreement; this was for territory, this was for me. And I wasn't some plot of land to spill blood over. "I'm not playing this game anymore. It's enough."

"It's not enough." Parker warned, "Gemma, he's dangerous."

"We're leaving." Alejandro looked at me, eager to convince me with the assertiveness that Parker hated. "You don't need to be here for this. We can take care of each other."

Never had I seen Parker's eyes so enraged, the whites enveloped like a horse ready to rear. Something snapped within his jaw. *Alejandro the caretaker? Alejandro with me?*

It was all so sudden.

Smack.

Alejandro grunted, his back slammed against the

stone like a fastball pitch into a mitt. I screamed as Parker shoved Alejandro against the marbled pillar beside him, releasing the most exerted power of brute force that could be felt at our feet.

"*Take* care of each other? Just like you *took* care of Natalie Brower?" Parker fucking growled as an unruly wave of hair set loose along his face.

I worried Alejandro's silence stemmed from everything Parker accused him of, his reaction so painfully still that it made me want to disappear.

Parker continued, "Since you're such a fucking savior, tell Gemma what happened. Tell her the truth about the girl from Belmont Hills."

I stepped away from my chair, distancing myself from the dreaded mention of someone new; of the very shadow that had followed Alejandro and me since I mentioned him to Parker. This wasn't just us anymore, this was bigger, this was a revelation, and it had a name: Natalie.

"Alejandro, what's he talking about?" I asked horrified and confused.

Alejandro calmed himself into a single glare that Parker couldn't replicate. He wasn't as composed, garnering all the looks of the audience around us, Camilla included.

"You and I… we're more alike than you even know, and maybe that's why I dislike you so much. But right now, we couldn't be further apart." Alejandro drew a slow, collected breath, his face far more disappointed than anything else. "I don't understand the choices you made, and you don't understand mine… but I know we have to live with them. And for you, that means letting Gemma go. You had your chance with her, and now it's over."

"Ok. We're done here!" I finally demanded, pushing them apart. I wanted to know the truth, but what I needed most right now was to get Alejandro and Parker away from each other as quickly as possible, even if that meant not getting the answers I wanted. Parker's hands began to shake, watching catatonically as I reached for Alejandro. "We're leaving…"

"Not with him you're not," Parker cut me off. "You and your safety come first. Alex knows nothing about that."

"Well, I do," I asserted, finding the courage to speak for myself. "This isn't about you two anymore, I get to make my choices. I get to live my life how I want it."

"He's dangerous—"

"He's not, Park. He's the other half of the story that people forget. I get to assess both sides, I get to see what works for me."

Camilla scoffed, "You should be careful, or you'll be the next mystery girl Alex is in court for, the next big scandal." She snaked her arm around Parker's bicep, alerting him to an uncomfortable look.

My ears began to ring.

"You will stop right now, Mila." Parker reprimanded her as I stepped forward, guarding Alejandro behind my back. This was it. I was so clearly on the other end of some imaginary line, belonging to some team that felt wrong in Parker's eyes.

"Why are you still here?" I spat at Camilla, feeling

defensive for my best friend. "You're not here for Parker, you don't even care about him. Not like how someone should. You're just using us for one of your pathetic articles."

"Don't flatter yourself," Camilla's red lips parted with a hiss. "Your life's suitable for some trashy magazine, but not for New York Prestige."

"That's enough, Mila," Parker flinched.

"It's true," she defended. "They're perfect for each other... both fucked up and damaged."

"Fuck you," I lifted my drink, throwing it as hard as I could into her face. It splashed everywhere, garnering a collective gasp as Camilla shrilled from the top of her lungs. Perfect black tears of mascara and vodka rolled down her cheeks, as my face burned with shame.

"Gemma!" Parker shouted.

"Watch your fucking mouth," Alejandro warned, his forehead now digging into Parker's. He came out of nowhere, snapping him back into the most chaotic moment of my life, as I pulled him off.

"Gemma, please... I need you to trust me," Parker choked, thinking of a defense, an excuse, some reason beyond everything I assumed he wish he could say but didn't. He reached for me, actually taking my hand into his as Camilla watched, her disbelief as scorching as Parker's touch as he pressed his thumb into my palm, delivering some desperate pressure to be felt.

Where have you been? I wanted to ask.

This wasn't us, this wasn't who we grew up to be, and all I could feel was the burn behind my eyes as he opened his mouth.

But nothing came out.

Just silence.

I waited, feeling everything, our bodies connected by the tips of our fingers, hopelessly electric.

"I need you to trust me, too," I finally exhaled, blowing out my one true wish, my words meeting his ears like the tips of birthday candles. In the past weeks, we'd been nothing but nasty to each other, slinging whatever stone and silent pout we could, but now, honestly, I just wanted to pull him into my arms, win or lose, I wanted to keep him, but I needed to walk away. *This isn't just for you, Parker, this is for us.*

"I don't want to do this," he gritted, "I just—"

"I want to make my own choices," I stopped him. "Everyone is always warning me, telling me what to do, how to feel. But I want to decide that for myself… no matter how unconventional it may be for others, or for you. It's my choice, my conflict to navigate, not for you to protect me from, because I need to learn to fall before I can get back up. And trust me, I know that you care, but tonight I need you to care less."

Parker rubbed his thumb along my ring, his gift from a time when nobody else existed but us. "I'm incapable of that, Butterfly." He painfully paused, his words falling down to our silver reflection. Didn't he realize that I always carried him with me, not only in my heart, but on my finger?

"It's ok…" I whispered. "Everything is ok, Rattlesnake…"

"It's not," he silently admitted. "It'll never be ok without you."

Camilla straightened up, her face wet, her lips sucked in with rage. "Let them go," she whimpered. "Let her figure it out on her own."

Parker stepped back as Alejandro reached for my hand, stopping the approaching staff members with a measurable glare.

"We need to leave," Alejandro directed, as everyone silently watched us.

There was nothing I could say, nothing I could feel other than regret for everything Parker said. I could never envision saying goodbye, but if I did, I imagined it in the somber way that finally came out of my mouth. No nicknames, no I love you. I shut my eyes and quietly fell apart, staring back with the final opportunity to see his face.

"Goodnight… Parker."

Chapter 9

ALEJANDRO

"Goddamn it." Gemma cursed to herself, her body bound to the leather seat as we pulled away into traffic. Her hands were shaking, crazed since the moment I slammed the car door.

"You're ok," I comforted. She had every sense to be shocked, treated like the object of disgruntled men. I hated that I was a part of that, a participant in the most gross resemblance of where we came from: a place of arguing, anger, jealously.

I reached over her waist, securing her belt with a click. Her arms stayed glued to her sides, her knees clamped together like a vice.

"I didn't mean for that to happen. I just lost control, and everything spiraled."

"None of that was your fault." I tried redirecting her attention, but she stared everywhere but at me: at her hands, the windows, the floor. "You did what you had to. You stayed afloat."

"That wasn't staying afloat, Alejandro. That was wrong. I can admit that."

"Admit what? That you're accountable for another's actions? Don't do that. This wasn't because of you."

"It was *only* because of me," she argued. "I'm the reason we're here; for the yelling, the shoving."

Gemma's frown appeared exaggerated, magnified by the passing shadows that eclipsed her beautiful face.

Each street we passed was a new set of lights, an ornate secretion of colors that highlighted the threatened tears in her eyes. As much as I wanted to console her, I couldn't, because the panic she had needed to be felt, it needed to be expelled.

My goal to push Parker, to break his facade, was horribly botched, and in the backlash, I was nearly destroyed. How could I ever tell the truth after what he said? He knew Gemma, had history with her, and the horror on his face was as startling as the strength he used to shove me against the wall. What if Gemma knew my secrets, what if she confirmed everything Sergeant Fields and Parker warned me of, that she'd fucking run if she knew the monster I was?

"I hate how I feel." Gemma formed her hands into claws, grasping at an imaginary ball. "I threw a drink at Camilla. I..." she stammered, tripping over her emotions, "I... *threw*... a... drink... at...Camilla..."

"She deserved it."

Gemma finally looked up, angry that I'd even suggest that. "She didn't, and I don't deserve to do that to myself either. I feel bottled up and shaken, like everything inside is just brimming to the top of some un-poppable cap. And I don't like that. I don't like that I feel—"

"Bad?" I asked, warning her not to say it. She was anything but, and the possible guilt she felt angered me. Gemma's eyes magnified into globes, my single word igniting her truth.

"Yes!" she admitted. "I hate it. It's in me, and it's rotten, and it stems from holding everything in and never speaking my truth. No matter how big or little it could be, it just sits there, swollen like a seed that never sprouts, and as much as I hate it, I always hold onto it, because that's who I am, and it's better than the alternative." She latched onto her seatbelt, twisting it in her hand. She was doing it again, suffering silently, enacting the same sense of concealed shock I noticed the first moment I laid eyes on her.

"Fuck that," I dismissed. "There are a lot of people who are bad, Gemma, but you don't get to call yourself that. Not with me around."

"What? You want to control my feelings too?" Her accusation stung. I wanted to reach out, to grab that auburn hair of hers, and yank it into a position to be heard.

"I won't control you, I'll break you," I threatened, knuckling the leather seat by her thigh. "Fear of the unknown is just fear of being seen, which is exactly what I do to you."

"And maybe you do it too much."

"You've already decided on what's easier," I reached towards the nape of her neck in the darkness of the car, and I didn't care that it startled her, because I liked it; the way she pulled her hands to her chest made her look as vulnerable as I desired. "You're committed to a routine that you feel you deserve, and you reinforce that every time you accept the idea that you're undeserving of something good."

"Yes, because things like this could happen!"

"Things like this? You stood up for yourself, and now you feel bad? I don't fucking think so. Feel however you want, Gemma, but I don't believe you could ever be so complacent; you just do it because it's easier than acknowledging how someone like me can make you live better than what you've ever settled on."

I found Gemma difficult to decipher in this instance, her fluttering eyes either of anger or perplexing curiosity.

"Acknowledge you? How? The only thing I could acknowledge is how you make me feel, but who you are is decided upon how honest you can be. Good, bad, I'm not sure… maybe you believe what others say about you, but I've always been in your corner. There was a lot said tonight, and I'm not sure how much I was supposed to hear."

I wanted to pull myself away, but resisted as she reached for my hand, brushing the black rose that sat over my knuckles. The truth was somewhere in the petals, a meaning I found with someone else, from a memory I wanted to forget: Natalie Brower, Belmont Hills, The Pierre Hotel. Not even I could hide this from Gemma, and my hesitancy was so robust that the city itself became mute.

"What the hell happened tonight?" Gemma corralled a strong silence, challenging me as she should. How could I really win her over after tonight? The only way was to give her the entire truth of the case, but was that a risk I was really willing to take right now? Neither of us were ready for that, so I answered honestly for something different.

"Everything Parker said and did was out of desperation."

"Don't say that."

"It's true. He's desperate enough to risk his whole career, and it's for you, Gemma. He'll say and do anything to keep you, and I don't blame him, because I'd do the same. Parker will only see me as one person. To him, I'm Alex Rivers—the celebrity—but to you, I'm Alejandro, your boss. Both sides are completely different, but both no better than the other. It's true that I have problems, and they complicate who I am."

"We all have our problems, Alejandro... but the closer we grow, the more I realize you're holding back. I've been patient with you, even avoidant, but I don't know if I'm physically able to do that anymore," the way she responded made me weak, leaving me no room to resign. She was still too kind, too completely perfect to ever fully be exposed to my world, to risk having her trauma mixed with mine. I had to be so *fucking* careful.

"What if Parker was right? How would that make you feel?" I brushed my knuckles along her bare shoulder. I wanted to see all of her, including her reaction, knowing at any moment her fair skin could burn red. "The lifestyle, the parties, the bullshit, everything he hates about me is still attached to the person I am because Alex Rivers is attached to me. I'll admit it, I am a dark cloud, and there are consequences to those who get close."

Gemma pulled my hand off her shoulder, caressing it into her own. "I can accept your truth."

"Can you?" I asked. "The choices I made involved

Natalie Brower, and they involved the parties I allowed to be thrown in honor of Alex Rivers… regardless, I tried to do what was right, to help others in need… but ultimately, despite my intentions, people got hurt. And here's an ugly truth; whether it's my fault or not, I've accepted that I was born to be the cause and consequence of everyone's bad decisions."

Gemma's face turned into a stern frown, still safe from the utter distaste I'd seen in Parker.

"And all the bad decisions that came into your life came from someone else? You were never to blame? I know you lose control, Alejandro. I've seen it. I've yelled at you because of it. So, how are your bad decisions any different?" she asked suspiciously, knowing that it couldn't be true. I hated that she had to hear me admit it.

"My bad decisions are always reactions. You've seen my knuckles… you know what I've done, and why I did it. I don't go out looking for men who hit women, but if I find them, I can't ignore them." I knew she read about me and the DJ out in Bushwick, about how bad I beat him. She had no idea how far it could've gone, how deadly that moment really was.

"I wouldn't want you to ignore that."

"I never would, and that's why I'm involved with Belmont Hills. It's a safe place for women to go… women who have experienced things that only you and I have witnessed at home."

Strike one. This made Gemma nervous. In a brief second, she rolled her shoulder, using it to wipe sweat from her ear.

"Like a shelter?"

"A home," I corrected. "A place for those who were abused, who suffer from trauma, who need rehab, or counseling. It's expensive, but they do a lot of good work. So, I donated to them, and that's where I met Natalie."

Strike two. The re-mention of Natalie made Gemma stare down at her ring, the one with that fucking butterfly on it. Parker and Claire made her believe that she was meant to be shy and timid, to be uncertain of what she could be. Fuck that belief. I wanted to push for more.

"But Parker wouldn't be upset about that… there's more you're not telling me. Why is he concerned for her?"

"He's not, it's more for her husband. It's extortion… and I'm not interested in giving him my money."

"Her husband?" she asked, shaken, swirling with a million different scenarios. I needed to see her shocked, I needed her to be absorbed in this sense of who I was and the life I carried—surprised, nervous, exhilarated. That way—when and if I spoke the truth about Natalie, about me and my past—she'd never look at me like Parker, but instead, like the confident woman I knew she was.

"Did you have an affair with her?"

"Is that what you think?"

"I don't know what to think." She cleared the stickiness of her throat. "I want you to tell me."

"No," I said dryly, "we never shared those feelings. I'm more in line with Parker than you think. When it comes to relationships, my interests only involve you… and if you want the truth about Natalie, then I'll need some truth from you too."

"That's not fair." She tried to pull her hands away, but I stopped her.

"I know it's not, but you have one foot in the door with Parker, and the other with me. And I'm too stubborn to let that slide."

"That's not true."

"It is. I saw how you looked at him. You're not just stuck on him, but on some inadequate sense of who you are. I believe in all your potential, and I'm not afraid of the work it takes to pull it out from you."

Gemma's cheeks radiated pink. I was getting closer, pushing her to the edge. "Don't say that," she begged. "Parker and I… we have nothing."

"If you can't accept that simple truth, then how can you accept mine?"

"Stop." Gemma tried to cross her legs, but I forced them apart, causing her head to pull back and her chin to tilt up. I pressed my thumb right into her cheek, correcting the direction of her red, open lips towards mine. The other side of Gemma was in there, somewhere, begging to be pulled out, and like a splinter, it would hurt to do so, but the immediate relief she'd have would be incomparable.

"I won't stop till you know it, till every inch of your body snaps like a whip: loud, strong, quick. A correction that'll make you know who you are and where you belong: a goddess shackled to the post of my bed." I ear fucked her, admiring the goosebumps that appeared along her neck and collar bone, teasing them with the delicate graze of my soft lips.

Strike three.

As soon as I met her eyes, I saw the most beautiful fear I'd ever seen. She was scared, not for her life, but with the possibility of forever being transformed. Each push was another click to the wheel of an old wooden coaster, one where Gemma peaked at its summit. The harder I instigated, the more uncertain she was. Would she collapse, or would she plunge towards the most thrilling existence yet?

"I don't know what to say," she cocked her head, obeying the firm control I held.

"I'll ask the questions… I'll get the answers." I hissed, watching as her hand fell to her thigh, reaching for my wrist. She struggled to decide, either to push me away, or to lead me inside her dress.

"We're here, Mr. Rivers," Charles announced, placing us into park. Gemma glanced at the Cassowary sign out the window, looking up at my high-rise penthouse at the top. She pushed me off, still resisting the need to explore who she was and who she could be.

The moment she walked out of the car, I knew she begged to be chased.

Someday she'd be able to handle my truth—the full truth—but right now she wasn't ready. I didn't want to be her monster, I wanted to be her angel, and that required her walls to be broken. And I'd fucking do that for her.

I'd leave this car and test her, over and over again, until she was prepared, until every atom of her being was saturated with the immunity of ever being afraid of me, exposed to the same exhilarating fear she displayed as I kissed her on the rooftop.

And in those moments I'd ask…

Do I scare you, Gemma?

And as soon as she'd say no—honestly and fully *no*—then I'd believe she could accept me for who I am. No more codes, flowers, or secrets. Just us.

Chapter 10

GEMMA

As much as I wanted to walk away from Alejandro, I couldn't. The persuasiveness of my body and the ability to yield its direction became weak as he followed close behind. His eyes watched every bit of my movements, their sensation indistinguishable from the hot summer rain that peppered my skin.

Not a single word was spoken, only felt, as the spell of his penthouse pooled between my legs. Up there, alone, felt like the meeting point for all the actions we craved to take, but only fantasized about. What would I do once I was there? Stand in the foyer like the night I measured his sweaty body? Nervous? Excited?

When Alejandro threatened to shackle me to his bed, it terrified me in the most spectacular of ways. Wanting to be vulnerable was different from being vulnerable, and the possibility of him ever doing that wasn't just hot, but intimate; an idea that produced a Parker-level fear: thinking I was desired, but really never was. And if I believed that, then what else would I believe? That everything would be ok, that I wouldn't be the next mystery girl as Camilla described; caught in the lawsuits, the fame, the crowds, the hurt, being the woman Claire warned me of.

I marched ahead in the hallway, pressing the button to Alejandro's private elevator as it opened immediately. I walked in, clutching my purse to my side, attempting to ignore him as he entered. I barely had a moment to think, as he smashed the button, forcing the doors shut.

My obsessive carrousel of fears—both from Claire and Parker—all competed with the swirling heat of anxiousness I felt. That heat, that *bubble*, splashed into my chest like a wave as Alejandro took hold of my wrists, shoving me against the wall, meeting my skin with his.

"Look at me," he demanded.

"What are you doing?" I gasped, forced to face him, the tip of his straight nose brushed against my ear.

"What I fucking need to," he inhaled my neck, stretching my hands further above my head. "Why are you so brave with Parker? How can you be so confident with *him*, but so shy with me?"

"I don't know." I lied, but he knew better.

"You do know, but you're choosing not to tell me." He pushed into me, keeping me still with the weight of his strong hips. I felt all of him, the cotton of his expensive suit a facade to the rock-hard torso and chest that enveloped my shaking body.

"So what? You're a mind reader now?"

"Maybe… I certainly have my guesses." He grinned.

"I'm sure you do, but I shouldn't even be here."

"Then go," he demanded against my rosy cheek. "I'm not your little friend, Gemma… I'm your reckoning. And as soon as you accept that, the sooner we can get to work."

"What? Am I some project to you?"

"My biggest one yet… and my life depends on it." He stopped my legs from closing, pushing them apart with the strong sweep of his own sturdy boot. The way his heel dug into the ground sent a trickle of hot, sticky sweat down my thigh. "You're so shy around me. Is it because of how direct I am?" he asked.

I tucked my chin toward my shoulder.

"Use your words, good girl," he instructed, biting softly, clamping onto the soft skin at the bottom of my jaw.

The elevator beeped loudly, filling me with insurmountable hesitation.

"No." I finally exhaled, centered by the tease of his citrus scent.

"Is it because I want to fuck you?"

"Partly," I admitted.

"And what if I wanted to use you up? To make you my plaything? To make that pink, little pussy of yours drool with cum? Would it make those cheeks of yours red?"

God, he was so hard, the tip of his cock indistinguishable between the buckle of his belt. I couldn't even reply, alarmed by how stiff his shaft felt against the silk-covered shield of my belly.

"Maybe." I wet my lips, my nipples pebbling through my bra and dress, hard at his words, eager to be sucked.

"*Maybe* isn't what I'm looking for. But I'm getting closer." His day-old stubble brushed against my skin, his voice even keeled, like the urgency had left.

"How do I know I can be safe with you?" I asked, uncertain of everything that was said at the bar, of the person who chained my arms above my head. Alejandro didn't skip a beat.

"You can't. In fact, you're not safe, because the person you are is a shell to who you can be. I want what's beneath." He said to the plate of my chest, his lips kissing, mapping its direction straight to my mouth. I shut my eyes.

"You think you know me, but I don't even know myself," I moaned as he freed a hand, carefully lifting my dress past my thighs.

He had to keep me from falling, from my knees bending into a position where I'd face his erection, where I'd have no choice but be both victim and servant to his pleasure.

"I know enough, I know whether I'm hot or cold… and I'll know what I need to right now, just with this," my mouth propped open, coaxed by the smear of my imperial, pink lipstick from his thumb. "Gemma…" he bit out. "Tell me you're mine. I need to hear you say it."

I wanted to scream.

Squirm.

Die.

He stole my breath, teasing at the possibility of a new definition of us. It was all too promising, a reality where I could be free from myself and my past. I had to pull myself away, my head turned as Alejandro's intoxicating charm shattered my confidence. He figured me out.

"There it is…" he admired. "The look I need."

"Of what?" I begged, not knowing what to say.

"The door to you. Those eyes, that fear. You'd rather be fucked like a toy than be fully seen, but maybe one is required before the other."

"That can't be true." My teeth rattled, a new sense of cold made me feel completely exposed, entirely read. He was right, I was petrified, and the more I tried to rationalize it, the more complex it felt. It made me want to run, but to also stay, to both beg for mercy and punishment, to be smashed like the jar I felt stuck inside of.

"It's more truth than you're willing to admit. It's a big feeling… but maybe, you're just a little girl." He teased, his blood-filled erection burning my entire body with how hard he pressed it against me. I lowered my hands behind his neck, a brace to hold onto.

"I feel little next to you… next to what *we* can mean." I neared his mouth, unable to reach the kiss I wanted to steal. "I'm nervous with what will happen afterwards…"

"After I fuck you?" he asked sternly, eyes pinned to mine.

I nodded again.

"After that, Gemma… I give you everything you already have with me, but refuse to acknowledge: a home, a place to rest your head, to cry, to feel, to be appreciated and praised like the incredible and deserving woman you are."

Alejandro's palm consumed my thigh, swallowing it up as he slowly slid his fingertips up and over my panties, teasing the spot right above my clit, but not touching it.

"I'm afraid of getting hurt, of not knowing the truth about who you are," I admitted. "But I'm willing to try."

"You'll do more than that. I'm not just persistent, Gemma, I'm effective. I'll get what I want, even if I have to fuck it out of you first."

He balled my panties into his fists, pulling them aside, exposing my cunt to the cool air. I was so fucking wet, spilling over my lips and onto his hand.

"You will be mine, Gemma. You *will* feel me; you will scream my name, not by choice, but by the demand of your own body." He warned one last time, testing how hard my shoulders could tremble, smiling once more. "Do I scare you, Gemma?" He clenched my auburn hair, yanking it to meet his eyes, evoking every root to tingle like the spread of a wildfire.

"Yes," I answered weakly.

"Do you want me to keep going?" he asked, as the elevator stopped and opened to his penthouse.

He could barely finish his question, my answer already causing his cock to swell.

"God, yes," I begged. "Never stop."

Chapter 11

GEMMA

"I'm rough, Gemma. Between these walls I don't play nice," Alejandro bit into my neck as he lifted me, cradling my ass with an all-consuming pinch. I loved how he carried me through the foyer, my legs wrapped around his waist, crashing me along a wall that spiraled a frame into a crooked mess.

"I'm done with nice," I cried, "I want bad." I was so lightheaded, panting as he shifted his lower hand to cup my mound, spreading me open. He couldn't stop kissing me, kissing me in a way that felt hurried but slow, his fingers digging into my sensitive flesh.

"Good," he grunted. "Rule number one: I'm not your keeper, I'm your fucking Papi."

"Papi?" I croaked.

Alejandro slid me off his waist, bent me over, and shoved me against the kitchen counter, causing my dress strap to fall off and my stomach to be wedged between the cold, white granite and him.

Smack!

A pop rang through the kitchen, as he slapped my ass. I yelped louder than the spank as he pinched me harder, making it sting.

"That's right. Say it when you're fucking helpless, and you need a daddy to tell you how to feel, because there are consequences for you not admitting that you're mine."

The endearment of ever calling him Papi—or daddy—was so fucking sexy. He was older and authoritative, a culmination of all the things I missed from my childhood, but never knew I needed, or rather, wanted. Still, this was different, sexy even.

"Consequences? Like punishment?"

"Only the worst and best kind. Something I've been dying to do."

"And will it hurt?"

"At first maybe. But I'm here to teach you a lesson." He answered to the back of my neck, squeezing my pink nipple into a delicate chaffed red, pinching it so damn good. "It won't be easy, but believe me, Gemma… today's pain is tomorrow's pleasure. Now, palms on the counter," he demanded sternly.

I eagerly complied.

Alejandro tore the rest of my vintage dress, ripping the silk down to my navel, restlessly removing his jacket and tossing his phone onto the counter. He was just as impatient as me, my purse already sprawled out of reach.

"What's my lesson… Papi?" I side-eyed his biceps as he meticulously rolled up his sleeves. All I could do was watch, silently awaiting as he removed each button on his shirt. The cosmic black ink that stretched along his arms branched onto his exposed chest, meeting the black angel wings on his pec. I desperately wanted to know whose initials were on his body, but he interrupted my thoughts.

"Your lesson today, Gemma, is that you need to be broken in… slowly." He pulled my dress past my hips, tugging it like the rein to a horse's bridle. I grunted, my ass yanked towards his crotch as he rubbed himself against me. "If you can admit I'm your Papi now, then someday you'll be able to admit we're more, because at this moment, you're not mentally ready for me… just like how this pussy isn't ready for my cock."

Ready for him? That entailed two things: his secrets and his affection. The pressure of everything felt unbearable, confusing me on what really made me leak. Was it the exhilaration of being handled so roughly or the staggering anxiety of the unknown?

"I can admit more, but I need your help," I pleaded, feeling his zipper brush against the top of my ass, blossoming open with his growing erection.

"I know you do…" He ironed his hands down my arms, ensuring my palms were still stuck to the granite, before tracing back up to my neck, brushing my hair off to the side. "But you can't just be fucked, Gemma, your body needs to learn to submit, to have that pussy be the little puppet to the tip of my finger… because if you took me now, the real me, it would hurt too much." His large knuckle tested the mound of my slit, brushing over its warmth. "Jesus, you're so fucking wet, dripping right through your underwear." He chewed into his own words.

"You're making me that way…" I shivered as he shoved my thong down to my knees, keeping my legs spread with the force of his outer thigh.

"I know I am. It's in my nature to make you wet,

because to me, you are, and always will be, my *Piedra Preciosa*… but since you can't accept that… then tonight you're something different and you'll be treated as such."

"Tell me, who am I?" I begged.

"My slut," with a cooled and determined growl, Alejandro reminded me of the power he held between my legs, as he—for the first time ever—swiped the silky wetness that dripped between my lips. It tickled until it didn't, as he reached my clit and rubbed it slowly.

"You're touching me," I choked, realizing that it was actually happening, that somehow his rough calloused hands were tender, smooth, inviting as he continued to tease me with the trace of his finger over my bare mound; every part of me fluttered uncontrollably.

"Fucking right I am, and it's what you wanted, it's the reason you shaved your fucking pussy, right? To be seen? Thumbed open for my eyes? To be teased? Trust me, this is more for me than for you… I need something, anything… just to stop me from wrecking you completely," he rasped. "I don't want to hurt my tight girl, but I can't promise you won't be sore."

My eyes fluttered in the reflection of the counter, captivated by how slow his fingers slipped inside me. I gasped as he pulled me up to my toes, curving himself to the roof of my cunt, hithering me into a response.

"You feel so big…"

"You haven't felt anything yet, but I'll make you beg to find out."

"Yes."

"Yes, fucking what?" he bated, slapping the lower

cup of my ass again, sending a shot that could be felt between my legs and up to my cunt. I literally fucking groaned. How could this man, a fucking daddy, a papi, be such the sporadic sexual bull? One moment he was dangerously kissing me on the edge of a building, the next he was bending me over, punishing me like some unruly little girl that made him impatient.

"Yes, Papi…"

"Good. And do you feel naughty? Having your dress lifted up, getting fingered like my dirty little slut?"

"Yes. Like *your* dirty little slut." I affirmed, his finger smacking the wet sound loose from my body, echoing amongst the walls. To feel like a slut, to be made to feel like anything other than a sister, was such a prize. His vulgar label was far more of a sexual lure, not taken as an actual criticism. A slut to him didn't make me feel shameful, but rather, a willing and hungry participant, a fucking animal in heat.

"Fuck!" I cried out as he fingered me harder, an unbearable punishment that exuded as much pressure as it did my urge to come.

"I bet your pussy tastes so damn sweet. God," he purred, losing himself, driving his finger faster and faster, causing stars to build in the back of my eyes.

He slipped himself out, wiping the wetness along the back of my thighs as he grabbed my hips, lifting them upward toward his face, my knees now placed on the counter. Starting from my pussy and up to my ass, his tongue licked me so slowly, so deliciously, that I thought I'd come undone from that single, dirty move.

"Do I taste ok?" I shuddered out, devoured by every

bit of his tongue that moved down my slit, preparing me just for him.

"Like my own fucking treat," he growled between licks before slipping me off the counter, forcing me to sit at the edge to face him.

His erection shifted, bursting through the top of his slacks and into the band of his black Calvin Klein underwear. He was huge, much too big for me, leaking a dot of semen into the fabric.

"I don't know how hard I'm going to come." I wrapped my hands behind his neck, whimpering. He leaned in, pressing his lips into mine, opening my mouth with the slip of his tongue. He was there, almost reaching my entrance, my legs spread wider for him as he reached to pull his cock out.

But then everything stopped.

Our frenzy felt like a quick memory, captured by the still rolling beads of sweat that fell over my chest.

"Who is it?" I stared at the screen that lit up our faces.

The room filled itself with a buzz, a rattling hum that came from his phone, an intruder to our moment whose name sat in fat, white letters: Miguel.

He paused for a moment, rededicating himself to the role of Papi, his enigmatic glare resurrecting some assertiveness that initially drew me to him.

"Rule number two, Gemma: patience begets pleasure." He carefully pulled away, sucking the taste of my wetness into his mouth that still sat on his fingers. He licked me off, enjoying a piece of me that relaxed the permanent brood to his face. I felt perplexed.

"I was so—" I stumbled, trembling with how close I was to coming.

"I know… but this is an emergency." He returned to the phone, lifting it into his hands.

"Is something wrong?"

"It's just…work."

"Work from Lina?"

He ignored my question. "I need to take this."

"Should I leave?" I couldn't help but stare as he massaged the bridge of his brow, unsure if the interruption was the reason for his scowl, or perhaps the person on the other line.

"Absolutely not. I don't want you going anywhere. You're my prisoner tonight, Gemma. I'll keep you in my bed till you're fucking raw. You understand?" His brute warning was met with the most charming smile.

I grinned back, an impressive feat considering my ruined orgasm. "Ok, then. I guess I'll just wait." I hesitated, as he quickly kissed me, tormented by his sculpted ass in black, fitted slacks as he left the room.

I covered myself as I sat up on the counter, lifting my dress, redirecting my focus to the name I just read.

Miguel?

I'd seen that name before when Lina visited me, so I assumed it was about the case.

I could hear the slam of the door in the distance, causing me to crane my neck for a quick peek of where he was. Regardless of how quickly he left, I couldn't ignore the sense of playfulness I still felt, the cunning little game of him being my daddy.

Maybe I just wanted to participate, be the little brat

who'd disturb his call. After all, what did he expect from me? I still tasted him on my lips, the smooth tequila he harvested, and the sweet and tarty tinge of cherries from his supple tongue.

But it wasn't until I hopped off the counter that I began to feel different. A shout? A hiss? The distant and harsh boom of his voice was a strange invitation that somehow pulled me towards the hall. He was arguing.

His reverberating tone made me hesitant to even approach him, exchanging the city-lit kitchen, for the eerily eclipsed hall that led to some forgotten spare bedroom. All of this, paired with the darkness, felt reminiscent to the shouting that caused me to hide in a closet as a little girl, raising some irrational fear but also some incurable curiosity. I shook myself away from the thought, fixating on his voice.

"Don't you ever threaten me..." I heard Alejandro say so clearly, *"I never hurt her, not like you."*

Her?

I stepped closer, my bare feet silent along the wood as I neared the framed light of his shut door.

He screamed at someone on the other end, a sudden and unimaginable car crash to my chest that made me turn and fall over myself.

"You're the killer," he slammed his fist against the wall, *"not me..."*

Chapter 12

GEMMA

he Big Hurt. That's what Claire would call it; the ultimate pain she'd warn me of before a depressive spell. *"It's a long way up, letting someone in, and a long way down, letting them go."* She would say this; living, breathing, and preaching these words the moment my father left us so long ago.

I didn't fear the feeling so much as the embodiment of how that event could shape me, stepping away from the hall, my chest constricting itself into a knot from Alejandro's words. *"You're the killer, not me."*

What the hell could that mean, other than how it sounded? I treaded quietly along the floor, more cautious as I backed away, trying not to panic, realizing the gravity of Parker's accusations. What if he was right, what if my version of Alejandro wasn't real? Could Alejandro be my *big hurt*? I didn't want to wait to find out.

I scurried quickly into the kitchen, passing the pockets of darkness and light, fixing what little dress I still had over my shoulders.

I had to move fast.

I had to leave.

I wasn't scared of Alejandro, not physically at least, but was totally and completely unprepared for what I'd say when I'd see him again. I couldn't ignore what I heard, and Christ knows I wouldn't be able to hide it. That's what scared me.

I lifted my shoes from the ground, reaching for my purse, but clumsily dropped it off the counter, spilling my keys and a tube of lipstick. Everything rolled away, scattered like loud glass marbles.

"Fuck!" I bit into my palm, flustered by such a stupid mistake, rushing to my knees to pick it all up.

"Where are you going?"

I shuddered, caught in the act of leaving; my emotions tied between running off in a fit of panic or remaining absolutely still. I calmly turned around.

"Home…" I answered to Alejandro who appeared from the hall, simultaneously stuffing my belongings into my purse.

Alejandro watched closely, his slacks fitted neatly below his abs.

"And why is that?"

"Because I'm tired… It's been a long night, and it sounds like you have a lot to sort out." Alejandro moved over me, stepping on a single sheet of paper that was out of my reach. I realized too late what had fallen out of my purse.

"What the fuck is this?" He bent over, removing the document from the heel of his boot.

"It's exactly what you think it is," I snipped. "It's us in a nutshell."

"That's bullshit, I'd never ask you to sign something like this. Where did you—"

"Lina," I interrupted, "she gave it to me today. But I probably shouldn't have been surprised."

"And what does that mean?"

"It means we have secrets, Alejandro. It means there is more to you than you're willing to share, and although I can't blame you for that, I also can't ignore what I just heard. NDAs aren't normal, we're not normal; and despite how I feel, I just can't help but expect the worst from you. And whatever it is you need from me, whoever you think I am inside, can't compete with this waiting game you're playing. I can't be trained to accept you just because it's convenient for you."

"Trained? I'm not training you, Gemma. I'm commanding you because I have the foresight to see where this ends, and that's already on a thin fucking line. Tell me what you heard and let me explain, but don't sneak out like a fucking child." He cut into me with a stinging dose of honesty I wasn't prepared for, pulling me to my feet. I hated that he held a mirror to me, to how I acted. I wanted so badly to do the same for him.

"Sneak out?" I asked. "Don't fool yourself, Alejandro. I'm not the one *sneaking* away to take heated calls late at night. Now let me go, I don't want to keep you from your *urgent* matters," I threw my hands into the air. "Or from god knows what." I turned around, attempting to slip on my heels as I made my way to the elevator, clicking it open.

"No." He persisted, forcing himself in front of me, blocking the entire width of the door with the stretch of his arm. He lowered his head just to meet my eyes, his body the perfect inverted triangle that stopped the elevator from closing. "You may want to run away, but I won't let you; I won't let you carry on with whatever story you created in your head." He stepped forward, forcing me backwards, "I asked you a question. Now answer me; what did you hear?"

Alejandro was always the man with all the questions, but he could barely answer one of mine. He pushed me in the most uncomfortable of ways, and maybe that was what he wanted.

"I don't want to say."

"Do it…"

"No. This is too crazy, Alejandro, this is… I don't know what this is or what it means, but—"

"Gemma…"

"*You're the killer, not me…*" I finally murmured, stunning myself before staring at the floor. It sounded even worse than when he said it, and I nearly stopped breathing. "It's just too much to ignore, especially after tonight. You have to understand, with all the people after you, the lawsuits and publicity, what am I supposed to think? Especially now after Lina came to me with this NDA. I can't help but wonder what she's protecting you from." I shut my eyes, unable to look, unable to say her name, but I forced myself to do so anyways. "And with Natalie…"

"Natalie?" he stopped me. "This has nothing to do with her, she's just… not a part of our story."

"Don't say that, Alejandro. She's a real person; there's history there, and it kills me that you've shut me out. I can't ignore that Parker mentioned her on purpose. He was trying to tell me something. Can you say the same for yourself?"

"I'd do anything for you, Gemma."

"Except be honest? Except be truly open?" The elevator finally shut behind him as I turned around, marching away from his body and into the kitchen. "I can't keep playing this game of tug of war with you. It's exhausting."

"Exhausting, like how you play so coy?" He stepped closer to me, but I stopped him, forcing my hand onto his body to keep him away. My resistance was met with the most startling complacency. He obeyed, leaning just enough for my palm to dig into his chest, allowing me to feel the relentless beat of his heart. Was he scared? Angry? He was something, but I wasn't sure if it was good or bad. "This isn't you; this is just your guard—"

"Don't you dare." I interrupted, frustrated with him, with myself. "I'm expected to be this open book for you to read whenever you want, yet my questions are evaded. And damn it, I can't rely on my interpretations alone, Alejandro, they will trick me every time. I see you, and I feel excited and hopeful, but I also feel everything in-between, including doubt. It's not my job to just fall, it's your job to also catch me." I pointed my chin to his, challenging him once and for all with the most direct stare I could muster. "You can stand there all you want and try and convince me, but the reality is that you don't trust me with your truth. I want to be there for you, but how can I when you're so unwilling?" I shook my head. "On the phone, you said you never *'hurt'* her—at least—not like how *'they'* hurt her… Who is *her* if not Natalie, then? What have you done? Why does everyone keep warning me to stay away from you?" I asked pathetically, unexpectedly weak from the idea that the truth could be as terrifying as I imagined.

"If I tell you now, you won't like it," he said.

"It doesn't even matter anymore. The fact is I'm used to getting bad news, so save me already and just spit it out." I rebutted, a strange and sad truth that came too naturally.

Alejandro flinched, and the bridge of his nose scrunched as he almost stepped back.

"I was afraid of this reaction… I didn't mean for you to hear that, it's why I walked away."

"To hide your guilt?"

"This isn't about guilt."

"You're right… this is about *her*, so you tell me right now what that means, or I'll leave."

He paused, the serious look on his face faded, replaced with an apologetic wince. His mouth opened, only to close, as seconds of silence passed between us. He licked his lips.

"*Her*, Gemma, is a script, not a person…"

Suddenly and horrifically, I felt foolish.

"How? How is that even possible?"

"That person on the phone was a studio agent… They're threatening to pull the plug on a project. It's something I've been working on for a while now." He brushed my hand, calming me as he leaned against the counter. "They wanted to voice their concerns, because my potential monogamy scares them. I didn't want that

Hollywood bullshit making you uncomfortable… but my discretion made it worse."

"Wait, that doesn't make any sense, why do they—"

"Alex Rivers is a lucrative persona," he cut in, "I need to be both, the good and the bad; the heartbreaker. You don't fit in with that, but I don't fucking care anymore." He pulled me closer, securing my position in front of his hard body. He answered so quick, so convincingly, that I still stumbled over my words. "They will kill *the deal*, not me, I won't bend for them, not against you. They think I'm hurting my image, but the truth is they're hurting the potential of another great movie, another huge paycheck."

"I'm not sure I believe you," I answered honestly, wanting to, but deciding not to pull away. "There are too many opinions in my head, too many versions of you that I still don't know. Like you've said, there are two sides of this story… and I don't know if I trust Alex Rivers." I could still hear Claire warning me, her silent stare fueling the roadblocks of my life. I was raised to fear it all, and it was hard to stop being that little girl, afraid without my protector, afraid to open up and stay on the path of a new beginning. I hated being so suspicious. "I'm so sorry…" I apologized, unable to look at Alejandro, embarrassed.

He grew quiet; my admission a subtle change to his demeanor. "You never have to apologize to me," his smirk faded. "I'm trying to be honest, but maybe I'm just delaying the inevitable, because truthfully there'll never be a *good* time to share, but that's not your fault. I just hope I don't dig myself deeper into a hole."

I looked up into his pitch-black eyes, where I could see for once, the waning of his walls. It took time as he said, slowly revealing that we were more than just the dark clouds from our past. Who was I to rush him into opening up, but in that same breath, how long was I willing to wait?

"Thank you," I said, looking back down at the floor.

"Don't thank me yet. It's my job to prove these things to you, to ease your heart into this world of mine. All you have seen, all you have heard is about my lawsuits, about The Pierre Hotel…" he hesitated. "And now, unfortunately, of Natalie, someone who got mixed up in the cost of fame. You've heard about the parties thrown in my name, those hosted by *Alex Rivers*. But now you need to see who he is, and how he's different from me."

"And how would you do that?"

"By showing you. I don't want to, but I owe you *my* truth, just like how you've shared *your* truth. Tomorrow, I'm hosting an event. The things you've been told about, the gossip, the madness, it will all be there. It's a party, intended to promote *Don Jefe*."

"A party?" I scoffed, nervously looking away. I felt the unwavering sense to curl into a ball, peeking behind the curtain of the infamous Alex Rivers was just what I needed, regardless of how scary it could be.

"A hotel riot, possibly." He grinned, but in a way that left me unsure. Was this excitement, or was this sarcasm? "You don't need to answer now, but at least stay the night." He picked up his phone, unlocking it with disappointment. "I'm expected to call back, to sort this out… I'm not sure how long I'll be."

I tried to smile but couldn't. Our magical moment was ruined because of me and my own insecurities. "I'll just sleep in the guest room," I said, reluctantly.

He gave a slight nod, as if he was defeated. Maybe he wanted me to spend the night with him, but whatever he had to sort out, clearly I wasn't privileged to be there.

"*Buenas noches*. Goodnight," he sighed into my hair, pulling me into a tight embrace.

"Goodnight."

Hoisting my chin, he looked at me one last time, kissing each cheek, my nose, then my lips before turning back to make his call.

I remained in the kitchen, my mind less focused on my stay and more on the upcoming party. An event promoting the inevitable release of his own tequila, seemed like a recipe for disaster, but how else would I see this man and his world, unless I decided to fall down this hole? I knew the cost, I knew the reward, even if I got the *big hurt*.

"Alejandro…" I spontaneously called out, causing him to stop along his path and turn around. One look at his endearing face was all I needed. "I'll be there tomorrow…"

Chapter 13

GEMMA

Hills and Health, read the subtext to an image of a colonial white mansion that was surrounded in pine oak trees and large, picketed gardens. There were no actual hills to be seen, but the *home* itself sat elevated on a series of speckled, stone steps.

I laid on my belly, surrounded by plush pillows in the guest bedroom as I finally decided to scroll through Belmont Hill's webpage. Its bright banner of green acres and manmade ponds felt more like a sanctuary than the forbidden secret others made it to be.

Three separate people brought this place to my attention, yet Alejandro never mentioned it once. Why? I pretended it was for some good reason, just like how the Joneses never let Parker and me watch *My Girl* on family movie night. Sure the film was traumatic, but not as much as the way Mr. Jones spoiled it, *"Imagine Parker getting stung and killed by bees… that's what happens."*

It immediately made me feel uneasy, just as I did now reading the treatments offered at the facility. Counseling and therapy, all centered on what?

Domestic abuse.

Mental health.

Post-traumatic stress.

It was my entire life wrapped into some indigestible nutshell. Triggering? For sure. And maybe that's why I was spared the details, not just about Belmont Hills, but about Alejandro's past. He was a good guy, and I reminded myself of that while reading the small headline to an Ithaca-based newspaper: *Donations Change Landscape for Those Who Seek Help at Belmont Hills.*

I could so easily forward this to Parker and rub it in his face on how I was right. I imagined being so blunt.

...

Dear Rattlesnake,

Please see the attached article that proves how closed-minded you've been. Take special note on how Alejandro's four-hundred-thousand-dollar donation has covered the expensive cost of this private women's facility. He granted access to an entire economic class of those who'd otherwise never meet the insurance requirements to attend.

See! What did I tell you? Alejandro is a good man, and all that good has been lost on New York Prestige! Of course they didn't report this, it doesn't perpetuate the bad boy reputation they like. And do you care? No, because you only care about what fits the narrative that suits you best.

Also, goddamn you!

I'm so annoyed that I even care about what you think; how your opinion is so important to me, and that your approval somehow means I'm making good choices.

Nevertheless, it's all true, and now I'm second guessing everything I encounter, like the conversation I overheard from Alejandro tonight. You wouldn't understand what that last sentence meant, and that's a good thing, because honestly, the thought of you being scared or worried for me, makes me want to cry…and I won't waste good mascara on such a pathetic but true feeling.

Ugh!

Goodnight, you jerk.

I love and miss you…

-Butterfly

…

If only I could say all that and more, my postscript being a laundry list of all the things I knew about Alejandro; a man who took a chance on me, who saw me and, despite my resistance, knew immediately that I was his. He wasn't just an actor, he was a generous person, someone who endured hard labor and arduous tasks, who loved his mother and the taste of cherry cigarettes.

I convinced myself that Alejandro was as innocent as I thought, studying a photo of him attached to the article I just read. In it, he wore a pair of dark sunglasses, his otherwise luscious hair tamed into a flat position, lacking its normal style. I could tell he didn't want to be photographed, his modest position more conservative with his arms crossed, obscuring the spot where his black rose tattoo should've been.

I twisted my leg over a pillow, inhaling the oversized shirt that I borrowed from him, sweet but musky, warm like suede. It bundled itself into the size of a dress, its soft white cotton sweeping over my bare thighs. You'd think sleeping in the luxury high rise of a dark New

York penthouse would be easy, but sleeping was usually difficult for me anyways, especially without my Andy.

I hugged my pillow, imagining it was the tattered fur of my little giraffe. I wondered if he was the exact distraction I needed, stopping me from thinking of the single, three syllable artifact that kept me awake.

NAT-A-LIE.

I squirmed in the cool sheets of my massive bed, wanting to dissect her name like some freakish lab experiment.

Her first syllable—*Nat*—paired ironically with my buzzing thoughts, her existence only a series of letters and sounds that held more of a warning than anything else.

Don't do this, Gemma—I lectured myself, simultaneously typing Natalie's name into Instagram. It wasn't just about seeing her face; it was about acknowledging my own insecurities and, somehow, shopping for the perfect identity to fit Natalie Brower was just what I needed. If I could just see that she was ok—undermining Parker's warnings—then I knew I could be ok as well.

Alejandro is just a good man, trying to do good things, I mused, tucking my knees to my stomach, curled on my side as a result popped up on my phone.

Instantly I saw who I thought she was, the perfect mundane image of a woman who otherwise didn't even know I existed.

Nat Brower - Brooklyn.

It didn't take long to memorize her face, the flow of heart-pounding blood fueling my brain with the power it needed to remember her forever: long black hair, freckles like little constellations between almond eyes and crooked lips. She wore a blue Dodgers Cap, its size much larger than her head could fill.

Alejandro is just a good man, trying to do good things. I repeated once more, deciphering how her troubled stare somehow perfected itself into a smile. *Are you ok? Are you safe?* I asked, disappointed by the privacy notice that blocked me from seeing more of her photos.

I wasn't sure if I felt better or worse, left with no conclusions on if Natalie was some foreshadowing figure on who I could end up becoming.

What if Alejandro really was in trouble, and that somehow, all of this—Belmont Hills, Natalie Brower, The Pierre Hotel—would lead to the end of us? There was only one person who could help, whose number I dug out of my clutch as I rolled over to the edge of the bed.

GEMMA

Lina... I don't need specifics about the lawsuit, and I don't need you to share anything outside of what you're able to disclose. I just need to know if Alejandro will be ok... and I don't mean financially, I mean physically. Just tell me, could he ever be taken away?

I asked in the best way I could, not even wanting to type out the word prison in the text message. The prospect seemed too real, too permanent and far scarier than the equally nauseating reality of him ever returning to California and leaving me behind, because

Alejandro was—in many ways—the strike of tailor chalk against my life, leaving his mark on all the perfect places to cut me into existence. Who was to say I wasn't the same for him? A half-stitched gown wasn't a gown at all; it was loose and unfulfilled fabric, and that's what we would be, if he ever left.

It scared me.

He scared me.

And the thought he could be in more trouble than he was willing to admit became unbearable.

GEMMA

Please, just tell me he's safe, that's all I ask. Tell me, and I'll sign the non-disclosure.

The ding of the elevator entrance was barely noticeable, traveling especially weak through the penthouse. I almost missed it, which was good, since it had been hours since Gemma had gone to sleep, and I didn't want to wake her.

Lina turned the corner of the foyer, approaching quietly on her bare feet. I sat in the dark living room, studying her approach, noticing the concealed look of concern on her face. She hid it well, tight under red lips, the guise of a pearly white blouse.

"You know I up-charge for late night visits," she greeted quietly. "Especially with instructions as unique as yours." I didn't return the smile she gave me.

"Have a seat," I pointed to the couch, leaning back into my large, leather chair. "I see you did as you were told."

"Heels in hand." She confirmed. I didn't need her clicking along the halls so loudly, or having Gemma know that Lina was here for business. "Long night?" she asked as I uncorked the top of an old bourbon bottle. I poured a measure into a small crystal glass.

"Frustratingly so," I said curtly.

"Must have made you thirsty."

"It made me a lot of things, but this one's for you." I

slid the drink across the coffee table towards her reach. "Drink."

Lina didn't hesitate, not showing a desire to please, but a casualness that she used to dispel our tension. I said nothing. I only wanted there to be silence.

"Surprised it's not tequila," she cleared her throat.

"Tequila is for celebrations and negotiations."

"And bourbon?"

"Bourbon is for problems…big ones." I laughed, showing more of an annoyed smile than I intended to display.

"Nothing is too big for me, Alex. I know why I'm here, and frankly, I won't apologize."

"Apologies aren't required in order to feel sorry, and believe me, you will feel sorry."

"I have a job to do."

"You have an obligation to abide by my rules, to approach any legal pursuit upon my approval and *my* approval alone."

"I have to protect you and this case! That includes whatever it is you disclose to Miss Harrison," she threatened to yell.

"You protect us equally. You have no right going behind my back and handing out non-disclosures. Not to her. Not without my permission."

"Equally?" Lina laughed, "And how equal is this relationship of yours, Alex? How equal is ours for that matter?"

"Whatever the hell you're trying to say, Lina, you better say it now."

"It means, my client-attorney privileges are not

being taken seriously. I'm a hell of a lawyer, but not if you're sneaking behind my back. And let me tell you, I know something happened tonight. Yes, I went to Miss Harrison's house; yes, I gave her the non-disclosure, but she gave me something too. Information about you and her meeting tonight? As if it were that simple, I could tell there was more to it than what she said."

"She doesn't owe you an explanation. I pay your bills; you answer to me. Always."

"Be that as it may, I still have my reputation to maintain. And that's not up for debate." She slammed her empty glass onto the coffee table, encouraging the most provoked glare I'd ever given.

"You need to keep your voice down." I licked bourbon off my lips.

"As I was saying, *Mr. Rivers*… If there's something I need to know about tonight, then I'd rather be prepared. I won't go back into Mr. Jones's office and get blindsided by him, not during this critical time of your case. I refuse to look like a fool." Lina wiped the tired mascara from her eyes, our silence interrupted over the pop of the liquor bottle once more.

"Gemma and I met with Mr. Jones tonight," I admitted with a testy sigh, "also with his *girlfriend*."

Lina rolled her eyes. I knew I challenged her professionalism, and that my habits would surely cause her hair to turn grey at any moment.

"Camilla?" she asked.

"How do you know?"

"I met her myself. She came in one morning when I met with Mr. Jones, and I just assumed."

"You must have hated her. I know how much of a headache those journalists at New York Prestige can be." I humored, but the reaction in Lina's face represented a level of high-pressured rage that nearly broke the dam of her patience.

"You met the opposing plaintiff's attorney and his journalist girlfriend…" she winced, "without. Telling. Me. First?"

"Absolutely."

"I would have advised *strongly* against that, Mr. Rivers. I would have told you no, *absolutely* not! And without me? Of all the things…"

"It's fine."

"No, it's not fine. What did you even discuss? Tell me everything. Now."

"This wasn't about the case," I corrected, knowing that the details of our bar fight would send her into a tailspin. She seemed unconvinced.

"I don't believe you," she took a larger sip of her drink.

"Probably because you're too smart. But this was something different. This was matters outside of the case… *mostly*."

"Jesus, Alex…" she scolded me in Spanish, frustrated like a little sister.

"Finish your drink." I demanded, instructing her to relax. "What was said was not as important as what I found out."

"And what could you have possibly found out?" She shook her head.

"That Mr. Jones is desperate," I said calmly.

Desperation often made men more dangerous. I wasn't sure if Gemma knew it or if she just ignored it, but Parker Jones loved her, and he loved her fiercely. That much I could tell, and his attempts to take her now seemed wild enough to ruin his career. I didn't care about the case, I only cared about Gemma, who I feared would see the truth in Parker, and that somehow he'd *try* and take her from me. And I only use the word *try* as a generous way of showing his efforts. I'd never let him have her, not really, because I needed her like I needed to breathe, and I'd do anything to keep her as mine.

"How desperate?" Lina asked.

"Desperate enough to mention Natalie."

Lina's silence grew to the point where I felt uncomfortable. Even if she was joking about up-charging for late night visits, I somehow gathered it would come true.

"You're kidding."

"I don't joke around."

"Well then, this changes everything." She pulled out her phone, swiping it open.

"What are you doing?"

"I'm calling the MelBrook Law Firm. This is a complete breach of contract. And in front of the press? No way." She began to dial.

"Stop," I slammed my drink on the glass table harder than I anticipated. "I pay you good money to advise me, but I'm the one advising you now. You're not making this call."

"Mr. Rivers—"

"You may be good at reading people, Lina, but not as good as me. He mentioned Natalie because Gemma was there, not because of some journalist. He was foolish, but not stupid. I'm certain he's already instructed that woman not to report anything she heard."

"That's ridiculous."

"Maybe. But believe me, I understand the logic in how you think. You're smart, Lina, and this isn't to say that you aren't wrong, and in any other circumstance I would agree with you calling. This—for now—is different."

This wasn't a battle between men, this was a war for Gemma, but she wasn't a woman to be won, rather earned. She—whether she knew it or not—carried all the power in the world. I was determined to show her that she was capable of conquering anything, my heart already included.

"So, Gemma knows now?" she asked, assessing how much damage control she needed to do or possibly gauging how many months of work had been compromised. "Have you told her what happened to Natalie?"

"That wasn't my fault," I snipped defensively, forgetting that I didn't need to explain myself to Lina.

"I know that... just wondering what Gemma knows."

"Gemma knows I made donations to Belmont Hills, and that Natalie is somehow involved with it. That's all for now."

"And your relationship with Natalie?" she asked. "Is there anything you told her about you two? To be frank, not even I understood the relationship you had with her."

I sighed, tucking my cuff closer to the black rose along my hand. Telling Gemma about my relationship with Natalie would never be easy, not because it was wrong, but because of what it represented. Natalie was so familiar, so sweet, and I cared for her in a strange and unmentionable way. It was never romantic, but something I treasured, like an old box in my heart I never knew I'd open again. I could still picture her face, her eyes, and smile, the moment I met her in the garden at Belmont Hills. She was a ghost before she even knew it.

And how could I tell Gemma that with Natalie there was a connection I didn't want to describe, or how our relationship itself was tied to something bigger and more private? I didn't know what I was more scared of, telling Gemma about what happened to Natalie Brower, or what she represented to me.

"She was just a friend, Lina. But I have a problem with how the press and that *fucking* attorney's office wants to use her name in some gossip campaign to earn money. I don't give a shit what they say about me, but I won't let them disgrace her like that. I won't let them smear her name in the tabloids, nor will I give her husband the satisfaction of settling." I wasn't ready to accept what happened to Natalie or how the world hurt her.

Lina for once didn't respond but instead accepted how adamant I was about refusing any settlement.

She finally spoke.

"You know if we don't settle, we'll most likely have to go to court."

I groaned at the idea of ever having to testify, of enduring those truly responsible for Natalie's hardships.

"I offered to donate to CSAP and to the National Domestic Violence Hotline."

"They don't want that."

"Of course they don't. I'm the bad guy… not them. They're just a bunch of greedy bastards who'd rather keep the money for themselves."

Lina concentrated on her phone, lifting it up, reading a message before looking over her shoulder.

"What is it?" I asked.

"It's Gemma… is she here?"

"Yes, that's why you need to stay quiet," I reminded, as she looked back down at her phone, trying her best not to smile.

"She must still be awake."

"What makes you say that?"

"She just texted me… and maybe not everyone thinks you are the *bad guy*." Lina's endearing look almost made me fidget. Christ, Gemma was by far the only person that could make me *this* nervous.

"You? What does she need? I can take care of it."

"Calm down, big boy. I know you could, but this is for me," she looked back at the screen. "She wants to know that you'll be ok, that you won't have to go to jail."

"Because of the case?"

"I'm guessing so. Whatever was mentioned tonight must have gotten into her head; although, spending all night at a precinct is enough to make anyone worry." She scrolled down and smiled again. "She'll even sign the NDA… just so you know."

Gemma, my good girl, *my* gemstone: strong and gorgeous, more valuable and treasured than anything else—yet guarded. She was my girl, even if she couldn't admit it.

"No NDA," I ordered. "NDAs are not normal, and all I want, Lina, is to be normal again," I emphasized, but she was already ahead of me.

"I already responded. I told her you would be just fine… that the whole thing was more of a misunderstanding." She clicked off the screen, locking it shut.

"Thank you…" I sat back into my seat, "and though I enjoy our conversations, Lina, be sure to listen to me now, I don't want you bothering Gemma unless it's necessary, and my secrets are not the problem." I warned, letting her know one last time that her boundaries were tied to an extent.

"Understood, Mr. Rivers," she agreed. "And from your text earlier, it seems we have bigger problems, anyways."

"Correct. You may need to fly back to L.A. tomorrow."

"So, Miguel called you tonight?"

I re-twisted the bourbon cork shut, uninterested in having another drink at the mention of his name.

"His timing was less than perfect."

"I still don't know what he wants. He's not asking for money; all he says is that you need to tell the truth, and, honestly, I don't know what that means, but it's starting to feel like harassment. Moving forward, I'm advising you not to take his calls. Let me take care of this, Mr. Rivers."

I nodded.

"Fine. Go back and sweeten the deal and give that drunk whatever he needs to let this go. He ever speaks to anyone about me, I'll come for more than just what little he has." I stared down into my empty glass, annoyed at the swirling circumstance that I found myself in.

Tomorrow was so important. It was my only shot to show Gemma the world of Alex Rivers was different than my own. Maybe that was why she was so afraid. I couldn't blame her. I was scary.

My entire life I was called a monster, starting from Miguel himself. Gemma had no idea how much I hid, which was why I had to lie to her after she heard my conversation today. Thinking about how I couldn't be truthful about Miguel tore me apart, and in that moment, I never hated myself more. No matter how I tried to justify it, it was wrong, but necessary, and I only hoped that she could forgive me, once she was ready to accept my truth.

I changed the topic. "Before you go, I need to make sure you delivered my package to Ivanna."

"The one you stole from Gemma's room?" she asked. "Hopefully you don't get arrested for that either."

"Stop," I grinned. "She doesn't know about it, and

I'd like to keep it that way. It'll change her life forever, and I don't want it spoiled." I admitted, feeling content that not all my lies had to hurt, but rather could help. I'd do that for Gemma; anything to make sure that her future would always be better than her past.

I hated this green door. I hated how its paint chipped and how its gold knob had lost its luster. It felt used; tainted by the oil of hundreds of hands, from hundreds of moments, by those who had come and gone; of Gemma, of when she was small, to when she was here with Alejandro, to me and now. I hated it. But most of all, I hated how it once made me feel, so impossibly helpless.

I closed my fist, delivering three loud knocks to its top corner. She must have known I was coming, considering she broke the rules.

A few seconds passed, and the sound of shuffling feet stopped on the other side of the door. She was hesitating, and I knew she was watching me through the peephole, but I was adamant about seeing her, transparent enough that she'd know not to fuck with me today.

The lock clicked as she slowly opened the door, revealing the same old darkness that always lurked behind her. "Parker?" Claire asked, speaking as if I had disturbed her.

"We need to talk." I replied, standing at least a foot and a half taller since the last time I was here as a kid. I didn't need to peer up; instead I glared down into those gaunt, grey eyes that once horrified me as a child.

"About what?"

"Our agreement."

"It's still good. I have no problems with you."

"You may not. But I do," I added sharply.

"I don't need to explain myself to you." She began to shut the door, but I immediately wedged my foot between it, my weight and strength far superior to the push of her small body. She looked up, annoyed.

"Don't make me get the landlord, Claire. I'd really hate to break into my own apartment."

"Stop," she spat. "This is my—"

"Enough," I warned. "You own nothing, you have nothing. It's my name on the lease, it's my name on the bills. You'll open this door, and you'll talk to me. Do you understand?" I tried to be civil, not wanting to scare her, but she was making it so goddamn difficult.

I was already so fucking tense, so angry and disappointed with so many of the bad decisions I made. I embarrassed myself last night, and I embarrassed Gemma. I had fought so hard to keep her safe, to keep her protected from an idea that was manifested within this very apartment. And for what? For it to go wrong, to be wrong? I was done with it, done with talking, done with assuming. I was going to listen to Gemma, I was going to give her what she needed, and last night she made it clear, what she *needed* was for me to trust her.

"Now open the door." I stated, removing my foot so Claire could close it, and release the chain. She opened it back up, revealing reminiscent smoke and shadows.

"I should ask if you're thirsty," Claire turned her back as I stepped inside. "It's already warm outside."

"I don't need anything."

"Not even water?" she asked, avoiding me as she fished a mug out of her murky filled sink. I didn't answer, my focus penetrating her back as she flipped on the facet handle. Everything was the same, untouched from years that had come and gone. Same T.V., same couch, same ugly kitchen, and shit-colored carpet. It had all the familiarity of a nightmare, the kind whose patterns and characteristics went unchanged like some haunted time capsule. "How about a beer?"

"Nothing," I reiterated.

"You sure? Men love beer. And that's what you are, right? A man coming over to assert himself?" She turned with the cup in her hand, taking a sip. I half-expected it to be the jelly jar I once drank out of, but it wasn't; still, the anticipation of it made me nauseous.

"I'm here because you broke our agreement."

"You said that already," she snatched a pack of smokes on her way to sit down. "I didn't bother Gemma."

"You did. And now, I'm bothered. I told you I'd pay for your medication; I told you I'd pay for your rent. Your job was simple, to keep your problems to yourself."

"It wasn't as bad as before." She removed a cigarette from the carton and placed it between her lips.

Bad as before? She was referring to when Gemma stopped her internship with Gerard to help her out. Claire was never good at keeping a job, and the one she lost four years ago had a bigger impact than expected.

She couldn't cover the cost of her meds without her previous insurance and was forced to take something less effective. That's when everything went wrong, and somehow, it became Gemma's problem again. Gemma was here for weeks at the time, until magically, Medicaid approved the right prescription, only, it *wasn't* magic. It was me, fronting the bills, sorting the paperwork with the landlord as well, making the arrangements to have Claire financially stable and self-sufficient.

I would have done it sooner had Gemma told me, but she was always good at keeping secrets. I couldn't blame her, I'd always done the same, not only about my promise to Claire, but about Alex, especially with his relationship with Natalie and the DJ out in Bushwick. I made it sound so vague to Gemma before, that Alex was just violent, avoiding how it all tied together. I said too much last night but didn't say everything.

"Not as bad as before?" I asked. "We had an arrangement. I pay for everything, and you focus on yourself. You were supposed to leave Gemma alone, and you were only supposed to call her to check on her. You were supposed to do what mothers typically do. Not dump your fucking problems on her. She's not your therapist, she's not your doctor. I made this easy for you, Claire, and what was my one stipulation? You take your fucking pills."

"It was a mistake." She lit her cigarette and took a quick drag, her hoarse voice deteriorated over the years. Her nonchalant response ignited so many feelings in me, like how she was unbothered by the fact that our agreement was broken.

My promise meant everything. And hers? It meant nothing.

"A mistake? What the hell kind of an excuse is that?"

"Not an excuse. It's just what happened. I forgot. So, enough already."

"*You* don't get to forget. *You* don't get to make choices, Claire. You lost that privilege once you took Gemma's away, and that's something I can't forgive."

"Well, you'll just have to deal with it, Parker," she snapped, using what little air she still had in her lungs. Everything grew silent as she tapped a blotch of ash atop a crystal green ashtray. "It happened, ok? My neighbor was the one that called Gemma, and yeah, it was a mistake. But the prescription has been filled, and I'm back on them, so you can leave now. I don't need some little boy telling me what do, and I certainly don't need him telling me how to talk to my own daughter."

"The fuck you just say?" I hissed, my viscous tone snapping her head into place. She looked back up, shooting a stare that I had replayed in my head since the day she burned my finger. It was anger, contempt, and panic, directed at no one, but everyone. Who did she really hate? Me? Gemma? Or herself?

"Don't act like you know us, Parker. Gemma and I are not like you. You'd never understand."

"What the hell does that mean?"

"It means your world is too different," she yelled. "She could never love you, because she could never relate to you. So give it up! And don't you dare come into my home and preach to me about agreements. You promised you wouldn't hurt her, yet where is she now? I know what you did, Parker. You lured her into your home, and why? To string her along, and break her heart? You're just a mistake waiting to happen, another disappointment like her father."

Her shaking face bordered on a tremor, sending me into a hypnotic flash of memories and fears, of regrets and choices I made. In the moment it took me to blink, I saw everything I ever shared with Gemma: our childhood, our friendship, the secrets, and the heartache I caused the night she confessed her love.

Keep her safe?

Claire never saw what I did; she didn't realize how Gemma appeared after the moments they shared together or how guarded she became as a person. I noticed, I always had. But Claire? She seemed oblivious to all of it—all the pain, frustration, and fucking deceit she caused. And in that instance, I pictured Gemma's eyes, their enormous size filled with unfiltered disappointment.

Something happened to her as a child, something she never wanted to share, and I knew it was Claire's fault. This unfathomable, despicable dread fell onto my chest, caught like some brick hurled off a tall bridge.

"You don't know how far gone you are." I yanked a chair out of my way, screeching it across the floor to get as close to her as possible.

She flinched. "Don't even—"

"Shut the fuck up," I leaned into her face. "You don't fucking listen, do you? All you care about is yourself, and I don't give a fuck what problems you have, because all I care about is Gemma. You understand me?" I pried the cigarette from her dry lips, mashing it in my hand, scarring itself into my palm. Its excruciating pain was far worse than any match that Claire made me hold, but I wouldn't let her take control anymore, and the pain it caused was minuscule compared to the years of my agonizing silence. "She can't help that she's your daughter, but I can make it less noticeable once you're gone." Claire watched as the ash fell from my hand, my thumb toying with the bits of black soot that stained my fingers. She didn't blink once, as I finally had her full attention.

"Gone?" she asked. "I don't understand."

"I don't need you to understand. You hurt Gemma."

"That's not true—"

"It is. Admit it now, and I might have mercy on you."

"Parker… it's not what you think," she defended, placing her hand up as if that could stop me. I pulled it away.

"It's everything I think it is. I can't imagine what she's been through, but I know it's been hell, and I know you're involved. And don't even try to explain it, because it's not your truth to share, it's Gemma's… Not that I would believe you, anyway. The only thing you can stand in your life is to hear yourself talk, and I'm done with that."

"You're no better…" she gritted.

"You're right. I'm not. But the difference between you and me is that I'll own the things I've done. I know I hurt Gemma. I thought I was helping by keeping this goddamn promise, but now I know how wrong it was.

But I'm gonna make it right again, because it's not about her past, it's about her future. If she wants to tell me what happened, then I'll listen... but I won't force her to, Claire, because I'll fucking love her regardless."

I crushed her pack of cigarettes, tossing it into the trash, before wiping my palm clean, smearing tar on the table before reaching into my pocket for the one thing I should have never accepted all those years ago.

"You're supposed to keep her safe..." Claire repeated, confused by the old quarter in my hand, unaware of how important it once was.

"Gemma doesn't need that. She needed that from her mother when she was a child, and you already ruined that. What she needs now, what she deserves, is the courtesy she's owed. She deserves honesty, she deserves a chance to make her own decisions, to have them respected, and I'll make sure she has that."

It was hard to confess, but the things I said were true. Gemma needed to make her own choices, and I needed to trust her. This wasn't about my beliefs, this was about true, unconditional love, about accepting whatever secrets she had, and honoring the decisions she made. I was never going to make another promise again, unless it was to Gemma, and this was me keeping my word.

"I told her you were dangerous... all of you are." Claire's words got caught in a choke, as an angry tear rolled down her cheek.

"You're right. I am fucking dangerous. But not for Gemma. And you should be scared, because I'm here for anyone that stops her from living the life she wants.

That includes you, Claire. Now stand up," I growled, tossing the quarter onto the table.

"I don't even know where you're taking me—"

"Doesn't matter," I interrupted. "You're not staying here anymore. No more rent, no more bills. You're going somewhere for help, *real* help. You already had a chance to make things better, and you blew it. Now, a decision has been made for you." I adjusted the cufflink near my wrist, my curt tone ending any debate. "You'll be staying at Belmont Hills. You're their problem now, and maybe someday, if you get the help you need, you can be part of Gemma's life again. You can't—I can't—interfere with her decisions anymore. Now move. I won't ask again."

Claire panicked at the command, shaking her head, "I won't go… everything I have is here. This is my home."

"You can either move yourself, or I can drag you downstairs to the car that's waiting. Either way, it's happening, and it's happening now." I gestured to the door as Claire slowly stood up, exchanging a stare that dared me to fight back. "Don't," I warned. "You said it yourself, Claire… my love is nuclear, and I'm done lying dormant. Fuck your promise. Fuck your punishment. I'm telling Gemma the truth. I love her. No conditions. No questions. And if I lose it all… if I lose her, then at least she knows the truth, at least in the end… it's her who got to decide."

Chapter 16

GEMMA

Vomit would look particularly awful on my new dress, but puking was almost inevitable with my nerves. Standing alone, jostled in a small, private elevator, I tried to recount the precise instructions Alejandro gave me.

Once you exit the elevator, there'll be someone waiting for you. Stay close to the walls, stay far away from the crowd. I'll find you near the private booth in the back. And trust me, Gemma, you'll be safe. I'll always be watching out for you.

His guide on how to get around felt more like an exit strategy, and maybe it was, considering I didn't belong here, fifty stories in the sky at a notorious nightclub called Venom.

Nervously, my heels planted themselves into a permanent position, collecting all the reverberated sounds of ominous electronic music above. It thudded along the steel walls, climbing into a peek that shook the contents of my empty stomach as the elevator came to a sudden stop.

Everything was magnified.

Hot.

Loud.

Booming.

The atmosphere of another world seeped through

the slow opening elevator door, overwhelming me with the eruption of light and sound. I gasped as a few men fell in, nearly knocking me over.

"It's not a wall, dummies, it's a door!" A graveled shout made its way into my ears, delivered from a person who urgently grabbed at my hand. "Watch your step, babe!" she instructed, guiding me over the tumbled drunks and scattered loose pills.

"Ivanna?" I questioned, recognizing the raspy bark and choppy, black bangs of Alejandro's assistant. She pulled me to the side of her long, latex-wrapped legs.

"Your personal bodyguard for the night." She leaned close to my face to shout over the music. "The elevator was a bad idea. It's in the middle of the party."

"Where's Alejandro?"

"Not here yet! Still taking photos outside. I gotta get you away from here though."

"Why, what's happening?" I followed Ivanna's lead as we approached a thick brush of molten bodies. I swiped at something wet that fell above my bright, red lips; hopefully it was just a drink.

"Once Alejandro arrives it's going to get hectic. Everyone is already fucked up."

"Didn't everyone just get here?"

"The party's been on for hours. You know how Alejandro is. He never shows up on time, and for good reason." She elbowed us further into the crowd, disobeying Alejandro's first request.

"I'm supposed to stay near the walls."

"That'll take too long, and we don't have much time. Trust me on this."

I tried shouting, but it was pointless as we trudged through a wall of people. I could practically taste their sweat, their obnoxious cheers so claustrophobic and sweltering, that it felt more like the gates of hell than an actual celebration.

"It's so loud!" I said, my body squished into hers. Music filled my chest, regurgitating itself up into the pulse of my eyes.

Ivanna looked up, her face doused in the swirling light of the industrial facade. "Keep your jaw clenched," she suggested. "It'll stop your teeth from rattling once the bass drops." She guarded herself from the sudden spray confetti. A pluming explosion of sound erupted into the crowd, covering us in an atmosphere of haze as the music crashed into my ears.

"How could this ever be considered a fun Saturday night?" I screeched, watching as a woman fell down, her thigh pierced from the stiletto heel of another person. I cringed, tiptoeing around her body.

"After a few drinks, it's ok."

"So once you're buzzed and unable to grasp reality?"

"And deaf…" she added, pulling me through the other side of the cattle-like masses. "Almost there!"

"I don't know if there's enough alcohol for this," I joked, hiding my blatant discomfort, as Ivanna gave my hand a reassuring squeeze. Everything felt like the vibe and cadence of a frat party; though bigger on the budget, larger on the venue. *God, what a bad memory, and an awkward one at that.* I nervously massaged the wings on my silver butterfly ring.

"Maybe you haven't tried the right alcohol," she sashayed through the curtained partition towards our private booth. We sat side by side, sheltering ourselves near large, potted palms and black steel decor. "*Tienes suerte en tu lado.* You're in luck, pretty girl, I got just the thing for you." She reached for the bottle that sat at our table, passing me a shot glass. "I know Alejandro isn't here yet, but soon he'll be in your belly," she teased. "Well, his tequila at least."

"This looks different." I noted, watching as Ivanna carefully twisted off the top.

"Because it is. This is his new signature recipe. Black label, 100% blue agave." She poured me a taste. "He hasn't shut up about this one and how it's his favorite. It's cute, really. He's barely that passionate about anything anymore." She mocked Alejandro, deepening her voice, "*Ivanna, I harvested this myself, it's on special reserve just for Gemma. Extra Añejo.*" She puffed her chest.

"Extra Añejo?" I laughed.

"Yeah, something about how it's aged. They stuff it into a barrel for a long time. I don't have the patience for that, let alone listen to Alejandro drone on about it forever," she waved off. "But it looks damn good, doesn't it?" She passed the shot to me, its amber hue much darker than the golden pyramid of tequila bottles that stood at the center of the club.

Slowly, I took a sip, letting its scorch spring from my toes and up to my lips. Its taste was completely different, immediately unique to anything I had before, warm like grass in summer, but dark and rich like smoked butterscotch. Perhaps it was the spice, being complex with intoxicating notes that I could hardly describe. I toyed with the inside of my cheek, realizing that it was akin to having Alejandro in a glass—the taste, the scent, the rush. I loved it.

I read the black subtext to Don Jefe's dark label. "*Piedra Preciosa*? What does that mean?" I asked surprised, wanting to finally understand the tender phrase that Alejandro had purred into my ear time and time again.

Ivanna arched a brow. "It's like a precious *gem*stone." She elongated its prefix: *gem*, *gem*stone, *Gem*ma. Alejandro was a clever man, but now I knew he was also incredibly sweet, having used the term of endearment the moment he saved me from Gerard. I was—for whatever reason—his *Gemstone*. I couldn't hide my smile.

"Look at you glow. Now, you're enjoying yourself," Ivanna gleamed. "There's something here for everyone."

"Maybe. I'm still deciding that." I used my palm to shield my reddening cheeks.

"Not your definition of exciting?"

"More or less. Exciting for me is guessing the Wordle puzzle correctly on the first try. Or an empty theatre for a newly released horror movie."

"You like horror?" her face soured.

"Of course. It's my absolute favorite."

"Horror is so not my thing. It's too… scary for me."

"And this isn't?" I gestured towards the empire of swaying bodies. Everyone rippled like an erotic wave, their moves indistinguishable from dancing or fucking.

Ivanna spoke into my ear, avoiding the need to

shout. "On first glance, yes. It's a lot to take in. I noticed right away you were overwhelmed, and you're not very good at hiding it either."

"Wasn't trying to."

"Good. It means you're being honest with your feelings. And that's something I know Alejandro needs."

"That's good for Alejandro, but honestly, I'm still deciding on what *I* need." I replied, unsure if this scene was something I could ever get used to, buckled by the noise of shattering glass and bouts of arguments behind us.

"It might be uncomfortable. But it's not everything. There's always more to us than what others see on the surface. It doesn't have to be perfect in order for it to be significant. It can even be something new we learn about ourselves." She poured herself a drink, finally giving it a taste.

"I like to think I know myself pretty well," I said half-convincingly.

"Maybe. But don't be so sure." Ivanna licked the taste of tequila from the corner of her mouth, the tops of her breasts rising in the corset beneath her blazer. She crossed her legs, the vibration of her skin-tight pants shifted the cushion below us, teasing alongside the hum of music that ran up my thigh and to my ass. I wiggled myself within the little spot where I sat. "You like porn?" she asked.

"Excuse me?" I literally laughed.

"Porn? Porno? Watching people fuck?" She nudged the drink toward the direction of my mouth.

"I don't know."

"Yes, you do."

"Well… everyone watches porn sometimes, don't they?"

"They do, even though most won't admit it. But I'm asking *you* specifically." She added, "I only assumed that you did. And since you like horror movies, I figured you enjoyed getting scared. My question's not so random… sexual arousal and fear can come from the same place. But why is that? How can two opposite feelings come from the same spot in the brain?"

I took a moment to really consider her question, wondering if it was possible for me.

"I don't know. Because we're complicated?" I guessed.

"Exactly," Ivanna tapped her head. "We. Are. Complicated. People can be two opposite things at once. Alejandro could be Alex Rivers, just like you can be two different versions of yourself. Maybe you don't like parties, but also, maybe you have been conditioned to not like them."

"I think it's preference," I admitted, honestly assessing that parties often carried unlikeable characteristics: loud noises, rough crowds, fighting, screaming.

"Remember, there may be good in the bad, and bad with the good. Don't commit yourself to being one person. Yes, you like horror, but maybe you also like porn." She jutted her chin towards a dark corner of the room, making eyes in a direction for me to follow. There in the dimly lit shadows was the distinct shape of a couple; rowdy but secluded. They were dancing slowly, grinding in the dark, the girl's dress hitched above her thighs. "So fucking naughty, wouldn't you agree?"

"I think I need another drink." I responded, observing the man's unbuckled belt, his cock out and stiff, disappearing inside the woman as they danced. They were fucking in the dark, their small moves sometimes interrupted with the quick, extra thrusts needed to get them closer to orgasm. Each pump caused the girls mouth to open wider, for her tits to bounce a little higher.

"I should join, show them how it's done." Ivanna popped a pill in her mouth, taking a swig of tequila.

"You would?" I asked, amazed by her honesty.

"Not before, but now I would. I was scared to try it in the past, but one day I discovered I actually enjoyed it. I found another part of me, babe." She shrugged, "I won't lie, the parties are crazy, but this shit isn't for Alejandro, it's for Alex Rivers, the character. I fuck around because I want to, but Alejandro is more careful than that, more astute with what he wants."

"And that would be me…" I confirmed, fitting myself into the most complicated relationship I'd been a part of.

"Bingo," she pretended to be inspired. "He's not subtle, though, neither am I. I'm sure he's been clear about how he feels. He doesn't get involved with this trivial shit, but let me tell you, he pays the price for it. It was good for when he was a young, single man, mostly because he had nothing to lose, but I'm not so sure about that now. He's not Alex Rivers, he's not even himself anymore. He's changing, or at least he's trying, and all of that stems back to you, Gemma."

"To me?" I responded truthfully, unsure of how to react.

"Feels like a heavy burden to bear."

"Only because you're still finding out who you are. You'll agree with me someday; you'll discover what it's like to be more than what you thought you were." Ivanna swiped her phone open, checking the stats of their latest social media numbers. "Who knows how long he'll pretend to be this Alex character, and honestly you shouldn't have to worry about it. We're so close to meeting our goal of eight million likes for tonight, and once we do, he'll leave this place, walking right out that door with you… *only* you." She smiled as the lights suddenly went out, cascading the venue into a loud, black pit.

He was here, and the fans knew it.

Alex Rivers finally arrived.

Chapter 17

GEMMA

"*I'm only going to ask this once, and if you lie to me… I'll blow a hole of sunshine through your fucking head.*" Alejandro appeared over the large projective screens that circled the club, showing a clip of an Alex Rivers film that echoed from above. He pointed a revolver at someone's head, clicking its hammer into position as everyone in the crowd chanted his name.

"I fucking love this scene," Ivanna placed a hand over her heart. "Alejandro hates it, but it made him rich."

"I've never seen any of his movies," I admitted, earning the most perplexing look on Ivanna's face.

"No wonder he likes you." She sighed, "Word of advice, you may want to plug your ears for this."

"*You wouldn't do this; you don't have the guts!*" The antagonist on screen shouted at Alejandro, who then appeared amused.

The crowd repeated each following word in unison, reaching a peak of excitement that bordered on cultish. "*Of course I do. IT'S ME, BABY… DEAL WITH IT.*" Alex pulled the trigger, setting off a barrage of lights and confetti that shot out into the pit of cheering fans.

The place exploded.

To everyone's surprise, Alejandro appeared in the

spotlight, circled by a group of bodyguards in suits. He waved subtly, his signature brood heightened from the collection of flashing cameras that went off in his face.

"Whatever happens, don't leave this booth," Ivanna warned. "It's safer here."

"I wouldn't dare." I shuddered, watching as fans reached for Alejandro, some throwing bottles in his direction to be signed. He ignored the chants, the confetti of broken glass, and people who tumbled toward his stage. A man from the balcony tried to get closer, falling, losing his balance as he attempted to descend from a drape. Alejandro wasn't kidding about how out of control it could get. "Is that guy going to be ok?"

"I guess we'll find out, but falling a few feet is fine. Besides, it's kinda fun, like that one holiday," she snapped her fingers, momentarily forgetting the answer. "The one where we eat all day and fight all night for gifts? Oh, Black Friday!"

"The holiday is Thanksgiving, but yeah… I see what you mean." The bass was so heavy that I held onto our bottle of *Don Jefe*, keeping it from rattling off the table. "What's he going to do now?" I asked nervously.

"What do you mean?"

"Does he jump from the stage and into the crowd? What else could possibly happen that creates the intense atmosphere I always hear about?" Not that I needed to see anything else, because I'd already witnessed my fair share of uncomfortable and painful moments.

"Alejandro?" She laughed. "This is it. You're looking at it." She pointed to the media montage of Alex

Rivers's fight scenes. He leapt off buildings and knocked out men, perpetuating all the cool shit that made people scream, but caused me to recoil. I hated action films, I hated the reactions they got, but by the look on Alejandro's face, he may have felt the same.

"I don't understand?"

Alejandro's long finger rested on the diamond cut corner of his chin, his face sharp as glass. I couldn't tell if he was excited or worried, maybe both.

"All people want is the action star, they don't care about anything else. So, this is all he does. He plays this exact montage anywhere he goes, and people pay big bucks for it." Ivanna clicked on her phone, beginning a timer that flashed on its screen. "We got less than an hour until we leave. It's the longest he'll stay, social media goal or not."

"Is this normal?" I asked, observing the screens above. The clips finished themselves, defaulting to a still shot of *Don Jefe*. A distracting parade of bottle girls appeared in the crowds, passing out autographed boxes of tequila as Alejandro stepped away into the shadows of armed security.

"He seems a little more generous today. He actually waved. Most likely just for you," Ivanna replied. "But honestly, I don't think he has it in him anymore. He'd rather be harvesting agave in some miserable field." Ivanna showed me the text that arrived on her phone.

MR. RIVERS

Shut the drapes. I'm almost there.

"That's my queue." Ivanna sat up, reaching over to

loosen the straps of our red curtains. She drew them closer, engulfing us with a quick red shield. "For privacy, of course… we'll keep the guards outside, but Alejandro is about to join us."

"Do you think it'll be ok?" I asked, unsure of the attention we could possibly receive.

"We'll be discreet, but that may be difficult with guards around."

"I can order them away." Alejandro appeared by my ear, kissing my cheek as I jumped from surprise. He put his leg over the booth and sat right behind me, drawing me into his chest.

"She's been on edge," Ivanna noted, pouring another drink.

"Of course she has. This place is fucking ridiculous." Alejandro unzipped his signature leather jacket, showing off a wisp of chest hair under his crisp, black shirt. "There was an altercation. Someone got stabbed near the bar."

"Another one?" Ivanna didn't even bother looking up from her phone, acting as if it were a normal thing to ask.

Alejandro signaled for the guards to move, leaving us less noticeable without their presence. "Yes, don't worry about it. Everything was taken care of. Did you start your timer?"

"Of course. Fifty minutes left in the countdown." Ivanna held up her phone.

"Your whole operation is like a well-oiled machine," I grinned.

"More like a bomb than a machine," Alejandro

slipped on his black aviators, appearing more as a shadow than a man. Still, even in the dark, his graveled rasp lit me on fire. I wasn't sure if it was intentional, but his boot tapped along my heel like a secret morse code of affection. "She looks good in daises, doesn't she?"

Ivanna immediately agreed. "I knew it when I saw it, it'd look perfect on her."

I pulled my hand along the satin that hugged my hips, wearing the dress he had Ivanna pick out for me weeks ago. It felt just like yesterday when I was in his trailer, trying so hard to throw him off. I still couldn't believe I wore that hideous orange turtleneck, but who was I kidding? Even the universe had a good laugh by spilling coffee all over it.

"I want to make sure everything's in order, you know how things get," he addressed Ivanna impatiently. "Go meet with Charles. I want the car ready now, just in case."

"You got it, boss," she stood up, focusing on her phone. "Look for my text. The second we hit eight million you can leave early."

"The sooner the better."

We watched as she disappeared back into the crowd of people, and although the room was deafening, Alejandro's silent stare towards my face felt a hundred times louder.

We exchanged a look as he grazed my thigh, the tips of his fingers touching invisible peach fuzz that drove me absolutely insane. I was lightheaded, and my lips tingled as the spot he placed his palm made me suddenly nervous. Would he go further? Would he rub me right over my panties in public? The suggestion alone drained all the blood from my ringing ears, pooling it between my legs, tickling the spot I knew he wanted to touch. That wasn't even the best part, because with Alejandro the key to his seduction always lied in his anticipation. I was never sure if he was going to play with me or not, because everything he did was sexual, everything he did was surprising and deliciously unpredictable.

"So, you like my daisies?" I asked innocently, brushing my pinky over one of the small flowers near my chest.

"Like them? I love them… but right now, I'd enjoy nothing more than to rip those little petals off your body. I saw you right when I walked in, and it made me hopelessly restless."

"Is that so? And what did you think?"

"About how frustrating it is to be me." The scorch of Alejandro's growl fell into the crevice of my neck as he splayed his hand further up my bare thigh, threatening to yank my dress off. Although we were curtained with privacy, I wondered if others could still somehow see us, not that I'd mind.

"Oh, really?"

"Of course, I'm not above saying that I'm a jealous man. That dress gets to hug your hips, and it makes me want to react."

"Then, tell me all about it," I taunted, but Alejandro didn't smile.

"Oh… I'd rather show you, good girl." He pulled me into his side, one hand possessively gripped onto my stomach, the other now so near my pussy, that I could feel the heat of his knuckle near my clit. "Guess I gotta be patient. It's not my strong suit."

"Apparently with tequila it is," I raised my glass. "Aged in a barrel? How could you possibly wait?"

"It took more than three years, but good things are worth the wait. How'd you like it?"

"Tastes like the sweetest thing anyone has ever done for me," I answered. "Can't say I've had a signature liquor ever dedicated in my honor before."

"So, the cat's out of the bag? Right, Gemstone?" He kissed into my ear.

"You're too clever for your own good. Which makes this all so odd." I leaned my head onto his shoulder, playing with the cuff of his jacket.

"How so?"

"This. The party, the people? They're all so happy. They're all out there losing their minds, but not you."

"If I'm being honest, the whole thing bores me."

"You don't really want to do this, do you?"

"No, and in fact, this is the last contractual party I'll ever have, something the sponsors of Don Jefe wanted. These events were always wrong for me to throw, but in the past served a different purpose. This Hollywood lifestyle was always a dangerous distraction from the problems I refused to face, but I won't allow it to happen anymore. Besides, at this point, Gemma, I'm only killing time."

"Until what, exactly?"

"Until I'm with you again," he answered, breathing me in, kissing the top of my head.

I shut my eyes, leaning further into his chest, his body supporting mine as my cheek touched his chin.

"You should be celebrating your hard work. This is your passion, something you share with your brother, right?" I reminded. "Is he here?"

Alejandro bobbled his head. Yes? No? "Not tonight…" he settled, "but he's the reason I'm here, and honestly, he's better off in Jalisco, especially after all he's been through, he deserves the rest he can get. Trust me, I wish I could switch places with him, sometimes."

"Then, why don't you?"

"Because there's something much better waiting for me."

"Like what?"

"Like you. I'd do anything for what we could be. I'd burn it all to the ground, if it only meant that I could keep you as mine for another second."

I paused, not immediately answering, ruminating in the pool of his candid forwardness. Alejandro had always been bold, but it never made it less surprising. "I would never ask you to do something like that. You've given up so much for this," I said, sensing how dangerous I could be to Hollywood, or even his fans. He placed so much power into me, the sheer thought of controlling his future made my palms uncomfortably wet.

"Others have given up more. It's no secret that I came from a broken home, but I've been blessed with a few good people. Ivanna, Lina, my mother included. Regardless, I can't hold onto something that's temporary, when all I want is forever." Alejandro tilted my head, studying the distance between my eyes and lips.

"I should be so lucky to ever be a woman like those you just mentioned."

"Who says you aren't? You're all I want, Gemma. No more past, no more issues, no more questions on who wants us or who hurt us. Just you and me. People made sacrifices for where I am now… and what would all their sacrifices be for if not to someday make me happy?" Alejandro looked at the bottle of *Piedra Preciosa.* "Happiness is a treasure, it's a gemstone… And fuck if I didn't find the most precious one of all." A strobe of light oscillated around the room, momentarily catching his face with its blood red shine.

I grew silent.

"Strong beliefs, strong tequila…" I admitted, moved by his words to the point of being quietly stunned. I just wanted to stare at him, to remember him like this. He wasn't the byproduct of hysteric fans and noises; he was the man who found my heart and turned my weaknesses into strengths. "Thank you," I said firmly. "Thank you for showing me this… for letting me in."

"You don't need to thank me, just tell me you'll try… try to accept the bad with my good." He buried his head into my cheek, whispering into it. "I want you to stay with me tonight, no conditions but one. You're free to choose any room that you want, to decide for yourself where you'll sleep."

"And the condition?" I asked, his tongue nearing my jaw as he licked his lower lip.

"The upstairs is mine… if you make it to my bed, if

you ever cross that line, I swear I'll take you as mine. No exceptions, no games. That's your choice, Gemma, and the move is yours to make, but just know I'm still hellbent on taking you." He cupped my face, leaning in for a slow, sensual kiss, one with enough pressure to melt the entire space around us. "So what's it going to be?"

I wasn't sure how to answer, his constructive hands desperate to shape me into the perfect example of who I ought to be; the good and the bad. Wasn't this his way of trying? And him bringing me here, wasn't that a positive step in the right direction? I took one look at the bottle, the one with my nickname on it, resonating on the fact that he took a piece of himself and included me in it. This was important to him, and it wasn't just about tequila, it was about showing me that he cared.

"I'll come with you… but like you said, I'll sleep where I want." I assured, "But I'll need to make a stop first. I have nothing to wear…"

"Then wear nothing at all…"

I looked down at my drink, blushing, resisting the small laugh in my throat. If I decided to stay, I knew I'd have to see Parker; I'd have to go home and pack a bag to be with Alejandro. I wouldn't let him take me shopping, I wouldn't let him sweep me away without a piece of my own belongings; and although I was frustrated with Parker, a part of me still wanted to protect him as much as he protected me.

"I'll need to go home first, and you have to let me do this." I requested, easing my hand away from his.

Suddenly, his face lit up, brightened by a text that appeared on his phone.

IVANNA

8 million likes. You're done big guy.

Alejandro smirked, dropping his phone into his pocket. "Then let's go together… we're calling an end to this party. No lawsuits tonight." He reached for the fire alarm against the wall.

"What are you doing?"

"Sending everyone home. We call the shots, Gemma… not the rest of the world." He flicked it on, causing a roaring siren to pierce the venue. Immediately we stood as house lights popped on and the music stopped. "Another success," he exhaled sweetly, directing me to an exit that was guarded by his staff.

His personality never ceased to amaze me, his character split into two distinct halves. Whether he excused it or not, there was a little bit of Alex Rivers in Alejandro. He was brash, confident, and did things with an unapologetic nature. I guess that was what made him so cool to others, but to me it made him the most complex human I'd ever encountered.

It was different.

He was different.

And maybe I was still unsure of what my future looked like, but I felt like I was getting closer.

Partly excited, partly reserved.

A little bit of Parker, a little bit of Alejandro…

How could seeing my best friend, the man I knew since I was a child, be as equally intimidating as the party I just left from? I self-soothed my anticipation, reminding myself that I didn't do anything wrong. *He* wanted to meet Alejandro, *he* initiated the first antagonizing words that set everything over the edge.

Still, I couldn't pretend like I didn't completely abandon him on the worst night of our decades-long relationship. That wasn't something I could let go of, along with how he said my name the night I left him.

Gemma… I could hear him so perfectly in my mind, and he

never sounded more broken.

"Just wait right here," I said to Alejandro, unlocking Parker's door.

"Absolutely not," he reached for the doorknob, holding it still. "It's not a good idea, especially with how he acted at the bar. I don't trust him."

"Well, he doesn't trust you either. I can't have another fight like last time. I won't allow it. Besides, it's late and he's probably asleep."

"And what if he's not?"

"Then… I'll be fast."

"What you'll be is safe, and I'll ensure that, even if I have to go in there myself." Alejandro removed his hand from the doorknob, willing it to stay shut with a pensive stare. Reluctantly, he brought his attention back to me as I opened it up. "If I feel like anything is wrong, I'll do what I need to." He said, stepping back into the hall, making space for me to enter. I nodded one last time, hoping it wouldn't have to go any further than this, quietly shutting the door behind me.

I wasn't sure what to expect exactly but was surprised to see that the lights were still on.

I secretly hoped I'd see his bedroom door shut, knowing it'd be way easier to pack my clothes without facing him right now. The truth was, I wasn't afraid of seeing Parker, but rather what seeing him would do to me.

What if I stared too long into those deep, emerald eyes? Would I be stuck somewhere between the past and present, lost on some old fantasy that felt more like a possibility now, that somehow, no matter what, we were supposed to grow old together? Because, the truth was Parker is, and forever will be, a mountain in my life; one I never came down from, one I built a home on. Honestly, leaving him didn't just feel strange, it felt impossible. He was in many ways my other half.

I thought all of this to myself, as the distinct screech of an electric drill startled me, its whine came unexpectedly as I turned the corner. I looked down the hall, and watched as Parker stood by my room.

I froze.

"Parker…" His name fell out of my mouth.

We'd only spent a night apart, but it already felt so long since I'd last seen him. His solemn expression flashed for a second, caught like a gorgeous ghost in the halls of my heart, tall and calm, forever mindful of the tender look he always gave.

"Gem?" The grin on his face grew into an unconcealed smile, as if he couldn't believe I was right in front of him. "You're here…"

Seeing him was so bizarre, as if all the worry I had, all the fear that festered in my gut, dissolved itself like sugar cubes in tea. Guilt slammed into my heart as a single tear rolled down my cheek.

"I'm so sorry…" I hitched, using three words for the all-consuming emotion I felt but couldn't say.

I'm sorry if I hurt you, I'm sorry if you worried, I'm sorry I was silent for so long and especially now… I'm sorry for what I'm about to do.

"Gem… no, don't be sorry. Don't waste your tears… not over my foolish behavior." He made his way toward me, wiping my eyes before pulling me in, warming me with the single touch of his hand on my back. My dress felt too formal compared to his cozy look; his soft, red shirt, almost salmon colored from years of use, wrapping loosely around his tanned biceps. "I missed you, Butterfly."

"I missed you, too." I hugged him.

He opened his mouth to speak, but instead followed my eyes that stared past him.

"Actually, you're back in time. I just finished putting it together." Parker moved to the side, presenting a new white door attached to the frame of my bedroom. He walked across a scattering of tools. "I may be better at tearing them down, than putting them back up though."

I followed close, covering my mouth with surprise as he grabbed the knob, twisting it, testing its ability to actually close.

"Not bad… for a city boy," I teased, bumping my arm against his.

"Yeah, not bad at all… took a while, but I wanted to make sure you slept well tonight. I know how much you hate sleeping with the door open."

I never felt worse, faking a smile to hide the sudden wave of insurmountable remorse that stole the tenderness of our moment. He was clueless as to why I was here, and the thought of admitting the reason made my mouth so incredibly dry.

"You look beautiful. Were you… out tonight?" he asked, not in a prying way, but with a genuine curiosity.

"Yes," I stepped into my room. "Alejandro and I attended an event in Soho, well… actually… we're going to spend some more time together. He's invited me to stay with him. I'm not sure for how long…" I blurted out, immediately grabbing an empty bag and hugging it against my chest. The room fell incredibly silent, as if that didn't say it all. I was *crushed*.

He remained speechless.

Did my admission break him? Was this the final straw to our long-winded battle? After everything we spouted at each other, the disagreements we had over Alejandro, over Camilla, was it possible that neither of us could accept the other person's happiness? Or, was it more? Maybe there was something keeping us apart, and that realization was as painful as spending the night away.

His eyes cemented themselves to the floor. "Gemma, who I was, and who I thought I had to be… was unfair to you. You don't need to be afraid of what I think of you. It's me who's afraid of what you think of me," he paused, "especially now. Part of me feels like… like I lost you…"

I winced, noting the subtle twitch at his cheek.

It absolutely killed me.

I'd gotten so used to wearing my own mask, that perhaps I failed to see he'd been wearing one too. I never once considered his own pain, or if there was any at all. He seemed so perfect from the outside, the unprovoked, regal lawyer of Manhattan. Yet, this was new; a vulnerable version of the invincible man who carried me and my sorrows for our entire lives. I placed my bag on the bed, freeing my hands as I drew near to him.

"You could never lose me," I pulled on his strong body, digging my head into his chest. "You're stuck with me forever, Parker Ellis Jones."

I joked around to hide the seriousness of how I felt; torn and confused.

He began to let go.

"I won't keep you waiting. Believe me, I've done that enough. I'll let you pack in peace."

"Wait…" I stopped him, wiping my eyes, not ready for another goodbye. "Just stay with me. Talk to me. I won't be long, I promise."

He stared at the bag, then back to me, "Stay with

you? I'd stay with you all night, Gem, so long as you'd have me." He graveled into my cheek, and regardless of his intention, he still gave me butterflies. I knew I should've apologized about the drink I hurled into Camilla's face, and for ignoring him the last few weeks. I was sick with the feeling of it all. There was so much to still discuss, but I didn't want to ruin the mood as the grin he suddenly flashed made my heart jump.

"I love that you still have him." He said, sounding relieved.

"Andy?" I exclaimed as Parker laid on my bed, holding my stuffed giraffe. "He's by my side every night, can't sleep without him."

"I guess five-hundred and twenty tickets was a good investment."

"I can't believe it took you fifteen tries to get him. Totally worth it though." I proudly reminded how Parker popped ten tiny balloons just to win a prize for me.

"Well, you just had to have him, and in a way, I felt like he'd take care of you in the moments we were apart, especially on the nights when you stayed with your mom. I couldn't be there, no matter how bad I wanted to be… but he could. It's funny what you think as a kid, that there's magic in the things you do, like I'd win him, and he'd somehow be indebted to me… that he'd return the favor and watch over my Gemma."

My fingers grew stiff as I raised a half-folded shirt up to my chest, praying with it. I couldn't believe what he said, and how it frightened me, like suddenly I missed the most important memory I never had. Didn't he know how many times Andy saved me from nightmares, that he wasn't just a toy, but an extension of Parker all along? Why didn't he share this before?

"Is that true?"

"Of course."

"I never knew that…"

"You never knew a lot of things, but that's my fault. I know I've been quiet… but I've always tried to show it. I'll never forget that one night you slept over, when you forgot Andy back at your mom's. We were going to the Hamptons in the morning, and there was no way that I was going to let you go all summer vacation without him."

"You rode your bike, carrying me on your pegs in the middle of Brooklyn after midnight," I replied, realizing how terrifyingly stupid we were at that age.

"Forty-seven blocks both ways," he brushed the unkept fur on Andy's head, "but that didn't matter, that didn't stop me. I would've ridden all night, had it made you happy…"

He took a sharp breath, his shoulders hunched.

I wish I knew what he was thinking, his face crinkled and upset, swallowing a lump in his throat that made my heart throb.

"Jesus," he mumbled. "I was just a boy, Gemma, and I should've never promised Claire—" He stopped. I caught him staring away, biting his upper lip. *Claire?* I leaned closer, placing my knee onto the bed, needing to understand. In what little time it took to open my mouth, he beat me to the punch, quickly and confidently cutting me off. "But I'm not a boy anymore,

I'm a man, and you're a woman, a beautiful one that doesn't need my protection. I couldn't see that before, but I do now, and that makes me feel safe, like I can finally say what I want to say…" Parker looked up at me, more gentle and serene than ever before. "Gemma. I've been wanting to—"

"*Preciosa…*" Alejandro appeared in the doorway, interrupting Parker as I looked over.

"Alejandro," I spoke loudly, still surprised that he actually came for me. "You were supposed to wait in the hall," I said frazzled, stuck between both men, afraid of what could happen.

Alejandro stepped into my room, cautiously focused, "I couldn't help myself; you were taking too long, and I worried."

Parker casually stood from the bed, carrying my bag. "Gemma was just about to leave, but you're both welcome to stay if she needs more time."

I stared at Parker, his calmness sexier and more compelling than the wolf I witnessed before. I took the bag from his hand.

"I think I have everything," I said as Parker placed his hand on my back, a sensation I'd never get tired of.

"I think so, too."

I cleared my throat as we made our way to the front door, opening it, before turning back to Parker, giving him a quick hug to say goodbye.

"*Better shake, Rattlesnake.*" I whispered in his ear, holding him, still unsure if I could ever let him go, his laborious sweat sweeter than not, aromatic like spring in Central Park. He pulled back, gently fixing the strap to my bag. I knew his voice would be devastating, but I yearned for it regardless.

"*Bye, bye, Butterfly…*" he said quietly, allowing me to turn away, to be free just like I wanted.

And then I left…

Alejandro reached out his hand, taking mine into his as we walked to the end of the hall. "He seemed to be in better spirits," he said, pressing the button to the elevator, allowing us inside. The doors closed, giving me a last glimpse of Parker's door.

"He did," I replied, unsure if that was true. He seemed to be at odds, both content and sad at the same time. I'd never seen him like that before, not with anyone, not even a lover. All of it left me with the most incredulous sense of awe.

I peeked down at my bag, unzipping just an inch to make sure that my belongings were actually inside, but then paused.

I nearly started to cry.

Sitting atop of my clothes, sheltered in the shallow glow of the elevator light was a familiar friend, a reminder of the man I loved since I was just a little girl.

Andy…

Chapter 19

GEMMA

Outside, the underbelly of an overcast night turned gold, shaping New York's clouds into a reflection of everything that lay beneath it. I wanted to stare at it forever, challenging my belief that nothing could ever distract me from such a rare and spectacular penthouse view. But that wasn't true, and maybe that's why I felt so bothered. This joy, this expectation I set for myself to be excited, disappeared, because no window, from no height, could ever produce enough dopamine to fight the looping soundtrack of Parker's interrupted words: *You're a woman, a beautiful one that doesn't need my protection. I couldn't see that before, but I do now, and that makes me feel safe, like I can finally say what I want to say…*

"It's been a long day for you," Alejandro said, guiding me into the living room. I pulled on my bag, drawing closer to his body, feeling restless. "Just remember, everything here is for you, Gemma, and please know you're welcome to anything you wish, my bed included." His not-so-subtle invitation was purposely gentle. I tried to hide the exhaustion in my voice, my disappointing answer already written on my face.

"I think I'll get ready in the spare room and call it a night," I replied hesitantly.

He didn't flinch as I watched his eyes, expecting some type of reaction, but instead received total acceptance.

"Then it's yours," he leaned down, kissing me softly, quietly letting me know that it would all be ok. "Goodnight, Gemma."

I shot one last smile before turning away, departing to my own wing of the house, slowly but surely leaving Alejandro alone in the dark. When I entered my room, I pressed my back against the door, shutting it with a quick lock.

"Fuck," I cursed, spitting a string of obscenities, physically gutted, frustrated. What the hell was I doing? *"Just stop it, Gemma."* I coached myself, flipping the light switch on, hurling my bag onto the bed.

I hated how conflicted I was, like the universe was hellbent on questioning everything I did. *Are you making the right choice,* it asked. *Don't you want to know more about what Parker was going to say?* He was about to tell me something, and I just walked away. Why did I *always* do that, why did I *always* allow myself to get caught up in a moment?

To top it off, this wasn't just about Parker anymore.

Two men cared for me, and I cared for them, but how would I ever begin to separate my feelings, or how would I know what's right or fair? Was *fair* even the right word to use?

Fair as in being hopelessly in love with Parker with no resolve?

Fair as in sharing Alejandro with Hollywood: his parties, his lawsuits, the secret of Natalie Brower? They were two different worlds. But perhaps, as Ivanna suggested, I was two different women: the carefree, and enamored Gemma with Parker, and the raw, honest Gemma with Alejandro.

So, *who* was I?

I removed my heels, rubbing my feet as my phone began to ring. Thinking it was Parker, I answered immediately.

"Hello?" I whispered, trying to hide my enthusiasm.

"Hey, babe!" Ivanna chimed through the other end, sounding almost surprised at the speed that I answered. "I was expecting to go voicemail."

"Of course not." I laughed. "Why would you think that?"

"Because that's what happened with Alejandro just now. I'm trying to get ahold of him. Figured you'd both *decline* your calls. You know, being that it's *bedtime*." Her assumption that Alejandro and I were sleeping together made me twist the strap of my bag.

"Absolutely not! I'm… just settling in."

"You sure? You sound out of breath," she pestered.

"What can I say? The city views take my breath away."

"Suuure…" Ivanna didn't believe me.

"I'm telling the truth!"

"So where's Alejandro, then?"

"Upstairs."

"Upstairs?" She sounded annoyed. "I swear… I'm getting blue balls just hearing this."

"Why?" I undressed myself, rolling my eyes. I pulled out a peach cami from my bag, placing it over my head and onto my body.

"It's the most upsetting display of delayed satisfaction I have ever seen. I swear... this must be some kink."

"No kink, just taking our time."

I faced a large mirror; its slim gold frame leaned against the wall, reflecting my body. Staring for a moment, I tugged on the cami that hovered above my hips and sheer black panties. With my hair pulled into a messy, top knot, I felt oddly sexy; just as sexy as Alejandro made me feel, and as hard as it was to admit, I craved to be devoured by him. But that's not to say that all we had was lust. He was more, something better, rivaling all the things I thought I knew about attraction, connecting us like destined magnets of dysfunction. Together, we weren't alone in our experiences, and I meant that far past anything physical.

"I don't understand you two, but I guess it makes sense. You're both so complicated. Match made in heaven."

"Or hell," I added slyly. "Are you calling me to drop off the suit tomorrow? I know you wanted to see it."

"Yes, but no. Actually... Alejandro's in trouble," she sighed.

"What? Why?"

"Because Lina is out in California, and she's been trying to get ahold of him. Of course, he's not answering, but it sounds urgent."

"Do you know what for?"

"She wouldn't say, but I figured you could be my messenger." I could hear her smile over the phone. "By the way, what are you wearing?" She hummed with the coax of her sultriness.

"Excuse me?" I laughed again.

"Humor me…"

"A cami," I answered, cutting the conversation short.

"Is that all?"

"No."

"So a pair of shorts too?"

"Not quite…"

"Oh, this is perfect. Are you in your panties, babe?"

"Oh my god," I squeaked, feeling completely exposed.

"I hope they're black, lacy little things. I bet Alejandro will like those."

"I'm not going to find out." I chewed on the corner of my thumb, staring at myself in the mirror. Ivanna had a way of making even the simplest question feel laced in sexual indecency. It was kind of fun, actually.

"Well, I need you to go find him. He needs to call Lina back. And if he's in trouble, then what better way to receive bad news, than from a half-naked Gemma Harrison."

"Please. I'm not half-naked." I grinned, sitting on the edge of the bed, lifting a book that sat on the nightstand. *Define a Daffodil: A Lexicon of Flowers and their Meanings.* How cunning but sweet, the worn spine of the encyclopedia looked well read. Did he read this just for me? It was tempting to go find him, just to ask about the book. "I'd feel a little self-conscious going up there with how I'm dressed," I answered.

"Don't… trust me, I can imagine how you look. I'm a fan after all."

"Flattery won't work here, Ivanna."

"At least poke your head out. Maybe he's closer than you think."

I did as I was told. First, placing my ear against the door before opening it, listening for any sign of Alejandro.

"I don't hear anything…" I said, allowing the cool air to seep along my feet and bare legs.

"Ok. So, go find him."

"I'm not sure if I should."

"Oh, don't be scared, Gemma. It's like hide and seek."

"I'm not scared." I claimed, not wanting Ivanna to know the consequences of what she was asking me to do. I slowly made my way through the living room before climbing along the staircase, remembering his warning from earlier.

If you ever make it to my bed, I swear I'll take you as mine.

I fought to dismiss it, knowing this could be important as I stopped at the top of the dark landing, hesitant to approach his large double doors. I called out his name but heard nothing.

"Well?" Ivanna asked impatiently.

"He might be asleep? His doors are shut, and I don't want to disturb him."

"Please, trust me. At least just peek inside. It'll be fun."

"Our ideas of fun are *way* different. It's been a weird night, ok?"

"Weird is a precursor to interesting," she coached. "You know you want to take a peek anyways. So do it."

A part of her was right, but the courage to take that next step felt dangerous, like I was entering the den of some notorious beast, damning myself to a sentence of tangled bedsheets and rough merciless sex.

Hesitantly, I twisted the silver knob, discreetly opening the door into a shapeless abyss. A small cast of light reached the enormous bed, the city's subtle glimmer burrowing into its sheets, opposite to the outlined glow of a shut bathroom door.

"Oh, he's in the shower…" I said shamefully, as if I already did something wrong. The dull patter of shower water reverberated in my direction. I wrung my hands together, keeping them low by my panties, my cheek securing the phone with my shoulder.

"Mmmm… lucky you," Ivanna hummed. "Get closer. He needs to know."

"How much have you had to drink tonight?"

"It's not my fault you taste so good," she whispered, alluding to the *Piedra Precicosa* she had drunk. "Remember what I told you tonight? About not knowing who you are, about taking a chance to find out?"

"This is different…"

"No, it's not. I shouldn't even be on the phone right now. Remember the couple at the club, the ones we caught *dancing* in the dark? Well, I'm over at their place… tucked in their bathroom, cleaning myself up."

"From what?" I asked.

For a while I just stood there, not sure what to do, my eyes shifting between the bed and the door. I was dying, brimming with a sense that I had been edging to climax for what felt like weeks now, knowing the smell of cherries alone could send me off into an orgasmic mess. *It'd be so easy, I could peek inside and see his body lathered in soap.*

"They brought me home, but we could barely make it past the elevator. And let me tell you, it was amazing."

"What happened?" I asked intrigued, my lips dried at her words.

I took a few steps closer, telling myself just to listen, to fuel my imagination of how Alejandro must look. Each step was an excuse, another image in my mind.

What if he caught me? Peeking like the little slut he saw me as, wearing a pair of small, black panties. And what if he liked it? I could be porn for his eyes, a reason for his erection to fill itself stiff with blood. Fuck, if I could just see him stroke that cock, slipping that fat tip through his strong grip. I'd lose control.

"A lot happened. At one point her boyfriend went to fix us a drink… and I couldn't help myself. Alone with a beautiful girl? Before I knew it, I had her against the wall, pulling her dress down. A few minutes and three rolling orgasms later, we were caught red handed, but that was part of the fun."

My eyes stood wide, realizing the door was opened just enough for a glance. Jesus, I bit my fucking lip as the shower grew louder, echoing the splashed handfuls of water that I imagined he cupped into his palms.

"And when you got caught?" I asked into the crack

of the door, tempted by Ivanna and the potential of what lied within the bathroom. The rush was far too intoxicating, the promise of Alejandro so thick in my gut that I could feel him inside. I squeezed my legs, fighting the urge to rub myself, my clit tingling and aroused.

"When *we* got caught, I made that little beauty get on her knees and lick my pussy. God, it always feels so good, especially while the girl is getting fucked from behind." Her confession came out in a desperate sigh, finding itself between my legs. I couldn't stop from looking; right or wrong, I had to see the man who dared to almost fuck me raw in my own closet. My knuckles cracked as I leaned in to peek.

"Oh fuck…" I swallowed, losing Ivanna on the other end.

Inside, Alejandro ran his hands through the waves of his wet hair, his eyes shut from the water that dripped down from his strong back to the dimpled cheeks of his firm ass.

My breathing quickened, captivated by the sight, his golden skin almost glowing as he reached up, scrubbing a spattering of thin, dark chest hair. He was, in every sense of the word, devilish— perfectly sculpted by design with his dark, menacing tattoos.

Alejandro turned around, his abs slicked with soap that poured down to the cut of his lean pelvis. He caught me with my hand inside my panties, pleasuring myself, fingering my cunt to his rock-hard body.

"I h-have to go…" I stuttered as Ivanna called out my name, her voice fading as I let my phone fall to the floor. If Ivanna could enjoy two sides of herself, couldn't I?

"Gemma…" Alejandro growled as I stepped further through the door. He was no man, he was a god, and spoke my name with both a promise and a warning. This was his world, his domain, and another step closer was the tacit acceptance of his complete control.

His rules.

His game.

Chapter 20

GEMMA

"You sneaking around? Think I wouldn't fucking catch you?" Alejandro locked me into a crude, unbreakable stare, beckoning me toward the tiled opening where his all-too-nude body stood.

I rubbed my hands together. "Lina's looking for you…" I said, caught in a yelp as he yanked my arm, pulling me into the shower. I gasped, flying into his wet, firm chest.

"I don't care about Lina. I'm busy right now… and so are you," he growled, his voice matching the pressured hiss of sprinkled water that soaked my entire cami. I drew my elbows in, shielding the excited goosebumps along my arms and breasts. There was no doubt in my mind that I was captured, completely helpless to an animal, to some primal version of a man who was stripped from his leather—naked and hard. He didn't want to just fuck me, he wanted to ruin me for other men, and I'd let him. "Didn't I warn you about coming up here?"

"Yes…"

"And you know what that means, right?"

"Yes."

"Yes, what?" The tip of his finger crawled under my

soaked top, brushing a tender spot right above my belly button.

"Yes, Papi," I obeyed, knowing whose house I was in, and whose world this was.

"Do you know what happens to good girls who get caught by bad men?"

"No…"

"They get disciplined, Gemma. And now that you've seen too much, you owe me."

"What could you possibly want?"

"Besides you on your knees? Every. Fucking. Piece of you."

He raised my wrist up to his face, studying my silver butterfly ring with utter contempt. "This is my game, and now it's show and tell, *Preciosa*. Do you remember my other rules?"

"Yes, Papi."

"Good, because here's rule number three, and I want you to listen closely to this, because for the rest of your life there will never be anyone else but me." Alejandro slowly twisted the ring off my finger, pinching it, contemplating the possibility of crushing its existence. For a second, I believed he could've destroyed it, but instead, tossed it wildly into the distance. I trembled in the water, shocked by the sharp consecutive taps it made as it disappeared into the dark. Not once had I removed it since I got it, and now, I felt just as nude as Alejandro.

"There's no one but you." I repeated his rule, as he squeezed my wrist, stroking my palm with his thumb.

"Perfect. Cause you know I'd fucking kill for you. Right?" I believed him, his arousal bundling at the bottom of my wet cami, the heat of his cock bent towards and across my wet stomach. "I need a good listener for this. Can you follow instructions, good girl?"

"Yes… I'll do anything for you," I said too eagerly, halted as he directed my hand along his hard torso, leading it down across trimmed pubic hair. God, he felt so good on my fingers, like he truly was all man, muscle, and veins.

He smirked, his erection jumping from my fingertips, visibly pulsing. "I want you to grab me, try and wrap your hand around my cock. You won't be able to hold all of it, but I'd love to see you try."

I did as I was told, gripping around the thick base of his shaft, the tips of my fingers unmet, holding what felt like muscle wrapped in silk. How would I be able to take all of him inside me if I couldn't even do it with my hand?

"Like this?" I asked nervously.

"Just like that. Now shut your eyes, and show your Papi where his little slut wants him," he instructed, swiping against my torso, his large tip smoothing a trail of clear semen across my belly button. He moaned.

"I want you right here." I stuck my tongue out, showing off the soft, pink spot meant just for him. "You think I could suck you off? That I could fit that full head in this pretty mouth?"

"You can fucking try. But when you gag, I can't promise I'll pull out. But you'll like it like that… I swear."

"And if I do, will you tell me I did a good job?" I raked my nails down to his navel, dropping to my knees in worship, his hard-on pressed against my full lips to be sucked. He affectionately brushed my hair like I was his pet, coaching me to lean my head against his strong legs. I liked it, being below him, being something to be praised, yet handled roughly, my knees pushed into a position that turned them red.

"I'll be fair, I'll tell you how well you've done, but only if you suck slowly, baby," he growled, shielding me from the beating water above. "Take me in as far as you can, and don't stop unless I tell you to."

For the first time, I licked the underside of his cock, feeling the velvety softness of his tip pop right into my mouth. Groaning my approval, I stroked him over my tongue, drooling over the hard vein on his shaft. Inch by inch he pushed himself further between my lips, causing my stomach to flutter and my neck to tense. I gagged, my chest heaving with a need to hiccup.

"Right there, baby," he fisted my soaked hair into a punishing, wet twirl, posing my head perfectly centered to his thighs. "I want to feel the back of your little throat, right where it's nice and wet." I blinked, loosening a stray tear, as my head bobbed in and out over his erection. Alejandro didn't even hesitate, rubbing his thumb along my cheek, licking my salty tear as if it were cherry cola. I loved that he did that, that he rocked his hips into me, that his strong dimpled ass flexed as he fucked my mouth.

"You can come if you want," I breathed, pulling him out with a suck. Fuck I wanted him to unload all over me: mouth, breasts, stomach, anywhere. "It's ok if it spills over my cami, or into my panties… you can stain them however you want—"

Maybe my permission was too much, as Alejandro's toes suddenly curled and his eyes immediately shut. He gripped me tighter, bracing onto the roots of my scalp like it was the only thing stopping him from coming. "I dare you to spit me out. Let's see if it can spill its way down to that little pussy of yours."

Fuck.

The difference in how his hips moved made me needy, how his cock head flexed over my filthy words. I reached between my legs, tracing circles on my clit, spreading myself open. I was the dirty girl, the whore on her knees who rubbed herself while sucking off the hottest celebrity in the world.

Suddenly, I screamed as Alejandro pulled me to my feet, his cock springing from my lips as he spun me around, shoving me hard against the cold shower glass.

"What the fuck are you doing?" he demanded.

I exhaled, "Rubbing myself. I can't wait any longer, you taste too fucking good."

"I don't care. Rule number four, no one makes you come, but me," he persisted. "Only I will make you scream," I arched my back, pressing my ass against his cock as he forced my cami down, exposing me to the mirror across from us. "Look at those perfect little tits. Keep them right fucking there, or else I'll suck them red." He slapped my ass so hard that it made my cunt swell, leaving me close to tears.

"Shit!" I erupted. I fucking loved it, my clit buzzing between my legs.

"*Shhh…* let it sting… let it linger till it starts to throb. Tell me, who knows best?" He spanked me again.

"Papi?" I whined.

"Fucking right. I'm your *Papi,* and I'm here to show you what good girls need."

"And what's that?" I feigned innocence.

"A rough fuck to crumble those insecurities of yours." He reached for my lace panties, not pulling them down, or shoving them aside, but instead, shredding them off like wet paper. I screamed as their tattered fragments fell to my feet.

"Alejan—" My lips were interrupted with a gasp, stopped as Alejandro slipped his perfectly long finger inside me, his palm cupped against my folds.

He dug so deep, fucking me so impossibly hard that it brought me to the tips of my toes. "Your little mouth struggled to take me, but you did so damn good."

"Did I? You sure, Papi?" I pouted my lip, sticking it out to be sucked. He leaned in, pulling it between his teeth with a suck, drawing its red, tender color to the surface.

"Yes, so fucking good… but how can I stuff myself inside you when your cunt is still too tight?" He sunk another finger inside. It was too much to bear, stripping the last bit of energy out from my legs. I fell back onto his chest, writhing myself against his hand. "I'll take my damn time, and I won't pull out until you're loosened up for me."

I tried to fight my building orgasm, my first true release that wasn't initiated by one of my sweet, vibrating toys. It twisted below my core, turned like a timer that was set to explode.

"I can't hold on anymore! Alejandro, don't stop. Don't stop!"

"Let it out. Fucking come on me." It all happened so fast, like a blur, hitting the right spot in perfect harmony as he repeatedly beat my pussy with a spank.

I bit my shoulder, feeling the wave of not one, but two hot orgasms. I was coming quicker and harder than ever before, the air escaping my lungs as he pulled himself out of me, greedily, hastily, sticking his cum-soaked fingers into my mouth.

"That's my girl. Tell me how good you taste."

I sucked his fingers clean, licking the taste of my pussy, my first time ever tasting the prize of my own orgasm.

"Tastes so good, but I want more."

"Can you take it?"

"I don't care. Just do it. I'd rather it hurt than not have it at all…" I begged as I was pulled back around, lifted into the air by Alejandro's brute strength. He kissed me harder this time, almost puncturing my lip, as he hauled me out of the shower and onto the counter by the sink. A puddle formed below me as I wedged myself against the mirror, flexing my torso into a crunch to see his erection right at the edge of my entrance. I needed to see him going inside me.

He didn't hesitate, combing the hair out from his face as he reached into a black, velvet box, pulling out a condom, ripping its gold label with his teeth, before rolling it on.

"Do I scare you, Gemma?" he asked, lifting my chin to shut my mouth. I didn't know it was open. I saw him —all of him—and a part of me was scared, not only sexually, but emotionally. Everything felt too good, like my body was made of stardust.

"Yes." I blinked, and he seemed to be content, as if he expected it all along.

"Don't you dare look away from me," he commanded. "I want to see your face when I slip inside you for the first time. I need to see how you come undone just for me." He pressed his palm down over my pelvis as drops of water fell from his tussled, black hair onto my stomach.

I wasn't prepared for what came next, feeling the expansion between my legs fold over, stretching from his perfect, round tip. It ached with every inch he impaled me, causing me to wince as my wetness engulfed the entirety of his erection.

"Hold it there… please," I begged as he pushed further, reaching a point that no one, not even his fingers had been before.

"I love the sound of your voice when you beg. Do it again."

Lifting my hands behind his neck, I sunk my nails into his shoulders, as he completely filled me up, making me whole.

"Please, Papi, I want it. That's the spot," I whimpered, his tip reaching a button that made my toes curl.

He didn't pump, or push, he simply pressed forward again into the spot itself. My pelvis twitched, the impression of his cock visibly contracting my insides with a long thrust.

"There it is…" he sucked in, his tongue stroking the inside of his lip. "That fucking look, my scared, beautiful girl."

I leaned my head onto his chest, his arms pulling me closer to the edge. "Alejandro…" His name fully escaped my mouth. If he stopped, even for a moment, I might lose my building release, and I couldn't have that, I needed more.

"You better be ready to fucking come. I don't think I can edge myself any closer," he lifted me up off the counter, fucking me across the bathroom and onto his dresser in the bedroom. "You feel so tight and so goddamn good, baby… and I don't usually come this fucking fast. Please tell me you're close."

I loved hearing him pant and was ready to come like he wanted, his anticipation to orgasm turning me the fuck on. I pushed my back against the wall, digging my bare heels onto his ass, helping him go deeper, to rock me in the most painfully sweet of ways.

"I'm so close. So, so close." I tried to keep my eyes from rolling, focusing on the mirror behind him, my hips still writhing. All I saw was us, not just fucking, but something more beautiful and erotic than I could've ever imagined. The kiss tasted different, the sounds and moans no longer so shallow, but deepened with pleas of praise. This was an indulgence, this was… *more.*

He slid me off the dresser, carrying me towards the unmade bed where he laid me gently, keeping his cock inside me, not once pulling out or stopping his thrusts as

I kissed his lips feverishly. I didn't want him to see how sensitive and willing my body was for him, never had a man made me do what I felt like I was about to do.

"We should stop. I feel like I'm going to—" My legs spread into a tremor, shaking as a flooding sensation began to pull into my core.

"Final rule, Gemma… you're mine to keep forever," he obsessed. "Don't hesitate with me. Don't stop yourself." Alejandro prayed into my neck, a kinder gesture of intimacy that forced me to kiss him.

"Don't be mad," I warned, my body building into a peak like a bursting, wet, fucking door. I fisted the sheets and bit into his chest, concealing something far too big and wild that I didn't want him to see. I couldn't hold back though, not even if I tried, not with how deeply he fucked. "Oh my god—" my breath was cut short, diminished by a mutual, never-ending moan that erupted in the room, "I'm going to come… I'm coming!" I cried out as a sudden rush of fluid escaped me, flooding the surface of Alejandro's hips with a hot, wet, gushing squirt. It was a pulsing, ravenous rush that circulated my body, shot like a cannon of electric waves. I recoiled from the constant rolling contractions that rippled between my legs and over his shaft, my heat trickling out into a dirty little puddle, caught between our glistening bodies.

Immediately, I covered my face, biting my lip, consumed with embarrassment and joy, a confusing mix of the most incredible orgasm I ever experienced.

Alejandro stretched himself over me, his firm chest heaving like wet slate from the city light outside. I awaited his words, wondering what he'd say when he saw what I did, our bodies no longer soaked from the shower, but from me? Criticisms? Disgust? Shame? I wasn't sure but found out with the most primal of praises as he coated his finger with my filth, licking it off.

"That's my good girl," he whispered, "my good *fucking* girl."

Chapter 21

ALEJANDRO

Gemma, my addicting, innocent Gemma sat below me, amazement etched on her face as she looked between my expanding abs and the glistening, beautiful mess we created.

Taking my time, I pushed deeper inside her, sitting in her heat, baptized with a reward that caused her to shield her eyes.

"God, I'm so embarrassed," she stuttered, attempting to rise up. I shoved her back down, excited and aroused by the burn of her red cheeks and even redder, swollen lips.

"You don't need to be embarrassed." I said, my cock still rooted in her wet pussy. My condom ballooned inside from how hard she made me come, and I didn't want to move, I only wanted to worship the smell of sex that perfumed our bodies. "Does it make you shy that you spilled yourself all over me? That I'm drenched in your cum?" I reached for her hand, pulling it towards my abs. I wanted the tips of her fingers to slide along the slickness her pussy caused along my pelvis.

"Yes, I think so." She grinned, biting the tip of her own finger. "I mean, I made a mess." She was genuinely concerned, innocently worried how I'd react. Didn't she realize how perfect she was, from the dip of her dimpled cheek to her wet auburn hair that fell across her chest?

"Maybe I like it." I confessed, savoring the sound of our damp silk bodies. "Maybe I like everything about you, every expression, every reaction, every fucking moan. Nothing from you is exempt from praise, nothing from you will ever go unappreciated. But shyness, Gemma, you know I can't tolerate that." I lifted her leg over my shoulder, her cunt wrapping tighter around my cock. She winced, adjusting to the new pressure.

"That's not a new rule, is it?"

My jaw bristled against her inner thighs as I licked the wetness at her calf, the very cum that had just jutted out from her body and onto my sheets.

"Not a new rule, but a lesson, and perhaps the most important one of all," I answered. "That one: there's nothing about you that you need to hide. You're perfect. Always were, always will be. And two: I won't ever allow you to hold back. When I tell you to come, Gemma, I fucking mean it." Slowly, I pulled myself out, rubbing my tip along the slippery rim of her pussy's snug grip.

"You were so deep," she swallowed. "Did you come?"

"Harder than ever before," I drew the condom off slowly. "If only I could've fucked you bare, then you'd really be leaking."

"Don't tempt me. I might just risk it all for you."

Risk it all for me? I almost bored my cock right back into her, tempted by the rotation of her hips and the awed crease of her brow. I was so fucking addicted, stuck on her erotic sighs, the goddamn tease drove me a new kind of crazy.

"I can't let you cool down just yet." I paused in contemplation, enamored by the pale glow of Gemma's toned stomach and breasts. Everything about her shimmered, her curvatures drawn by stark black shadows, begging to be covered, and stained. I placed my hand over her pelvis, stopping her from moving out of the perfect place I needed her to be. "You think you've made a mess, but you don't know a fucking mess until I show you."

I twisted my wrist over her body. One drop. Two drops. I poured myself out of the condom and onto her stomach, drizzling the entirety of my orgasm until it spilled over her hips and onto the bed.

"Fuck, it's so hot," she said excitedly, reaching down, toying with the pool of white semen that sat above her navel. "And so... slick," she added, propping herself on her elbows.

"Now we're both filthy. There's no need to feel ashamed for expressing how you feel, and how you feel is fucking incredible. We're meant for each other in every way, just as it should be. That is..." I paused, smearing cum I just spilt up to her nipple, pinching it with my thumb. "Once I fuck you again, and make you come like the perfect girl you are."

"Alejandro," she gasped.

Gemma felt weightless as she guffawed into a screech, helpless and enthused as I flipped her over onto her stomach.

"You like that? Being forced to come?" My cock slid

up between her ass, jacking me off, my tip still leaking onto her bare back. She moaned as I reached towards the nightstand, pulling out a condom from the drawer, ripping it open.

"Yes!" she cried. "I don't want to hold back anymore."

"You won't have a choice." I hummed in her ear, taking pleasure in the scent of her fresh skin, her perfume lost from the shower and sweat. "I want you on your knees, soaking my cock like your little cunt was made for it."

She fisted the sheets, pushing her ass back like a heart-shaped saddle for me to mount. "Just fill me up. I promise it's all I need. You'll hit that spot, the one I'm still feeling." Her leg shook, her cheek pressed into the pillow as she looked in my direction.

"Fill you up?" I rolled the condom over my cock. "You mean like this?" I thumbed open her folds, spreading her wide, her pussy puckering with a contraction I needed to feel. Slowly, I plunged my tip inside her, taking rigorous mental notes of what I saw and of what I wanted to remember forever. It was the sound; the tender and wet friction of latex and flesh; like the drip and suckle of a freshly bit peach. It was as if she sucked me in, her wild *inhale* pulled my cock further and deeper.

"Just like that," she whimpered, aching.

"You holding your breath, baby?" I noticed, her toes curling as I pulled out slowly, only to thrust in again, her pussy smacked like a Blow Pop.

"I can't help it," she exhaled.

"Why not?"

"I normally do. But not during sex."

"Then when?"

"When I…" Gemma bit into the pillow. "When I touch myself, sometimes I hold my breath. I don't know I'm doing it though. I only know it happens when I get close."

"Close to what?"

"Close to coming, just like before. But I could never get myself there with other men…" she whined, our sweat rolling into shared beads between our bodies. "I don't think I can hold on any longer."

"Then don't." I demanded, lifting her back to meet my chest. She gasped, her arms hoisted like wings, restrained and braced for the pump of my hips. Fuck, now would be the time to use the cuffs on her, to chain her wrists into an unmovable position. She'd look sexy as hell but already felt too damn good to move anywhere but in and out of her body.

"Christ, Alejandro." Her voice drowned out by the pound of my hips. She never held her breath during sex, but she never knew what true sex was, what *true* fucking could be. She held it now because she was close, her milky cunt leaving slick lube along my condom. I'd look for it as I fucked her, measuring her pleasure by the size and covering of what she leaked.

"Look at yourself." I kissed her balmy neck, my cheek guiding hers toward the standing trifold mirror in the corner, the one I installed when she took my measurements. Back then she refused to come to my room, but now she was here, right where she belonged, and I thanked Christ for such a merciful fucking gift. "What a sight, a beautiful fucking sight," her breasts raised in the reflection as I clawed at her stomach, my cum still dripping over her belly button, rolling down from the vertical line of her torso and towards her inner thigh.

"I look like—" she leaned her head back, pushing herself harder against me. "A fucking. Dirty. Mess."

"Just like us. Perfectly messy, just how I like it. Just how we are. Now come for me."

"I—" She held her breath.

"Give it to me. Another and another. Wet this goddamn bed." Her body jerked as I fucked her harder, my knees digging into the soaked sheets of her release, nearly losing balance with how mercilessly I railed her cunt.

"There!" She yelled out, "I'm coming!" My cock slipped out, all of my weight and size freed between her legs as a pool of warm liquid poured out from Gemma and over my cock. My erection pulsed, no longer inside her, but coming regardless, filling my condom again as she squirted over it, soaking me.

"Good fucking girl." I growled, holding her from behind, controlling the loose tremor of her body. I pressed my mouth against her shoulder, foolishly biting her in an attempt to be closer, to fucking consume her.

We panted, collecting our breath between kisses.

"I can't believe it." She reached between her legs where my cock sat erect, placed beneath her, stiff against her clit. She pinched the tip of my condom, stroking the last bit of my cum into it. "I know you're out of me, but I still feel you, throbbing."

"But you're emptied." I praised, elated how her wetness pooled around my knees again. "Now relax, baby. You've done *so* good," I supported her loose body, her muscles puddling against me. "You know that I'll take care you." In a quick but gentle move, I cradled Gemma, lifting her into my arms as she laughed, exhausted.

"You, take care of me?" she asked, her eyes much bigger in the dark as they expanded to take me in.

I sat her onto my small midcentury dresser, propping her up, ensuring she didn't bump into the brass knobs. She watched me unroll my condom, her face frowning as I tied its end into a knot. I think she liked what I did earlier, and the minor change of expression may have been because I didn't spill it all over her.

"Yes," I reached over a tufted chaise by our side, removing a white blanket from its arm to wrap around Gemma. "I take care of you, and I take care of *us*. Us as a couple, us from the press, the world, and from anyone and anything that could ever threaten what we have, because what we have, Gemma, is far more incredible than what anyone could ever hope for."

A brief silence lulled as I wrapped the blanket around her shoulders. She didn't immediately respond.

Maybe the thought of *us* as a collective was finally settling in. From the drawer by her side, I pulled out a fresh set of sheets and a spare towel to clean her.

"Those are really big feelings to share," Gemma grinned, breaking her gaze from mine, directing it toward the floor. She didn't seem shy or embarrassed, and for once, her eyes escaped the fear that I felt had been holding her back. I didn't know if it were fleeting or not, but I cherished it nonetheless.

"Spread your legs for me." I commanded, rubbing her knee as she parted herself slowly. I ran the towel along her chest and down to her navel, gently padding it towards the lower half of her body. My cum dripped dangerously close to her pretty pussy as I swiped it away. She didn't seem to mind, and I wondered if she would have allowed it to fall right over her clit if its course continued. "Do you mind that I share *big* feelings?" I leaned my head against hers.

"I'm…" she paused, "I'm just not used to it, I think."

"That's a shame. You deserve to know all the pretty things that you bring to this world. The purpose you give me." I brushed her eyebrow, her hand raised towards my chest, checking the sturdy pulse that still raced for her.

"And what would my purpose be?"

I kissed her deeply, selfishly taking my time memorizing each intricate curve of her body. She was mine, and for that I was grateful, along with the truth I was about to share.

"Well, for me… it's everything. It's what I've looked for and always wanted. It's you, and as strange as it may sound, it always has been. You have been out in the world, and I have been waiting, searching for this feeling, like everything will be ok. That's purpose,

Gemma. It's the possibility that I can truly be myself someday."

Gemma's timid smile dropped.

Did I say too much?

"I thought smokers enjoyed a cigarette after sex?"

She changed the subject, the depth of my confession maybe more than what she could handle.

"Some do."

"But not you?"

"Of course me. But I told you, I won't smoke in front of you." Gemma fidgeted with a pack of *Tranquillo's* by her side, which may have prompted the question.

"Even if I told you I don't mind?"

"Yes, even if you say you don't mind."

I knew better but watched closely as she opened the pack and pulled one out.

"I don't know if I should tell you this," she sighed, dragging the cigarette across her bottom lip.

"Tell me what?"

"A secret. An embarrassing one at that. I'm not even sure how you would look at me if I told you."

"I know the feeling, but trust me, I'll never stop looking at you the way I do."

"And how is that?"

"Like it's the first time all over again." I confessed, dropping my shielded glare, no longer disguising my nervousness, but making it known. I had her now, so my face finally relaxed.

Gemma hid her blush.

"Well, the night I came by to measure you for your

suit, when you caught me snooping. I actually had something in my hand, something I stole from you." Gemma ran the cigarette down my chest, unprepared for how suddenly I caught her wrist.

"A thief? Just like when you stole a box of pants from your school auditorium?"

"Worse," she admitted. "I stole one of your *Tranquillos.*" She faked a pout. Goddamn, she was so cute, and it frustrated me.

"You're a bad fucking girl," I worshipped.

"Maybe I'm both, bad and good. Maybe I'm realizing this myself. I think it's your fault, Mr. Rivera-Marquez."

My full name from her lips reminded me of our professional relationship. To me she was Gemma, my good girl, but also, to the public eye she was my employee. This made me her boss, the very boss that just spilled his hot cum all over her stomach like a dirty fucking canvas. It was all so perfectly indecent.

"Stealing?" I playfully scolded. "Oh, Miss Harrison, how could I ever forgive that?"

She shrugged, batting her eyes, "Guess I should have known better."

I removed the *Tranquillo* from her fingers. "So, you have a special cigarette of mine?"

She nodded, the tops of her breasts rising as I traced the tip of the cigarette along her chest and down to her stomach. "If you get a special cigarette, then so do I." I licked her lips. "Maybe it'll be my last cigarette. I'll only need one more, one that is sweeter than any cherry."

"Tell me, what would that be?" Gemma's stomach

prickled with goosebumps, as the filter teased the lips of her perfectly spread pussy, still filled with arousal, seeping the clear lube that made my cock hiccup in excitement.

"The taste of your cunt," I eased her shoulders as I ran the cigarette against her opening, lathering her taste onto its tip.

"Me?" She bated.

"All you, baby. I'll smoke it when I need it the most, and I'll think of you. Only you. And how amazing you make me feel." I slightly penetrated the tip inside her just enough to appreciate her taste for later. It made me grit my teeth.

"I'm still so wet." She swallowed, shivering as I pulled it out and placed it behind my ear. Her hazy eyes begged to be fucked again, but also competed with their need for sleep. I had exhausted her, and as selfish as I wanted to be, nothing brought me more pleasure than seeing her taken care of.

"You'll need your energy." I rubbed her chin. "If you think tonight was good, then wait till tomorrow, and the day after that."

"And after that?" she asked, watching as I carefully pulled the old sheets off, lying fresh ones down.

"And after that. I have big plans for us."

Gemma grew quiet again, watching as I tucked everything in, making sure it was clean and dry.

"Alejandro?" she asked as I finished smoothing out the sheets, making my way back to her.

"Gemma?"

"What does *us* feel like to you? I didn't mean to shy

away from your feelings earlier. I guess, I'm still just surprised to hear them. It feels nice, and I wouldn't ever want them to go away, but then again, some things can feel both nice and scary all at once."

"Scary?" I asked, drawing the fuzzy blanket closer around her arms.

"Yeah. Scary as in, getting my hopes up. Tonight was so great, and honestly I haven't felt this way, ever. Well, I've never been *this* intimate with anyone. Have you?" She looked away, shaking her head. "Never mind. Don't answer that."

"What if I want to?" I corrected the direction of her worried eyes.

"It's just… I feel like I'm slowly discovering who I am. Maybe I'm a little bit of the person from my past, but also, maybe I'm someone different. Someone I only am when I'm with you." She grazed her fingers along the angel wings on my chest. I knew she wanted to know more about the A.A. initials that they held. "I'm sure it's already happened to you. You're older and more experienced than I am, and maybe I'm just trying to catch up."

"My experiences are different than yours, but trust me, there's never been anyone like you." I looked down at her hand, her finger circling the feather-like strokes of my tattoo. We stood in the dark, just like at The Met, the moment she opened herself to me and shared unreciprocated pieces of truth. I owed some in return, even at the cost of my discomfort. "The A.A. is something I look at before bed, and immediately when I wake up. It's a reminder of the sacrifices that were made to get me where I am today."

"Was it a lover?" she asked again.

I shook my head. "A love but not like that. One that was lost too soon." I lifted Gemma into my arms, her body still wrapped in the blanket as I carried her to bed. "It's just not easy to talk about, but how can I criticize your shyness when I'm being so timid?"

"That's honest of you." She turned to face me as we laid in the cool fresh sheets.

"I'm usually better at looking at others than within."

"Within is where the good stuff is."

"But also the bad." I admitted, combing her hair. I just wanted to make her feel comfortable, and it was the little things she did for me that told me she felt the same. It was her attention, undivided and committed, prevalent even after waiting all night for me to get out of jail; her willingness to be accepting, to see me at a party and still stand by my side. She was all the good things I never deserved, loyalty included, sticking up for me even with the disapproval of her best friend. I knew I could feel safe with her, but my own insecurities always had a way of creeping in. Mostly, I feared what she feared, that it would all go away with the slip of a tongue. "Always. Alma." I exhaled slowly.

"Always, Alma?" Gemma repeated quietly.

"It's my mother's name. The tattoo is for her, and it's a reminder for me to do better, to be better. I always thought the reason I did things was to honor her, to make her proud, and serve her memory. Always for her. Always for Alma."

Gemma snuggled against me, as I pulled her in closer. Our bodies seemed to fit so perfectly, so equally close and impenetrable. It was all I could say, a little at the time, a fraction of the broken story of my life.

"I love that," Gemma finally spoke. "And I love that you shared that with me. You can share anything with me, Alejandro. Please know that. I know we try our best to be open with one another, and I know in time we will. I swear I can be patient, like you have been with me."

I was certain she wanted to know more about how I lost my mother. I could share it all, but all I cared to share was how she made me feel, and wasn't that what really mattered? I cared, and I wasn't afraid to tell her that, I was only afraid to lose her.

"Someday…" I squeezed her tighter, kissing her forehead.

"You're allowed to keep secrets. Just know this, I'll never stop looking at you the way I do." Gemma echoed my own words to me, I couldn't help but chuckle, curious as to her answer.

"And what would that be, Miss Harrison?"

"That you deserve to feel the way you make me feel. That I am worthy of something more," she cooed. "I'm not scared of you, Alejandro. Not anymore."

Her eyes began to close as she nuzzled my chest.

Falling asleep.

Listening to my heart.

An incurable thrum meant only for her.

Chapter 22

GEMMA

Did last night really happen?

The rough love and tender kisses?

The dirty words and endearing truths?

It was all so wicked and divine, so impossible to believe, but once I felt the cool sheets in my grasp, I knew this wasn't a dream.

It was real.

We were real.

I slowly found the courage to wake up, revealing the Manhattan sky, lit like an auburn fire settling on the white linen that wrapped around my body.

"You're awake," Alejandro marveled, gruffer with the first use of his voice. I glanced up, taking in his peculiar bedhead and thick, long lashes as he pulled me into his naked body.

"Have you been watching me sleep?" I asked, giddy at the thought, his hands caressing my arms like honey on porcelain.

He kissed my cheeks between words, his confidence hidden in the modesty of a whisper. "Watching you, dreaming of you, thinking about last night, and god, how bad I *still crave* you." He reached below the sheets, drawing a line along my breasts and to the curve of my hip. Each touch reminded me that my skin was still naked and vulnerable to his command.

"Craving me? Geez, you must be so hungry then."

"Starved," he scooped me up.

I screamed in delight.

Alejandro flipped me onto my back, leaving me little room to resist, but giving me little desire to either. He stopped as my eyes went huge, his devout attention sinking into the center of my pupils.

"God…" he said above my lips.

"What?"

"Nothing. It's just… you look so innocent. Just like when you followed me out of Gerard's."

"You mean when you stole my designs?" I laughed. "What choice did I have?"

"Your designs? I wasn't stealing those. I was stealing *you*." His hips parted my legs, his body burrowing into a space almost too small for such a large man. "And then you smiled. I'm not sure if I could ever find the words to tell you how you made me feel that day… but I sure as hell can show you."

The sheet slipped down as he tossed me further up the bed, exposing my breasts to his insatiable, lust-filled eyes.

"Let me feel you, the real you. No condom. Just the tip, that's all I'm asking for, Papi." I begged, freeing my hand to run my fingertips along his back. I knew it was dangerous to ask, but the risk of his cock fucking me bare turned like a spring in my stomach, his hard, red tip already brushing along my slit.

"Don't taunt me, Gemma. You don't know how fast

I might come while I'm inside you… and Christ knows you couldn't wash me away."

"Who says I would? Now. Fuck. Me." I surprised myself with the slight jut of my hips, accidentally pushing his erection into my pussy. "Just like that…" inaudible words perched from the back of my throat. I dropped my hips, causing his cock to fall out and onto my pulsing clit. I looked down at my wetness smeared along the top of his crown. Alejandro was so aroused, his dick brimming with precum. I rubbed it away, allowing its sticky slickness to part between my fingers before sucking it off, wanting more.

"*Mr. Rivers!*" A spry voice echoed along the penthouse, carrying up to our bedroom—his bedroom —from the foyer downstairs. My eyes widened as I tried not to laugh.

"Fuck…" Alejandro groaned. "It's my scheduled room service."

The thought of an unknowing observer ever hearing my screams felt naughty, almost enticing, and I knew already with just a few more thrusts, that I'd come.

"Again," he covered my mouth as I tried not to scream in pleasure. "Let me just feel a little more." Alejandro positioned himself closer, tempting me with the realization that I could easily slip him inside again with the raise of my hips. He twisted my lips shut as the man called out once more.

"*Mr. Rivers, I have your breakfast, sir!*"

Panicked, wet, and far too horny, my greedy self wanted to take all I could with what little time I had.

The pressure of his entrance weakened my knees as the springs of the bed squeaked.

"Stay nice and quiet, baby. You don't want to get caught having that pussy stretched, do you?" his finger pressed onto my tongue, pacifying me with a gag. I sucked it good just as if it were his cock, and I didn't care if the man downstairs heard. I just needed Alejandro to fuck me.

"*Sir, I need your signature!*" The man's final shout rattled me, encouraging me to push further, taking more of Alejandro than what I should've. He hunched forward as I swallowed his length, pulling the entirety of him deep inside my pussy.

"God…" he exhaled, taking the sheets off the bed as he drove himself into me.

I flexed my stomach, containing the tailspin of tingles that twirled below my belly. "I want to squirt on you, Papi," I begged, rushed from the fear of being caught and the pleasure I felt.

"Come on me, baby, go ahead and I'll lick you up. You'll be my fucking breakfast." He bit into his lip, letting me know that he was close too. It made me so wet, so terribly reckless.

"Wait. No, we can't," I finally admitted between heavy breaths, prompting him to slowly pull out completely. I couldn't think of anything hotter than his cum seeping into the deepest parts of me, but the risk of not having any birth control was as terrifying as it was sexy.

"You don't know how badly I want to come inside you. How loud I want this bed to be. Fuck if he hears, or if anyone does for that matter. I just want to see how that pussy looks when it's filled with my cum." He closed in on me, aggressively sucking my bottom lip, as if to satisfy how sexually frustrated he'd become.

I stopped the tremor in my leg, stiffening my toes as he caressed my heart-shaped face.

"Soon!" I promised. "But not now. Go get ready, and I'll take care of the man downstairs." I scooted back as Alejandro fixed his hair, rising up from the bed with a stiff, pulsing erection.

"Better you than me," he grinned.

I shooed him away as he moved into the bathroom, allowing me just enough time to throw on a robe, open the door, and relieve the man downstairs.

"Coming!" I sang out, tying the silk belt around my waist.

A short man in a uniform smiled, presenting a cart filled with food.

"My apologies, Mrs. Rivers," he greeted. "I hope I didn't disturb you."

Mrs. Rivers? The sweet man's foreign accent made me wonder if he actually knew who Alejandro was. The idea of ever being married to him had my idiotic heart beating far too hard against my chest. I snorted, thinking of the inherent charm of how that sounded; *Gemma Rivers,* or more authentically, *Gemma Rivera-Marquez.* I didn't correct him, I merely played along as I came down the stairs, barefoot and all.

"No disturbance in the least bit." I lied, knowing my orgasm was not completely lost, still tipping at its edge. It was as if I could explode at any second, too hesitant to move, afraid that I might leak out while standing beside this stranger.

I took the small clipboard from his hand, signing the receipt with my now fake married name.

"Thank you, ma'am," he smiled, taking my signature. "Please enjoy."

Oh trust me, I was enjoying my time and possibly far too much. A trickle ran down my thigh the moment he left. I sighed out in relief, wiping my leg with my robe as the elevator door shut.

"He's gone!" I shouted up the stairs, curiously peeking beneath the covered plates on the cart. A puff of steam rose when I lifted the lid, revealing a stack of pecan covered pancakes and bacon. My stomach growled, having just realized that I hadn't eaten last night, but instead, dunked back tequila shots at a very revealing Alex Rivers party. Actually, it wasn't as bad as I pictured.

Sure, the scene was crazy, but it seemed simpler now that I experienced it. Could everything else be this easy? Honestly, I didn't even feel nervous anymore, because what Alejandro and I had was much stronger than any crazy party; and maybe this was our real beginning, like the start of us being a happy couple. Was that what we were now? I mean, per his final rule last night, I was *his*, but to what label? Girlfriend? Lover? Did that even matter at this point? Of the list of pros and cons, this certainly felt like a pro; nights of hot sex, mornings with tea and pancakes.

I could do this the rest of my life, I told myself, trying to ignore the absence of my butterfly ring. Casually, I looked down at my finger, recognizing the white tan mark left in its absence.

It'd be weird to go look for it, trying to avoid my sudden desire to seek it out on the bathroom floor and put it back on. I was allowed to be happy. And I was, wasn't I? With Alejandro finally opening up, I had to give him some credit, considering he told the truth about his chest tattoo. He was a good man, he had to be.

I wheeled the cart towards the kitchen, switching the T.V. on, listening to the morning news.

"You checking the weather?" Alejandro entered, asking as I fixed the table.

"Actually, the traffic," I clutched my robe with a smile. "Just wondering how much time we have before you're needed on set."

"They work around me, besides, I'd much rather hear about your plans." Just like the centerfold of Gentlemen's Quarterly, Alejandro leaned against the cool, white counter, shirtless, his hard obliques contracting as he playfully plucked the bacon from my mouth, taking a crunchy bite.

"Your suit," I mindlessly replied, distracted by his body. "It's finished, and I need to drop it off with Ivanna today, but I need one last fitting with you, just in case. I think she wants to inspect it before your event." I gushed as he unabashedly studied the way my robe loosened itself, exposing my cleavage.

It took everything in my power not to reach out and grab him by the belt loop of his pants. His smile turned into a small, manly laugh, as my stomach began to gargle.

"You're a busy girl, you know that? But you'll need your energy." He motioned for me to sit down at the table, my thighs still aching from the night before. "Make sure to eat every bite. I want you strong for later," he instructed sweetly, forking a slice of pancake into my mouth.

God, I was in instant heaven.

"Forget about later," I said between chews, my mouth now full of syrup and pecans. "These pancakes are already like sex. Seriously, they're incredible. Reminds me of Benee's down on Fifth." I downed another scoop, chewing much quicker than flattery would demand. Alejandro poured steaming tea into my empty mug.

"So, you're a breakfast fan?" he asked, shoveling a heap of hash browns into his mouth. He ate just as quickly as me, if not faster. I swore we'd choke at any moment.

"Well, sorta. It was my favorite meal growing up, but mostly because it was the only one I was guaranteed besides lunch." I sat quietly, slightly embarrassed to admit it. I hadn't even thought of Claire until now or how hungry I'd be as a child after not having any dinner from the night before. Luckily, Parker had always brought me a sandwich for lunch. Well, actually, he'd also bring me dessert. He never forgot me like Claire did, and the more I thought of it, the more I realized how he never missed a day of school for me, even when he was sick. "My school provided a free one, usually oatmeal, but every Wednesday they'd add a banana…" I trailed off.

Alejandro looked down at his plate, keeping a light smile that felt more disappointed than humorous. "At my home, breakfast was a competition, not a promise. One stack of tortillas, one stick of butter. When it was gone, it was *gone*."

His passive admission was said so matter-of-factly, so unconcealed. I supposed I was rubbing off on him, allowing him the courage to talk about things he probably didn't care to share.

"Maybe you can take me to this Benee's?" He beamed. "You can order for me and show me what's good."

"Parker and I always get breakfast there; it's normally our Saturday tradition." I covered my mouth, my fork clanking loudly against the plate.

Parker? Seriously? What an idiotic moment to share my experiences about the man who was hellbent on ruining Alejandro's life. His calming presence had subdued me so much, that I couldn't filter the stupid words that fell from my mouth.

"I didn't mean to say that…" I hesitated.

He looked away, brushing his dark eyebrow with his thumb. "You know, breakfast is fine and all, but you don't need to feel weird about the traditions you already have. I appreciate that about you. But maybe we need something just for us… *our* own breakfast tradition."

Immediately, I was intrigued.

"Ok, yeah. Like maybe, we can try a new pancake place each weekend?" I suggested as a long, loose strand of syrup fell from my lips and down into the opening of my robe. "Shit!" I hissed, reaching for a napkin. I went to wipe it off, but Alejandro stopped me, slowly reaching for my wrist, pulling it down.

"Pancakes aren't a bad idea, Gemma, but I think syrup could be a much better tradition," he said into a kiss on the back of my hand, reaching for the steel bell of dark maple syrup. "How about something that suits both of us? Something sweeter, something more satisfying?" he proposed, his words formed into a promise as he dipped two fingers into the bell.

"Just for breakfast?" I asked innocently, raptured by the intricate detail of black stone and vines tattooed along his arm.

"Don't be so modest, it can be breakfast, lunch…" he rattled off, lifting the sticky, sweet syrup up to my lips. "For dinner, in the kitchen, in the bedroom, along the walls, or wherever we want." He slithered into his final word, "Suck."

It was a command, and I did as I was told, parting my lips to taste his finger. It was sweet, still warm as it coated my tongue, licking it wet as a sappy drop fell from the corner of my mouth and onto my chin. While it was sticky, it was subtle enough to keep my attention on Alejandro who didn't dare look away.

"It can be something to fill you up, but to also keep you wanting more." His finger fell out of my mouth and down my neck, connecting a line of spit that reached my chest.

"How much more?" I asked as he snatched the loose

belt around my waist, unraveling its knot like an uncoiled snake.

"So much fucking more." My robe blossomed as I sat still, unfolding to my bare, naked body. "Jesus, Gemma, you're so fucking gorgeous," he said painfully.

I clung to the sides of my seat, the small curve of my tummy sucked in, covered in my own spit. "Am I?"

"Of course, and so fucking sweet, but you know that, right?" Alejandro snatched the leg of my chair, screeching it along the floor, dragging it closer to him.

I flinched.

"Oh fuck…" my legs parted as Alejandro began to finger me. "Just like that." He massaged the top of my cunt, a sensitive spot that caused my leg to stretch out across the tiled floor.

"Remember all my cum on that sexy stomach of yours?" He growled, tilting the bell over my body, allowing a small line of syrup to leak over my chest and down to my shaved pussy.

I nodded, blazed by the dueling contrast of warm syrup and the cool room that gave me goosebumps.

"Oh my god, it's so fucking sticky," I gasped, biting back a smile.

"It's a fucking mess. But I think you got me addicted to messes now." Alejandro dug his hand into my thigh as he got on one knee, sticking his tongue out, stopping the syrup from going too far, as it drizzled itself onto the tip of my aching nub. He hummed my name right into my sensitive clit, radiating it up with the flick of his tongue.

"You cleaning me up?" I shivered, placing my legs

over his shoulders. He jutted my ass forward, causing me to slouch into my chair.

"Can't let this get inside. I better suck it off those pretty lips." He lapped me up softly with the firm press of his velvet tongue on my asshole. From there, he untangled every sense of insecurity, relishing the entirety of his lick that parted my folds. I dropped my mouth, completely consumed, my robe falling off my shoulder. I wanted it; I wanted *him*, deep inside, fucking me like a dog in this very chair. This anticipation, this hair gripping, nail digging moment silenced itself into a sudden and sharp ring in my ears.

"What the fuck?" Alejandro barked, his chair falling to the floor as he stood up. His scowl of pleasure morphed into genuine distaste as he pushed himself off, blistered by the shouting man that appeared on the T.V. behind us.

"Alex Rivers is not who he says he is. Don't be fooled. He's the reason his mother's dead!"

Chapter 23

GEMMA

I clutched my robe, absolutely stunned as an older man with thick grey hair and darkened skin spoke vehemently into the camera. His piercing eyes seemed undeniably familiar; his cadence a rolling blend of the man who stood beside me.

"What the hell is he doing?" Alejandro turned up the volume, filling the room with the loud image of an angry crowd; a rallying community who stood behind the single man who spoke equal parts Spanish and English. I was lost in the translation, the sound and faces on T.V. so present, that it left me feeling totally exposed.

"*Tiene una mecha corta.*" The man struggled to explain, chopping into his own hand. "*It's what he does. He doesn't just ruin lives, lo robas también… I'm ready to tell everyone who he really is…*"

I stood up from my seat as Alejandro rushed to the counter, grabbing his phone. "Jesus Christ."

"What's happening?"

"It's Lina… forty missed calls?" He swiped at his screen as a searing wave of panic rushed over my chest.

"Yes, she called and I tried telling you, but I…" I shouted, but Alejandro barely noticed, typing a string of wild texts to his phone after attempting to call Lina.

"Fuck. She was supposed to take care of this. He's not supposed to be on T.V."

Everything about Alejandro suddenly terrified me, his voice, his panic, but nothing as much as his grueling apprehension. He paced across the kitchen, but I was positively frozen, stuck from the feet up as Alejandro threw his phone against the wall.

"Alejandro?" I asked, completely sick with what the man said next, a devastating confession that made me lean against the counter to keep myself from falling.

"He's not an actor… he's a killer!"

My hands began to shake as I backed away from the screen, from the thick, white letters that ran across the bottom of the channel: *Miguel Rivera - Father of Alex Rivers comes forward in daring accusation of mother's murder.*

"I don't understand?" I asked disoriented. "What the hell is happening?"

Ruins lives? Killer?

He ignored me, still fixated on the angry man on the news.

And Miguel?

He wasn't some studio agent, he was Alejandro's father—his 'dead' father—and now, nothing Alejandro said made sense, because nothing he said was true.

Immediately, I thought of Natalie Brower, The Pierre Hotel, Belmont Hills. I faced him, petrified of the truth, but brave enough for the answer. Was Parker right all along?

"Look at me!" I yelled, pulling him away from the screen, his eyes glistened with red blurry mist. "Please just tell me what's going on. Let me be here for you, let me do this."

Alejandro smashed the remote against the counter. I flinched as fragments of plastic scattered about.

"You want to know what's happening?" he shouted at the T.V., pointing viciously at the man. "He's a fucking liar and a drunk! Goddamn it. *No me busques porque me encuentras*," he swore under his breath, losing me in the translation. "He'll do anything to ruin me…"

"Liar? I don't know who the liar is, or who to believe, because you're the one that said you weren't a killer. Jesus, there was never a script, was there?" I realized out loud. "You made me believe Miguel was a studio agent, that what I heard was a misunderstanding," I reached for his arm. "If there's something to say, then say it, but don't shut me out!"

"There's nothing to say," he shouted. "That man is lying." He fired through the room, pulling a shirt over his body.

"Then so are you!" I retorted. "Alejandro, you are running away, you are hiding. Goddamn it, just talk to me!"

"This isn't about you, Gemma… this was supposed to be on my time, not his, and now it's fucked. There's so much more to what he's saying, and I have to stop him before he ruins anything else. I told you before, I'd protect *us* from anything and everything, this included." I finally caught his arm, using every bit of my strength to pull him back, but he couldn't even look at me, not like he had just moments ago.

"Whatever it is you fear, it'll never be bigger than the

support I'll give. Remember that?" I shouted. "You told me that when I was terrified to go back to Bushwick, and it made all the difference. Now the same is true for you. Stop pretending to be so helplessly alone, it's *not* true." Damn it, I couldn't just let him leave, not like this, not without a fight.

"No, this is different. This is bigger and more compromising to us and our future." He stood motionless, the chaotic volume in the background still playing during our one chance to make things clear.

Alejandro turned away but I hugged him from behind, feeling the shaky deep breath he took that shook his body. My fingers splayed at his chest, pulling his large frame into my tiny one.

"I won't say it. Not at the cost of what it all leads to. Trust me, what I'm about to do is for your protection. There are things that you could be liable for, something darker, something I hate to remember. Don't ask me to do this now, because if I did, then I'm afraid you'll never look at me the same way again," he said below a whisper.

"Don't say this is for me. I'm tired of being protected, I'm tired of everyone believing they know what's best for me. I won't accept that. Not from you, and especially not right now!" It was all happening so impossibly fast, swallowing the efforts we made to get to where we were. I hugged tighter, but he loosened my grip to pull away. It hurt so much. "So everything that was said about you was true?"

"No."

"No? No is not good enough. No is just something

you tell yourself, because it's easier than explaining the truth."

"And you think you could handle the responsibility of my truth? Gemma, if I don't fix this now, I may never be able to come back. I need to go," he said, talking to me as if I were naive.

"You're a child," I said with a croak. "When I wanted to leave, you said the same thing… and that's what you are. A hypocrite."

"I'm not a child. I'm just saving one from the reality of who I am and who I've become. Tell me that doesn't scare you," he demanded, beating his chest with the ball of his fist.

"I'm not scared of you, Alejandro, and I'm not sure if I ever really was. I was scared of who I could be, but I think the same is true for you."

"You have no idea," he growled, stepping closer to my body, allowing himself for a brief moment to be open.

"I don't need to know everything about what's happening in order to know how I feel, which right now is a hell of a lot braver than you're acting. You thought I was scared of you all along, but now I think it was you who was scared of me," I said, my ironic statement meeting the most scornful expression.

His lip trembled, mad at either me, or himself, or possibly Miguel.

"Yes, I'm terrified of you, Gemma," he swallowed. "Terrified of losing you permanently. And I won't let that happen."

"And you'll lie to keep your belief safe?" I challenged

him once more. Whatever this secret was, it was enough to make him look away, to drop his hands to his gut, as if stopping some wound from bleeding.

"I did what I had to. And I won't do it again. Ever. And that's why I'm leaving." He gathered his phone, stuffing it into his back pocket.

He was running away, just as Parker said he would. I was given all the warnings, but still I ignored them, and now I was afraid it'd ruin me. How could I tell Alejandro that my father did the same thing? That if he left right now, it would be the cruelest reminder that all men leave, that I was destined to slowly—but ultimately—be abandoned like Claire, begging for a man to stay.

I stepped closer, needing to feel him, to calm him down, but he tore his arm away again. "I'm ending this for good now. I'm doing this for us, and I swear it, I'll be back. I'll be your good man, no matter how fucking long it takes, and someday this will all make sense, but… just not now."

He punched the button inside the elevator, his entire rage latched onto my gaze as he disappeared into the eclipse of solid gold doors, leaving me alone, the T.V. loud between the new silence that followed and my reflection in the elevator doors.

Broken.

Just like Claire.

Chapter 24

GEMMA

The strap of my duffle bag began to pinch the skin on my shoulder as I entered Parker's hallway. My baggage somehow felt heavier than when I originally left, and in some ways that was true; the once excited feeling that fluttered in my stomach now sat heavy on my chest. I was wrecked since the moment Alejandro left this morning.

"Where are you?" I checked my phone for what I thought was a vibration.

Nothing.

My face lit up, brightened by a string of unanswered text messages that I had sent Alejandro. No responses, no clues, just the single message I received from Ivanna, just hours after Alejandro left.

IVANNA

Ordered to be in L.A., have no idea what's going on. Phones are being confiscated. Try not to worry. It's going to be ok.

I leaned against the wall, biting the edge of my thumb, staring out a dark window of a late New York night. I wanted to send Alejandro one more message, one more chance to reach out.

GEMMA

> Giving you space… Here when you're ready.

I stopped myself from typing. *Here when you're ready?* Was I really going to say that? The phrase felt like an evocative reality of my life thus far with Parker. Was I waiting for another man, sitting *here* for his convenience? After all I'd fought to conceal, after dropping my guard and letting him in, I was left here again, alone, and unsure of the man I just spent the night with—an *accused* murderer.

I looked down at my phone, edging closer to Parker's front door. I didn't know if Alejandro would ever be as open as I'd been with him. That hurt me to admit, but also empowered me with one truth; that being there for someone and waiting for someone to come around were two different things; the latter being the bane of my existence.

I erased my message for something new.

GEMMA

> Giving you space. If you need me, you'll have to come find me.

It was harsh, but once again I had to protect myself from the world, from an outsider. I sent it, leaning my head against Parker's door, swallowing the lump that sat in the back of my throat.

Shit.

I rotated my butterfly ring along my finger, having found it earlier under the clawfoot tub in Alejandro's bathroom.

Now that I was back, what would Parker say about my late-night return? As if he needed any more reason to hate Alejandro, this would surely send him into a spiral. And what about me? After everything he warned me about, would he say those four dreaded words? *I. Told. You. So.*

I composed myself as I walked inside, greeted with the sound of jazz that came from the kitchen. My fake smile soon turned into a real but timid sigh, as the smell of toasted bread welcomed me at the door.

"Hey Park, I'm home!" I sang out, determined to set the mood of my nonchalant return, my greeting interrupted by the sizzle of butter that sauntered from the kitchen.

"Gemma?" Parker turned the corner, his dimpled cheek creased with a radiant hello. "What are you doing here? I thought—"

"It was just for one night, Parker," I waved him off, dropping my duffle bag to the floor. "You know how forgetful I am. I misplaced my toothbrush, figured I'd come back." Yes, a perfect excuse, traveling all the way back with packed bags for a toothbrush. I smiled bigger, as if it were totally plausible, and not totally absurd. A hint of suspicion washed over him but faded so quickly that it almost didn't matter.

He didn't judge, he didn't say what I expected, he only seemed grateful to see me. I couldn't describe this feeling, this surreal realization as if I were safe at home all along, back in my bed after a particularly torturous nightmare. It was as if he knew what I'd been through, pulling me in for a hug, relaying with touch that no words were needed.

"Can I feed you?" he asked. "I have something here that I know you'll love."

"You want to feed me?"

"Of course, baby…" he answered, his single word like a dog whistle to the tingled sparks that erupted above my elbows.

"… Sorry?"

Did he say baby? Even if it was a mistake, it somehow caught my heart on fire, awakening every inch of my body like an unanswered late-night call.

"*Maybe…*" he overcorrected, "*maybe* you can tell me what you think of it?" He looked towards the kitchen. "The dinner that is." He distinguished his posture, but I could still feel the excitement in his voice as he held me close. I followed his lead as he let me go, taking my seat at the counter as Parker circled over to the stove.

"I hope you're hungry." He said, cooling himself by unbuttoning his shirt, his fitted grey slacks still belted but his tie long gone.

Parker tossed a clean dishtowel over his shoulder, cranking the heat below the skillet as music continued to play behind his movements. I absorbed the aesthetic, the array of colors and smells, the steam rising into the light.

"Wait a minute, this isn't…" I looked around the kitchen, realizing how special the meal really was. Everything I suspected was here: a large loaf of sourdough bread and a small wheel of golden Époisses. "Mama Meg's grilled cheese?" I asked. This simple sandwich was more than just an American classic, it was culinary porn.

"She brought everything over for her favorite girl. She was going to make it for you, but I insisted."

"She was here?" I pouted, genuinely sad that I had missed the one person I could truly call a mother. I missed her so much: our inside jokes and recipes, our time drinking sangrias on the dock for Fourth of July. I imagined her arriving in a sparkly St. La Vie dress, scolding Parker on the lack of food in the fridge.

"She was. Actually, she planned to also whisk you away to go thrifting, but she settled on a rain check." Parker laughed to himself. "I told her you're busy at work. She's very proud of you."

"Well, I have always been her favorite, you know."

"You're everyone's favorite, Butterfly," he shot an intentional wink.

He could've told Mama Meg what was happening and who I was with. Surely she knew Parker was on this case, especially since his father, Al—a legal savant—was so invested in keeping up with Parker's career. Parker was considerate, but more so than that, he was thoughtful and looked out for me, even when I wasn't here.

"Thank you," I said quietly, captivated by his control in the kitchen and the vein in his bronzed arm that bulged as he lifted the skillet, flipping the golden sourdough onto the plate.

"You're welcome." He reached for a large knife, slicing the sandwich into two steamy halves with a crunch. "I hope it's good. This is my first time making it actually, and you caught me practicing... I just wanted it to be perfect before you came back," he said, still professionally dressed from a late night of work, preparing a dinner I originally thought was just for him, but was intentional for me. He placed the plate on the counter and smiled, "For you."

I looked down, conflicted, knowing Parker was probably hungry, but gave me the sandwich regardless.

"For you, too," I said without a second thought, patting the seat by my side. "Come sit with me, we can share." I handed him my other half as he walked over, taking my first big bite of food since this morning.

For a while, all there was, was crunching. Comfortable, quiet, chewing. For the first time today, I took a deep, relaxing breath.

"So... did you have fun last night?" Parker asked swiping crumbs that fell onto his lap.

"Umm... you know, not bad." I shrugged, sparing the obvious details.

"Not bad? Hmmm... let me guess, no pizza and horror movies?"

I laughed, "Actually, I'm not sure if Alejandro even likes horror movies."

"Well, I'm sure he likes pizza..."

"I hope so. Who doesn't?" I asked, realizing I didn't even know that. I knew he liked bacon; he had it this morning. He was a tequila fanatic, a cherry enthusiast, but outside of hot dogs from a New York street vendor—the first true meal I ever shared with him—I wasn't sure what else he actually enjoyed eating. Jesus, the realization was almost embarrassing, essentially admitting to Parker that I barely knew Alejandro.

"He seems like a pineapple on pizza kind of guy," he teased. "You know, considering he's from L.A."

"Is that what they do over there?"

"Eh, it's the West Coast. Who knows what they do? I only know us."

"Us as in New Yorkers? Or us as friends?" I watched as Parker's audible chew turned into a rough swallow of jagged bread.

He waited to reply. "Just... us," he confirmed quietly.

I didn't know why that made me want to cry. *Just us?* Our story?

There was so much we shared, this sandwich being the least of them. Our time, our passions, our loves and hates. Parker knew me as the person, not as the trauma I lived, and I always wanted to keep it that way.

"There's a lot about us... between us," I replied.

"A lot of foods included."

"And plays."

"So many plays," he laughed.

"And other things... like the tooth fairy?" I reminded, the story of how Parker would bring a quarter to school whenever I lost a tooth. I never got one under my pillow, and he knew that.

"I told you already, the tooth fairy got used to you sleeping over at my house. Honest."

I smiled at all he had done, at all I knew about him and us.

God, there was always something about Parker that I

could never find in anyone else. I think it was his smile; a forever unchanging bookmark to the boy I spent my entire life with. Sure, he matured, his assertion more confident, his face more defined with sharp bone structure, but I could still see the kid in him, the one who used to wear comic book shirts and who'd drive me around on the pegs of his bike.

I caught Parker quietly studying my face, his charming grin sheltered by the way his palm mantled his cheek. What was he thinking about, and did it have to do with why I was home so suddenly? Typically, he'd give his two cents on my situation, but this time he didn't. For now, I wasn't the subject of his protection, but rather, the partner of his attention, and for some reason it made me want to share something about myself—not everything—but just enough.

"Did you see the news today?" I asked, almost inaudible compared to the thorough chews of sturdy sourdough bread.

"I did," he replied.

"I don't think it's true… what they said about Alejandro. Do you?" Suddenly his opinion mattered a great deal. Parker became quiet, licking sweet pepper jam off his thumb before answering.

"I think this Miguel guy has a defamation suit coming his way. But no, I don't think it's true. I know a lot about Alex, but this accusation seems unlikely. Maybe it's worth looking into his family, something I hadn't considered until now." He carefully folded the napkin in his hands, only to wring it. "Gemma, I'm afraid I said too much… that night at the bar. I shouldn't have mentioned anything about the lawsuit he's involved in. I do consider Alex to be liable for a lot of things, but I don't consider him as the direct cause of them. The people he's hurt are the ones that got caught up in his lifestyle and already had their own issues. Those he actually hurt, the assaults, are from fights between other men."

"Like the DJ out in Bushwick," I added.

Parker paused.

"Yes… just like him, but that's a different story. Trust me, Gem, if I ever suspected that he was capable of anything like that, I would've never let him anywhere near you. I know you don't need to hear that, and I know you're capable of taking care of yourself, but I don't think I'm so disciplined to do anything other than keeping you completely safe. Honestly, that's been my biggest challenge," he admitted.

"What has?"

"Holding back. I know I've been difficult, but worse, I've been hurtful and wrong. Guess losing control makes me ugly, and you don't deserve ugly. I know what you're worth, and it's not what I've given you. I could have done better. No, I should have done better."

"That's too kind—" I started, but he was quick to correct.

"It's not. Not for someone who deserves the world." He looked down at his thumb, rubbing the corner of his nail. "Is that why you came back? Because of the news?" he asked, and the thought of admitting it out loud was too hard, so instead, I nodded.

"I think he needs a moment to process this," I said,

picking crumbs off the crust. "As do I. Adjusting to a different personality is new for me, compared to what I'm used to."

"Adjusting's never easy, especially if you've been adjusting for the wrong reason. Believe me, I recently figured that out, and now I'm ready to fix it," he said reluctantly, glancing down the hall and back to me, pivoting the conversation. "You know who would make you feel better? Mama Meg," he said, almost in a cute rumble. "We're driving up to meet the parents tomorrow; annual Hamptons trip, remember?"

My heel slipped off my foot, smacking the floor when I eagerly stood up from the stool. The sheer opportunity of going back home, to the place and family that accepted me as their own, was far too exciting.

"*We're* driving up?" I asked, assessing the way Parker asked the question.

"*Parker,* do you have a shirt I can sleep in?" Camilla's voice appeared through the hall as she stepped out in a towel that wrapped around her bust. She stopped as she saw me, her hair still damp from the shower. "Gemma?" she barked out my name. "I thought…" She looked between Parker and me, and then down at the sandwich in my hand.

My stomach turned, knowing how our last interaction ended.

"Hi Camilla," I choked out, the bread caught in my throat as I expelled her name in a brute cough.

Parker interjected. "Camilla's coming too. One of her pipes broke at her apartment, so I told her she could stay here while it gets repaired." Parker half-smirked, uncomfortable like the rest of us. Camilla didn't have a post-sex glow, but rather a disappointed frown, clueing me in that nothing had happened between them before my arrival. She glared at me, as if I were the shit-flavored cherry on her already awful sundae.

"I don't want to impose," I shrugged.

"You wouldn't be. If anything, you'd be expected. Like you said, you're Mom's favorite." Parker shook off the ridiculous notion, "Your room is still there; Mom and Dad miss you, and I know you miss them."

Camilla shot a weird look, a new one of threatened emotions. As much as I wanted to spare her, I was tired of saving others at the cost of my own feelings. I did miss being with my family, and I wanted so desperately to leave the city—Camilla or no Camilla.

"Ok, sure." I nodded. Parker wasted no time in showing his excitement, his smile beaming as he stood up.

"Perfect, I'll let Mom know," Parker headed towards the hall to grab Camilla a shirt.

She faked a smile, turning to follow suit, scurrying close to Parker's side.

I took another bite of the crispy grilled cheese, accepting that the trip would be weird, but not caring, nonetheless. Tomorrow I'd be back in the Hamptons, and nothing could take that away.

THE
HAMPTONS

S outh of the Montauk Highway and sheltered beneath the sparse elms of a secluded road, I cranked up the A.C. inside my stifling, hot Range Rover. Mila dug her hand into a bag of salt water taffy whose label read, "Sag Harbor," the place where we stopped to load up on cheap candy and cold sodas.

"That's the new Continental GT." Mila chirped, noticing the fifth luxury Bentley to pass us by. She placed a yellow banana taffy out of the bag and into the cup holder, removing it from her favorite flavor of choice: watermelon. "That's the one I'd want, completely pearl-white, but as a convertible instead." She tugged on her NYU sweater, stretching its sleeves to the base of her thumbs. Despite hating the cold air that I finally turned on, Mila maintained that she still wanted to sit in the front.

"I didn't know you liked cars," I answered, casually looking in the rearview mirror, my eyes taking shifts between the road and Gemma in the back seat.

Unlike Mila, Gemma didn't wear a sweater. She wasn't cold, she was hot; maybe even dewy with sweat. Her bright red single-piece bathing suit sat below a pair of loose denim shorts, that were ready to be pulled off at any sign of the beach. Everything about her was bright:

her top, her yellow Birkenstocks, even the red framed sunglasses that covered her beautiful hazel eyes. Everything about her felt like summer, including the smell of coconut sunscreen on her long, gorgeous legs.

Mila smiled, but Gemma didn't, her expression more distant than the space that laid between us, resistant to a pout I felt could appear at any moment. I never wanted to see her sad again, to see the jut of her full bottom lip begging to be sucked, to be comforted with a kiss that would make her smile, or rather, that would make *me* smile. Fuck.

"My grandfather owns twelve dealerships up in Jersey," Mila replied, returning my attention back to the road. "I've been around nice cars my whole life, but nothing like these. We had money, but not Hamptons money."

"I don't believe that," I laughed. "I know a rich kid when I see one." While I was being modest, I knew how spoiled Mila could be. We were still learning about each other, but I knew enough from experience to see when someone had expensive taste.

"Not like you! You have *Parker Jones* money."

"And what is *Parker Jones* money?" I asked, almost scoffing.

Mila waved around. "Hello? This!" She pointed to a gated mansion whose perimeter was shrouded in juniper trees and private ponds; its massive shiplap garage spacious enough for twenty plus cars.

Gemma followed the motion of Mila's hand, then laughed out loud. Mila furrowed, unamused.

"I don't have Hampton's money. Not even close."

"You're totally rich."

"I'm comfortable," I admitted.

"Your parents are rich, that makes you rich too."

"Not at all. That's their money, not mine. Anything I have I've worked for on my own."

"Parker used to deliver newspapers as a kid," Gemma spoke up, offering a credential of sorts to show I was telling the truth. "He always made his own money. Mama Meg wanted him to be raised the same way she was."

"Poor?" Mila asked, assuming the complete opposite of what Gemma was saying.

"No," Gemma took offense. "Humbled by the worth of a hard-earned dollar." She quoted Mom word-for-word, as if she was indoctrinated with not only her mantra, but her lesson.

This was no surprise to me, seeing how she knew Mom so well, her recital a telling sign of how close they were. Sometimes I wondered if it was Gemma and I that were the best friends, or more so her and Mom.

Mila ignored Gemma, as the tension between the two continued to fester. Mila never apologized for her behavior that night at the bar, and Gemma never apologized for tossing a half-filled martini into her face. It wasn't just awkward; it was especially tense.

"Why would a kid like you need to deliver papers?" Mila asked, placing another banana taffy into the cup holder.

"For money," I answered.

"Well, duh. But for what reason?"

"Many reasons. I always had my priorities straight

back then. I knew what I wanted, and I worked for it." My vague answer seemed to disappoint Mila, her face less than satisfied with my response. It was better than admitting the truth, how it all was secretly intended for Gemma's birthday gift.

I looked back at Gemma, watching as her small fingers braided the end of her ponytail. Constantly she would check her phone, picking it up and placing it down. I hated that she was in the back seat—both physically and symbolically—displaced by Mila. Gemma should have been by my side. This was our trip, our time, our life, yet I clouded it up with some fucking promise that I was eager to erase from existence, and goddammit I would. I'd fix this, I'd fix us.

Gemma reached out, looking as if she wanted to pet my arm. But she didn't. Instead, she grabbed a handful of peach gummy rings which acted like a barrier between her and Mila.

"It's true, Parker always had his priorities straight," Gemma continued, her sweet voice virtually grazing the hair along my neck. "He would always save money for wax-paper trading cards."

I couldn't help but smile at the semi-embarrassing admission.

"Wax paper what?" Camilla scrunched her nose.

"They were comic book trading cards that came with gum. Wax paper is what kept them fresh," I responded.

"Gum?" Mila laughed, leaving me unsure if she was making fun of me, or if she found it endearing.

"Yeah, it was really good gum, actually," I defended.

"You're such a dork. But I love that about you." Mila leaned over and kissed my cheek.

I didn't want her to do that in front of Gemma, actually, I didn't want her to do that at all. Fuck if I just didn't think that, and the guilt it caused. It wasn't like I couldn't have invited her, her apartment was practically unlivable, at least until the plumbing was fixed. I smiled and forced a laugh.

"I just *really* wanted this one gold Spider-Man card, but never got lucky enough to get it."

"Oh, a *gold* Spider-Man?" Mila chimed in, "Of course. I could understand that. I always wanted gold trophies as a child, so a gold card sounds pretty on par."

"Trophies?" I asked.

"Yes. I used to do pageants growing up."

"I'm really not surprised," I joked.

"Good. You shouldn't be. You're in the presence of *Little Miss Manhattan 2014*." She sarcastically raised her nose into the air. She was being playful, but Gemma was quick to interrupt.

"I don't think he's a dork," she snapped back.

"Excuse me?" Mila cleared her throat, feigning interest while looking down at the shuffled music that played on my phone.

"It wasn't *dorky* when Parker collected cards. It was fun and something we did together, and it had meaning. Parker was obsessed with superheroes, he always wanted to be one, he always wanted to do what was right."

Gemma's sweet words were an unintentional stab in my gut. I wasn't a hero, I was a coward, and at minimum a complete fucking idiot that didn't deserve another moment of either of the girl's time. I chewed my tongue to distract from how warm her comment made me.

"He will be a hero, once he takes me up to Montauk during this trip. Isn't that right, Parky?" Mila smiled to herself.

"Is that where you want to go?" I asked, confused by the plans we never discussed, and the newfound nickname I immediately despised.

"Yes! On a date night. Oh, we can eat oysters again," she replied. I was at my tipping point, and it took everything in me to restrain a simple frown.

"That sounds good," I kept my composure.

"And what do you want to do on your vacation here, Gemma?" Mila asked, her question a not-so-subtle attempt to single her out.

"Relax, I think…" Gemma reached for another peach gummy ring. I clenched the steering wheel harder. "Actually, I think I'll go running while I'm here. The scenery is just too nice to pass up."

"Running?" I couldn't conceal my excitement. "That sounds great, Gem. I'll definitely join you."

"In the morning?" she asked, leaning between Mila and me, crossing the leather armrest that made Mila roll her eyes. "Sounds perfect."

"You guys run?" Mila asked, more surprised than not.

"Parker was the captain of Columbia's track team," Gemma said flatly.

"I didn't know…"

"Gemma and I used to run everywhere out in

Bushwick, this was way before I could afford my own bike," I responded, but my answer only confused Mila more.

"I forgot you were from there. It all seems so weird. You're a kid from Bushwick, yet you have a house in the Hamptons. I mean, your family was rich enough to send you to Columbia, yet you had to deliver papers for money?" Mila snorted.

"Parker paid for school," Gemma cut in again, answering as if my life were a series of Jeopardy questions. "Well, his track scholarship paid for it."

"You got a scholarship?" Mila almost shouted.

"Like I said, anything I had was because I worked for it. I'm not joking when I say Gemma and I ran everywhere. She was essentially why I became so good."

"Don't tease," Gemma playfully slapped my arm, her peach-flavored lips close enough to smell. Mila appeared to not care for the gesture, her face less than impressed.

"It's true, Gemma, had you not gone to FIT I bet you would've gotten a scholarship too. You saved me over three-hundred-thousand dollars in student debt, all because I could run."

The stockpile of banana taffy was beginning to brim over the edge of the cup holder. Mila said nothing, fixated on my phone and the random playlist I had. Suddenly, only after the momentary pause of an Alton Ellis song, did the reminiscent sound of a creaky door and bubbling potions come on over the speakers. The unmistakable drum pattern of a 1960s pop song rolled along as Mila stuck her tongue out.

"Ewww," she pretended to gag, motioning to switch the song.

"NO!" Gemma and I shouted, startling Mila enough to drop my phone. "It's the 'Monster Mash'. *Don't* change it."

"This song is so weird though. It's summer, not Halloween," she shook her head.

"It's our favorite song." Gemma poked between the seats again, singing a part of the lyrics as I laughed.

"Gemma and I would listen to this every year before trick-or-treating. Still do." I corrected, "Well, we don't trick-or-treat, but you know what I mean. It's the best."

"Remember the year Mama Meg took us to the Hamptons for Halloween?" Gemma reached over to turn the music a little louder.

"The candy bars were way better out here than in Bushwick."

"They were king-sized, but that wasn't all we got. One of the neighbors even sent us home with an uncooked prime rib."

"And a bottle of Cabernet Franc," I added.

"We pretty much had a barbecue later that night."

"I didn't get any trading card gum though," I joked. "I *still* want that golden Spider-Man."

"What did you dress up as?" Mila interrupted, turning the music down to its original volume. I pretended to try and recall, cocking my head to the side. I didn't really need to think of it, I knew the answer immediately, but didn't want to appear too eager to admit it.

"Frankenstein," I swallowed.

"Of course, you two and your monster movies." Mila sighed. "And Gemma?" she asked, not really to Gemma but to me.

"The Bride of Frankenstein," Gemma responded, caring very little about who Mila's question was directed towards. "You should have seen my wig. It was about three-feet tall."

Mila tossed another banana taffy into the cup holder. "Well, I still don't like this song. It makes me feel like I'm in a black and white movie."

"What's wrong with that?" Gemma asked.

"Nothing. It's just weird and creepy."

"It's not creepy. It's fun. The song is literally about monsters who wake up *just* to dance. It's surprising."

"What's so surprising about it? The fact that two adults still listen to it?" Mila scoffed.

Gemma ignored her, "It's surprising because the monsters are doing the one thing you'd never expect them to do. When you think of a monster, you'd naturally assume they'd be up to no good. But this isn't the case. Instead of wreaking havoc, they do the opposite. *They—just—dance.*" Gemma enunciated each word passionately. "I love it. It reminds you not to judge a book by its cover."

Once again, I looked in the rearview mirror, watching as Gemma leaned back into her seat, unbraiding and re-braiding the tip of her ponytail again. I couldn't help but grin, my heart literally on the verge of beating out of my chest, divulging in a sudden fantasy of her and me.

This could be us, driving up to the Hamptons every year, living for the most mundane conversation, because even the mundane with her was thrilling. I wanted her; I wanted us; I wanted every fucking thing I could get, down to the nuisances and joys of children—*our* children—ones we'd take to the Hamptons, ones that we'd sing the "Monster Mash" to and go trick-or-treating with. We could be a family, and I could grow old knowing that I married the woman I loved and lived the life I always wanted.

But what if that was all too late?

What if I had already ruined it and was none the wiser? I couldn't keep my eyes off her, desperate to see her smile once more, to see her disguised pout be displaced with genuine joy.

"Well, I guess you're just brave," Mila exhaled, mildly annoyed. "I'm sure nothing scares you or creeps you out."

"That's not true," Gemma shot back.

"Is that so?"

"Yes… lots of things scare me."

"Name one."

"Gemma doesn't need to name anything," I intervened, trying to alleviate the mood with a nonchalant shrug of my shoulders.

"Sure she does. What scares the girl if not monsters?"

Gemma thought for a moment, staring out the window, taking a small but noticeable breath. "I don't know… thunderstorms scare me."

"Thunderstorms?" Mila laughed. "That's classic.

Horror movies don't do it, but a bunch of noisy clouds do?"

Gemma continued to look away as I stared at her, forgetting how long it had been since I looked at the road. She remained quiet, her fear of thunder was a long-known fact. Even as kids in the Hamptons we would share the same big bed in the largest room of the house, cuddling during any storm that came our way. I'd hug her while sleeping back then, just as I would now if she needed it, as if I could resist.

"Well, there's a chance of rain tonight, so you may be in for something spooky." Mila's taunt garnered no reaction from Gemma. She turned to me and asked the same question. "And what about you, Frankenstein? What are you afraid of?"

The simple question felt much heavier on my mind than I assumed she expected. I feared a lot of things, but what I feared the most was the same thing I did the day I broke down Gemma's bedroom door. What I was scared of, and what I was absolutely terrified of, was a life without her.

"The future," I answered, focusing towards the back seat until Gemma caught me looking. My heart pounded in my teeth, her attention like lights that caught me stealing in the dark as I refused to look away. We stared at each other, holding a gaze—

"PARKER! Watch out!" Mila's sudden shout redirected me back to the road, causing me to turn the steering wheel sharply to the left.

We skidded loudly, the brakes screeching throughout the entirety of my ears as we swerved out of the way of a passing skunk. My harsh slam of the brakes halted our speed, yanking our bodies forward in unison as we came to a powerful stop.

I shouted, then cursed under my breath, "Fuck…"

We all sat quietly, numb to the now displaced cheer of "Monster Mash" that finished in the background. The car hummed, the engine much calmer than the rest of us.

"What the hell was that? Jesus, Parker, you won't need to be afraid of the future if you keep driving like that!" Mila's face was absolutely red as she pulled off her NYU sweater. I guess she was hot now.

Outside I watched as the skunk made its way to the other end of the road, its tail stiff in the air like a flagpole. The brief and awkward silence was interrupted as Gemma began to laugh uncontrollably. My chest continued to pound, filled with adrenaline, my hands borderline shaking from the moment. But Gemma's laugh made me grin, until it made me smile. Spontaneously, I started to laugh too, unable to escape the contagiousness of her voice that eluded Mila.

"You two are so ridiculous!" Mila rested her head against the passenger window, exhaling a loud huff.

I pulled back onto the street, turning the corner to the last stretch of road that led to my parents' house. I could see it in the distance as Gemma continued to laugh.

"I can't disagree with what you're saying, Camilla." Gemma smiled. "Parker and I are just too similar." She noted, an indisputable fact that made Mila's face still in contemplation.

Up ahead, Mom stood behind the large, gated entrance that concealed the sprawling beach front estate. She waved beside the white hydrangeas and tall cypress hedges, her high cheekbones creased in a smile as she sipped on a sangria. Gemma rolled down the window as the gate began to open.

"*Bonjour mademoiselle!*" Gemma placed her finger above her lip, pretending it was a mustache, affecting a French accent. It was an odd exchange that her and my mom had, another quirk and greeting they shared amongst many others.

"*Bonjour ma Patate!*" Mom replied, howling into a laugh.

"*Patate?*" Mila asked, escaping the attention of a now distracted Gemma.

"It means potato," I explained as I pulled forward, passing my mom and up into the driveway. "It's a whole thing between them, with potatoes, actually. This is just another character of theirs... a French fry or something."

"Potatoes?" Mila sat confused.

"I love them," Gemma answered as we parked. "We all do." She reached over to the cup holder. "We even like banana taffy," she added, lifting one out for herself before jumping out of the car. She shut the door, and I could hear her and Mom laugh as they met for a hug.

For a moment, it was just Mila and me, alone for the first time the whole trip. Outside was loud and fun, but here in the SUV, it grew quiet.

"I didn't know you liked banana taffy," Mila spoke softly.

"I do."

"I also didn't know you liked comic books as a kid, or how you earned your own money, or that you even got a scholarship." Mila looked down at the sweater in her hands, fidgeting with its tag before looking up towards Mom. I couldn't tell if she was nervous about meeting her, or instead, sad about knowing so little about who I was. "I also didn't know you were afraid of the future…" Suddenly, she seemed more somber, and the shift in mood made me worry about what was happening. More than anything I wanted to do what was right and deliver the information gently to Mila, but somehow I always made things worse. Was this cruel, worse than leaving her home with no plumbing? I wasn't sure anymore, and now it made me feel sick.

"It's ok, it takes time to know someone. I didn't know that you liked luxury cars so much, or that you did pageants."

"Yeah, but you weren't surprised," she was quick to reply, "and that's different."

"How so?" I asked, but Mila paused, her silence more of a contemplation than a need to hold back.

"It's different because *I* was the one that shared that with you, not because someone else told you about it. *Someone* who knows you so well." She picked up a banana taffy, staring at its waxy cover. "You didn't ask, but we also share something in common too. We both fear the same thing: the future." She twisted her lips, subtly hinting at something we both didn't want to say. I feared my future with Gemma, and undoubtedly, Mila feared her future with me.

"I'm having fun, aren't you?" I repeated the words she once said to me on the night the fire alarm went off. Back then I had asked if she *cared for me*, wanting to gauge her reaction, hoping to buy more time in my attempt to develop feelings for her. We were still barely dating, but maybe she cared more than I even realized. Now, I worried my feelings still hadn't changed, I was still hopelessly in love, but not with her.

"Yes," she replied.

"Then like you said before, let's enjoy what we have right now. No sense in worrying about the future," I added. "It was a silly thing for me to say."

"It's not silly. Gemma's right, you know. You weren't dorky." Mila unwrapped the candy in her hand to take a bite. "I can like banana taffy too, we can like it together." She began to chew, immediately jumping out of the car to meet Mom.

I sat alone, stewing in the trouble I caused, and on the hearts that I broke, and would continue to break. There was a lot I had done wrong, and now, there was a lot I had to make right.

Chapter 26

GEMMA

The pressed linens at the Joneses' Hamptons home remained uniquely crisp; a defiant look to their impossible softness I knew I'd sink into tonight. This, of course, was the essence of the Jones family: a pristine but impeccably comfortable group of hosts. I fixed my hair using the same large, gold mirror that hung in my bedroom—the one I used to share with Parker when we were just kids. That felt like ages ago, but being in here made it seem as if it were just yesterday.

"Gemma, dear!" Mama Meg called from the kitchen. "I need my butterfly girl!"

"Coming, Mom!" I hollered, combing back my hair, turning my body for a final check before leaving. The minute we arrived I knew I wanted to switch my outfit. We spent so much time at Sag Harbor that my bathing suit felt less than dinner table ready.

"I hope you're hungry." Parker half-knocked at the doorframe, leaning in with a grin, eyes matching the hue of his mossy-toned polo that hugged his biceps.

"Starved." I tucked my turtleneck into my tweed skirt, revealing the hint of thigh that Parker peeked at. He looked up confidently, as if he wanted to be caught. I glanced at my shoulder, laughing to ease the tension.

"Room hasn't changed at all, has it?"

"I'm not sure if it ever will. It's been the same every year since we've been kids."

"Too bad I'm downgraded to the spare bedroom down the hall. It's not nearly as comfortable as this one."

"Would you like to switch?"

Parker was quick to shake his head, "Nah, I wouldn't dare. You get the best here, and I'd rather you stay in the bed that we used to share. Besides, that'd mean a lot more to me."

My mouth grew dry, parched from the imagined thought of us as adults: grown, illuminated by the bright light of a Hamptons blue moon, cuddling under the cool sheets of our old bed.

What a wild and spontaneous image.

"Well, it was built for two," I played it off, diffusing any intentions he may have implied.

"Still is," he gleamed, his purposeful stare acting as a challenge. Every second we held our glance carried another meaning. One second was friendly, two seconds was attentive, three seconds bordered on suggestive, and four seconds—well—four seconds was something entirely different, something that made me daydream of the impossible.

"Are you here to escort me?"

"Absolutely. Any chance I can get," his cupid lips twisted. "But I'm also here to let you know that what Mila said in the car was true. There might be a thunderstorm tonight."

"It's ok."

"I'm sure it is, but if it isn't, I'll be close by. If you come look for me, I won't be hard to find. I promise." By the way his thumb traced the pad of his fingers, he seemed to be restraining some need to reach out. Did he want to take me by the hand? The arm? My waist? I folded my hands together as he made way for me to pass. "Let's get you downstairs," he said, leading me through wainscot paneled halls and exhibited family photos.

Mama Meg was already calling out to me as I made my way down the stairs, her voice pitched with an obscure Mid-Atlantic charm that had since been lost on newer generations. "There she is!" she shrilled, her tiny hips sashayed towards my direction, wrapped in a tweed skirt and cream-colored blouse. "Twins!" She beamed, comparing our outfits with the motion of her hand. "It's like looking in a mirror, honestly." She laughed, turning towards Camilla whose arms crossed along her chest.

"Please! I know a St. La Vie skirt when I see one!" I drooled over the gorgeous cowl cut of its design.

"A steal from a little shop near Washington Square Park," her hand cupped the side of her mouth, protecting some egregious secret, "Thirty-two bucks."

"Lies!"

"Dead serious! But forget about the bargain, I love your color more. Tahitian gold?" She pointed toward my skirt.

"Gazpacho," I batted my eyes, enacting a caricature of snobbishness that we often assumed. None of it was serious, and all of it was for fun, but I wasn't sure if

Camilla could tell. We emitted a fake haughty laugh, clutching the nonexistent pearls on our necks.

"Isn't it just divine?" she asked Camilla loudly, attempting to pull her into our playful banter.

"I prefer red," Camilla replied timidly as we smiled. Mama Meg was fast to respond, not letting the moment grow awkward.

"Well, if red is what you prefer, dear, then I have just the thing for you." She palmed my hand ushering me towards the marbled island. "Now, I already had three glasses, but only to ensure the batch tasted perfect." She gestured towards Camilla, beaconing her to get closer as she pulled out a pitcher of sangria. "But testing doesn't count for drinks."

"Or for cookies," I interjected, opening a grey cabinet for three fresh glasses.

Parker made his way to a decanter of small batch bourbon in the corner, pouring himself a drink. "Try not to burn the kitchen down. God knows you ladies would go up in flames from how strong Mom makes those things."

"There's fruit in them," she retorted. "It's practically doctor-approved." She stirred the pitcher with a wooden spoon, staring daggers as the assorted berries and sliced oranges swirled.

Parker waved her off, exiting the massive archway towards the backyard, passing by the windowed walls that faced a quiet beach and manicured hedges.

Outside by the grill stood Albert Jones, Parker's father and now retired Chief of Justice from New York's federal court. His rather stoic demeanor was only softened while at home, in the presence of family or charbroiled burgers. I could see the creases in his face, the smile lines raised as Parker joined him, mouthing inaudible words as they clinked glasses. His white polo matched the silver tone of his hair, though his body defied age with its rather sleek and toned build. He was Parker, but in the future, still anchored in youth with cunning wit and devilish good looks.

"Now, don't be shy," Mama Meg poured hardy portions of sangria into our glasses. "This potato salad won't put itself together." The table was spattered with clean white bowls and ramekins of spice.

"Chives?" I questioned, assuming my role in the process we built throughout all these years.

"Saved them for you, dear," she smiled, combing the short brown hair behind her ear. "I know you love the crunch they make." It was true, they gave me some audible satisfaction as I chopped. I began my task, peeking up as Mama Meg turned to Camilla, her thick, black glasses as chic as her red, sangria-induced cheeks, magnifying the same green eyes Parker inherited. "You girls must get along so nicely, seeing how close Gemma and Parker are." She inquired innocently, as Camilla took a long, noisy sip. My chopping felt impossibly loud, pounding against the wooden cutting board as Camilla cleared her throat.

"Of course…" she straightened her posture. "We're like a little family."

We certainly were like a family, one for a Lifetime reality show.

"She puts up with me. I know it's not easy being in a

relationship with a third wheel." I laughed to myself, tossing the chives into the large bowl.

"It's manageable," Camilla replied hesitantly. "Actually, Parker and I are talking about getting a place together, starting fresh when Gemma moves out."

Mama Meg and I shot an instant look at each other, puzzled, her crooked smile discreetly asking, *Did you know about this?* While my wide and unblinking eyes responded, *Absolutely not!*

"Well," Mama Meg shot back the rest of her drink, letting out a breathy cough, as if she swallowed down the wrong pipe. "You know, you're the only girlfriend that Parker has ever brought to the Hamptons. Not including our Gemma, of course. This is just as much her home as it is Parker's."

"Not a girlfriend though," I smiled, defusing Camilla's angsty glare.

Mama Meg winked half-convincingly, assuring me as if I were too stubborn to admit something. She was right, though; Parker had never brought anyone here. In the past, he had countless girlfriends, none of which lasted longer than a week. Usually the women he found ended up being far too clingy for his taste and before I knew it we'd be back to our normal traditions as if we didn't skip a beat.

"Let's not get caught up on semantics," Mama Meg laughed. "Important thing is, you're all happy and coexisting."

"Well, it hasn't been too bad, actually, considering Gemma spends all her time with—" Camilla was about to mention the one name that would open up a slew of questions I wasn't ready to answer: Alejandro.

"*Work!* I spend all my time at *work!*" I shouted, cutting her off in the most obvious way. Camilla squinted, parting her lips as Mama Meg mistook her stirrer for a straw, completely oblivious.

"I got burgers for my buttercup!" Al shouted, appearing with a tray in hand. Parker followed, scanning the kitchen suspiciously, possibly feeling the thick tension I just caused. Al leaned over and gave me a kiss on the cheek. "Camilla, Parker mentioned you don't eat red meat, is that true?" he barked louder than maybe he intended. Years of being an authoritative figure saturated his voice to be more intimidating than it really was.

"Well—" Camilla's crooked smile broke as she tried to recover from the question itself.

Al interrupted, "You're not on the witness stand, hun, I'm only asking to make sure. I made you a turkey patty. I hope that's ok."

"Smile, dear," Mama Meg reminded Al, coaching him to adjust the permanent scowl he earned as a judge.

"I am smiling! I had four glasses of fifty-year-old bourbon, who wouldn't be?"

"I had to take over the grill," Parker brought over a tin-foiled plate. "He kept forgetting to flip the burgers over."

"Flip what over?" Al asked, tossing a maraschino cherry into his tumbler, turning on the radio to his favorite Motown hits.

"The patties, Dad."

"They're on the plate," Al pointed, misunderstanding in typical inebriated fashion. I laughed as Parker shook his head, leaning closer to my ear.

"I made sure yours was cooked how you like. Grilled with mustard, two slices of American cheese." His brief but secretive tone brushed along my skin. "You make the potato salad?"

"Yes," I watched as his finger swiped a scoop of the creamy mix for a quick taste.

"You did good, Butterfly," he quietly praised, filling me with the most stomach-warming pride.

"What were you all talking about?" Al chirped.

I was quick to shift the conversation to food. "About how hungry I am. I'll grab the plates." I motioned for Camilla to take the bowls, and Mama Meg the sangria, waving them towards the dining room.

I needed to collect myself before being back around the others, biding time as I carefully grabbed a stack of dinnerware, their porcelain clatter a welcomed distraction from Al's unanswered question. When I returned, the family was already clinking glasses, reaching across the massive wooden table that silhouetted the sunset outside.

I sat down next to Parker, unfolding my napkin as Al spoke. "How are things down in MelBrook? Still on track to making partner?"

"I'll know after summer. There are a few clients we're still trying to secure."

"Tri-Tech Security?"

"Well, that's not really public knowledge yet, but possibly."

"I heard they're buying out four subsidiary companies. They'd be like the Amazon of security firms. That'd be huge for you, Park." He pointed his fork like a wand, shooting the good juju through the tips of its end.

"Knock on wood. I've been combing through the contracts and ensuring it goes through. But once again, that's not something anyone should know about, yet."

"And how is that one case going?" He dabbed a glob of ketchup onto his burger, simultaneously sipping on his bourbon. "Alex Rivers, right?"

Shit.

Parker turned to me for a second, then back to Camilla. Not even the juiciest of gossip could've pulled her attention away as she stared at the photos of Parker and me all over the walls.

"Still in pre-trial conferences, discovering if there will be a settlement or not." He spoke clearly, but not before taking a big bite of his burger.

I followed his example, stuffing a big chunk into my mouth. I chewed with my cheeks filled, trying not to choke.

"Hmmm. Settlement is cleaner, but where's the fun in that?" Al spoke as if settlements diluted their honor. "I'm assuming you threatened to sue further if taken to trial; plaintiff's never want to pay court fees. Let that son of a bitch know you're coming for him."

The breeze from the Atlantic rolled through the large, parted doors, settling upon the cold sweat that ran down my neck. I pretended not to hear, but my uncomfortable chewing said otherwise. I couldn't blame Al; he was only trying to show support for Parker. I, on the other hand, couldn't help but feel everything: worry for Alejandro; nervousness for Parker; and concern for Camilla, whose expression warped further into distaste. My history with Parker was everywhere, rubbed in her nose with glossy black and white prints. She gave me a side glance, stabbing a forkful of fresh greens on her plate.

"We mentioned that," Parker answered quietly, sensitive to my presence. He seemed more level-headed, no longer chomping at the bit to assert his inevitable victory in court.

"Personally, I think he should be charged criminally, I think there's enough evidence to avoid any acquittal," Al asserted.

"And what do you know exactly?" Parker talked through his food.

"How he beat up the Plaintiff out in Bushwick, the victim's husband?"

"Our old stomping grounds," Mama Meg grinned.

"Excuse me?" Parker nearly choked.

"Yeah, Michael Brower. What was he? A DJ? The whole thing seems messy. Can't believe that poor girl though, Natalie. I'd hate to be her husband right now. I'm glad they're seeking restitution."

I swallowed whatever I mindlessly stuffed into my mouth, clutching the cloth napkin on my lap. What the hell did I just hear? The DJ out in Bushwick was Natalie's husband? My head began to spin as this tangled web of history unraveled itself before me. Why wouldn't Alejandro mention that? Both men had spoken about the incident before, but never enough for me to form any conclusions on my own. The whole situation began to feel more confusing than revealing, and Parker must have noticed, watching my reaction before cutting in.

"Once again, this is something we can't talk about. And how the hell did any of this come to your attention? There are non-disclosures all across the state."

Al shrugged as if it were some simple explanation. "I stopped by your office and talked to Tommy. He mentioned how the team wasn't pressing charges for the assault out in Bushwick but increasing the amount in damages instead. Not a bad move."

"Oh, I love Tommy. How's he doing?" Mama Meg chimed in with a smile.

"Fucking Tommy." Parker tossed his napkin onto the table.

"Language, Parker," Mama Meg snipped. "And enough of this jibber jabber. These cases are so boring, not something for dinnertime talk." She stirred the ice in her freshly filled drink.

I sighed in relief, still rattled at the revelation of how Alejandro's involvement with Natalie Brower seemed deeper than I realized. Who were they to each other, and had he gone out to Bushwick that night just for me or for the DJ in particular? I wasn't sure anymore, I wasn't sure of anything, having still not checked my phone since arriving, committing myself to leaving it alone once I left the car. The truth was I was far too scared to look, bothered by two possibilities: either

Alejandro had reached out or he hadn't. Both options I hated.

My clouded thoughts momentarily parted with the sudden graze from Parker's warm hand. We reached for our silverware, accidentally touching pinkies before pulling back. It could've been nothing, but the way we quickly looked up into each other's eyes made it feel as though we were about to get caught.

Camilla glared between the both of us.

"I'd rather focus on how great it is having Mr. and Mrs. Spuddington back in the Hamptons," Mama Meg clinked her spoon against her sangria.

Parker and Al groaned loudly as I dropped my fork.

"Mom," Parker pleaded quietly, "not this again."

Mama Meg shooed him away, fueled by the power of alcohol to share childhood stories.

"What is this now?" Camilla asked in a nervous laugh.

Mama Meg shoveled a scoop of potato salad onto her plate. "It was the summer of 2003. Gemma and I signed up for the Fourth of July Hamptons Hoedown and volunteered to bring potato salad. Could you believe it was the first time she'd ever had it? Honestly, Gemma was so proud of the creation, that she wanted nothing else to eat." Parker buried his face into his hands as Al got up to get another drink, burping loudly as Mama Meg continued. "Of course, Parker followed her example, he was absolutely obsessed!"

Camilla's glare was replaced with a distant stare, and I wondered if it had anything to do with how Mama Meg elongated the word obsessed.

"That's not true," Parker sighed as I held in my nervous laugh, but Mama Meg shushed him.

"You don't know anything; you were obsessed and still are." The whole room grew fiery hot, and I wanted to scream and die all at once. "They ate so much that we warned them they'd become spuds. But that didn't stop them. I think all of the Hamptons ran out of potatoes by the end of that summer." She rubbed Parker's back, sighing with reminiscent endearment. "We started addressing them as Mr. and Mrs. Spuddington and even had a wedding right at the dock. Do you remember you two dressed up in the backyard? That cute little kiss and the vows!"

My palms grew terribly sweaty as I nodded, bracing for Camilla's impending punch.

"Vows?" Camilla asked, clearly not thinking it was as cute as Mama Meg did.

"I promise to be your truest love," Al howled, returning with a fresh glass of bourbon, reciting the words Parker declared an eternity ago. "I had the legal authority to make that come true too. No prenup either, good job on you, Gemma," he winked at me as I sucked in my lips.

"Ugh! They grow up so fast." Mama Meg sighed, her face now aglow by the tabletop candles as the nighttime shadows swept into the room. "Gemma even wore my ring," she toyed with the diamond on her finger. "You know it's yours, honey, when the day comes," she smiled at Parker and me so lovingly.

"Mom!" Parker barked, looking over at Camilla who now shoved all her potato salad to the side of her plate.

"What?" she cried. "I'm your mother, I just know these things." She held her hands up as Al shook salt all over his plate. I essentially stuffed the entire burger into my mouth, hoping not to be asked any more questions.

Camilla wiped her lips with the cloth napkin, scooting her chair back with a loud screech. "If you'll excuse me."

"Fuck," Parker grumbled, looking over at me with a worried stare. I stared back, my mouth still full, nodding as if begging him to go check on her. He understood, glaring at Mama Meg. "No more Spuddington talk," he scolded, then turned to Al. "And you, no more case talks, please."

Al failed to listen as Parker stood up to chase Camilla.

"I thought it was cute," Mama Meg looked back at me for approval. "You like the burger, hun?" She moved on as if she said nothing at all. I wanted to say the food was incredible, but I couldn't even taste it. I couldn't enjoy anything really, not fully at least. Sure, there were moments, instances, where I was luckily distracted, caught in some fantasy of how I envisioned everything to be. If it wasn't Parker on my mind, then it was Alejandro, the very two people who had taken real estate on my entire life. But it wasn't just them anymore, it was *others* too, people that I now knew because of them; Camilla and Natalie included.

Alejandro had always been secretive about his past, but now it was leaking out from the bourbon-fueled lips of Albert Jones. Something so private was said so nonchalantly, and now I couldn't *un-know* it. What the hell was up with Alejandro and Natalie Brower, and why couldn't he tell me more about her or the DJ he beat up? And if this wasn't enough to think of, I was now also concerned for Camilla. I looked down at my plate, my mouth still filled as I finally answered Mama Meg.

"Everything's perfect," I replied, unintentionally dropping crumbs from my mouth. "Ab-so-lute-ly perfect…"

I pulled Andy towards my chest, listening to the pattering rain of a mellow Hamptons storm. It wasn't too bad, not unbearable like the idea of knowing if Alejandro finally reached out or not.

It'd be so easy to do the things I wanted, to check for Alejandro's reply, to peek into the life of Natalie's husband. I knew I could but reserved myself at the possible cost of doing so.

"Should I look at my phone?" I asked Andy, holding him in my hand, unable to sleep. I turned his little head from left to right, answering 'no' to the question.

I placed him on the pillow beside me, exchanging him for the very thing he warned me against. "I'm just going to hold it, in case it goes off." I excused myself, questioning my sanity as I explained my reasoning to a stuffed giraffe.

I rolled over, but stopped when I spotted the cherry cigarette I'd stolen from Alejandro on the floor. *It must have fallen out from my bag.* I wasn't sure why I thought it was smart to bring it, hopelessly wanting just some small part of him still close by. Honestly, it was all I had at the time, and the desire to taste his cherry lips suddenly felt like some unreachable itch. I lifted it up to my nose and shut my eyes, making everything much darker, and in the brief exciting moment, imagined him finding me all over again, lost in the shadows amongst the rain-filled night. Doing this was a bad idea, compelling me with the strangest desire to taste Alejandro once more, to do the unthinkable, to leave this house, brave the rain, and smoke this cigarette.

Andy fell over as I stood up, landing on the electric blue numbers of the bedside alarm clock. It was late, well past midnight, and I knew I had to be quiet, silently passing the door and hall as I made my way down the shadowed staircase.

Initially, I wanted to get out as fast as possible, but stopped myself as I reached the bottom, overtaken by the need to peer into the living room by my side. I didn't know why I did this, or why I was so surprised by what I saw, but the sight itself felt calmer than any puff of cherry smoke.

There in the dark, peacefully undisturbed was Parker, doing as he promised, staying close by in case the storm became unbearable. *That was sweet of him*, I thought to myself, watching as he lay on the couch, covered in the warmth of a fluffy, grey blanket.

I stopped from getting closer, his ambient calmness like a remedy to my sleepless night that I so desperately needed. I knew if I were to lie within the nook of his body, that I'd instantly start to dream.

"Parker?" I whispered quietly, gauging the deepness of his sleep.

He didn't respond.

I leaned against the arched doorway, admiring how the soft breaths he took exchanged themselves for the rise of his chest. As the rain fell and the light poured in, he seemed to glow like an angel; his hair unfixed, falling loosely like golden waves onto his pillow. There was something so perfect about his imperfect sleep; the way his lips parted, how his hands curled underneath his cheek.

"Parker…" I said once again. *Parker, Parker, Parker.* I couldn't help but repeat his name in my mind, saying it without anger or disappointment as I had the past few weeks.

Twisting the cigarette in my hand, its filter brushed against my butterfly ring. In my palm were pieces of Alejandro and Parker, two men who inspired two different Gemmas. I wanted the cherry kisses and to be someone's Butterfly, but romanticizing both versions didn't make it any clearer on what version of myself I still wanted to be.

Was it possible that Parker felt like I did with Alejandro? Completely locked out of my life as I ran from my past? I worked so hard to keep that inside, and now it made me wonder if I was in the wrong this whole time.

This quiet realization was short lived, immediately fleeting as the loud clink of a dish jostled itself from the kitchen, catching my attention.

I wasn't alone.

A small pendant light broke through the archway across from me, an insignificant accent to an otherwise darkened house that floated above Camilla. She sat at the counter, raking her fingers through her long, black hair, allowing it to fall over her striped cotton pajamas.

Jesus, she made me nervous, especially after the complicated dinner that ruined her night. I was sure she wanted to be alone, and I was sure her embarrassment from dinner never left. Honestly, I felt bad, and although it would've been easier to walk away, I knew there was something I had to do. I tucked the cigarette into my front pocket and clutched my phone.

"Can't sleep?" I asked quietly, not wanting to startle her. She seemed unfazed, peeking over her shoulder before turning away.

"I guess… something like that," she stirred a small cup of tea with a silver spoon. "And you?"

"Just thirsty," I lifted a cup off a rack that hung below the cabinets. "Wanted some water."

"Water? You're not going to *throw* that in my face too, are you?"

Ouch.

Her words didn't have their usual harshness attached, yet they stung, nonetheless. I couldn't help but feel guilty, but forced myself to acknowledge that it was Camilla who was always determined to put me down first, not once making an effort otherwise to be friends. Typically, she always seemed so confident, but right now she was different, more guarded in a way that made her appear so uncomfortably visible.

"I don't want to cause trouble. I just want to make sure you're ok."

"I'm perfect…" she massaged her temple, hiding the

swollen puffs below her eyes. "Just like that stupid sleep mask on your forehead."

"What?" I knitted my brows, snatching the silly mask off my head. It read, "*Wake Me for Pizza,*" and I thought it was cute, hardly warranted for such a nasty remark.

"Why do you hate me?" I questioned impatiently.

"I don't…"

"Yes, you do. And don't say that you don't. I tried to be nice to you. I tried to be accepting of your relationship with Parker. I see how happy you make him and that should make me happy too, but it doesn't, because you're so unbelievably mean." I stepped closer to the counter, more confident. "You hate me, and I don't know why. But if there is something I can do to fix it, then just tell me, but don't punish me because it's easier for you to be mean than honest."

Camilla stuck her hand out, halting me. It looked like she wanted to cry, but ran out of tears.

"I don't hate you, Gemma," she gritted. "I'm just… threatened by you."

I jolted back.

Threatened? Me? The girl in the pink, silk pajamas with the squeaky voice? That was ridiculous, I literally had nothing compared to her.

"That doesn't make sense. How can—" I barely asked before she cut me off.

"Do you think it's easy? Being with a man who only talks about how amazing his friend is? His *best* friend? About how you two share so much history and traditions? And it's not just the inside jokes and quirks either, it's the way he stares at you, Gemma. It's nauseating."

"He absolutely does not stare at me."

"Oh, Gemma, please," she scoffed. "I've been compared to you since the day I met him, since the second I stepped into his office and saw your photo on his desk. I've never been enough, living in the shadow of the *fabulous* Gemma Rose Harrison."

"We're just friends."

"Friends? Yeah, right. It's so much more than that."

"He chose you. What else is there?"

"Me? How could I ever be the one, when the one isn't me?"

"Camilla, you're wrong," I defended, guarding myself from ever accepting *that* truth. God, I was so uncomfortable, her words like jabbing needles to my skin. All I could do was hunch my shoulders. "Parker doesn't stare at me like he does you. There's no one else. It's you…" I reached for her hand, surprised by the warmth of her palm, and the fact that she didn't pull away, but instead, choked back a sob.

"If you don't see it, Gemma, then it's because you're *choosing* not to." A tear rolled down her cheek. "I mean look at the guy, he's sleeping soundly on the couch. That's for you. I know it is. I'm nothing but a second choice, because Parker totally has feelings for you; the whole family does, and that's the truth, and, god! I can't believe I'm actually crying in front of you."

She turned her cheek away from me, her tears nearly contagious, a foreign feeling I never knew was possible with her, yet here it was.

The truth was, I loved Parker, and beyond that I had already told him so. But at the end of the day, from years and years ago, despite his sweet rejection, the answer remained; Parker didn't feel the way I did.

"Um… are you hungry?" I calmly let go of her hand, palming a tear from my cheek before turning away.

"Are you serious right now?"

"Of course. I'm asking for a reason. You might not know this, but Mama Meg only makes comfort food, and that's exactly what you need. Did you even eat dinner?"

"No. Obviously."

"Then you can't think straight." I stood from the counter. "You're a smart girl, Camilla, but I'm telling you right now, you're wrong about me and Parker."

I made my way to a tin pan by the fridge, lifting its lid before pulling out a pair of forks from a drawer.

"I'm not wrong…" she sniffed.

"You are. Trust me. If Parker wanted me, he could have had me long ago, but that's just not us. Things… are different, have been since we were kids." I placed the tin between us as I passed her a fork. "Sure, we're close, but not in the way you're thinking. Have you ever asked him about it? I'm sure he'd tell you." I dug my fork into the gooey center of the room temperature strawberry pie, chipping its crust.

Camilla stared at the fork, not yet touching it. "Of course not. It would just make me look insecure. I don't want to seem like some obsessive psycho… like how I did tonight," she looked completely mortified.

"Tonight was nothing… and you're not a psycho. We are allowed to have feelings and insecurities. You should have just asked him, he's a very open man. But if you won't, then I guess I'll just tell you myself." I chewed a little harder with what I was about to admit. "Back in college I told Parker I had feelings for him. I thought what you thought; I was absolutely certain he liked me too, but it wasn't true. He was nice about it, but the rejection stung. Bad."

The room would have been silent, had my heart not been pounding in my ears.

"He rejected you?" she asked a little too hopefully, finally lifting the fork to take a reluctant scoop of pie. "What did he say?"

"That…" I paused, then recited the words that still killed me to admit out loud, "I was like a sister to him."

If I believed for a second that we were on any type of friendly terms, this was it, the way her face lit up, her open mouth matching the size of her pupils, like she was enriched with the holiest of gossip.

"Sister?"

I nodded.

She took a quick bite before grimacing. "What a jerk!" Her statement made me snort. She was actually just as appalled as I was, both of us now concealing our laughs.

"I know! I was mortified, still am actually," I admitted, sheepishly toying with the sugary red filling. "But he made it clear that there was nothing between us, at least, nothing you have to worry about." I was good at pretending to be casual, but saying it out loud was as painful as it was humiliating. For a second, I was reliving the horror of that night, attempting to brush it off as if it were nothing, but my desire to make Camilla feel better suddenly had the opposite effect on me. Honestly, it hurt like a reopened wound.

"Relationships are weird. They can make you think and act in ways you never knew were possible, or worse, worry about issues that never existed."

"You're not wrong," I rested my fork along the tin. "And for that reason, I owe you an apology. I shouldn't have thrown that drink at you, Camilla. What I did was unacceptable, gross, and shouldn't have ever happened. I'm really sorry," I said, reeling from my confession, but adamant about setting our differences aside. Camilla sat suspiciously quiet, swallowing a rather large piece of pie before nodding.

"At least it was a martini," she replied with a coy smile. "Can't say I hated how it tasted." I covered my mouth as we both held in another laugh, trying our best to be quiet. "Gemma… I'm sorry, too. I let my thoughts get the best of me and that wasn't fair to you. That's not me, and I apologize for that. Sincerely." She slid the tin towards my direction, delivering a truce over pie and a single-worded question, "Friends?"

I took a stab at a loose strawberry, popping it between my lips. "Friends."

Camilla wasted no time in pulling the tin back, taking hold of the pie that moments ago was resistant to. "Now, if the boys could just be on good terms, then we could redo that night at the bar. A proper double date, with drinks in our hands, not on our dresses."

"Eh, I wouldn't hold your breath. Us girls have common sense, but not them. Especially with everything going on."

"And how is Alex?" she arched an eyebrow. "I know he's going through a lot, but so are you."

I remained quiet, shrugging my shoulders. I wanted the appearance that everything was ok, but I was never good at being on the spot. I pulled my phone out, resting it on the counter.

"We had an argument, or at least I think it was an argument." I stared down at the dark unopened screen. "I needed space, or maybe he did, but since coming here I haven't checked my phone. I have no idea what's going on, or if he's even tried to reach me."

Camilla cocked her head, "Uh-uh. You just alleviated my own self-doubt, and now you're going to stop yourself from knowing the truth of what's on that phone? Let's find out right now."

"Andy would disagree with you," I said under my breath.

I was so clearly stalling.

"Who?"

God… help me.

"Never mind, it's a joke."

"Whatever, just turn the phone on! The truth is the truth, and it's better than letting your mind come to its own conclusions."

I tapped my teeth with the tip of my nails, quietly contemplating if it was even the right thing to do. Camilla was totally right; my hypocritical actions were now hurting me more than helping me. "I know. I suppose you have a point," I answered, hesitantly reaching for the power button. Maybe she was just the edge I needed, the push to do what I was afraid to do. With all the spontaneous effort I could muster, I decided to just turn it on. Quick. Decisive. Done. I looked away as the screen began to load.

"Well?" Camilla eagerly leaned closer. "It's on!"

I frantically swiped at my screen, my apps appearing like a burst as I cradled the phone in my hand. I dropped it between us on the counter, showing everything we needed to know in a flash.

There was nothing.

My air fell out in a sigh as I opened my texts, showing only the previous messages I sent before.

"Not tonight," I smiled, pretending not to care.

"Gemma…" Camilla broke the silence immediately. "These things are complicated. I'm sure it will—" A loud ding rang from my phone, shocking us both as I fought to silence it. "Who is it?" she asked more excited as I stared back down at my phone.

"I don't know. But, it's an email."

"Is it Alex?"

"Wait… this doesn't make sense…" I said to myself, shocked at a message I had to re-read three times before continuing, assuming it was some cruel joke. Camilla grew nervous as my hands started to shake.

"Gemma! Who is it?"

I tried to answer, forming into words that wouldn't sound as ridiculous coming out as they did in my head, because honestly, it was unbelievable; acknowledging a name I'd only seen on countless bags, shoes, and dresses across New York.

It was my hero.

My idol.

The man who lived in my heart and in my closet, whose legendary name had been passed down from Mama Meg.

"It's St. La Vie," I mumbled. "He wants to meet me…"

Chapter 28

PARKER

It was hotter than the typical summer day at eighty-four degrees, but damn if it didn't look fucking good on Gemma's long, smooth legs, and how they shimmered in the bolstering heat.

"Smiling and sweet, or brooding and bold?" Mila asked another question, chomping at the tail end of her pink glitter pen.

"Both," Gemma answered, leaning over the adjacent poolside lounger to peer over Mila's shoulder.

"No peeking!" Mila shouted. "And you can't answer 'both'. You can only pick one." I dunked my head under the clear turquoise water, pushing myself off the edge of the pool towards where the girls sat. "The answer to this can make all the difference, so choose carefully," Mila guarded the Cosmo magazine that her and Gemma bought this morning. Gemma flipped a page of her Vogue magazine, then stopped to seriously consider the question.

"What are you guys doing?" I ran my hands through my wet hair.

Mila lowered her white, cat-eyed sunglasses with a devilish grin. "It's a Celebrity Soulmate Quiz, and now that Gemma's going to be a big star with St. La Vie, her dating pool just exploded exponentially."

"I am *not* going to be a star… he just wants to meet, and I'm not even sure for what yet."

Gemma's modesty paired eloquently with her bathing suit, a flesh-tight halter top with matching white bottoms. Not even the decency of her look stopped how hungry I was for her, or how that sheer knotted coverup above her navel begged to be undone with my teeth.

"Celebrity soulmate?" I joked, hiding the subtle dismay on my face. One Hollywood man seeking her attention was already bad enough, but now all of them?

I dunked my head under the water again, exhaling a few loose bubbles before rising back up to hear Gemma's response.

"Smiling and sweet," she finally replied. Mila pursed her lips while jotting the answer down.

"Netflix and chill or dancing and disco?"

"Ohhh, Netflix for sure."

"Arms or eyes?" Mila asked, but I already knew the answer. *Eyes,* I mouthed to myself, leaning over the edge, my back baking in the sun.

"Eyes!" Gemma answered, shimmying in her seat.

I knew her so well, what she liked and what she didn't, her habits, her fears, her joys. Of course, I wanted to tell her this, but first I had to get through this trip. I knew it would be painful, but once we got home, I'd be honest with both girls, accepting whatever consequences came my way; positive or not.

"I like both!" Mila said. "But I can say that because I'm not taking the quiz. Isn't that right, Parker?"

"Your rules," I smiled. "You both can pick whichever you want."

Mila shook her finger. "No, just me. Like I said, I'm not taking the quiz. But, I'm picking both because they remind me of you: green eyes and big arms." Mila adjusted the strap to her yellow bikini, flashing an untanned portion of her already tawny skin. She winked at me, her brow raised through the dark shades of her glasses.

"I've seen bigger." Gemma stuck her tongue out at me, then looked at Mila, both of them cackling like schoolgirls.

"Come closer to the pool and tell me that." I warned playfully, splashing water towards them. Mila tossed a towel in my direction, but I caught it, placing it below my bronzed arms like a pillow for my chin. I finally started to feel relaxed.

"Few more questions." Mila cleared her throat. "Towering and tattooed, or brawny and bare?"

Brawny and bare, I answered to myself again, knowing she'd pick it.

Gemma chewed on the corner of her lip, taking her time to dog-ear a page in her Vogue. "Towering and tattooed," she smiled, and I almost swallowed water. I turned to her immediately, completely caught off guard by her unexpected response.

"Dark and desirable, or sandy and stylish?" Mila asked.

"What the hell does that mean?" I interrupted.

"It's a hair question," Mila squeaked.

Gemma paused again.

Sandy and stylish, right?

"Hmmm…" she contemplated, "let's go with dark."

Gemma flipped the page to her magazine and gasped, "Ugh, look at this St. La Vie dress! I had no idea it was featured in this issue." She held it up for Mila, who returned an elongated *ooohhh* of a noise.

"Since when do you like dark hair?" I reached towards the bowl of peach gummy rings that sat by their side. I popped one into my mouth, savoring the cocktail of sweet candy that perfumed the chlorine and jasmine scented air.

"Dark *is* desirable, babe," Mila interrupted, using the braid of her hair to wave hello. "How could anyone resist?"

They both laughed again, their sudden friendship becoming more startling than the answers Gemma just gave. I had no idea what happened between the two, considering last night was a complete disaster.

"Ok, last one!" Mila declared. "Dependable or spontaneous?" Gemma considered the question as if the results could come true, looking up at the shade of a bellowing palm tree.

The air silenced itself, disturbed only by the gentle laps of pool water that rocked by my chest. I sat harbored like a steady boat, her words like the passengers I needed in order to fulfill the purpose of my existence.

Say it, Gemma, tell me, please.

Why was this answer so important to me, and why did it feel like my life depended on it? Yes, I tortured myself with even the smallest of gestures and words, my mind burned out from years of asking and contemplating: *is this right, is this wrong?* I just wanted things to be easier, and to shake the dust from the fucking shelf I put us on.

"Dependable," Gemma finally answered, sparking another jot of Mila's pen into the magazine. She began to tally up the results as I back-stroked away from the edge, submerging my ears into the water, muffling them to not appear so desperate for the results.

"Oh, this is interesting." Mila hummed as I stood up in the deep end, pushing off towards the peach rings again.

I reached in the bowl and fished one out, my brow creased from the sun. I wanted my name to be on the list, no matter how impossible that was, shamefully pining for Gemma as she took a look at me.

Thank god I was in the water, hiding how my cock responded to her. I pressed myself against the pool wall, forcing it down while fantasizing about dragging her in, untying her top, and biting the tip of her tits with an insatiable suck. If she could just reach into my trunks and set me free, I'd let myself stand stiff between the thin, wet polyester bikini that protected her from me accidentally slipping inside. Jesus, I was so restless.

I bit off a piece of candy.

"Who's the lucky guy?" I asked. Mila peeked up from the magazine.

"It was close, but I like the results," she assessed. "It says here: *'You're a homebody who loves quiet nights in, one who prefers the comforts of a sweet and reliable cuddler, rather than a naughty night owl. Although you like peace, you also desire a little spice. You need someone who can keep you on your toes with a tatted and toned body,'"* Mila wafted her face. *"'Your celebrity soulmate is: Chris Evans.'"*

"Where can I claim my prize?" Gemma wiggled her eyebrows.

I chuckled to myself, her adorable expression making the muscles around my mouth ache into a smile.

"He'd be perfect! It would be like we were dating twins!" Mila pointed the magazine in my direction for comparison.

"I don't think so." I stretched my neck, feeling the sun resting on my wet cheek.

"Same body, same radiant smile," Mila protested.

"Same sweet guy," Gemma added, incorrectly labeling me as something I wasn't. Still, her casual recognition felt like an award, a trophy for a test I cheated on. "Who came in second?" Gemma asked, returning to her Vogue magazine.

"It doesn't matter," Mila replied, "number one is the best."

"Tell me. I'm curious." Gemma maintained, licking her finger and turning a page.

"Eh… the score was off by two points, not your type."

"Oh, come on."

"Chris Evans really is sexy though, don't you think?"

"Camilla!" Gemma laughed, "Who came in second?"

Mila mulled over the page, her words almost too fast for me to even register. "Just… Alex Rivers." She blurted out, as if to remove the name from her mouth.

My ears began to burn.

"Oh…" Gemma pretended not to care about the name that nobody wanted to hear. The mere mention of Alex deflated the mood like a vacuum of fun, the girls' giddy laughs now stifled into a suffocating silence.

The very mention of that asshole annoyed me, my abs and arms particularly hardened, aggravated by the imaginary left hook I pictured giving him for the thousandth time. Briefly, he had Gemma, and within that small amount of time, he managed to hurt her, it was so apparent. Telling Gemma that I loved her like a sister was by far the biggest, stupidest mistake of my life, but at least I had always trusted it was for the best. I couldn't imagine this was true for him, not with his history, not with his tendency to leave when things got tough. I hated him, maybe even as much as I hated myself.

"You're coming with Parker and me to Montauk tonight!" Mila quickly added, "I won't take no for an answer. I already did my research and found us a place that's known for their coconut shrimp and double cheeseburgers." She reached out and rubbed Gemma's shoulder. "You like burgers, right?"

"Love them," Gemma smiled, but I gathered the mention of Alex sat heavy on her heart. She was so good at hiding her feelings though, something she thought she could do around me, but I knew better. I didn't like to pry; I didn't want to make her uncomfortable, but I always sensed when she was hiding something, and damn it if it didn't make me want to dig deeper, to finally get uncomfortable. I'd never shame her; I'd never let her believe that she was anything but loved. Didn't she know that, even without my confession? Didn't she know I was always completely and utterly here for her? I wanted to prove it over and over again.

"Mila, dear!" Mom came out from the large French doors, tossing a lime in her hand. "I've come to steal you!"

"*Steal me?*" Mila asked, her otherwise vibrant nature shier around my mom, possibly intimidated.

"Don't worry, I'll bring you back. I've always wanted two daughters, and luckily now I have them. I'm going to show you my secret margarita recipe, which will now be *our* secret recipe."

Two daughters? Guilt twisted in my stomach. Mom was showing her a secret recipe, forming traditions, building bonds. That was unfair to Mila, considering what I knew I had to do. I wanted to stop it all but was helpless at the moment.

"I'd love that… Mom," Mila said, flashing a timid but bright smile.

Mom covered her mouth with excitement as she helped Mila off the lounger. "What an angel! You want one too, Butterfly? Parker?" Gemma nodded, but I shook my head.

"Not a fan of tequila." I calmed my stomach, reminding the crowd of something Gemma already knew so well. I could tell she wanted to tease me, but she didn't, instead she gave me a sly grin as she pulled her sunglasses down.

I rolled my eyes as Mila laughed, her and Mom's excited chatter faded away as they returned inside, leaving me and Gemma alone. She put her magazine down and lifted a peach gummy from the bowl, garnering a newly sweet aroma as she bit into its center.

"You hot?" I dunked my head back, allowing the cool water to fall over my shoulders as I rose back up.

"Warm," she answered. "Kinda sweaty, actually."

"You want to get in the pool?"

"Hmmmm… maybe."

"Maybe? Don't be shy." I taunted, gauging her reaction. Something about the word shy made her hesitate, almost giving me a double take.

She shook her head.

"I'm not shy," she lifted herself from the lounger to sit near me. She placed her feet into the pool, distorting her toned legs into rippled mirages of untouchable treasures. "Just don't think about pulling me in, Parker Ellis Jones!"

"Like this?" I grabbed at her ankle, my large hand shackling it with a playful and mocking tug. She laughed and almost screamed.

"Park! You're going to get me wet!" She kicked water up with a splash, her hand placed onto my shoulder for leverage. A new and clammy heat rose to the surface of where she touched me, her soft fingers digging into me as if to keep her safe.

It's ok, Gemma, I won't pull you in, but don't think I don't want to, don't think that I lack the strength to yank you down into my arms, because I have it and I'd use it. Maybe I want you wet, maybe I want you to feel the cold, so that your breath will hitch and I can catch it with my lips, mine against yours, stolen and cherished like I always dreamed of. I'm here, I'll always be here, just give me time.

"You're right, you are warm," I commented, her hand retreating as if our playful touch was somehow wrong.

"And you're cool," she replied.

"Feels nice though, right?" I lounged by her thigh, resting near her side with my arms propped on the edge.

"Feels great. Everything feels—"

"Simple?" I asked, earning the most appreciative grin I'd ever seen on Gemma's face.

"My new favorite word."

"Simple is a luxury," I muttered.

"It really is. I know this more than ever before."

"Well, it's better to know it now, than to take it for granted like me."

She grew quiet, but smiled, moving to my face, the tip of her fingers twirling a curl of wet hair on my head.

"Your hair is getting long."

"I know. Does it look bad?"

"No. Not at all. It has that signature boyish wave to it. You're the embodiment of vacation right now."

"I'm actually relaxed for once." I admitted, not just being away from the city or the case, but because of now, finally getting to be alone with Gemma, my one true love. I wanted to know she felt the same.

My gaze traveled along her arm, its porcelain hue now pink, ripe before the adornment of bronzed skin. Maybe it was the coolness of the water or the graze of my arms against her thigh, but I couldn't help but notice her nipples were hard, shaped into perfect nubs against her top. I swallowed, this vision and the toned curves of her sun-kissed stomach made my cock throb fuller with a rush of blood.

"Please don't stop," I shut my eyes.

"Stop what?"

"Touching my hair like that. It feels nice. Keep going." I continued to rest my head by her side, looking up to her, pleading.

"Come here," she urged me closer. "Come rest between me."

Gemma opened her legs, creating enough space for my neck to enter. I moved closer, placing myself between her thighs with my back pressed against the pool. I couldn't see her face any longer, but her smooth-shaven legs draped over my shoulders, positioned as if I were carrying her through the crowds of a packed concert. Slowly and with intentional grace, Gemma combed the waves in my hair, raking them back into a more tamed position.

"Mmmm…" I hummed. Her touch was calming, mixed with the smell of sunscreen and candies which wafted in the air.

"Is that nice?" she asked, her smile evident in her voice.

"It feels like the best part of getting a haircut. I could just fall asleep."

"Try not to. You're far too big for me to pull you out if you start to sink." She gave my hair a tug. Bad play, Gemma, because that tug alone would be enough for any man to go insane, to take his woman into his own bed and ravish her until she doesn't know which way is up.

"Well, if I do, then don't try and save me. I think I'd die happy, considering how good I feel right now." I laughed, comforted by the sway of her feet which lied beneath the water and against my ribs. "You're so pink." I noticed, resting my cheek against the inside of her thigh. "Do you need more sunscreen?"

"I think so," she decided, still combing my hair. "I don't want to get too burned; I'll end up looking like the Phantom of the Opera."

I chuckled to myself, "Hey, the Phantom gets a bad rap, and even though Raoul was the better choice for Christine, he's still my favorite character." I defended, expecting my brief comment on the characters to pass. I was ready to fall asleep on her thigh.

"Raoul the better choice?" she questioned, humming to herself. "I'm not too sure about that. I don't think it's that simple."

"You don't think so? Even after all they shared in common?"

"Well, the Phantom and Christine shared a lot together too, you know?"

"I know, but Raoul and Christine have their childhood memories to bond over. Do you think she could have been truly happy with the Phantom?"

"I think it's possible. They share a bond that others don't understand. He helped Christine grow as a person, he guided her to chase her dream, making it all possible."

"Is that all?" I asked.

"No… there's more of course. He's important. Not a parent, but older, wiser, more persistent." She traced her hesitation into my hair, a distinct figure-eight, like the infinity I'd love her for.

"Persistent or stalking?"

"Stalking is harsh. He was there for her, an angel, a father figure when she needed one the most." I didn't comment right away, sensitive to the mention of a father figure, especially in the context of Gemma's life. My knuckle grazed the outside of her calf, hoping to relax her as much as she relaxed me.

"Is that what someone needs in order to feel true love?" I asked, hoping for a clue.

"I don't know anymore," she answered.

"What about his secrets? Do you think it would be worth it for Christine, dealing with a man in a mask, one who has hidden his ugliness from the world?"

"I think so. We all hide something we find ugly about ourselves… and who knows? Sometimes that ugliness is what attracts us to others."

"Maybe," I countered. "Or perhaps the ugliness is just so familiar that it starts to feel safe. But isn't that fake? Should Christine just live the rest of her life in the sewers below the opera house, just because of what the Phantom provided? Or is it better for her to take *one* more lesson from him, grow *one* last time, and live the life that we know she deserves?"

"Depends on how she views his ugliness."

"How so?"

"Well, for starters, the Phantom is totally misunderstood. I think we're drawn to the shock value he provides, but underneath the mask is something else."

"Then what is he?"

She hesitated. "A man, someone who's capable of love… *true love.*" Gemma's stance made me irrationally weak, the word *love* a galvanizing trigger to kiss her.

"And Raoul?" I asked. "What about his love? He would die for Christine."

Gemma let go of my hair, her soothing touch now absent from my scalp as she leaned back onto her hands. "Maybe Raoul would die for Christine, but the Phantom would *kill* for her."

Immediately, I almost responded, my words like instinctual vomit, that I could barely hold onto. *I'd kill for you too. I'd die and live, breathe and see, do and be anything I needed to be in order to have you, to hold you, to keep you forever.*

"And if you were Christine?" I squinted up at her face. "Who would you pick, Gemma?" My cheek still laid along her thigh, my lips so near her flesh that I could kiss it, and I would, I'd show worship to a place where I was thankful to rest.

"I don't know. That's a hard question, but I think I would pick—" Gemma's words were interrupted, averted to the rolling wheels of a large suitcase.

"If it isn't my favorite non-couple!" Tommy—fucking—Romero walked through the back gate, shooting a wide smile that made Gemma scream.

"Oh my god, Tommy!" Gemma and I were completely stunned, unsure of what he was even doing here. He sauntered by, lifting the shades of his large Ray-Bans to give us a view of his goofy wink.

"What are you doing here?" I asked surprised, annoyed with his timing.

"He invited me," Tommy pointed at my dad, who came out with—what I assumed was—one of Camilla's newly produced home-made margaritas. He took a long sip, before starting to choke.

"Tommy?" Dad practically barked. "What the hell are you doing here?"

"*You* invited me, sir." Tommy repeated, his smile dropping. "Remember? Last night?" Dad shrugged until Tommy scoffed, "You don't remember calling me, Mr. Jones?"

"Calling?" Dad took a long, hard look at his green margarita, removing the straw from his mouth. He examined it for a moment, looking back and forth between Tommy and his cocktail. "Jesus," he complained, "I got to stop drinking so much."

"There's plenty of room! We're going out for burgers tonight!" Gemma got up from the pool, leaving my side with an unsettling splash. She hugged Tommy and proceeded to lead him away into the house. Dad followed behind, signaling another round of margaritas to be made. Not soon after, everyone's voices began to fade, leaving me in the sun, silently baking.

I wiped my face once more, eyeballing the Vogue magazine that Gemma was reading. I noticed the single dog-ear that she used to mark a page, its bent corner creating a noticeable gap. I reached for it, assuming it was the article on St. La Vie, but frowned as I opened it up, observing the cologne ad that Gemma marked, its unsettling dark colors circling along the portrait of a smoldering and arrogant Alex Rivers. Below him was a quote, one that made my stomach turn.

"IT'S ME, BABY, DEAL WITH IT."

"Fuck you," I growled, annoyed that his presence was not only ruining my vacation, but Gemma's as well.

I pushed away from the edge, dunking my head under the water for a moment of peace. I exhaled, slowly allowing the bubbles to leave my lips, to sink like the ship I envisioned myself as earlier. I sank to the bottom, where I stared back up, the surface of the water no longer still, but beautifully cracked into shattered rays of light. I laid my back towards the bottom of the pool, my hair waving like grass in the wind, contemplating everything I thought I knew but maybe didn't.

Why did Gemma pick dark and desirable, towering and tattooed?

Why did Tommy have to interrupt? Why couldn't Gemma have just picked Raoul?

I exhaled a few more bubbles, facing the final ugly question I hated to ask: why was Alex Rivers right?

His fucking words played over and over again in my head, the magazine feeling more like a message for me, than an advertisement for cologne. I wasn't the only man in Gemma's life anymore, and I knew things had changed. There was Alex now. It was *him*, and just as he fucking said, I would have to *deal with it.*

"I'd give Tommy a chance if I were you," Camilla said, applying a fresh swipe of red lipstick as I washed my hands in the empty restaurant bathroom.

"Tommy?" I laughed.

"Yes! He's totally fun, and I think he likes you." She held the lipstick out like a cigarette, offering me a puff. Its label read *Pouty Princess,* which was possibly the most fitting title ever.

"Tommy likes everyone, he's just a flirt."

"Yeah, but he shared his food with you. A man doesn't just offer up an onion ring, let alone four of them." Camilla looked back at herself, squinting in the dimly lit, nautical-themed mirror. I never considered what she said as proof of being *liked* in that way. If only she knew Parker had already done this for me countless times before, purposely ordering pepperoni pizza with the intention of giving me his toppings. "Men don't just feed you for fun. It's like evolutionary mating stuff, you know, like hunters and gatherers? Read the signs, girl."

"The only sign I'm reading is that one," I pointed to a decorative placard, its painted letters shouting; *There's plenty of fish in the sea.*

"He's sexy," Camilla defended. "He looks just like Freddie Prinze, Jr. You've seen *She's All That*, haven't you?"

I chuckled, removing paper towels out from a small tin cubby. "To me, he's more like Freddie Prinze, Jr. from *Scooby-Doo*. More of a goofball friend than the smart, dazzling jock."

Camilla shrugged, "Good point. I guess he's kind of a downgrade."

"No, I'm not saying that at all. Of course, Tommy is gorgeous, but not like that."

"Not like what?" Camilla's mood was more playful after three long island ice teas. "Like Alex?"

"I wasn't trying to compare." I lied, attempting to avoid the topic, but was failing miserably.

Of course I tried not to think of Alejandro, of where he was or what he was doing, and although I completely avoided the internet, I still saw him everywhere, even in the darkness of Camilla's own provocative eyes.

"I don't blame you. Alex is hot. Like, *really, really,* hot. Honestly, his composure during that god awful bar night was super attractive. Don't tell Parker that though. He'd probably have a fit. Alex is a very assertive man, and it's sexy."

"He certainly is." I quipped, quietly staring at myself in the mirror, succumbing to the tingle from the beers I had.

"Do you like assertiveness? I mean… long term, could you see that working for you?"

"I really don't know. Can't say I haven't thought of

it." I fixed a braid in my hair, trying not to be so emotional. "It's hard to see the stars when the clouds are in the way, you know what I mean?"

"I understand. As you may know, Parker and I have had our fair share of clouds. Granted we haven't been together that long, but still, I've seen enough to know how I truly feel about what we have." Camilla pumped a small dot of soap into her hands before washing them. "Everything about him makes me nervous and excited all at once, like every piece of his life is a test that I'm eager to pass. I want to know all of him, and protect the pieces I cherish so much, like the things I find most in common with him. To be honest, it feels like we have the same deep desires, like we're both so eager to prove something, that our desperation becomes some chaotic magnetic force. Maybe I like it because it's familiar."

"I get that…" I agreed, recalling the indescribable force that drew me to Alejandro. There was something about him—about us—that made me feel like it was ok to be me, but maybe, it was a lot of what Camilla was saying. "When I'm with Alejandro, I feel like I found a piece of something I had lost, some ill-conceived idea of a guardian, some authority that sees past the secrets and codes I put myself through. I feel like I'm being deciphered and appreciated all at once, and I don't know where it comes from, but it terrifies me. I feel like our story isn't finished. Then again, maybe it's—"

"Love," Camilla interrupted, opening the large wood door with its clanky brass handle. "I know that feeling, because I'm feeling it right now… with Parker."

For a moment I lost my balance, trying desperately

to follow Camilla out of the bathroom and into the bar. What the hell did she just say? Love? Her sudden confession caused a sticky wave of sweat to wash over my chest, like at any moment I could melt into the grooves of the shiplap floors. Maybe it was just the drinks, but my fingers seemed to nervously shake as I hid them in my back pocket. Camilla spoke her truth with such vivid confidence, yet I stood behind, literally following her direction with confused and uncertain thoughts on Alejandro. What did I feel for him? Was it love? Was it something else? Whatever it was, it was different from Parker, who made me feel things on such a magnitude that I still couldn't get over it.

"Thought you guys fell in!" Tommy shouted from the beach, garnering a laugh from Camilla as we left the bar filled with colorful paper lanterns. I removed my sandals before walking outside, digging my feet into the cool, grainy sand.

Parker looked up, his face iridescent from the large bonfire, caught in the scope of a low hanging moon and shimmering sea light. "Beer, Gem?" he asked, fishing out a Corona from a bucket of ice. He popped it open before I could say yes, reading my mind, knowing what I wanted before I could answer.

"Don't get her too drunk," Tommy hollered, having already had a six-pack himself. "We don't want her getting sick again."

"I've only had three," I scoffed playfully. "Plus that night I had too much scotch, not beer. You know how strong those are."

"Bourbon," Tommy corrected. "It was a three-hundred-dollar bottle of Blanton's." He patted the old, cushioned couch he sat on by the fire. "Come sit with me. I'll keep you warm."

"It's summer, no one is cold." Camilla teased, calling Tommy out as I sat by his side.

"We can still be cozy," he maintained. "Bet this looks familiar though, doesn't it, Park? You guys remember?" He took a long sip as Camilla leaned against Parker's shoulder.

Parker said nothing.

"What's familiar?" Camilla asked.

"This couch," Tommy waited for a reaction, and when we said nothing, he sighed. "Oh, come on. You guys really don't remember?"

Parker and I looked at each other, locked into a brief moment that was just for us. Of course we remembered, the evidence concealed itself in the form of a quick hidden smile.

I shrugged at Tommy. "Actually, it was a little different."

"Ours had tiny brown flowers on it," Parker added.

"Lilacs to be exact." I recalled, remembering how fitting they were at the time, a flower for both youth and innocence.

"You two owned a couch together?" Camilla asked.

Tommy shook his head. "The frat owned it. Big and ugly, but comfortable as hell."

"It's what's on the inside that matters, and the same is true for couches." Parker flicked a beer cap.

Tommy waved him off. "Whatever. We had one just like this on the roof of the frat house. Him and Gemma always went up there together. One boring, old couch for two boring, old people." He belly laughed, leaning closer to the fire, his hair dangerously close to the flame as he reached for a new bottle of beer. "I tried to get rid of it, but Parker threw a fit."

"I don't throw fits. I simply said, 'no'. Didn't I?"

"I object, your honor. It was more like, '*noooooooooo*....'" Tommy mocked, clenching his fist, dropping his knees into the sand. Parker laughed, and I smiled, learning something new about him. "You'd have thought we were throwing out Gemma herself. He was such a baby about it," Tommy slurred, scooting closer to place his arm over my shoulders.

I blushed, madly embarrassed, but also flattered, not ever immune to Tommy's goofy charm.

Parker stared at Tommy's hand, his attention fixed like a directed arrow caught in a cocked bowstring, while Camilla arched her brows, as if saying, *see, I told you about Tommy.*

"Why didn't you pursue Gemma in college?" Camilla kicked sand over Tommy's espadrilles.

"With *Daddy* Parker in the way? There was no chance! No one could even look at her, let alone try anything else. He was *way* overprotective. Right, Gemma?"

I hesitated to answer.

Way overprotective? Parker always made sure I had money to come to the parties, to eat food, to be safe. Yes, he was protective, and maybe that's what I wanted when I was younger, but I wasn't sure anymore if it was what I needed.

"It's true." Parker inhaled, answering instead. "I was too much. Gemma didn't need a protector. She deserved better." He toyed with the top of his beer, thumbing its opening.

Did he really just admit that?

Agreeing to something he fought vehemently against weeks ago, as I shouted it in his face.

He left me speechless.

"You were just being the good big brother," Camilla defended. "There's nothing wrong with that."

Parker looked at Camilla, surprised by the term *brother*, his face caught in disgusted shock, as if completely disappointed in what was said.

"Well, look at me now. I got both the pretty girl and the couch!" Tommy flashed a victorious grin, but Camilla reached over to slap his hand away from my shoulder.

"No touching!" she snipped. "She's taken."

"By who?"

"By Alex Rivers. They're totally in love… well, at least Gemma is."

Still leaning back in his seat, Parker's face froze at this new misguided information, furrowing in her direction. It was as if Camilla herself were a splash of cold water dumped onto him, his O-shaped mouth formed for some set of words I knew he wanted to say but couldn't get out.

"I didn't say—" I stuttered, my explanation cut short as Tommy sighed.

"Another six-foot monster? As if Parker wasn't bad enough."

"I love monsters," I quipped quietly, as if tagging our appreciation for horror movies would somehow make it better. It wasn't, and if anything, it sounded like I agreed with Tommy.

Camilla squealed as a waitress from the bar brought over a s'mores kit, handing over four metal roasting rods to Tommy with a wink. She had essentially blocked the view between me and Parker, shielding my embarrassed smile. Everyone seemed fine, but I knew I was being awkward, chugging an empty bottle of beer that I'd already finished. Parker sat up, massaging the back of his neck while Tommy passed out marshmallows.

"I'm not that hungry," Camilla wobbled her head, breaking a piece of Hershey bar to chew on. "I'd rather dance. Parker come dance with me."

"Good luck!" Tommy laughed. "Parker can't dance."

"I can dance," Parker disagreed.

"I've never seen it, and we had parties all the time."

"I mean, I've danced before," Parker hesitated, knowing damn well the only time he had ever danced was with me.

The eighth grade Bushwick Beaver Ball was hardly as lovely as its *lovely luau* theme, but we went together nonetheless. Originally I told him no, not because I didn't want to go, but because I didn't have a dress—or any dress up to that point. But that didn't stop him from taking me, instead, he tried to match me as much as possible. While others girls wore gowns and boys had suits, Parker and I wore everyday clothes. I tried to dress myself up, braiding my hair, wearing my most valuable second-hand Paul Frank top to match his orange Knicks jersey, and in a way it kinda worked. We looked like a couple, and regardless if we were both sweaty or stepped on each other's feet, the moment David Cook's "The Time of My Life" came over the intercom, I knew it was the best decision I ever made.

It was the first time he had ever touched my hips, drawn me near, and stared into my eyes without saying a single word, but he didn't need to, because I was already convinced that we were meant to be together for the rest of our lives. This happened like a dream, a three-minute moment with green tinsel backgrounds and partially deflated beach balls. It felt good; it felt right; but most of all, it felt like the first time that either of us had the courage to do anything at all, that was, until he gave me my butterfly ring. After that, it seemed like neither of us made a move, until the night that Tommy reminded everyone of—the one with the three-hundred-dollar Blanton's bourbon.

"Come on, don't be a beach bum, Parky. Dance with me!" Camilla pulled on his arm.

"I kind of just want a s'more right now." He removed his marshmallow out of the fire, single handedly assembling his sandwich.

"You prefer that over dancing?"

"Well sure, have you ever had one before? They're so good."

"Not this again," Camilla exasperated to Tommy.

"What's he doing now?"

"This whole, '*flavor can change your life*,' thing he's done before," she groaned. "He once offered me a peach gummy ring, and when I refused, he gave me some lecture about how it could change my life. He was so dramatic on their sensation. I'm sorry, but a candy can't make you feel everything you described, as if eating one could just make you '*die happy*.'" She mocked, giving air quotes.

The brief and sardonic tease caused me to grow silent, the mention of *dying happy* felt so specific from today, with the peaceful awe Parker showed while resting along my thigh. Peach rings were our thing, our tradition, and his feelings towards them felt so heavy, so purposely poetic.

I removed myself from their attention, staring at the tips of my teal, painted toes, concentrating hard to avoid the swarm of fluttering wings in my chest.

"Dork," Tommy laughed under his breath. "These two are wallflowers, Camilla, but I'll dance with you."

"Really?" she asked, lifting up from her seat.

"As long as Daddy Parker says it's ok," Tommy took Camilla's hand, twirling her into a giggle-filled spin.

Parker didn't look at anyone, he just poked the fire with his metal rod. "I'm not your daddy. And you certainly don't need my permission. No one does."

Tommy handed me his marshmallow and crackers, practically chasing a screaming Camilla before Parker could finish his sentence.

Quietly, I placed a cracker on my knees, building a layer of chocolate before squishing down a large, melted marshmallow. The fire popped into specks of light as Tommy and Camilla slowly disappeared, their singing and dancing far too distant to be heard over the calming crash of dark foamy waves.

Parker and I were quiet, but not too quiet, as Mazzy Star's "Fade Into You" played faintly from the empty bar.

"Die happy?" I teased, blowing on my s'more to cool it down.

"Happy doesn't even begin to describe it," he returned, his voice as soothing as the ocean. "It's much more than that."

"Then, what is it exactly?"

Parker paused.

A wave crashed again, fizzling before any response.

"It tastes like home, it tastes like something so simple, so meaningful, that I can't help but crave it every second of every day," he answered seriously, licking the chocolate from his finger. "But when I have it—that single bite, that single moment—feels irreplaceable."

I didn't respond, I only stared at him and listened, his eyes seeking me through the flames; their color much darker than the night, but vast and full just the same.

"Like being a kid all over again?" I finally asked, but Parker didn't answer.

Camilla shouted from the shore, not deliberately getting our attention, but doing so nonetheless.

"She's wrong, you know." Parker looked out at her.

"Who's wrong?"

"Camilla... what she said about me earlier, about me being a *good* big brother; it was complete bullshit. There's a lot of things I should have been in the past, but a brother was never one of them, and believe me when I say this, Gemma, I'm nowhere close to that." The s'more in my hand slipped away and tumbled into the sand, as I suddenly lost my grip.

"Shit," I muttered, ruminating on his words.

Parker cracked his s'more in half and handed it to me. "Here, Butterfly," he grinned. "Eat."

I took it from him, my mouth dried with the echo of Camilla's expertise: *Men don't just feed you for fun. Read the signs, girl.*

"Thanks," I mumbled.

"You never have to thank me. You're too kind, you always have been, especially to me."

"That's not true," I said quietly. "You deserve kindness, Parker, you're my best friend."

"I know what I am," he scolded, "and you're doing it again. You're sweet, and you're kind, and you deserve so much, and if I could say sorry to you every day I would, because complete recognition of my faults is everything that you deserve."

"You really don't have to say that—"

"I'm sorry, Gemma," he interrupted. "I'm so, so sorry... I think about that night, about you and me, about what it took for you to say what you said and how I let you down. I don't think you know how much I still live in that moment... if I could just go back, if I could just stop myself before ruining it, before hurting you... I would; I'd save you from my decision." He looked down at my spilt dessert, his voice barely above a whisper. "But I can't... it's sand on a s'more now. I wasted it, and I ruined it. And then I brought you to meet Mila, surprising you like it was some goddamn great idea to make you feel better, to make you feel like you weren't some effect on my life when the truth is, you're the *greatest* effect on my life."

My fingertips literally burned, scorched from a set of nerves I never knew existed, but were somehow alerted by Parker's honesty. "You think about that night?" I asked worried.

"Every day of my life. I think about you, and how wrong I was to spiral us into this situation, how it was you who took all the chances, you who was brave, when all along I made you believe something that wasn't true, because honestly, I was afraid of hurting you. That wasn't just wrong, that was evil, and I accept the consequences of that and the insurmountable work that it'll take to earn whatever ounce of trust you give me… that is, *if* you choose to give me any."

I tried so hard not to pout, my shoulders inevitably dropping like the abandoned strings of a marionette. If I wasn't his sister, then what was I? What had I always been? He wasn't here to protect me, to guard me from some terrifying feeling; and in fact, I was terrified, nervous at what he was saying, an apology that felt like an admission.

"Do you love him?"

I couldn't blink as Parker asked the heaviest question I'd ever heard.

"I don't know," I answered as open as I could. "I don't know what I feel, but it feels important."

"And are you open with him?"

"Maybe… He knows a little about me, about Claire. I was open as much as I could be at the time, but I think that has stopped. We haven't talked in days… and now I'm just exhausted."

"From what?" he asked, genuinely begging to know.

"From everything… from the lies, from the secrets, from the darkness."

"And to fix it… to fix everything, Gemma, where would I begin? Tell me, Butterfly." His voice fell out: smooth and soft, desperate in the most pleading whisper that made me ache. I couldn't help but answer so bluntly.

"I need honesty, Parker, and not just from myself, but from others."

My words appeared to pop whatever bubble we found ourselves in, removing the delicate staring contest that was intruded on by others.

"Come on, Gemma!" Tommy ran up and pulled me by my arm. I forced a smile, doing my best to conceal the previous drop in my face, and the surprising tears that appeared from nowhere on the corner of my eyes. "I'm taking you dancing!"

"I'm not any good," I shied away, but he wouldn't let me go.

"I'll teach you. It's fun." He shot a quick look at Parker and sneered. "Sorry bro, you had your chance! She's taken now."

Parker broke his attention from us as Tommy pulled me out into the moonlit beach, spinning me around. I laughed but kept my eyes back at the bonfire, focused on Parker and the orange light that lit his face.

He watched me, quietly and purposefully, his confession floating in the air. I wasn't his sister, and his words were tortured with an apology that crumbled everything I was told to believe. Why would he do that? Why would he force himself to carry such a feeling, such a burden? And what would he do now, now that I wasn't sure how it made me feel, leaving me to wonder if I could ever forgive him?

Chapter 30

PARKER

Mila had been listing ideas of things we could do here, and so far her suggestions hadn't been great. I stared up at the ceiling in bed as she continued to read them out loud.

"How about canoeing?" she asked excitedly, her glasses slipping down the bridge of her nose as she scrolled through her iPad. "Can you imagine Gemma and Tommy on one? How cute!"

"Cute?" I couldn't believe what I was hearing, still hung up on how dangerously close I was to ruining this trip, to confessing everything I ever felt to Gemma. I couldn't even handle how the smallest tease, mention, or imagined instance without her drove me insane. "You scolded Tommy tonight for being forward, and now you're wanting to set him up?"

"Better than Alex Rivers," she scoffed. "Gemma deserves better."

"Please don't mention his name," I said to myself, checking the alarm clock, feeling totally anxious. Why wasn't it morning by now, why couldn't I just be on my run with Gemma? I felt so completely distant from her, and after the bonfire, she'd been totally checked out. She wouldn't look at me, stand by me, or even say goodnight to me. Gemma knew something was up, and now it felt like we were in a weird place.

Was what I said too much?

Fuck.

It was, and I knew it would be, but between Mila and Tommy and their constant mention of Alex and Gemma, everything began to reach a point of unbearable restraint.

"Don't be such a baby." Mila burrowed her cold feet near my thighs, seeking their warmth.

"I'm not. It's just… can't I have a vacation without any mention of Alex, or a reminder of work? Or you playing matchmaker?"

"Do you have something against Tommy?" She furrowed.

I tried not to sigh.

"Of course not. He's my friend and… I just can't see the two of them like that."

Mila snaked her legs around me, her attention still glued to a top-ten list of romantic things to do in the Hamptons. She brushed herself against me, her panties and bare skin uncomfortably close to how confined I felt. I was becoming physically pinned to the mattress and plush white sheets.

"I can totally see it," she tried to convince me. "Oh, my god, they would have such cute babies! We could be their godparents!" She swiped at her screen. "You know there's an app for that? I can put their photos together and see what their children would look like. Can you imagine? Gemma's auburn hair, and Tommy's tan skin?"

Oh, fuck this.

"I need a drink." I tossed off the comforter, escaping the potential of what some god-forsaken app could do to my mental state.

"Could you bring water?" Mila asked.

I nodded, desperate for any sensory feeling other than what confined me to this room; cold wood floors, brushed nickel door knobs, and now, the sound of laughter that came from downstairs.

I could hear Mom howling from the kitchen as I made my way down, taking special note towards the hall, right on Gemma's open bedroom door. She couldn't have been asleep yet, and in fact, I didn't think she was even in bed.

I walked faster to get to where everyone was.

"Hey Parky!" Mom snorted from the kitchen counter, repeatedly bombarding me with Mila's new nickname for me. I shook my head, begging the universe to be called rattlesnake again, a more meaningful attachment given to me by the woman that stood right beside Mom.

Gemma looked up, silently surprised, her eyes big before darting back down. Really? This again? She didn't even say hi.

"What are you guys up to?" I fixed my voice, sounding as casual as I could be.

"Puzzles and chit chat." Mom sipped on a late-night cup of coffee, absolutely buzzing with caffeine.

"Of what?" I asked, this time directing my attention right on Gemma.

She couldn't avoid me now.

"Labradors in a boxing ring," she answered down to the puzzle, giving it a quick smirk before hiding it away.

Just look at me, I thought, *just tell me we're ok, even though I know we're not.*

"Dad and I are thinking of getting a dog," Mom announced, piecing together a collection of cheering poodles. "What should we get?"

"Get one like Parker!" Tommy made his way in, slapping my shoulder, his long plaid, pajama pants much louder than my grey sweat shorts. He looked like Christmas in the heat of summer. "A dog that's loyal to a fault. But smart."

"Not too smart," I replied, inching closer to Gemma, being as inconspicuous as possible. I just wanted to be near her, but fought to keep myself from staring. Her hair was pulled into a perfect knot, her pajamas a loose silk top that I wanted to wrap my arms around. As she leaned across the counter, a small peek of flesh appeared through the buttons of her shirt, teasing the spot right below her breasts. Even though I couldn't see them, I knew she was wearing shorts underneath the thigh-length shirt, but the illusion that she may not have been drove me absolutely mad.

"What do you think, Gemma?" Tommy asked.

"About what dog they should get?" She looked up at him, meeting his eyes, making me envious.

"No, what dog do you think Parker is?"

"A lying one," she tossed a sly smile at Mom, who almost spit out her coffee. Everyone thought it was a cute joke, but to me it was the most honest retort she could've given.

"How about a German Shepard?" I replied to my own defense, the only dog that Gemma ever could talk about while growing up as kids. *I want to be what you've always wanted.*

"Those are a little too protective, don't you think?" she asked me, stacking puzzle pieces like poker chips.

"They can be brave too. Doesn't that count for something?"

"They shed too much!" Mom interjected, turning to Tommy as they discussed potential names for a dog they didn't even have.

Gemma focused herself to a corner of the puzzle, a particular image of Corgis eating corndogs.

"I found a piece of their paw." I smiled with my voice, considering she couldn't see me. She switched to another corner of the puzzle, walking around my body to the opposite end of the counter.

She was right next to Tommy now, sharing the space with the bump of their shoulders.

Christ, all I could see was what Mila saw, a perfect couple, with adorable kids. I tried not to crease a cardboard piece in my hand, keeping my eyes down to the image below us as I made my way back to Gemma.

This was starting to get obvious.

"Ok, the German Shepard is a good idea," Mom conceded out loud. "But it's too big. I need something smaller, but that could match the family?"

"Something grumpy, like a lawyer and a judge." Tommy said, checking Gemma for a laugh.

She didn't reply, but side-eyed me as I leaned against the counter, resting by her side.

God she was warm, unlike Mila's cold feet, and as awful as it was to imagine, I pictured Gemma and I calling it a night, returning back to the very same bed we used to share. Wouldn't that be so nice? So absolutely perfect; like the end of a story that finally had its happy ending.

Tommy and Mom continued to talk as I turned toward Gemma's face, her pineapple makeup wash a teasing scent I fought to inhale.

"Mila is thinking about canoeing tomorrow," I said, hoping for a response.

"Mmmm," she hummed, unenthused.

She was giving me nothing.

"How about Madoo Conservancy? I can take you to see the flowers?"

"Me or everyone included?" she asked, snapping a puzzle piece into place.

"You know what I mean."

"I don't," she whispered, "and that's the problem."

"Not a problem… just something we can talk about."

"I think you've said enough tonight," she trembled for a second as Tommy announced to the group.

"Oh! A Schnauzer would be perfect. Small, but dignified, cute but also a curmudgeon old man."

"I love it." Mom already opened up her phone, searching for breeders. "What do you think, Gemma?" she asked, and I begged the same thing.

What do you think, what you do feel? And goddamn it, don't hold back right now!

Without an ounce of self-preservation, Gemma

looked up at me, hurt by who she saw before her, screaming with a look that held a million different interpretations. I ruined her puzzle, her night, her trip, and maybe our friendship. All that came through was the small drop in her voice, one I knew she hid so well.

"I think… I'm going to bed." She responded, turning away from the counter, and leaving the room.

As obvious as I was, I turned to follow her, Mom's eyes meeting mine with the most suspicious smile. She didn't need to say anything, she already knew the tension in the room, the obvious truth she so unapologetically declared at dinner last night. And she was right, I was obsessed with Gemma, but that didn't phase Tommy as he stepped in my way.

"Hey, can I get a second?" he asked, backpedaling as I left the kitchen.

"Um, ya." I looked up the stairs, seeing Gemma already reaching the top before I could catch her.

"I need to get your opinion."

"If this is about Tri-Tech again, I already told you, I put in a good word with MelBrook."

"No. I don't care about that," he waved away. "This is more serious, but it's hard to talk about."

"Well just say it." I looked back and forth, between Tommy and the empty stairs, losing complete sight of Gemma.

"Just don't be so defensive."

"I'm not."

"Well, you will be."

"Tom," I sighed, grabbing him by the shoulders,

fighting the urge to shake him. "I promise I won't be, but come on…"

Tommy cringed before whispering, spitting out his secret like a pile of sunflower seeds. "I want to ask Gemma out!"

God kill me now.

I didn't respond to Tommy's antagonizing statement. I only squeezed his shoulders to keep from falling down. I wasn't a religious man, but I was willing to pray to make this stop.

"Gemma?" I let out, redirecting my focus back to the stairs, taking my first step up. As much as I wanted to throw Tommy out the door, I trained myself back to my goal. I had to get to Gemma, and what difference did it make that Tommy liked her, too? Everyone did, and everyone should, and as unpleasant as it was to hear, I couldn't fault my own friend for wanting my opinion.

"You guys are so close! I want what you and Camilla have."

"Trust me, you don't," I said, climbing the steps.

"Yes! I do. And Gemma is amazing. I think she likes me; she was totally shy while dancing tonight."

"Dancing isn't her thing."

"Well, that's why I'm asking you. What can I do?"

Besides nothing? I thought, feeling on edge as I reached the top of the second floor, unable to even entertain the idea of coaching Tommy on how to ask Gemma out.

"Just… be yourself?" I settled, doing the best I could. Tommy seemed bored by that.

"That can't be enough. Wouldn't she like a grand gesture?"

Fuck. Gemma's door was now closed, the light below her frame snapping into darkness before my eyes. She literally ran away from me, as I peered over Tommy's shoulders.

"Don't get a boombox and hoist it over your shoulders," I begged.

"Oh… that's not a bad idea."

"It is."

"Well, a song would be nice. Does she like the guitar?"

"You don't even play." I scolded, lost in where this was even headed, before doubling down on the idea to get him out of my way. "Ok. Fine," I submitted. "It's not a bad idea, but you'll need help. Dad has one in his study, and if you ask nicely, he may let you play it."

"You think?" he asked hopefully, his beer-ladened optimism something I wish I could inherent.

"Yes. But bring him a drink. I'm sure he's in the office now, and maybe you can still catch him before bed."

Tommy didn't even thank me, essentially pushing me off to the side as he rushed downstairs, making his way to bother Dad. I didn't mind whatever plans he had, far too focused on shaking the nerves out of my hands as I finally made my way down to the darkest part of the hall, reaching Gemma's door.

I listened closely, not quite putting my ear against the wall, but hesitantly waiting for any signs of her on the other end. To be honest, I was really afraid of knocking, of hearing her disappointment again. Did she even like me anymore?

"Gem?" I whispered, my forehead leaning on the door.

It remained quiet.

I reached to knock but not before I heard her faint voice.

"Sorry, Park…" she said from far away.

I could tell she was already in bed by the distance alone.

"No, no. Don't be sorry. I'm just… checking on you." I squeezed my eyes shut, going nowhere in my conversation. I hated this reminiscent feeling, this stupid memory of me outside Claire's door, of the moment Gemma shut me out with tears in her eyes. It was happening all over again, her voice matured but somber, urging me to test the doorknob, regardless of if I knew it was already locked.

"I think I just had too much to drink tonight," she said, her voice a little closer. Was she out of bed now?

"Is there anything I can bring you?"

"No…"

"Well…" I hesitated at the sound of shuffling feet that inched closer in my direction from the other end of the door. I already knew there was nothing she needed, nothing physically at least, and as uncomfortable as it was to whisper, I asked the most opaque question I could muster. "Is there anything I can say?"

I leaned further into the crack of the door, my shoulder brushing against the spot I hoped she was touching on the other side. Without its barrier, without inches of wood, we'd be chest to chest, eye to eye, mouth to mouth.

"I don't think so," she finally replied, an answer I couldn't accept.

"I just want to know how you feel… I want… more." *I always have,* I wanted to add, but paused, unable to commit to the sentence, not wanting to scare her away. I placed my palm above the knob, begging to reach the other end, to grab her by the arm. There was so much I wanted to say, but couldn't, not like this, not without meeting her face and telling her like a man. "This is our home, our room, and I don't know how to fix tonight, and I'm … just…"

"Just what?" she asked, her lips close, her mint flavored tongue sweet against the crack from where we both spoke.

I can't hold it in any longer.

"Just…tell me we're ok." I begged, and I knew she knew I begged. I wasn't just asking anymore; I needed this.

"Parker?" Mila exited the bathroom that was down our hall, wiping toothpaste off her lips as she called out my name. Gemma stayed quiet as Mila adjusted her glasses, looping her arm with mine. "What are you doing down here?"

I shook my head, "I, uh…"

"No water?" She laughed, pulling me aside, apart from Gemma and away from our room. "It doesn't matter. I found a winery we can go to tomorrow. It's super cute, and apparently a popular wedding venue."

"For Gemma and Tommy?" I scrunched, asking

defensively, hearing the ill-attempted strums of a guitar down the stairs in Dad's office.

Mila laughed at me. "For no one, I'm just saying it's pretty," she leaned her head onto my arm. "What else could you ask for?"

Everything, I answered to myself, a list of wants and needs that had gone unfilled for far too long; for this trip to be over, for Gemma to be happy, to get the answer I wanted, but didn't receive as Mila pulled me away.

I didn't need much anymore, settling on the brief smile I caught Gemma giving Mom back at the counter while working on the puzzle. That's all I could have for now. That and the hope of getting us back to where we were, something I'd resonate on while falling asleep, wishing it was her that was by my side, back in our old bed, back in our old life.

My lungs were on fire, finally reaching a point where I could almost forget about last night. *Almost.*

I couldn't believe Parker, not only at the bonfire, but afterwards, pursuing me in the kitchen, standing so close to me, provoking a need for me to fall into his arms.

God, help me, I tried to stay distracted while running; fixated on the crunch of gravel, the fight for breath, the incinerating heat and sweat that covered my chest and ears, but the harder I pushed myself, the more I focused on why I was pushing in the first place.

There is no us, I am just a sister. I told myself again, placing myself back in the role I'd gotten accustomed to, because that's what felt safe now, predictable even. As the sister, I could never be let down again, I was already as low as I could get, because after all that had happened in my life—the heartache, the trauma, the inability to finally get ahead—I wasn't sure I could survive another let down, especially if it came from Parker.

"Gemma!" A rushed voice shouted from behind, startling me to quicken my pace.

I pretended not to hear him but was surprised by how close he was as he appeared by my side. He certainly was the same old track star from Columbia. "You ditched me."

"Hey," I flashed a quick smile to Parker, my throat dried from the lack of air. "Sorry! I was up early… I thought I could squeeze in a run."

"Without me?"

"Well, not on purpose," I continued defensively, trying not to look at him. It was so hard to avoid being trapped by his attention, possibly becoming vulnerable to whatever he could do or say.

There's a lot of things I should have been in the past, but a brother was never one of them, and believe me when I say this, Gemma, I'm nowhere close to that. Fuck. Not even my breathing could help me ignore what he said last night.

"I see you're feeling better… Christ, Gemma, you're fast."

"I want a good work out," I said. "I mean, I have to hurry up. I have to leave today."

"Leave?" Parker scrunched his brow. "I don't understand."

You wouldn't, and I don't need to explain myself, about how every hope I have is just another letdown waiting to happen. I was just anxious, my fear a byproduct of every experience I ever had. Abandoned by a father, abandoned by Alejandro, warned by Claire, affirmed by Parker.

I came to the Hamptons to get clarity, but instead acquired a new set of questions and uncertain futures. Alejandro still hadn't reached out, Parker was changing before my eyes, and St. La Vie was now wanting to see me. Shit. I was so unprepared, unable to focus on something that I should've been excited for.

I had to leave the Hamptons.

I had to go back to Manhattan and concentrate on this one opportunity, because if I stayed here, if I stared too long, I'd never want to leave.

I had to lie.

"St. La Vie's office messaged back. They're bumping up the meeting."

"Ok. I'll take you." Parker offered.

"No. I'm fine."

"Why not? This is important."

"Yes, but this is your vacation."

"It's *our* vacation. Besides, I can spend it how I want, and if that involves taking you home, then so be it."

"It involves Camilla, too. You can't just leave her behind."

"She'll understand," his sprint turned into a jog. "Will you slow down for a moment?"

"You're a runner. Just keep up with me."

"That's not why I'm asking. We need to talk."

"About what?" I barked, but didn't mean to, playing ignorant to the fact that last night was huge. I could already feel my eyes water.

"About my apology… about last night, about these past few months."

"I forgive you," I lied. "Can I just borrow the car and you drive back with Mama Meg and Al?" I asked, bypassing any mention of how I felt.

I wasn't sure if I could truly forgive him or what that would even look like. All I knew was that I was more disoriented than I was mad. It didn't feel good.

"Will you just look at me?" Parker pleaded.

"Not right now, Parker."

"Why not?"

"Because I want to run," I answered.

"And run from what exactly? You're acting weird."

"I'm not acting weird, Parker."

"You are. You're doing it again," he sighed.

"Doing what?"

"Hiding!" He exhaled loudly, voicing a stinging annoyance that made me stop abruptly. I turned to finally face him.

He was absolutely frustrated, his toned arms riddled with sweat that darkened the collar around his grey Colombia shirt. I hated that he made me stop, and all that he affirmed. This wasn't the vacation I needed, and I couldn't enjoy it, not anymore, especially with how his eyes trained themselves onto me.

"I'm not hiding," I finally let out, breaking our momentary silence.

"You are, you always have been. I blame myself for that. But I won't let you ignore what's happening to us." Parker still tried to catch his breath, his large chest heaving with a rise of muscle. I remained silent, angry at the charm of his tussled hair, its shape formed by a breeze that sifted through wild blue junipers.

This was what I was afraid of. I couldn't look away, I couldn't ignore all that I ever felt, the good and the bad, the admiration and the fear. Claire was right about a man's love and how it could hurt. Parker's hurt the worst, and the pain always came from not once feeling that he loved me the same.

Even this moment brought me back to a fantasy with

him, an imagined possibility that this could be us, living a life as a couple. Running, laughing, matching our routines.

"I need to go. Ok!" I blurted.

"Wait, where are you going? Gemma… can we—"

I didn't let him finish, I couldn't, so I just ran; ran until everything felt sore and the pain took me somewhere far from the possibility of ever being the sad, college girl on the bathroom counter again, my pace even faster, quicker than what it was before. Parker called out my name, a momentary shout before he began to chase me. I breached the tunnel of trees, making my way down the hill of a green pasture, private land unbeknownst to whom, but gorgeous and rich, as the Joneses' home sat in the distance.

"Faster…" I told myself, pushing my speed.

Parker quickly caught up, our descent powered by gravity and determined legs as the family dock appeared in my line of sight.

I ran harder than I did with Alejandro, different than the night we escaped a mob of fans on a busy New York street. That felt like a lifetime ago, a dreamlike memory that I instinctively compared to this. Yes, it was thrilling, but also so entirely different. Here, with Parker, there were no screaming fans or honking cars, but the stakes were higher now than they were back in the city, and getting caught here felt like it would change my life forever.

"Gemma!" I shouted once more as her sprint turned into a hasty walk. She ignored me, purposefully kicking a patch of grass as I drew closer, annoyed. "Gem, what the hell is going on?"

"Nothing, Park." She raised her hand in submission, turning away from me.

"Don't say nothing. That's bullshit and you know it."

"I already told you, I forgive you."

"I don't believe you, and I'm not asking you to. Jesus, you can't even look at me."

"I have nothing to say."

"How's that even possible?"

"Because Park!" She cut me off. "What am I supposed to say? As if I didn't have enough to worry about, to obsess about. I can't spend another second deciphering and misinterpreting things from you. I've done that enough!"

"Good. Cause I don't want you to. I don't need you to anymore."

"Why? Because you decide now is a good time?" she shouted, walking through the sandy grass, lifting her shirt over her black sports bra to wipe sweat off her forehead. "It's always on someone else's time. I'm always here, waiting and wishing for someone to say something, to make some move because I'm tired of trying to read between the lines. And it hurts. I won't do it, and I won't forgive you. I won't forgive you for how I was made to feel and what I was made to believe all those years ago. Fuck you, Parker!"

"Yes, fuck me. Fuck everything I did and said because all of it was shit. I won't blame others for the decisions I made, despite doing everything I thought was right. But I won't let you walk away from me. Not this time, goddamn it." My weight creaked along the old planks of the dock, drowning out the gentle laps of water against its base. I prayed she wouldn't jump in, leaving me no choice but to do the same. She drove me fucking insane.

"I get to shut out who I want, when I want. You don't get to decide for me."

"Fuck that. I won't decide for you, but I won't be ignored either." I warned as she stopped at the edge, unable to move any further, stuck between me and the abandoned harbor.

She sighed loudly.

"I already told you, I have nothing to say…" She focused on the pillar before me, on a small set of chipped initials carved on the top of its surface.

Gemma and I had remained at this dock longer than I could remember, not in person, but encapsulated with two simple engraved letters I carved the summer we turned eleven years old: *P & G.* I thought of all the times we had spent here, the memories that this very spot held, and what the future would bring. Would us— the Hamptons and the moments— ever end? Would time be as kind to us as it was for this pillar, keeping us together like unbreakable initials?

Soon things would begin to change, no matter how difficult it'd be to face, and I wasn't sure anymore what would come next.

"Look at me, Gemma." I tried meeting her face, but she rolled her shoulder away.

"No. I don't want to see you…"

"No? What, you just want to ignore me, you want to hide and keep things to yourself? Well, I've tried that, and it doesn't work. It just makes things worse. It's not a way out."

"What I need is distance."

"You always need distance. You always need to say and do things to protect yourself, and when push comes to shove, you shut off. I can't reach you; I can't even try because you'll freak out."

"Because you don't know what I've been through!" she shouted.

"And you don't think I know that?" I yelled, my eyes burning as I pointed to my chest. "You don't think I have some ounce of an idea? I've been watching you since the moment I met you. The way you move, the way you dress, the flowers, the meanings, you don't think I see all of that? Cause I do, and I feel it, and I've fucking lived in silence for so long, holding onto some stupid idea that I knew what was best for you. I was wrong, Gemma, so goddamn wrong, and you hiding is just the same."

"Me hiding is not the same. Mind your business, Park."

"I won't," I growled. "I won't stop until you hear me out."

"About what? About me hiding? How about you hiding the fact that both you and Camilla are planning to move into a new place together once I'm gone?" This time her misty glare found mine, opposite of the bay that seemed calmer than the dock we stood at.

"What?" I barked, utterly confused and completely upset.

"Yes. You two. The couple. You're moving in with each other. She told me and Mama Meg."

"I never said anything like that to her, it's not even true. Mila just told you to—"

"To what?" She cut me off. "To make me jealous? Poor Gemma, the lovesick puppy? Well, it worked, Parker, and I hate that it did, and I won't allow it to anymore."

"You have to listen to me—"

"No!" She turned around, shoving me aside as she began to walk away. I couldn't even keep my shit together, the sight of her back boiling an uncontrolled frustration in me that I never felt before in my entire life. She was so goddamn stubborn, and in turn, made me lose any consideration to what was even appropriate. The few creaky steps she took didn't last long as I caught her hand, pulling her back quicker than she could even comprehend. She gasped, the force so sudden, so impossibly strong that she was nearly lifted from her feet.

"Parker!" she screeched.

"Shut up and look at me. Tell me exactly how you

feel and don't you ever run away from me, from us, from this." Finally, forced to confront me, I stared at how Gemma's lip began to tremble. I wouldn't dare let her leave, locking her arms in place, my body scorching the bare flesh below her crop top. "I've lied to you, and you've kept me in the dark. And I thought this could wait till we got home, but not after what happened last night."

"I don't know what to say, Parker," she whimpered, her face as sad as it was nervous, a gut-wrenching look I fought so hard to stop from ever happening. It made me want to cry, to finally fucking explode like I was warned not to so long ago.

"Tell me anything, tell me what you can. Tell me you're mad or angry, just don't leave me here. Don't walk away from me or else I'll die." I begged. Gemma struggled to pull away, but gave up as her arms grew limp into mine.

"I hate you, Parker Ellis Jones," she gritted, giving me the most hurtful honesty that brought me to tears. "I hate you. I hate you. I hate you."

"Good," I snipped. "Fucking hate me. Feel whatever you need to feel because I am incapable of doing any less myself. I don't care what it costs me. I *don't* care that it's nuclear, and that it could ruin everything, because everything already is." I began to choke, my words and feelings pouring out like a bucket of water, emptying me out until all that was left were the final important drops of everything I ever had.

Pain.

Hurt.

Resolution and peace.

I couldn't live without her. I couldn't even breathe another second or say another word except the ones I repeated in my head like a sickening mantra that got me through life. It broke me, and I knew it broke her too, but I couldn't help myself as the Earth grew quiet and the waves stopped just long enough for me to hear the unbearable skip in Gemma's heart.

"Dammit, Gemma… I'm in love with you."

Chapter 33

GEMMA

In a moment of weakness, I allowed myself to feel everything I ever experienced with Parker. The love, the pain, my confession, and the letdown that proceeded that college night so long ago. How he brought in Mila, how he made me believe all the things that tore my heart apart, but that also built it back up. It was good, it was bad, but all in all, it was the sweetest torture that I would never wish upon another person, but also, never wish away.

"I. Hate. You." I enunciated once more, cutting with a curtness that made my tears break into streams.

"You're a liar," he cursed. "You said it yourself last night, Gemma, you wanted honesty, well here it is. I knew it since we were kids. I knew it before our sleepovers, before our family trips, before peach gummies were ever a thing, and far before I ever put that ring on your finger, because the longer I think of it, the more I'm certain I knew it *the* day I first saw you. I knew it before I even knew what *it* was." Parker lowered his voice, competing with my own pleas to stop. I couldn't run, I couldn't look away as I called his name.

"Parker…" I begged.

"You aren't *just* my best friend or my first-grade

crush. You're so much more than that… you always have been. I'm sorry it took so long, I'm sorry that I was the one who got us to this place. Please don't hate me, Butterfly…" he dropped into a whisper as he leaned his head against mine. "Because I'm so in love with you—*every* version of you—starting with the girl who sat next to me on that field trip, who wore the denim overalls and sunflower buttons, to the person I see now, the woman, the purpose of my existence."

"Please, don't say that," I cried pathetically, the salt of the water stinging my eyes, illuminating me with the golden light it reflected. Why was this happening now, a single moment that turned the lump in my throat into a ball of combusted fireworks? I couldn't speak, I couldn't even think of how everything I ever wanted had just happened, how scared and alive I felt, completely obliterated as Parker's stoic stare remained unapologetically on me.

"I love you," he repeated, relaxing into the relief it gave him. "I love you. I love you. I love you," he said it over and over again, slowly, as if each confession lightened his heart, his hands cupping my cheeks, brushing away my tears with the stroke of his thumb. "I was a coward before, too scared to say out loud what I always knew was true, that you, Gemma, are the only woman I'll ever love."

"Do you mean that?" I asked one last time, knowing that what was to come had the potential to break me, to take everything about us and change it forever.

"I really do. I'll never forgive myself for what I did,

but I will spend every moment of my life fighting to make it better, fighting for you. I'll never stop saying it, not now, not ever," he said, slowly leaning in, anchoring his hand to my lower back.

My mouth parted, separated by the firm and restless kiss of Parker's full lips, lips that I'd only fantasized about, whose taste and touch pulsed like red embers in a strong wind. I cried, excited and scared, lost in the pressure of his strong hands that pulled me flush against his hips. Every second was telling to how long he wanted this—needed this—striking me like an unforgiving bolt of lightning.

"Stay with me… pick me. Let me be yours," he whispered, helplessly pulling into me, his lashes grazing my own.

"Yours?" I murmured, tears still streaming down my face.

"Yes, I love you so much…" he continued, as if incapable of stopping, releasing the decades held secret with five little words.

I sobbed and wasn't sure why, the exact reason going beyond anger, and stretching into relief, comforted in his arms and on his lips, his taste finally revealed in perfect flavor, like the first chew of a sweetened mint. I couldn't believe I was tasting Parker, and my skin pebbled with bumps.

"Parker, I—" I couldn't even finish, distracted by the figure that stood beside us, watching every ugly detail of what we did.

It was Camilla, slowly removing her headphones down to her neck, clutching her phone in her hand.

"Gemma?" She broke into a sob, questioning either me or the disbelief she had towards Parker.

"Fuck," Parker exhaled, not once letting me go. I stepped away though, unable to cope with how cruel the sight was.

What just happened? My mind still sat in a haze as I realized how everything looked, how awful it was. This wasn't love, this was betrayal.

"Camilla, let me explain—" I didn't know what to say, but she interjected.

"Friends, my ass," she hissed. "Fuck you… fuck you both!" She turned away, running through the path leading to the Joneses' home in the distance.

Parker stood quietly, anguished with being caught, impatiently saying my name, "Gemma—"

"You have to go to her!" I interrupted, wiping my eyes. "This was wrong, this shouldn't have happened, not like this."

"Don't say that. I don't regret telling you, I don't regret how I feel."

"It doesn't make it right. No one needs to get hurt, not anymore." I looked at him for guidance, aching for some resolve. Parker kissed me, but did I kiss him back? "Fuck, Parker. There is more to this than just us." I cried, unable to fully confess why. "There's others we have to think of—"

"If not Camilla, then who?" He pulled me back, blatantly ignoring the fact that Alejandro still existed. "He doesn't change anything, just like Camilla doesn't. This is it, I won't stop fighting for you, not ever again."

"I know you won't…" My whisper came out so

defeated, holding onto his eyes as I struggled to find the right thing to say, but could only land on the words that were needed, "Just go to her," I begged. "Make this right…"

"Mila, Stop!" I shouted, already having slammed the front door, now chasing her upstairs. This was so fucked, an unfair punishment to everyone involved, but especially to Mila. I could hear hollering already, the empty house void of Mom and Dad, but not to Tommy, who came out carrying a guitar.

"What's happening?" he asked but recoiled as Mila shrieked in my direction.

"Don't follow me!" she screamed, barging through our bedroom door, immediately lifting her suitcase.

"I have to!" I shouted, pulling the suitcase away, "I can't just let you leave. You deserve better, and you weren't supposed to see that."

"That?" She turned to me, using a sweater as a whip, slapping me in the arm until she got closer, replacing it with her fist. "I trusted you! You made me believe everything was ok. And I believed that!"

She punched my arm, her soft blows beginning to sting as I latched onto her wrist.

"I know!" I growled, pushing her against the bed as we tumbled over, clothes scattered and all. "You have to stop hitting me. I need you to listen."

She turned her cheek, pulling me away, using every

bit of her force to shove me off. I'd never get physical with her, but the way she yanked a photo off the wall had me on guard.

"You don't get to ask anything from me," she warned, her final declaration met as she smashed the frame against the floor, sending the entire room into a deafening silence.

Unlike Gemma, Mila was not afraid to stare in my eyes, her rage completely un-avoidant, challenging me to speak. We just stared, our chests heaving, our teeth clenched.

"You have every right to be mad." I pointed to myself, "But you and me, we always knew this was a risk. I knew you needed information on Alex Rivers… and that's why we got close."

"No!" She held out her hand, her finger shaking on its own accord. "You always thought that. Yes, this was supposed to be fun, this was supposed to be new, but when the hell did I ever agree to being disrespected?"

She pinned me into a corner, shouting the undeniable truth I couldn't avoid. There was no excusing what I did, and owning it was all that I could do before she began to burst into tears.

"And what was the goal?" she returned, my eyes redirected to the corner of the room, "To bring me to your home? To meet your parents? You're as dumb as you are good looking, and that's saying a whole hell of a lot." She yanked the suitcase back into her possession, tossing loose clothes and unfolded sweaters into its shell.

"I couldn't just leave you in the city. You had no place to go."

Mila laughed, until she cackled, her wide eyes exploding into an epiphany. "Oh my god! You actually think you did me a favor?"

"No. That's not what I meant."

"Yes, it is. Tell me right now that what I saw downstairs was an accident... that you weren't planning that all along?"

"Not like that Mila, I'd never intentionally hurt anyone." I argued, as she swiped a scoop of banana taffy off her nightstand and onto the floor, reaching for her belongings.

"That's the problem with you, Parker. You never mean to do anything wrong, you're just cursed to do it," she slipped a shirt over her sports bra, yanking her ponytail through the hole, "but you've caused more problems than you ever created solutions. And as much as I hate Gemma for doing what she did, I hate more that you led her to believe that she was anything more than what you always claimed. So congratulations... you've fooled two girls who are in love with you." She pouted, casually, hopelessly, blurting out a truth that almost caused me to stumble.

"You love me?" I whispered, confused by the rhetoric we always told each other, of the illusion I sold myself. This was supposed to be painless, this was supposed to be a fling, and as much as I forced it to be more, I knew it was never going to be anything else.

"Yes," she admitted sternly, sniffing, "I do. And despite what happened, I can't say that it changes how I feel. So whatever your intentions were, just know how it affects others, because you have just acquired a shit storm of problems." She zipped up her bag, slamming it on the floor.

I stood in the doorway, knowing that just across the hall Gemma was packing up, she was probably about to leave at any moment. As awful as I was, I couldn't let Gemma or Mila see each other again, or allow whatever that encounter would look like to happen. I remained adamant about what was just said.

"What problems?" I cocked my head.

Mila rolled her eyes at me, making me feel even more like a naive child than she already did.

"Like the one out in L.A. right now," she scoffed. "You think, for one second, that Alex Rivers is going to let you take Gemma from him?" she asked, honestly expecting an answer.

This really took me back, the outsider's perspective that Alex could ever be a threat to me and Gemma, only validated everything I ever feared. Did Mila really feel that way, even after she knew what I was capable of?

"Don't think of that…" I shook my head, hating the direction she steered us towards.

"Oh, I will. Because that man will kill you, Parker. Let him find out what you just did, and see what happens. Because the truth is, you should be worried, just like how Gemma should be worried about me." She began to wheel her bag in my direction, but not before I could step forward, blocking her path. Man or woman, I'd never let anyone make such a claim.

"What the hell did you just say?" I warned, triggered by her undisguised threat.

"You think you're the only one with big feelings,

Parker, that only you can defend someone you love? I can't let her just kiss you… I can't let *her* do that to us." She bit into her own lip, her eyes glossing into a heartbreaking red.

What the fuck did I do? How could I have brought so much pain into her life, into Gemma's, into my own? And now, what? She had a vendetta, all because of me?

"This isn't her fault," I exhaled, holding Mila by the arms, physically stopping her from stepping another inch.

The roll of a bag rattled behind me, thumping along the wood floors of the hall that stretched to the bedroom in the distance. Mila looked over my shoulder, her laser-focused scorn sought on Gemma, who with Tommy's help made her way down the stairs to leave.

I didn't get to say goodbye, but the last look she gave me tore me apart. It wasn't just sad, it was helpless, and the side effect of everything I was told I'd someday become.

I was the bad guy.

"I kissed her," I admitted to Mila, guiding her chin in my direction. She pulled away, denying the truth with the look in her eyes. "I'm sorry."

"Don't apologize to me."

"I don't care. You need to hear it. I'm sorry, and what I did was completely wrong, but this isn't about Gemma, this is about you and me."

This was so personal to her, such an attack on everything she had claim on. And after her and Gemma started to get close, the rug was pulled beneath her, and it was because of me.

"I can't ask you to forgive me, but I can't let you leave without telling you how wrong I was, and how there will never be a way to make up for what I did… but it ends here, and I'm sorry that it does."

Mila paused, amused by a thought that she held to herself. "You get to control a lot of things, Parker, but you won't control me. This isn't over, and in fact, it's just beginning."

"Stop," I warned, but Mila pushed me aside, taking her bag all by herself as she began to walk away.

"Don't worry, Parker, I'm only after Gemma… but as far as Alex is concerned, you better prepare for a war." She looked back, swiping at her phone for an Uber. "And trust that I'll be there to facilitate it, every step of the fucking way."

MANHATTAN

New York

"Everyone here goes by their first name. Miss Dawson from HR is just Elizabeth, Mrs. Aziz from accounting is just Farrah, and St. La Vie is just Henri." The tall, dirty blond man laughed to himself, his soft center tucked into a fitted floral top. He clutched a book to his chest, navigating me through a row of half-dressed mannequins and elongated cutting tables.

It was finally here, the sound of heels on glossy concrete, shears against fabric, the conglomerate of workers huddled around a single unfinished dress. It was everything I wanted, tied into a bow of the biggest St. La Vie logo I'd ever seen embedded into the wall. I wished I was as excited as my host, appreciative of every minute detail of the place I'd probably never be again.

But I wasn't.

And in fact, I wasn't even mentally here, seventy-seven floors above a busy, Manhattan morning. I was gone, back in the Hamptons, reliving the details that competed with the distraction of overpriced coffee and leather handbags.

"And what do others call you?" I pinned my attention to the man whose dimpled smile and bright, baby blues flashed in my direction.

"Mr. Davis." He grinned, tripping over a bolt of fabric. "But my friends call me Dean."

"Hope that includes me," I joked, enjoying how friendly it was to be around him.

"Oh, it does. I can tell we're gonna be friends." He opened the glass door to a massive corner office, its wall of windows crowded with bookshelves and clothing racks. I did a quick once over, admiring the candid photos of St. La Vie, posing at Lake Como with Oscar De la Renta and Donatella Versace.

"You can tell that already?" I stepped inside, wiping my palms on the skirt of my yellow, two-piece blazer set, drying them on the intricate floral pattern.

"Of course. I like your style." He began to organize the large desk where I sat, removing a pile of Vogue magazines to make room for the book in his possession. "I knew it the instant I saw you. You're a real human being with color and glow. Not another New York vampire."

"Well, I did just get back from the Hamptons."

"That must be it! You look like one of my cousins. She's a California beauty just like me." He searched around, lifting a pack of cigarettes off the desk and tossing it into the trash.

"Is that where you're from?"

"Laguna Beach," he answered, sprucing the bounce of the cushion on a chair. "I haven't seen a palm tree in over a year."

"Our beaches are way different here. Have you been?"

"I've been planning to, but this old grump keeps me prisoner at work. Which beach do you prefer?"

"I've only ever experienced the Hamptons, mostly near the Wiborg area," I answered, trying my best to be as personable. *I've only ever had Parker, too*, I thought to myself, simultaneously balancing two amazing kisses in my head. A carousel of images flashed before me; kissed on a roof by Alejandro, us at The Met, his penthouse, his shower, all of which collided with Parker, with a lifetime wish that was granted by the single most magnificent kiss.

My phone chimed with an alarm, sending me into a panic as I immediately reached for it. I thought it was a text, or at least hoped for it, but my face dropped at the generic calendar reminder that popped up instead.

"You ok, girlie?" Dean asked sympathetically, taking a seat on the edge of the desk. "You look worried, and that makes me nervous."

Worried? More like exhausted. It'd been forty-eight hours since I left the Hamptons, and I hadn't gotten an ounce of sleep since. Between Alejandro's scandal and Parker's confession, I barely had time to think of anything else, other than getting past this very moment, of course. I still had no idea what was happening back at the Joneses' or with Camilla, having insisted with Parker that I needed a few days alone to figure things out. He respected my space, and I hadn't heard from him since, but maybe now a part of me wanted that text to be from him, or Alejandro, who remained completely unresponsive.

"I was just hoping to hear from someone," I

admitted. "And you shouldn't be nervous. I'm the nervous one. Honestly, my last interview didn't go very well… which I'm not sure is a good comparison, considering I'm not sure if that's what this is."

"Whatever it is, *it's* good. I'm not sure what happened in your last interview, but I can tell you right now it was meant to be."

"Well, I'm still deciding if it was a blessing or a curse." Meeting Alejandro that day brought a whole new perspective to my life, but also, a detour to my fate. What if he hadn't stolen me from Gerard, where would I be now? Would there've been other opportunities, or would I have still been jobless? Would Parker still have confessed his feelings?

"Trust me. Things happen for a reason, but if we roll with it, we can conquer it." Dean hurried over to the fridge for a bottle of water, passing it to me as he returned. "Believe it or not, I'm quite introverted. Well, I used to be."

"That seems surprising."

"Oh, I know… and I think I would've stayed that way had I not taken a chance on something that scared me."

"I'm guessing it was this job?" I asked, unable to think of anything more intimidating than working for the greatest designer of all time.

Dean wafted my question away, his nose wrinkled. "God, no," he replied. "But it is ironic that you'd say that." He rolled his eyes to the ceiling. "Are you one of those ocean people? Like you can swim in it and not care?"

I shrugged. "I guess so. I don't mind it, really."

Dean slapped his thigh.

"See, I envy that. To me that just feels so impossible. When someone says they can go into the ocean, it feels like a superpower."

"Lucky for you we're in a skyscraper." I played along, garnering a small laugh from Dean. He took a moment, sipping from his Perrier, before placing his finger over his lips, excusing himself with a swallow.

"Well, let me tell you, back home in Laguna, surfing is all the rage, and the day my friends tricked me into going on their little surfing retreat, I nearly died. You can only cancel on people for so long. Introverted or not, you start to look like an asshole," he shrugged.

"It's nice they got you to conquer your fear." I said, finally sitting back into my seat, feeling the smallest ounce of relaxation. Dean snapped his finger, causing me to spring back up.

"My friends? Honey, no. They were no help… but a stranger was. Let me tell you, finding the one person in your life that can push you outside of your comfort zone, who can see your potential, is completely priceless."

"A stranger?" I asked, reminiscent on the story, of how enamored he looked. I didn't know the scope of Dean's fear, but I knew the reward of concurring it, just by the look in his eyes.

"A stranger back then, but not anymore, because here's a secret for ya… if I hadn't gone that day, if I hadn't trusted that stranger with my deepest fear, I would have never have met the love of my life."

"Seriously?" I physically leaned forward in my seat, captivated.

"As serious as I am about avocado toast. Go to California and find out what that means."

Dean laid it out so simple for me, like the path to all my answers was as easy as trusting others. Maybe that's how he learned to deal with things, and I appreciated the effort he gave me as a stranger, though I wasn't sure I could relate, or if trusting others would do the same for me. I mean, how could I do that with Alejandro now, especially with how mad I was at him?

I was mad, wasn't I?

Jesus…

Sad, mad, worried, what difference did it make? It wasn't just some fear to concur as Dean suggested, it was here—now—interrupting my interview, piled on by a kiss from Parker. And what would I tell Alejandro if I ever saw him? Did I owe him the truth, and if so, what was it; that my kiss with Parker was a mistake, or that it wasn't? Not knowing was the worst part.

"I guess it's easier to relax when you have a stiff drink. You may be serious about your avocados, but New Yorkers are serious about their Manhattans," I said lightheartedly, eyeballing the bar cart in the corner, not thinking he'd take me seriously.

"Shit! Where are my manners!" He turned quickly. "Henri may be French, but don't expect any expensive wine. He's as much as a basic bitch as me." He fixed the perfect swoop to his hair, styled like a proud rooster. "Rosé?"

I looked over my shoulder, making sure we were

alone before checking back with Dean, "Are you allowed?"

"Of course. I'm in charge of delivering the designs and making you comfortable." He pointed to the book on the desk. "I already did half of my job, now I'm just trying to do the other." He worked on uncorking the bottle, turning his back as I eyed the book.

"Could I take a look at them?" I asked, curious to see what was inside.

Dean looked over his shoulder, giving the most perplexing shrug. "Well, of course. You can have them back if you want."

"Back?" I opened its pages to see what was inside. I couldn't believe what I was seeing—a stack of my *own* designs piled in a row, my initials inked at the bottom of the pages. It was everything, my colors, my patterns, my floral obsession. "Wait... I don't understand."

"Personally, I love them," he clinked the glass that found its way into my hands. "I'm rooting for you, friend."

"How did you even get these?" I blurted, more shocked than upset.

"Alex Rivers! He... gave them to Henri. I thought you knew."

I looked up and around the room, searching for an answer, getting stuck on a photo on Henri's desk. It was one of him and Dean, sitting on surfboards, kissing.

"Alex gave these to Henri?"

"Yes!"

"And wait, you're his assistant?" I clarified, getting

my answer from the narrowed expression on Dean's face.

"Actually, he's my husband..." A dulled French accent greeted from behind, entering into the office as I turned around. Henri St. La Vie pushed his way through the door, holding a stack of mail in his hand. A lady followed close by, taking feverish notes, on whatever he said before walking in. "I see Dean has already driven you to drink."

I put the glass down quickly.

"Gemma was nervous." Dean waved away, as if to brush off the criticism.

Henri adjusted the transparent frames of his glasses, fixing them against the bridge of his large nose. He swiftly kissed Dean on the cheek, making his way around the desk in a hurry. "We're due downstairs at New York Prestige in twenty minutes, they are running a featurette on upcoming fall fashion." He picked at his nails, not once making eye contact. "They're wanting headshots and a confirmation of our attendance to the party this week."

Henri then looked at me, his attention so intimidating that I nearly reached for my drink. I didn't know what to say, but I hoped my nervousness wasn't as noticeable as Dean had announced.

"I'm sure Gemma knows all about it," Dean grinned.

"About a party? Wait... New York Prestige is here?" I turned to look backwards, imagining their logo slapping me in the face.

"We share the same building. What do you expect

from the busiest skyscraper on Madison Avenue? Lots of style here, lots of fashion." Henri answered, digging into the trash to fish out his cigarettes. He rolled up his sleeves, simultaneously lighting one up for a quick smoke. I hardly noticed the otherwise triggering sound of the lighter, but Dean rolled his eyes, obviously annoyed by the habit.

"You kept us waiting." Dean scolded.

"Did I?" Henri scratched the sides of his dark peppered hair, using the tip of a single finger.

"Not at all." I assured, clearing my throat, "I'm Gemma. Gemma Rose Harrison."

"Mmmmhmmm." Henri looked away, discovering an old coffee cup to store his ashes. He flicked the tip of his cigarette, taking back the book of designs I just held a moment ago. "Gemma, Gemma, Gemma." He repeated, testing how my name sounded, drawing a line under my signature, his finger tapping on a sketch of a colorful summer dress.

"It's nice to finally meet you." I added, silently gauging the suppressed domineering effect he had on the room. He was very slow to respond, almost transfixed to the collage of paper and color he held in his hands, his expression positively unamused.

"Lilac is a loud color for spring," he pointed to the design, still not looking at me. "Used…"

"I personally—"

"Periwinkle is more subdued," he interjected. "More universal for day and night. My comment wasn't a question…" He leaned over and removed a red pencil from his drawer, leaving a note on the design itself, "And you want to be a designer?"

"Is that a question this time?" I asked, making sure he wasn't just talking to himself. He rested his chin on his palm and grinned, taking another hit of his cigarette.

"If you want to be one, I can make that happen for you."

"It's my dream… *St. La Vie*." I mustered, saying his name without sounding like a gushing fan.

There was something about his accent, about his scruff and candor that made me as steady as glue. I blamed it on his eyebrows, thick, black arrows that were likely formed from years of contemplative thoughts and fashion conundrums. He was intimidating in the best fucking way.

"Just call me Henri," he corrected. "And everything I do is for me. It's not nice to hear, but it's true. This included. Well… sort of," he flicked his cigarette. "When I heard Alex Rivers was getting a suit created, I was excited… that is, until I wasn't. You could imagine how disappointed I was… seeing how I personally reached out to him myself. I figured I should've at least been considered. So I reached out again, and what did I hear? Your name, of course, Gemma Rose Harrison, a person—who for some reason—equaled the end of my single opportunity to design for Alex."

"It made him a bit restless," Dean confirmed, but Henri shot a pensive look. It was weird to hear my full name leave Henri's mouth, but it was even more weird to imagine that I'd beaten him to an opportunity. Henri didn't seem to like this narrative.

"I was insistent on designing for Alex Rivers," he corrected, "but felt a little displaced to be honest. He's such an icon, so ahead of his time, and sure his actions are unconventional, but I consider them avant-garde," he shrugged. "But even men like Alex Rivers can be bought. I knew I could have him, but I wasn't sure of the cost."

"He doesn't do things for money," I said, looking at the book in Henri's hands.

He appeared disappointed.

"He certainly does not. Can you guess what his price was?"

Right away, my name popped into my mind, but I'd never let that answer leave my lips.

"I don't know," I said, avoiding the possibility of ever sounding vain.

"I'm looking at it." He pointed the book right to my face.

"And he gave you my designs?"

"It would appear so, but make no mistake, Gemma, what I'm about to offer you stems only from a favor. I have promised Alex Rivers I'd give you a chance to work with me, in exchange for his time in the future… and I certainly plan on cashing that in *very* soon."

I tried to shrink myself, my toes curling from the sudden attention. I looked back at my designs, recalling the only moment that Alejandro had an opportunity to take them. I caught him sitting at my desk, the night we set off the fire alarm. He must have stolen them then, just for me, a complete surprise. But was this what I wanted? A favor?

"I don't want to be anyone's charity." I finally admitted, feeling unsure about the whole deal. It felt cheap, like there was nothing to earn.

"I don't do charity. I give opportunities. When a Miss Castillo dropped off your portfolio, I had my doubts about what I had agreed to, but I'm not too sure about that now." His weary mood flashed for a moment as he leaned into his chair, crossing one leg over the other. He seemed to be so confused by me, as if I were the first bite of a new meal, his pallet deciphering the flavors into either bitter or sweet. "You have talent, Gemma, but it's unharnessed. You need help, you need guidance, and I can provide that for you."

"I had no idea he did this for me," I said to myself.

"Well, I'm happy he did. And if that wasn't confirmation enough, then the approval from my design assistant sent it over the edge," he smashed out his cigarette flipping through the mail he brought. "Do you know a Miss Dana Myers?" he asked, the name completely shocking me.

"Dana?" I leaned across the desk, startling Dean. "As in *my* Dana from FIT?" I asked, stunned to hear the name of my old college best friend, my personal relationship coach from the night I told Parker I loved him. I immediately took a sip of my wine. "She's not even in New York anymore! I haven't heard from her in years." We lost touch after graduation, her trip around the world not starting with Paris, but the UK, working with Sarah Burton at the Alexander McQueen headquarters. Time and distance were never kind to us, but there was never any hard feelings, just warm regards.

"That's right. She's been in our Paris location for quite some time now. But I'm planning on relocating her back to New York… that is, of course, pending your agreement to what I'm about to ask." He made eyes at Dean, who nervously smiled. "Listen carefully, because I don't like repeating myself, and I certainly don't like asking twice—so I won't do either—but you have a chance to do something here. I'm working on a project, something outside of fall fashion week that you can be involved with."

"In what way?" I asked, nervous by how serious he looked at me.

He pointed his finger like I was a child, highlighting the importance of my attentiveness. "It's a chance to earn my endorsement, to get your feet wet with the crowd, designing and learning how to fix your mistakes. It's a paid position, full benefits and salary… mind you, you'll be spending lots of time here, working with me in this very building."

"The one you share with New York Prestige?" I thought of the obvious person I could run into if I accepted the offer. What would that look like? Sharing a space with the woman who hated me again, Camilla?

Henri reached for a small booklet, opening it up. "Don't answer just yet. I don't need impulsiveness, I need certainty. Take a few days and think about it," he ran his finger down the list of a page then looked at Dean. "Let's pencil in a future meeting, but get our front office to at least begin the paperwork for Gemma. That way if she decides to stay, we can move ahead, and quickly."

"I appreciate that," I replied, perplexed as to what I was offered. "This just feels like a really, *really* big deal. Even sitting here is odd in itself. And all you've seen are my drawings. Is this a good idea?"

Henri nodded slowly. "Maybe not, it's a risk, but that's how you get great rewards. Sure, it could go horribly wrong, but I've already accepted that, and you'll need to do the same. Besides, Alex Rivers clearly saw something in you… that must count for something," he assured.

"Ok," I nodded hesitantly. "I appreciate the time to consider this."

"Don't thank me yet. You still have to choose. We all get a little time in life to make our choices, but, at some point, a decision has to be made, and once we do, it can make all the difference in our world."

I agreed quietly, surprised by another chime of my phone. I looked down again, faced with an equal predicament that finally appeared.

"Is it the person you hoped to hear from?" Dean asked as I slowly faked a smile.

"I think it is…" I read the message on my screen.

ALEJANDRO

I'm here, good girl… I'm ready to talk.

The corner of Seventy-fourth Street and York Avenue was eerily quiet, it's pothole-riddled street acting as a divide between ancient brick buildings and newer—more refined—condo complexes. I double checked the address Alejandro sent me before getting out of the taxi because this location didn't seem right.

"*I miss you,*" he texted before giving me the address. I revisited the message again and reminded myself how hard this was going to be. Of course I wanted to say the same, but how could I? I wasn't just mad, I wasn't just frustrated, I was hurt. And what would I say anyways? *I miss you too, Alejandro,* but also, *goddamn you.*

I was completely unprepared to see him as I reached the dark entrance of what appeared to be an abandoned theatre. I imagined him waiting for me, brooding in the corner like some defiant usher, scowling and dark. But he wasn't. He wasn't even here yet, and the realization that I was alone somehow raised the anticipation of meeting him even more.

"Hello?" I called out, making my way into the poorly lit lobby, its old concession fixed with assorted candies and a glowing case of popcorn. I got no response, aside from the symphonic hums of "Pure

Imagination," that lulled with the cadence of a tin can from the speakers above.

Everything was dark, fitted with old red curtains and peeling gold pillars, its shadows like vacuums that could suck me in to the single hall that appeared below a sign that read, *The Guardian Theatre.*

I avoided it, ignoring its flickering incandescent bulbs as I studied a collage of fresh-faced teens that covered a wall for cast members. "Kevin David Taylor," I read one name tag to myself. "Age fifteen, enjoys singing, his pet iguana Lizzy, and playing Tevye from *Fiddler on the Roof.*" I smiled at his goofy grin, his unfixed bedhead stuck in the air as if posed from a storm.

Above him, written with brass letters, was a declaration, an honorable homage to those of great financial contributions. There was just a single name that hung below in a thin, silver plaque.

I knitted my brow, studying the photo attached to the name, feeling completely confused. I knew the person listed under the donations, or at least I thought I did. I only saw their face once, but it was so vivid, so burned in my memory from the emotions I tied to it, that I could never forget them. They had long black hair, lonely almond eyes, and a freckled nose, but it was their smile that caught my attention, distinctly crooked with a crease that pulled more on the left than it did on the right.

It was Natalie Brower, only it wasn't.

"Alma Marquez?" I read the silver plaque out loud.

"That's my mother," the unexpected response settled itself from across the room. I turned around to face

Alejandro, who stood by the hall—no smirk, no smile—looking just as frustrated as me. He stared at the plaque and then back down in my direction, his body wrapped in a green Henley and black jeans. "Hello, Gemma."

"Don't say my name like that," I warned, unappreciative of the gravitas he gave. I didn't want him just somber, I wanted him on his knees, righting the wrongs he committed.

He didn't like my response, his aggravation apparent with how he readjusted his strong jaw. "I say your name the only way I know how. With everything that it makes me feel."

"And how does it make you feel?" I asked. "Let's see if it compares to my experience. Does it feel like abandonment? Like the person you trusted just walked out of your life? No phone calls, no texts, no indication if you were safe or not. Nothing."

"I didn't just walk out," he argued.

"You did! And that's not all. You shut me out." I stared up at him, angry with each word I spoke. I hated that I sounded like this, that I was weak and needy, and as much as I was tempted by the urge to lunge forward, to allow myself to be engulfed by his size and strength, I resisted. My overly cautious tendencies were back again, agitated by the sight of the man who worked so hard to tear them down. Did he see that now?

"Don't be so stubborn. I couldn't stay there and look you in the eyes with everything going on. I owed you more than that, and I'd much rather have left to *fix* the problem than compromise us." Alejandro stepped closer, only inches from me now.

"Please," I laughed. "This was not about us."

"Is that what you think?"

"It's what I know," I snipped. "You left me!"

"No. I avoided the one thing that could hurt us, Gemma."

"And what's that? Your fragile ego?"

"My fucking lies," Alejandro peered down, unable to hide the effects that either I or his trip had. Whatever he'd been through, whatever he had to do, carried a taxing expression, his fang pinching his lip to the point where I thought he'd bleed. "I couldn't say what I needed to. I couldn't be the very thing I demanded from you, which was honesty… if I stayed, I would have continued to lie about everything. I didn't want that. I didn't want to give you anything less than what you deserved. This was never just about you or me, this was about us, and that's the uncomfortable truth."

"Not for me it isn't." I harshly corrected, no longer accepting excuses. "You don't get to tell me what I'm comfortable with."

"You're right. But I get to say when enough is enough. Any longer and the damage done would be irreversible. And maybe it already is, but I had to prepare for *so much* just to have this moment with you. Gemma, I had to do things. I had to clean a mess that not even Lina knows about." Alejandro stood asserted, his manner far more telling and convincing than his own words.

A strand of hair fell loose as I shook my head, and while Alejandro attempted to brush it back, I stepped away, refusing him.

"Don't touch me."

"Please don't say that."

"Then don't do it again. I'm not sure if I should even be here." I whispered to myself, searching his face for an answer, before turning away.

"Here? You're right, you shouldn't be. Where you are is because of me, emotionally, mentally. I challenged you to be honest… living vicariously through the idea that someone—people like you and I—could actually be free from our past. I always thought you weren't ready for what I had to say, and I thought I could mold you into the person I knew you were inside—someone who could accept me unlike anyone else ever had. But now I may have been wrong. Maybe it was something we needed to do together, not one person at a time. You just wanted to show me how much you cared, and I let you down."

My shoulders dropped as I shut my eyes.

"That's all I wanted, Alejandro," I muttered. "I just wanted that chance to be there for you… and you robbed it from me."

"I know. I fucked up. I fixed what I had to, and I knew it had a cost. But now, I'm afraid I broke something else in the process. *You*," he confessed. "If I'm going to make this right, then it starts with honesty. It starts with meeting the expectations I had for you. I can be honest, Gemma. I can be open."

I looked away, uncomfortable with the idea of forgiving him so quickly. Why was he so difficult to read? Admittedly, it was impossible to tell if he was acting and that was hard to ignore, especially since we were in a theatre.

"If you're so willing to be open, then tell me right now… where have you been?" I finally asked, expecting the truth.

Alejandro took a deep breath, indulging in a pause I knew he needed. "I've been in L.A. I had to meet with Lina and my agent to develop strategies for when my father went live on T.V. My whole team and I have been on damage control, in the talks with press to combat the things he said, which you need to know, first and foremost, are completely untrue… Lina wants me to file a suit for defamation, but it's not worth the trouble anymore."

"Anymore?" I asked, his admission sounding nefarious.

His face remained stern.

"He's safe, Gemma," he assured, as if my suspicion became too much. "He just wanted to tear me down. He got that. He has everything he ever wanted now, and in return, I have his silence." I could see the tension in his broad shoulders relax, lowered in the admission that clearly made him uncomfortable to discuss. "He's back home. He won't bother us."

"It was never him who could bother us, Alejandro. It was our inability to trust one another that was the problem, always has been. I wish you let me help."

Alejandro shook his head.

"Letting you help meant bringing you into Miguel's world, and it'd be far too triggering for us. I know how you feel about thunderstorms, Gemma. They're frightening, they're loud, they're everything that makes you want to hide away. Miguel is my thunderstorm, and as much as I wanted you there, I'd never let that man have access to the only light in my dark life." Alejandro stared down at my feet, the tips of my heels meeting his boots.

"Your past is a part of you…" I replied, "but it doesn't define you." I placed my finger under his chin and raised his eyes towards mine. I knew it would be hard for him, but I had to ask the question, I needed to know how honest he was willing to be. This was his chance, his opportunity to show me the best he could, not through one of his explosive reactions, but through his words. "Alejandro, why did your father say those things about you… what happened?"

He looked past me, his firm grip reaching beside my shoulder. My back pressed against the wall as I looked up, watching as his thumb ran across the silver plaque with his mother's name.

"It starts with her…" he answered, "*Alma Marquez.*"

I looked back up at the photo, at the face I knew I'd seen before. "I've seen her…" I admitted, "she looks just like—"

"Natalie," he agreed. "I know…" He opened his palm to me, an invitation to take a chance and follow his lead. Hesitantly I accepted, placing my hand into his as he slowly, carefully, began to lead me into the dark hall that I originally avoided. "That's why we're here, to tell you about my past. About how it led up to everything I ever did. About Natalie…"

I hated to admit it, but once Alejandro laced his fingers with mine, I felt safe again. He was willing to show me his truth, his tenderness as gentle and as calm as his melancholy eyes.

"At your mother's house, you had asked me if I was ever afraid of becoming something that I couldn't control. Do you remember that?" With his free hand, he slowly pulled back the thick crimson curtain, guiding me inside.

"I do…" I reluctantly rested my head along his bicep, having no sense of direction as we took the first step to a set of stairs. Was this his Met, a culmination of dark halls, leading to the equivalent of my Latchkey Rose, a painting I showed him that represented all my grief? I was so scared and vulnerable then, and now, somehow, it started to feel the same for Alejandro.

"Similar to you, I never wanted to become the same dark cloud I grew up with. I feared it, still do," he said as we ascended, hearing the distant laughter of children. A new light took shape at the peak where we climbed, its glow split by another curtain. "For me, this was my father. His disease, his pain, was something less hereditary, but bred in a home that I hated more than anything in the world."

"His disease?" I asked, his nodding head assuring me with the faintest of outlines.

"Being with him, thinking of him, was always like walking in the dark. I'd already felt completely shut out, as if I didn't exist at all, or worse, like I only existed for him to despise." We took our final step as he pulled the curtain aside. "But not Alma, she was my light."

A cast of theatre lanterns revealed a hidden amphitheater, whose size was far larger than the tiny lobby would suggest. We were in the balcony, staring down towards a wooden stage, its dilapidated charm painted with Greek gods and olive branch wallpaper. Below were a few excited children, their chatter shushed by parents who attempted to corral their belongings.

"I never wanted to be someone else," Alejandro said, sinking into a foldable, velvet seat. "Well, not at first. One thing just led to another. It just made sense. Acting came easy to me, because I always pretended to be something I wasn't as a child."

"We've all done that at some point." I replied, but it didn't seem to resonate.

"Do you know what it's like to be eight years old and have the whole world see you as powerless?" he asked. "It's such a hopeless and little feeling to have, thinking nothing can save you from it, and for the longest time that's true, but then, suddenly you're someone else, like St. George on a stage wielding a sword. In that moment you have power, you have purpose, you have safety; safety in a way that real life could never provide, because in a play you already know how the story ends. You get to save the princess; you get to defeat the monster that terrorized your life, and the lives of those around you. And in turn you are praised, because you're not just a kid, you're someone else, someone better, a person who can do the things you never could before. That's an intoxicating type of attention, because it only reinforced the delusion that it was better than being me," he said. "Truthfully, acting wasn't a dream of mine, it was just the beginning of a long line of distractions and, in many ways, a means for survival."

"I knew you didn't like acting anymore… but I never could have guessed that—"

"That acting was just me running away again?" He laughed to himself, his broken smile as white as it was dismayed. "Like I always do when things get tough? Like I did with you? It's no secret that I can't bear the responsibility of anything that goes wrong. I have fought to avoid the consequences of my actions for as long as I could, because being blamed for everything wrong was always my purpose with Miguel."

Alejandro wrung his silver band around his finger, displaying a new tick of nervousness I hadn't seen before. Normally he would have pulled out a cigarette, cooling his poise with a long, sweet drag, but since he didn't, I reached out and calmed his hand with mine. He wasn't just quiet, he was contemplative, choosing each word carefully.

"I've never talked about this…" he said, leaning into my hair. "I don't do this, Gemma. I don't ask for help. I don't share this side with anyone."

"I know." I eased in, showing the relatable branch of circumstance that somehow bonded us together. It was sad, it was tragic, but it was ours. "Living with pain is like carrying a piece of broken glass. I know this, because I carry one too, but no matter how similar they may be, no two pieces are ever really the same."

"It doesn't feel good," he added quietly. "It's hard to share when you think someone won't understand that what's inside is too unique to be told."

"Yes. It's scary and real. And how others define bravery is just an illusion. You don't need to open up in order to be brave, because your willingness to try is already enough. I admire it because it's something I still struggle to do."

"But you have… I've seen it. You were vulnerable when I asked you to be, and I'm not sure how to do the same. I don't know how to start."

"Start anywhere. This is your story, Alejandro, and for once, you can tell it how you want."

The children below laughed again. We watched for a moment, shielded in the shadows, hidden in the darkness where we seemed to find our strength.

I shut my eyes, trying to imagine the world that Alejandro wanted to share, whose roots and weight could pull him back into a familiar, sticky, black dream.

"The moment I realized I existed—my first memory ever—came in the middle of an ordinary night," he hesitated, letting out a collected sigh. "It was strange. Before that moment it was just darkness, and then suddenly, it was like I was plugged in. I opened my eyes, and I knew *just* enough about where I was to be instantly afraid. Maybe I was two, a little older? I suppose I liked cowboys, because I had them on my pajamas, both knowing this and realizing it all at once, waking up alone, as my mother screamed for her life."

Alejandro stared straight ahead, ignoring how attentively I watched as he rubbed his thighs. I knew what nightmares were made of, but what he said next scared me the most.

"I could never forget it. I'll hear that noise in my head till the day I die. The scream. The spit. The sound of a wet sob. It's not like anything you can imagine, until you hear it for yourself, and when you do, the only thing you can possibly assume is that someone is being killed. That was my first thought, my first memory, that my mother—whoever she was, wherever she was—was going to die. Then, it all happened so fast, as if I had no control over my body, running into the kitchen, stopping near the hall. I was too young to see it, but I don't think I could ever be old enough either—watching my mother on the floor, motionless, begging a man to stop. I couldn't even stare as she shook her head at me, because all I saw and all I heard was Miguel, and his voice, Gemma, *his fucking* voice scared me, but not as much as the sound of his fist against her cheek. He was just hitting her, over and over again; and it's not like how it is in the movies. It sounds heavy, like a bat beating against a bag of sand—dull and wet—her stomach large, filled with what I knew was my baby brother inside. I wasn't supposed to be there, and I certainly wasn't supposed to get sick, to vomit on myself, to have Miguel notice me and yank me by the jaw..." Alejandro motioned with his hand, hooking his thumb and finger into a vice. "He pulled me to my mother, and you know what he said?"

I couldn't even nod as I clung to Alejandro's arm, stopping myself from sliding into my chair. I was terrified, witnessing the moment as if I was there by his side; little and afraid. I shook my head against him.

"That it was my fault. I was the fucking reason my own mother had welts on her eyes and cheeks. He dared me not to cry, and warned, if I did, he'd hit her harder. So I held it in, my breath included. And why? Was it because he came home drunk? Because he was an abusive monster who deserved to die? Yes, but what the fuck does that even mean or matter, because in reality he didn't like being told what to do or that he was the problem. It was all because of me. I stopped him from being loud; I spoke when I wasn't supposed to; I left the lights on, or the juice out, I played with my toys too excitedly, or stayed up too late. Alma would try and stop him from hitting me, not that it always worked. But he would hurt her—not because he was a piece of shit, not because he was a drunk—but because of *me.*"

"Alejandro…" my words got caught in a disbelief that I couldn't express, losing any possible way to make him feel better.

"I shouldn't be telling you this."

"Why not? These are your experiences—"

"But you're a survivor too, Gemma. It's not fair to talk about this… to bring you back here. It can't feel good. It's one of the reasons I couldn't let you in."

"Don't worry about me," I pleaded.

"I'm not worried, I'm just cautious. I wanted so badly for it to be over with, to avoid how it used to make me feel. I suppose once he got on T.V., once he said what he said… I worried you'd be next to believe it because I certainly did."

"It's ok. I know things are complicated, I know things are—"

"Muddied?" Alejandro cut me off. "The truth is less about what happened and more about how I feel. And trust me, I have felt the effects of Miguel for *so* long, that it's all I know… and now, all I can do is fight to remember how it used to be with Alma," he remained focused.

Regardless of how endearing the memories of his mother may have been, he seemed to have been immune to their effects, as if any smile reserved had already been used.

"And what was that like?" I begged for some light in his life, some soothing side that could ease his expression, but it didn't.

"There was never a moment I wanted to leave her side. She's the reason we're here today." He looked up, admiring the chipped paint of the old domed theatre. "I would help her any chance I got. Joining her in the fields at work, picking onions, potatoes, but my favorite was always the cherries. It's the only good memory I have, a time where my brother and I would be outside… away from Miguel, in the rare moments where I could pretend to be anyone else, as long as it wasn't me. Assuming an identity was kind of my thing, much more important than you may even know."

"You did it to keep yourself safe. You were just a kid."

"That's what my mother said too. She always

insisted I was too creative, too vivid in my imagination to be in the fields. That's why she took me to St. Andrews, and asked if I could join the parish so that I could be part of their plays. I hated it."

"Didn't it help though?"

"No, it was just another secret to hide from Miguel, her tithing what little she had to the makeshift acting school the church provided. And why would I really want to be there, participating in a place where people prayed to a god that I felt never existed? The priest always said *he* worked in mysterious ways, but watch your mother get hit enough times, and things start to feel less mysterious. It's fucking negligence. But despite all that shit, I did as I was told, I played the parts I was given, and slowly I got good at them. Any time my mother came to see me, she would smile from the crowd. That's what I held onto, and that's what I believed in… and from there, the dream was born."

"To be an actor?" I asked innocently.

"No. To be someone different… to pursue the only distraction that could keep me alive. My dreams aren't like yours, Gemma. They aren't aspirations. A dream to me is literal, like when you fall asleep and lose touch with reality. That's what I was seeking. But like I asked long ago, what is the cost to chase a dream?"

The warning was less for my future and more of a bleak reality he faced. He was telling me the best way he could, the only way he could. "It costs a life."

"And not just your own sometimes," he added. "The plays, the acting, my involvement in the parish, it was all an attempt to give me some normalcy, and Miguel knew nothing about it… until he found a playbill with my name casted inside." The cold drop in his voice was met with the turn of his cheek. I knew he didn't want to say whatever was on the tip of his tongue, so I waited.

"I'm so sorry," I whispered, knowing his unfinished sentence was darker left unsaid than it was complete. I couldn't imagine what happened after Miguel found out.

"Me too. Sorry to you, to my mother… to my brother who I tried to protect. To the boy who stood in the kitchen with vomit on his cowboy pajamas, the one who needed to escape, but ended up causing more harm than good."

"You did what you could."

"But it cost me everything. Gemma, I showed a need to escape, and my mother saw that, refusing to let me work with her. That meant keeping the secret, sneaking me every day to the parish, driving me back and forth to do so. And she did it, never complaining because that's how much she cared." Alejandro hunched into his seat, leaning over to his knees so that he could look onto the floor. He spoke to his boots, faltering between words. "She continued to take me to class, to work the cherry fields, and every day she'd pick me up. No matter what. Until—"

The last family from the stage left the building, exiting through a loud steel door. It slammed with an echo, sending the amphitheater into a strange new silence. We were completely secluded with the implications of what Alejandro didn't say.

"There was an accident…" he mustered inaudibly, the image of what he'd seen that day visible only as his sharpened cheekbones hardened, restrained from tears, as he started to blink. "It was raining, and she still went to work; she still took me to the church. And had I been there with her, working in the fields, not living some fantasy, she wouldn't have had to come pick me up. She wouldn't have been driving on that fucking road… *for me.*"

I turned closer to his body, offering the condolence of my head along his shoulder. Though his eyes glossed over with the most vivid red I'd ever seen, he didn't cry. He stopped himself, an impulsive control that may still have been there from when his father refrained him from ever doing so. I wasn't as strong.

"Miguel blames me. He thinks I killed her, because of my dream… because of the sacrifices she made for me… and I guess that's true. If it weren't for me, she would still be—"

"Stop…" I cooed sweetly, unable to bear the thought of the blame he placed on himself. "You did nothing wrong. What happened wasn't your fault, and don't you ever believe what he told you. That's the *disease* he wants you to have." I said, realizing how similar we were. Despite the avoidance we gave to the past—not wanting to become the things we feared—we still somehow got caught.

I fought so hard to avoid the memories of growing up alone with Claire in a house I hated being in. I was too young to hear the things she said, the paranoia and fear she instilled in my little head. I had neither the tools nor the power as a child to manage that life, to navigate her depression. It changed me; it scared me; and ever since then, I lacked the ability to differentiate her disorder from the trauma I experienced as a child. I knew it wasn't her fault, but the impression still burned in my mind: the long nights of screaming, the weeping, forcing her to eat, to cook and clean, the dread I had of falling asleep, of making sure my door was locked. It was everything I hated, stemming from a single night that my father left, the moment my life changed forever.

"Your mother saw a talent in you that the whole world now gets to see. She instilled your desire to help others, to be better. Don't let one person blame you for what your mother fought so hard to protect you from. She had nothing but pride and love for you, I just know it."

"Or shame," he argued. "There's nothing to be proud of when my life is *spent* clearing my name, settling in court, reinforcing a reputation of getting others hurt... it happens because of me, and it's expected regardless of how it happens. But every year is another theatre, another quiet place for the youth, an opportunity to help. I donate to them, but never under my name, only my mother's, letting her do for others what she had done for me, to make dreams come true for those less privileged. But I have to do better."

"And you're trying," I argued back. "I know you are."

"It's not good enough. You were wrong about the disease my father gave me. It's not the self-hatred that I can't stand... it's the anger." A line along Alejandro's cheek wrinkled into a scowl. "Whatever rage he had, whatever *fucked* up loss of control he had, I also have.

Gemma, I can't stop myself. When I see someone get hurt, when I see a woman, *any* woman, abused or mistreated, it makes me sick. I see fucking red, and I can't control myself."

"You're just trying to help…" I scrambled for words. "We can find a way for you to control it."

"That's the thing, I'm not sure that I can. I try to counter the bad I've caused with these acts of charity. You know it's not just theaters I give money to, it's places like Belmont Hills, as well."

My breath stilled at the mention of Belmont Hills. So much had circled around one place, around one person. I didn't know how to respond. Alejandro grew quiet, his final words an uncomfortable admission.

"I hate Miguel, I hate what I've become and how people I love have been hurt. I went to Belmont Hills to try and make things accessible to women who couldn't afford that type of protection, protection I couldn't provide my own mother." He looked at me, folding his hands together. "That's where I met Natalie… That's where this lawsuit began."

Chapter 38

ALEJANDRO

9 months earlier

"Stop it, Alejandro," Ivanna said my name with a warning. "You know you can't smoke here."

"Give me more credit," I pinched the tip of my cigarette, lifting it to my nose. I just needed the scent in order to feel calm, inhaling it one last time before tucking it into the front pocket of my jacket. "I need a break soon."

"What, too much walking?"

"Too much talking," I answered, following Mrs. Patricia Blair, the director of finance services at Belmont Hills.

"We've already met our fourth quarter goals, thanks to you, Mr. Rivers." She announced in the middle of her tour, guiding us along lush green fields and graveled stone paths. She pointed to two large oak trees; their bases affixed with two new benches. "We just added those with some of the funds."

"Those are pretty!" Ivanna chimed in, but I just stared, contemplative to the sereneness that provided little reassurance to how I felt. Nervous.

It was wrong for me to be here—a *man* at a sanctuary for women to feel safe. I tipped my Dodgers cap down, as if that and my dark aviators would somehow make me, the tall, broad man, less menacing.

"How else have the funds been applied?" I interrupted.

"We're adding a new meditation pond in the southeast corner of the complex, additional trees for ambiance—"

"How about for guests?" I clarified.

"The patients?"

"The women. The reason this place exists." I looked around the tunneled path of maple trees and carefully manicured lawns. Everything was shadowed but accented with perfect patches of sunlight. Sure, it was all so peaceful, but I knew that wasn't enough to help. "My assistant provided me with the statistics sheet of your admits. It feels a little low, based on the demand."

"We try to accommodate as many people as we can."

"As many rich people," I corrected, identifying the luxury escape this place portrayed.

"Sure, costs are high. I'll be the first to admit that. We're a non-profit organization, but our therapy involves the complete immersion of a *particular* environment."

"That's nice. But my donations are for those who cannot afford this place. I want it to be more accessible to them."

"We want that, too," Mrs. Blair agreed nervously, "and believe me, your funds are in use for those patients now."

"Good, because Belmont Hills isn't the only

benefactor of my charity, but it certainly has my attention. I think we can agree that access to help isn't a privilege, but a human right. Can't we, Mrs. Blair?" I asked, making my stance clear that landscape was the least of my priorities. She smiled at me, its impression weakened by my otherwise stern voice. I didn't mean to sound so curt, attempting to hide my typical frown.

"Of course, Mr. Rivers. Our goal for the coming year involves the expansion of our grounds. That includes increased housing and caretakers. We hope to meet that financial goal and eliminate any costs for our guests. We're serious about this, and I hope you can trust me." She nodded firmly, treating me with all the respective assurances of a board member. I didn't need that, I just needed to know my contributions would make a direct impact.

"Happy to hear," I answered, looking back at the grounds.

Ivanna hung back as Mrs. Blair continued her lecture on the therapeutic qualities that nature provided. "You could be a little more kind," she complained.

"I am. I just need a cigarette."

"I figured you'd appreciate this visit. I know how much charity matters to you. *This* especially." She murmured as if this was the context of our visit. It wasn't, and being in New York was less about helping and more about entertaining an annoyance.

"That's not why we're here," I groaned.

"No. But I knew it would entice you to come out. The producer has been very adamant about this project."

"I have enough projects."

"The agave fields?" she asked in a way as if I were silly for even alluding to it. "You're an actor, Alejandro. Let's get you acting."

"I'm whatever I need to be."

Ivanna knew very little about why I did the things I did, but she was intuitive enough to know that I was almost too focused on much needed distractions. Maybe she was concerned, maybe she knew that I was slowly escaping away into something that took a toll on my body, considering the fields weren't as forgiving as the comforts of a multi-million-dollar movie set.

"You spend too much time in Jalisco. Your knuckles are ruined from the field work, I can't imagine the rest of you."

"I'm used to it. It's what I enjoy," I reminded her, reminiscing on the only thing that brought me pleasure outside of cherry-flavored cigarettes. In the fields I was too burdened with labor to think about how awful it felt to have accomplished nothing—at least nothing of importance to me. I didn't want to buy park benches or fountains. I wanted to help, to right the wrongs I couldn't as a child, and for whatever reason, that feeling never went away. Ivanna could never know that though, she could never know about me or my past; about my mother, my brother; about Miguel. I rubbed the back of my neck, my boots thumping loudly along the graveled path.

"I just think it would be good to divide your focus. I know the movie is only in preproduction right now, but there are things you need to consider. The director loves you and just wants to do lunch. You read the script, didn't you?" she asked, and I nodded. "Well, it's good, right?"

"It's the same thing I've already done before," I said, unimpressed with another senseless film with explosions and violence. I couldn't even recall the name.

"It's the same thing that people love you for. The director is going to want to persuade you, and—*once* he does—we'll need to get the ball rolling. I've scheduled us to look at apartments this evening in case you say yes." She smiled, pulling her phone out to confirm a list of potential places. "That sounds fun, right?"

I shrugged, unwilling to give her a final answer. I had no plans on doing lunch, nor did I plan on staying in New York. Ivanna didn't even know I had already rescheduled our flight back home after this tour.

"You really are a great help to us, Mr. Rivers." Mrs. Blair addressed me once again, stopping near the front entrance of the massive home where everyone stayed. "We're really wanting to highlight the importance of donations and bring awareness to the needs of others." She looked over at Ivanna, her eyes seeking some preemptive permission, "We were hoping to grab a few photos… you know, something to show at our next charity event." She fidgeted as Ivanna looked at me, watching as I massaged the front pocket of my leather jacket. She knew I was anxious to leave.

"I'm sorry, I'm not too sure if we—" Ivanna began to apologize, but I stopped her, not wanting to hurt the chance that my appearance could raise more awareness and donations.

"I actually have to make a phone call," I lied, being unintentionally stern. I wasn't trying to be rude, I just needed a second to myself. "Ivanna... why don't you follow Mrs. Blair inside. I want you to inquire further about their expansion project. Let's make it happen for them. No matter the cost. I'll take the photos. Just give me fifteen minutes, and I'm yours." Mrs. Blair could barely contain her smile.

"I don't know what to say, Mr. Rivers. Thank you." She reached out to shake my hand, hugging a clipboard to her chest. I turned to leave, but she wasn't done yet. "Oh! Take your call in the garden around the corner. The dedication you gave us is placed there. Mind you, it's temporary; the official sundial, that will replace it, isn't in yet." She looped her arm around Ivanna's as she guided her back into the house.

Finally, I was greeted with silence I hadn't had since boarding the plane. This reassured me that I wasn't meant for New York. There was no place to think, to be alone, to redirect my focus onto something as enjoyable as a sweltering field. I would only take a few photos, then I'd leave for good.

I turned the corner of the covered porch, making my way down the steps towards a newly installed picketed fence. Behind it were rows of purple and blue flowers, their colors crowned amongst thick green leaves and tiny dots of bundled white petals. I stepped closer, fishing out my cigarette, placing it between my lips. I took a moment to appreciate what they did with the space. It was all new and alive, defiant to the emerging crimson leaves that sat in the trees above. I lit my cigarette, snapping the lighter shut with a click, sucking in its sweet cherry taste.

The tremor in my hand seemed to calm itself, my eye catching the small paper sign taped to the fence.

Jardín para las Almas Buenas: Garden for Good Souls.

The play on the word *Alma* was a secret in my heart that I never wanted to share. I bent over to test the soil, measuring its brittle crumbs between the pressure of my fingers. "A garden for *good souls,*" I laughed, committing myself to never step inside. That wasn't for me, that was only for the worthy, for people like—

I stopped everything I was doing, immediately paralyzed from who I saw.

"Hello?" The smallest of voices came out from the garden, its invitation laced with a cautiousness that startled me into a cold sweat. I couldn't even finish my thought, the very person I was thinking of stood up from the garden. It was her. Alma. My mother.

"Shit." I blinked, my cigarette falling from my lips. As foolish as I felt, I immediately thought she was a ghost, or maybe an angel, something far beyond what I actually ever believed in. But it was true, it was her. Dark, long hair, freckled nose, and dimpled cheeks. Everything about her was the same as Alma, but nothing more so than her eyes. Lost. Distant. Weary from a lifetime of experiences that only I and others of this unique circumstances could understand. "I'm so sorry." I stood up quickly, my previously settled anxiety once again on fire.

"No, I'm the one that's sorry. No one's allowed to be in here yet." She combed her hair out from her face, looking far younger than me, younger than what I remembered my mother even being. I stepped on the cigarette, extinguishing it.

"Please. You don't need to be sorry. This is your space. I shouldn't even be here." I became uncomfortably aware of myself, tugging on my leather jacket to cover my tattoos, as if being a man in a place like this wasn't intimidating enough. "I'll leave."

"No. It's ok." She stopped me, filling me with a strange sense of conflict. I wanted to go, but I wanted to stay. I just knew it was wrong.

"I'm trying to be respectful." I cleared my throat.

"Mrs. Blair seems to trust you," she said, almost soothing me with a courtesy she didn't need to extend. I turned to face her as she got closer, making her way through the garden. "I knew there'd be a tour today. I saw you guys standing on the porch."

"We won't be much longer. We just finished up, and I needed a moment to myself, so I snuck away."

"No better place to be than the garden." She smiled, lifting a small book in her hand with a shrug. I tried not to stare, but I allowed too much time to pass, that it bordered on awkward.

She turned away.

"What are you reading?"

She looked down at the book, her eyes shut with embarrassment, "*Define a Daffodil*," she held it up. "A book on flowers and their meanings."

"Do you garden?"

"Not before. I mean… sorta now. It's just peaceful. It

keeps my mind busy." She edged herself closer, approaching the entrance I refused to cross.

"I get that."

"Do you garden, too?"

"In a way." I offered a gentle smile, my appearance still unintentionally hidden with a pair of shades and a ball cap. I couldn't tell if she knew who I was or not, and I preferred to keep it that way. "My mother was a field worker. I helped her pick fruit and vegetables growing up."

"And now?" she asked.

"More or less. I work with agave, but it's less forgiving." I massaged my hands, their bruised, red hue still in the midst of healing.

She looked at them and pouted, "You should try flowers then; they're less painful."

"Not really my thing."

"Somehow I doubt that. I can tell you're a flower fan."

"How?"

"You looked stressed on the porch, but not so much anymore."

"Maybe it was just my cigarette," I pushed back the bridge of my sunglasses.

"Maybe you just need some convincing." She laughed so sweetly, so tenderly, her giggle similar to Alma's with a rasp. I never wanted her to stop talking.

"What flower do you recommend?" I took a step closer. "Asking as a beginner looking to be convinced."

She took a moment to survey the space, taking my question to heart. She ran her hands around their assorted colors, plucking a single stem of tiny white flowers.

"It might not be what you were looking for. But maybe it's what you need," she answered, handing me the flower. She reached out, extending her arm in a way that allowed me to observe the scarred lines that ran the inside of her elbow. She was an addict, her track marks healing like long, pink constellations. If she was here, then it was for a reason that already disturbed me. What the fuck had she been through, and who the hell had been there for her? My stomach burned again with an ache that I could never get rid of, her sentiment sticking in my head. *It might not be what I was looking for, but what I need.*

"And what is this?" I raised it to my nose.

"Sweet Alyssum." She looked down towards my boots, her shyness more contagious than I expected.

"What does it mean?"

"Calm energies… or at least, that's what the book says."

Calm energies; it was such a contrast to my intrusive thoughts. I knew I could end the conversation here, I could turn and walk away and forget this moment. But that opportunity passed as soon as I realized it, my mind made up, dedicated to the possibility that I could be redeemed. It felt wrong, it felt deceitful, but this woman, this face, felt like a second chance at saving Alma. I wanted to hug her, to tell her how sorry I was, that I wasn't big or strong enough to help before, but now I was.

"Calm energies are just what I need."

"Have I convinced you?"

"You have." I smiled.

She squinted from the bright sun, her face creased, and her brow glistened with sweat.

"It's not safe to be in the sun unprotected," I said, lifting my hand to remove my Dodgers cap.

She flinched.

Her face instantly caught in the sudden terror of my raised hand. Fuck. Clearly, I triggered something in her, some lifesaving reaction to block me. This wasn't a coincidence, this was her life, something she had grown used to. Someone had hurt her, and that made me want to kill whoever was responsible.

"I'm sorry... I—" I stammered, my words both apologetic, and upset at what I'd done.

"No, I'm sorry. I overreacted." She shook her head when she didn't need to. I twisted the cap in my hand, staring down at it in a moment of brief thought.

"May I?" I asked, slowly lifting the cap up. She lowered her head as I placed it on her, securing a shadow that protected her from the sun. "Please know you don't have to apologize. It's not an overreaction... it's not something to be ashamed about. It's up to me to be careful, not for you to excuse my actions."

"Thanks..." she squeezed the brim of the cap, testing its sturdiness. It was far too big for her head, but it helped, and her fear soon turned into a smile. "I can't just accept this, you know."

"Sure you can. I insist."

"If you insist, then I insist, too." She handed me her

book, the small, worn cover peeling at the edge; it was well loved.

"I can't." I shook my head.

"Nonsense. You can, and you will. It's not every day you turn a big man into a flower lover. Plus, it'd make me happy."

Make her happy? I'd do anything to help, anything to make her smile and feel better. My intention felt strange, knowing she wasn't my mother, but wanting it so badly to be true that I made myself accept it. She was just like Alma, and just like Alma, she deserved the life she never got.

"If it makes you happy," I said, flipping the pages, accepting the brief moment of silence that overtook our conversation. I knew what I had to do. "What's your name?" I asked, desperate to make her unique, to believe she wasn't really my mother.

"Natalie." She reached out, her open palm ready for a shake, "Natalie Brower." I placed my hand in hers, its size consumed within mine. "And you?"

"Alex! We're ready for photos," Ivanna shouted from the porch, startling both Natalie and me to turn and look. She laughed, seemingly puzzled by a sudden realization.

"Alex?" she asked, hinting with a surprise of who I might actually be.

"Rivers…" I added. "Alex Rivers." I released her hand, capturing the smile that reminded me of the only good moments I had as a kid. This wouldn't be the last time I made her smile or the end of us. I'd help her, I'd make sure she had more than Belmont Hills. "See you later, Natalie."

I turned and made my way to Ivanna who arched a brow.

"Mingling is not the best idea," she cautioned as we walked along the porch towards Mrs. Blair and a man with a camera.

"I was cautious and considerate. Besides, she's safe from the sun now." I tucked the book she gave me into the lined pocket of my jacket. "You were mentioning apartments. Which ones did you have in mind?"

Ivanna grinned, feeling as if she had succeeded in some masterplan to get me to stay. She pulled open her phone, giving it a long swipe. "The first is actually a hotel. They expressed interest in hosting you."

"Hotel?"

"A penthouse."

"What's it called?" I faked a smile for the cameraman who began to wave as we approached.

"The Pierre Hotel. *Super* famous. *Very* posh."

I shrugged at the suggestion, not really caring where I'd stay.

"Give them the green light," I answered. "And tell the director I've already made up my mind. We're staying in New York."

Chapter 39

GEMMA

"Once I saw Natalie, I knew I *had* to help her… and whether she wanted it or not, I was going to keep her away from the one guy who could hurt her."

"From Michael Brower?" I asked as Alejandro shot a surprised look. I knew he wanted to ask me about that name, about how I knew it, but the pieces had already clicked together. The only likely reason was Parker, and I could see that realization on Alejandro's face as he slowly started to nod.

"She kept his name from me, probably for the best. You have to understand, I didn't know much about Natalie at the time. She was guarded like us, but I knew she had addictions and that her husband was an enabler. Regardless, after she left Belmont Hills, I did the one thing I probably shouldn't have…"

Alejandro licked his lips, soothing them.

"Is it what caused the lawsuit?" I asked.

"Not directly, but it was the beginning of it… the tipping point. I made a deal with her…"

"A deal? What could you have possibly wanted?"

"Everything I couldn't give my mother…" He answered quietly, the faintest hint of regret choking in the back of his throat. It wasn't just an honest feeling, it was an honest reaction, and I felt it in my heart, knowing that behind the leather, behind the grimace and scruff, was a broken boy. He clenched his teeth, annoyed with the vulnerability that he wiped from his eyes. "She promised to never see Michael again… and yeah that was nice, but I needed guarantees. That meant keeping her close by, that meant taking responsibility for her safety… which was why I *insisted* she live with me at The Pierre Hotel, agreeing to give her a safe place to stay so long as she stayed away from him."

"That couldn't have been an easy decision to make…"

"It was the only right one."

"But since she came from Belmont Hills, it meant she was better, right?"

"You don't leave treatment better… you leave more equipped. I know these things are difficult to navigate, and maybe I bit off more than I could chew. My own father was an addict, a drunk, but he never tried to get better. I never knew what it was like being around someone in recovery…but I did know what it was like being around a woman who was abused."

"It's not a trauma you can fix… it's something you survive." I muttered—mainly to myself—resonating on the silence that followed. It was the very statement I believed since living with Claire. I wondered if he could hear the hesitancy in my voice as I guarded it.

He tried not to pout.

"Survival wears many faces, and often it's not the one you expect. What we show people, and how we feel, can be two different worlds, and Natalie's was no different… she was just better at hiding it."

"Better than you?"

"In every way," he nodded. "She made it all so simple; so natural to get along, to appear so open, and in many ways she was. Without ever needing to, she shared so much about her story—about Michael—about the things I could never forget, *things* she still had nightmares over. Telling me this only strengthened my belief that taking her in was the right thing to do, and honestly, I trusted her alone…I trusted her with everything. It didn't matter that I was gone most of the time, or that I worked weird hours… because I believed things were ok. But that was Natalie. Instead of ever asking for help, she showed me some performance of strength. I can't believe how naive I was, to ever think that what we had was good."

"Was it ever?"

"Selfishly maybe?"

"I'm sure you were just trying to help." I said, seeing the blame take over his face. He never looked so uncomfortable, my assurance almost impenetrable to his dropped eyebrows.

"It was good, because I believed it was good, because I believed that just keeping her away from Michael was enough. And why would I ever think otherwise? The first couple months were great—easy even. She was eating better, sleeping well, lecturing me on the importance of waking up early, trying in her own way to make me into the morning person that she was."

"You? A morning person?" I gently joked,

attempting to see a grin on his face. He twisted his lips, showing some shyness that I wasn't accustomed to.

"It wasn't so bad," he answered. "And even though I teased her about it, I secretly appreciated what she did; how open she became, how she confided in me. Most days she'd talked endlessly, more than I ever knew someone could. I'm a listener though, so it didn't bother me."

"I've always appreciated that about you."

"If only it were as useful as it sounds."

"It is… it's important. It's what everyone wants."

"But it's not what everyone needs. I'm good at listening to others, but I'm even better at reading the signs when something's wrong…at least I thought so. Who even knows anymore? I couldn't even tell what was happening under my own roof. I never could have guessed it…"

"Guessed what?" I asked, Alejandro's voice laced in disgust. His knuckles cracked.

"It's just… the morning she left me, everything was different. No smile, no endless talking, no fucking spark-in-the-air that she always brought into the room; the same spark I grew so hopelessly addicted to… She wouldn't even eat breakfast, let alone look me in the eye." He looked at me for some validation, "You know how perceptive I can be, not that she wasn't obvious enough…"

I nodded. "Perception is what you do best."

He didn't seem to like my response.

"What I do best is ruin a good thing; ignoring—against my better judgment—what I should've done. I shouldn't have pried, I shouldn't have left her alone while filming some senseless movie, but most of all, I shouldn't have overreacted when—that very morning—she got sick and threw up… because it was my job to show her how safe living with me could be… not scary, not scolding, not all the things I did when she came out of the bathroom… *pregnancy* test in hand, tears in her eyes." Remorse washed over his face, a look that was difficult to watch. I placed my palm over his, soothing the small tremble he tried to hide. "Goddamn it… she was seeing Michael again, and I found out about it." He squeezed his eyes shut.

I knew he wanted to stop talking, to wish this away. He looked so guilty, mentally bearing more than what he could physically hold onto.

"Sometimes we go back to the things that hurt us… not because of desire, but because of fear," I grew quiet.

"And sometimes, it doesn't need to make sense in order for it to happen, because trauma is a monster that doesn't just die…and I instigated that… I could have made it better, but instead made it worse, because the unfortunate truth was, Natalie and I shared something in common. We were both runners; scared of disappointing others, of being the brunt end of someone's anger. But I'm too impulsive, and even though I knew she'd run, I still said everything I felt. I freaked out knowing it was a bad idea, because all I saw was my own fear; my mother on the floor, pregnant and weeping, getting beaten by Miguel…"

As we silently sat shoulder to shoulder, I wondered what—if anything—I could do for him. Just sitting and listening always made me feel so powerless, as if talking out loud could help reverse the hands of time and fix the problems that already happened. I saw that he was in pain, but more importantly, I saw the honesty in his intentions. Whether he wanted to accept it or not, there was good in him.

"You weren't just helping her, Alejandro, you were trying to keep her safe," I defended.

"Well, I wasn't, and that's what kills me. I lost her, Gemma. Me. It was my job to look after her, and instead, I scared her away." Alejandro sunk into his seat, his fingers stretched across his knees. He looked as if he was going to crawl out of his skin, shuddering. "You'd think a lifetime of pretending to be someone else would have prepared me for that, considering I was supposed to pretend like I wasn't crumbling every second she was gone."

"That feels so impossible."

"It was fucking unbearable, but it got so much worse weeks later, on the one night that brought it all together… the one Parker tried to warn you about."

My stomach turned into a pit, hollowed by a sense of dread that had lingered around our relationship since the moment Parker begged me never to see Alejandro again. It wasn't just the cautious red flags, it was the headlines, the secrets, the party that somehow tumbled into a lawsuit that entangled everyone I now knew. My mouth went dry.

"The party?"

"Another goddamn event I was pressured into, one

that would've never happened had Natalie still been with me."

"But why The Pierre?" I asked, already hopeless.

"It was just a venue, Gemma. With the movie in production, and my reputation on the line, it was just another motion to go through... another ridiculous request to promote an Alex Rivers film that got out of hand. I'm just a face to people, it didn't matter what others said about me anyways."

"It matters to me," I said quietly. "You're better than what others say. You're not just a movie star that can be discarded easily for entertainment, because what I see in front of me is so much more; a living, breathing person with feelings. You aren't this shell, Alejandro... they're wrong about you."

"No one's wrong about me," he graveled. "I am who I am. And regardless of how much I tried to distance myself that night, it doesn't excuse that I still allowed it to happen."

It broke my heart how his shoulders folded in, "I hate seeing you hurt."

Alejandro shook his head. "No. Nothing could hurt me anymore, not like that night at The Pierre. I've already been hurt enough, starting from the moment I left the party—leaving to search for Natalie—to the moment I got back home...alone."

I sat sheepishly still, aware of how quiet the entire theatre felt, the sound of blood rushing in my ears, interrupted by a deep chest-expanding breath.

"I don't know if I have the courage to say it... how I came back home... how the place was empty and trashed, how little I cared," Alejandro said from the bottom of his throat. "It was already so late, and I remember everything moving so slowly, pulling out my second pack of cigarettes that day, removing another *Tranquillo* to smoke. I hadn't even lit it when I walked into my dark bedroom, not bothering with the lights as I laid in bed…"

He caught me staring, our eyes locked, unbendable to the tears that sat there. He seemed so hesitant.

"You don't have to tell me." I tried to comfort, but he looked away.

"If I don't tell you, no one ever will. Because I'm the only one who knows the truth, that Natalie came back for me… and I still don't know if she was scared or angry, or if she wanted to apologize or cuss me out, because everything I ever wanted to ask or know was gone. I saw her, her eye caught in the flick of my lighter, split open from a punch…" Alejandro's body leaned into mine.

"What?" I said under my breath, my eyes blinking.

"It wasn't supposed to be like that… *She* wasn't supposed to be there. She came to my house, my party, a place where an addict should never have gone. And all I could do was whisper her name—over and over again—until I screamed it…shaking her, lifting her, begging and praying. But she never looked away, she never blinked, she just stared; her mouth filled with foam, my Dodgers cap in her hand…. a needle in her fucking arm."

Alejandro furrowed his brow, grief torn on his face, the corner of lip twitching. I couldn't help but swallow a sob, my face buried into his arm as I hid my tears, seared with the image he painted in my head.

I just couldn't believe it, Natalie Brower, the girl from Instagram, the one everyone mentioned but no one could speak of, was a real person, someone who lived and breathed, who had an effect on the world and on Alejandro. And now she was gone. The secrets, the trial, the party and damages, all a mirage to what really happened. I began to feel sick.

"I'm so sorry, Alejandro." I struggled to compose myself, feeling only a fraction of what I imagined he carried inside.

How he looked at me, how his scowl etched itself into my heart as I cried, was something I'd never forget.

"I never wanted you to see this… to know this hell, let alone relive it. It feels like I lost my mother twice," he traced his finger across the black rose on his hand, stifling a breath I knew would break the tears in his eyes. I sat silent, mourning with him.

"Is this one for her?" I finally asked, brushing my thumb over the sorrowful black rose tattoo. It all made sense now; his knowledge on flowers, his ability to decode my dresses, their meanings held as closely to me as they were to him. It all stemmed from something more tragic.

"It is."

"But I just don't understand. None of this is fair… not what happened to her, to you. I don't understand the lawsuit, I don't understand how something so well-intended could ever go so wrong?"

"It was never about right or wrong. It was about

punishment. After that moment it all just fell apart. It was me who found Natalie in my bed, it was me who called for help, but it was me who got arrested. They saw the bruises and assumed I hit her… That's just how it's always been. People see me a certain way… and they're right. I am violent, I am dangerous, but never to her, never to you…"

"We have to fix this. I can talk to Parker. There's nothing here, nothing to charge you with."

Alejandro shook his head against me.

"It's not so simple, *Preciosa*. Sure, they couldn't charge me with anything, but there are other ways of making me hurt. It wasn't until a few months later that I finally got the name that Natalie never wanted me to know. I was being sued for wrongful death, being held liable for the party that caused her accident, by Michael." The unfathomable smirk on Alejandro's face peeked with a disbelief that he still carried, as if this was all some sick joke. "He didn't even attend her funeral, not that I would've recognized his face at the time, but I knew if I ever saw him that I'd kill him. So I stayed away, because I am my father's disease."

"That's not true…" I argued. "Alejandro, you're a good man."

"Good? Bad? None of it matters. It's my fault that my mother died in a crash, and it's my fault that Natalie died at my penthouse. I just keep thinking, if I never met her or tried to help, she'd still be alive, and I swear, I spent my whole life trying to make things better, trying to save others. But not once did I ever think I could save myself… not until I met you."

I was unprepared for the desperation in his grip as he held my hand. How could he see that in me? Despite it being the kindest thing I'd ever heard, I somehow couldn't accept it. Just like he said, good, bad, it didn't matter what you were told because sometimes, all that mattered was how you felt.

"I'm damaged… I have secrets, too, Alejandro." I argued against myself, but he wouldn't allow it.

"You only think that because you've been taught to think that. Just like I've been taught to believe everything is my fault. But I had to show you what I saw, because what I saw was hope, and if I saw that in you, Gemma, I prayed that you could see that in me too, because you are perfect, damaged or not… I want us," he pleaded an honest truth that had always frightened me.

But he was right.

We were the same.

But even I knew that a complicated path caused a complicated future, and that was something we were destined for.

My eyes welled with tears.

"When you live with fear for as long as I have, it becomes comfortable. What's the point of being vulnerable with another person, when you already know how much it can hurt? If I ever let that guard down, if I ever let *us* happen, who's to say it wouldn't just destroy me?"

"Maybe it's just something we have to face, and I wouldn't want to face it with anyone but you. When Miguel came on T.V., I was forced to protect us. I know how I did it was wrong, but I'm trying the best that I can, and I'll do anything to prove to you how honest I can be… how desperate I am to keep you as mine, because we have something worth growing here." Alejandro reached up, taking my hand in his, placing it over his heart. "You asked me about my tattoos. The one on my chest, the wings, and the initials… there's more to it than I told you."

"The As?" I asked.

"Yes. The first 'A' is for Alma, that's still true."

"And the second?" I asked, holding in a sense of suspense that nearly closed my throat.

"The second 'A' is for someone else… something I have never told anyone ever, because the truth of it changes the very existence of my life, and of those around it. I want to tell you tonight, to give you my whole truth."

I quickly looked away.

What did he have to say, and how would it change us? The pressure he produced was so laced in anticipation, that even waiting felt like some form of torture, making the back of my neck swelter with a line of sweat.

"The entire truth?" I asked.

"Yes. All of it. Come to dinner, then at home we'll talk. I swear." He stood up, asking for permission to take this chance with him again.

I wasn't sure where he would take me, or what he was going to say, but he was the bravest I'd ever seen him, and the promise of even sharing another second of that felt as hopeful as it did daunting, because for once, I felt like I could be fully honest as well.

"Do you really swear?"

"I do."

"Then… so do I," I said, accepting his offer.

He nodded, but he wasn't prepared for what I had to say, just like I wasn't prepared for him.

Alejandro was going to tell me his truth, and I would tell him mine, not just about my childhood, but about Parker, about the single kiss that scared me to even think about.

Because honestly, it changed everything, especially for what I had to admit—that my feelings for him now, were just as real as they were for Parker.

"I know tonight was a lot, but that's not a reason to keep us from appreciating all that's to come." Alejandro gestured to our table, reserved in a private section surrounded by windows. Our table wasn't as dark as the others, adjacent to large, digital billboards outside. Being in a high-class New York restaurant usually involved some privacy, but people seemed to stare. They knew who we were—or at least—who Alejandro was.

"Appreciate? I'm not sure if we should even be out right now," I said, taking my seat across from him.

It was hard to think of anything worth celebrating, my brain still foggy from the theatre. A party of five businessmen looked in our direction, their faces illuminated by candles like miners in a cave. They stared as if they knew all of Alejandro's secrets, mine included.

"Being stared at is nothing we can't handle, especially after the things we've been through. But, if you're uncomfortable, we can leave." Alejandro caught me looking at the table of men, of course he knew I was nervous.

"No." I answered half-convincingly, still assessing the feeling I had, settling on the word *uneasy*. "Being this close to Times Square seems unlike you. Remember how that turned out last time?"

"Don't worry about that, or about these people. They'll stare all night long with or without our permission. We'll take your best champagne," he said out loud, reanimating the gawking host who stood by his side. I didn't blame her for checking him out, he was beautiful, and every woman thought so, despite the label of *killer* that had taken his life by storm.

"No tequila?" I laughed.

"Not this time. Though I like where you're headed."

"Then why champagne?"

"Seems fitting, wouldn't you agree?"

The waiter returned, twisting the cork off a pine-tinted bottle. It popped loudly. Alejandro didn't move— I, on the other hand, flinched at the unexpected sound —and as hard as I tried to brush it off with a nervous laugh, he wouldn't let go of my gaze.

His continuous observation always left me wondering, was he appreciating me, or figuring something out? Given the recent events, I figured some admission of guilt was plastered on my awkward face, because holding onto Parker's kiss felt like a bomb strapped to my chest, the snip of its wire some test of skill I wasn't prepared for. One wrong word, and everything would be up in flames.

I stroked my neck.

"Remind me why." I said, taking the crystal flute from the waiter's hand.

"For your new position with St. La Vie. I wanted to

celebrate you and your accomplishments, and for the many more to come."

"Of course!" I blinked, my champagne nearly slipping from my sweaty fingers. "Oh my god. Yes."

"Don't tell me you forgot already."

"I'd never! I mean, I still can't believe it. I can't…" I couldn't respond, having almost no time to consider the job offer since the moment I received Alejandro's text.

"You can't what? Believe that you're gifted? Validation was never needed, but I'm sure it feels good."

"Validation isn't exactly the word I'd use. It's a great opportunity, but there's a lot I have to consider."

"What could you possibly have to think about? Isn't this what you always dreamed of?"

"Sure… but it wasn't exactly the way I pictured getting it. I mean, I spent my whole life dreaming of that moment, imagining climbing my way through some grueling internship, earning it like anyone else would. But it's not that at all, it's just a favor… and it's not even for me, it's for you. St. La Vie wasn't shy about making that clear."

"And that's a problem?"

"It screams nepotism… it feels dirty."

"It's an open door. There's nothing wrong with that."

"Don't get me wrong, I'm grateful for it. I just don't know if it's right for me."

"At least he was honest about it, and that's what I told him to be. Would you rather he lie to you? Wouldn't that feel dirtier than knowing up front?"

I chewed on the thought and how uncomfortably close it was to my secret. Did he already know?

"I suppose you're right. That doesn't sound good either."

"Trust me, it would be much worse. I got you in, but now you need to do the work. Don't look at it as a favor. Look at it as an opportunity to prove yourself, and you can trust that anything he says—any compliment or criticism—is real. The favor is to bring you on board, not to coddle you like a child."

"Guess that's a good excuse to cheers to then… to me… the non-child who'll *consider* the chance of a lifetime." I lifted the champagne to my lips for a long, much needed sip, allowing the bubbles to rest on my tongue before switching the topic. "Oh, and by the way, you stole my sketches… again," I teased.

"Borrowed," he corrected. "A big distinction."

"How so?"

"Stealing is so permanent. It's guaranteed to be gone forever."

"And how would you know I'd ever get them back? What if St. La Vie never called?"

"As if that would ever be a possibility. Plus, if that were to happen, I'd steal them back."

"How brazen," I replied, relishing the confidence he always maintained. Correction. It wasn't just confidence; it was an absolute.

"I knew you'd get them back. No one steals from you, and no one especially steals from me. Whatever gets taken, always gets returned."

"Is that true for everything?"

"Everything," he answered, his words as stimulating as the tickle from my champagne. "Because what's mine is mine, Gemma, that includes you. And be glad I *borrowed* those. Your talent is far too valuable not to be shared."

My expression softened, ignoring the compliment, but focusing on how he claimed me.

In his mind I was his.

I belonged to him, and nobody could take me away.

It made me so nervous.

"Yours, too. Like you said before, we're not so different."

"So, you finally agree?"

"In some ways… yes," I conceded.

"Told you so. But like I said, you're better, Gemma. Your talent is from something that you love, and I admire that. Don't do anything just to survive, not like how I did." He made eyes towards the leather-bound menu that sat by my side, waiting for me to pick it up. I looked at him suspiciously before opening it, causing a thick magazine to fall out onto my lap. I stared for a long second. "This is just the beginning. I know being here is a little silly. As you've said before, no self-respecting New Yorker comes to Times Square. Getting this close to the crowds has always been a concern, and maybe it's symbolic, but I chose this place for a reason. To show you I'm not afraid to go where I'm uncomfortable… so long as it's with you, because this is the new me."

In my hands was an unreleased issue of *New York Prestige*, its cover graced with the enticing lure of

Alejandro's face, an impressionable look I first saw months ago on a billboard while running barefoot through New York. My feelings for him had changed since then, no longer angry, but excited, enamored by him in a tuxedo, his fingers steepled to his lips. In bold white letters against a smoky backdrop read: *Say My Name, ALEJANDRO RIVERA-MARQUEZ: Meet the Man Who Killed Alex Rivers.*

My words couldn't come out fast enough, "Is this—"

"That's right," he resisted the most handsome of smiles. "I won't feed the world what it wants, or be the man they think I am. I'm taking it all back, once and for all." He sipped his champagne, his sincerity delivered like a promise. "Tomorrow will be different as well, after the Tonight Show, I'll be hosting a party for the magazine's release of my issue; however, it won't be like the ones I've had in the past." He looked out to Times Square, at the sheer madness of lights and colors. The large crowds gathered, laughing amongst pitched horns that blared in traffic. He stared at it, as if it were his last time, saying goodbye, not to the place, but rather the aesthetic of his wild life. This wasn't running away; this was standing his ground. No more chaos, no more *noise.* "It'll be a black-tie affair, invitation only to the socialites of both *our* worlds, New York and L.A. Sophisticated and calm; no bullshit."

It all made sense now. This magazine—the reveal of his name—it was all the prelude to a new man, the same one I knew he was all along. Tomorrow he'd walk the red carpet, not as Alex Rivers, but instead, Alejandro Rivera-Marquez, wearing the suit that *I* designed for him, the very thing that brought us together, a chapter to our story that was finally coming to an end.

"Page forty-two," he directed. "Paragraph three, line four." I immediately looked down, agreeing to his command as I flipped the pages, "Read it out loud."

"*Alejandro Rivera-Marquez isn't the only shocking news to hit the celebrity world by storm. Not only does the man have a new name, but also a new girl…*" I stopped, my mouth dropped open.

"Keep reading…" he requested sweetly, as I focused back on the page.

"*Gemma Harrison is a rising designer, set to be featured in Alejandro's future looks, and rumored to be in possible collaboration with the world renowned St. La Vie. Alejandro has declared himself officially off the market, stating he's never been happier than with the 'Gorgeous Gemstone' Gemma.*"

Officially off the market? My heart both fluttered and sank, the article being far too surreal to be true. I promised to be his, but being his was still such a unique place to be.

It was clear I wasn't supposed to be shared or stolen, and as much as I wanted that to be true, things were much more complicated now, especially after the Hamptons. I picked at the corner of the magazine's thick, glossy page.

"Is this true?" I smiled, still overwhelmed.

"Of course it is. I wanted it to be true since the moment I saw you, when I noticed that there was purpose in everything you did. You couldn't imagine my intrigue, discovering the most beautiful puzzle I needed to solve, the one person who was hidden like me, like an actor in disguise trying to be someone else. And to say I was desperate would be an understatement. It's the very reason I drove out to Bushwick, hoping it'd bring me closer to you, that I'd capture some small piece of who you were and where you came from."

"There was never anything out there for you to find." I admitted to myself, reluctant to acknowledge all that he did, and the beautiful, unapologetic intention he set forth.

"That's not true. Remember these knuckles?" he asked. "Remember how bloody they used to be? The story you read about me online?"

"About you and the DJ from Bushwick." I answered vaguely, avoiding the name I knew he probably hated.

"Your effect is much stronger than you realize, and though I didn't mention it at the time, the confrontation I faced out there was something you saved me from. You know by now that it wasn't just some DJ, because out there in some club, written on a tiny marquee was a name of a person I couldn't fucking walk away from. Michael Brower."

"I… remember the photos." I added quietly. "You're different though. You fight to protect, not to hurt."

"There was no one left to protect that night," he admitted. "I can be honest about what that meant to me. Paparazzi or not, I knew once I saw Michael, that I was going to hurt him. It was revenge, nothing else, and as soon as we locked eyes, I was gone…" he stopped himself, before murmuring, calmly and regrettably. "I. Wanted. To. Kill. Him. And honestly I would've if it hadn't been for you… if it hadn't been for why I was there in the first place."

Alejandro appeared at peace, and even though what he said was violent, not once did I feel sick to my stomach, not like when I saw Michael Brower's bloodied face in that article.

"Why me?" I whispered, the magazine still splayed in my hand, the chatter of guests ambient to our secluded spot.

"I don't know." He answered honestly, still perplexed himself. "I don't know why you, or why we even met. But it feels bigger than me. Why did you lose your job? Why was I walking into that exact shop at that exact time you were? It's almost like the universe can only kick someone down for so long until it gives them a break… or rather, a sign. I wish I had an answer for it, but I don't; I only know it happens once in a lifetime, and that when it does, you're never supposed to let it go. So I won't, and I didn't… which is why I didn't kill Michael… because as soon as I got to him, I was terrified at the idea of ever losing you. It was you, Gemma… you that pulled me through, you who was more important. And it's not what you said or what you did, it was simply just *you;* your existence so magnetic that I could only feel it, but not see it. You are so much like me, but you're the good I never had."

To think he even thought of me this way, the stubborn girl who put up a fight against his charm, who yelled at him, who rejected him, made me feel guilty. How could he be so accepting after all that? I couldn't be that valuable to someone, not me. "I don't think anyone has ever said anything like that to me before," I admitted.

"Well, maybe no one has seen you like I have. That's the reason you're my gemstone… I know this may feel like a lot, but when I tell you I've changed, I have. Telling you what I need to tonight won't be easy… but I need to get it off my chest, because I'll be gone soon, and you deserve to know it."

"What do you mean gone?" I let the magazine slip into my lap, not willing to lose him again.

"The studio booked me on a press tour for the next three months. I leave for L.A. in two days. But I want you to come with me."

"Well, I…" I couldn't wrap my mind around the sudden news. Of course, I couldn't leave, not without knowing what I wanted to do with St. La Vie first. But how could I let him go? The few weeks apart from each other felt like forever. What would three months do?

"It could be fun," he interrupted. "I can finally take you to Pink's Hot Dogs, show you the coast, get you tan like me," he laughed innocently. "I know you have St. La Vie, I know you have your roots here, and I can't ask you to tear them away so easily, but I'm too selfish not to ask either."

"I'm not sure if that's a good idea—" I admitted, but not before he stopped me.

"Don't answer…" he said. "Tonight, I only want to show you how important you are to me, to let the whole world know, starting here," he pointed down at the magazine. "This is more for you than for them. I have the courage to be who I am, because of you, and if you stay here, just know how committed I am." I looked out the window as if the answer would be floating out in the billboard's flashing in bright, pink letters. He took my silence in, not once looking away from me, "I just want to tell you my final truth tonight, and for us to both be honest with each other. And if you stay in New York, that's ok too. Either way, I'll be back, because nothing can keep me away from you. New York… is only borrowing you," he said, sounding so convincingly, that even I believed it.

Still, I didn't move, concentrating on all the impossible ways I could fix what I'd done, but settling on nothing. I thought of Parker, my childhood, my neck burning with an ache that needed to be soothed. I wanted to tell Alejandro everything right now, to blurt it out like bile that turned my stomach.

And what did he want to tell me, what more could there possibly be to the man whose life had already been a series of traumas? Was it like mine with Claire? Was it worse?

I took a moment and, without a second thought, committed myself to a small but necessary step. "Ok… Let's talk."

Alejandro's phone chimed at the table, averting his attention. "Damn," he muttered, apologizing. "It's Ivanna, she wants me to take a call tonight with the studio. It's about the tour."

"Of course." I pretended to be as casual as I could possibly be.

"We can pick up some food on the way back, but we have to leave. Is that ok?"

"Sounds great," I lied, folding my napkin onto the table. Truthfully, I didn't like this, and I worried about leaving, about getting closer to confessing what happened in the Hamptons.

"Let me just use the restroom real quick." I said, not waiting for his response, but standing as soon as I could.

I had to get away, I had to find some moment alone to figure myself out, to snip the proverbial bomb still strapped to my chest. I never felt more self-conscious than now as I barged my way into the empty bathroom, gripping my hands onto the sink.

"Goddamn it, Gemma." I scolded myself.

Telling Alejandro about the Hamptons would make his plans to leave all the more difficult. How would he react to both the kiss and me staying here? Would that look as though I picked a side? I hadn't picked anyone, not yet at least, and the more I thought about it, the more it hurt.

The only answer I continued to fall on was being honest, honest in a way that he expected from himself and St. La Vie, convincing me that it would always feel dirtier to be lied to than to admit the uncomfortable truth.

Decidedly, I'd stay with Alejandro, I'd tell him the truth and deal with the consequences; that'd be my first step. And as much as it'd hurt, it'd at least be in my control, my choice, my action. I dabbed my face with a paper towel, twisting it into a ball before tossing it into the trash.

I took one final breath before leaving and making my way back to the table, stopping.

I was immediately confused, unable to decipher everything I saw in the split second that it took for me to turn the corner.

Alejandro was staring out the window, his back turned from me, captivated by a large billboard in the middle of Times Square.

Below in the streets people pointed, fixed on *Celebrity Breaking News* that flashed across the crowded streets. It had Alejandro's name all over it, but it wasn't about him. "No…" I whispered, "not like this…"

It was a photo of me and Parker.

Us on the dock.

Stuck in a kiss.

The kiss.

"How?" I asked inaudibly. Alejandro stood motionless, fixated on everything I wanted to confess, but still hadn't. My own words, my own perspective, instantly stolen by a single image, amplified for all of New York to judge.

Alejandro turned around, his lifeless eyes void of any emotion other than disgust.

"Gemma?" his voice hardened as he said my name.

"Alejandro…" I reached for my neck.

The wrong wire snipped.

The damage done.

Chapter 41

GEMMA

"Goodnight."

That was last thing Alejandro said to me, a stale and distant word that lacked the spark he shared while congratulating me with champagne last night. And after the restaurant, *after* the moment where he turned around and whispered my name, he said nothing else. All we shared was an agonizing silence.

Silence in the car.

Silence in the elevator.

Silence *all* the way up to the penthouse, where we eventually parted ways to sleep in separate bedrooms. It was in that moment, there in the spot where I once measured his body, where Alejandro released the disappointed word that tore me apart.

"Goodnight."

And despite how angry he may have been, I knew better than to assume he was deliberately cruel. Alejandro's silence wasn't a grudge towards me, it wasn't some juvenile cold shoulder. It was worse. It was a silence that could only come from when you don't know what to say, so you say nothing at all.

I couldn't believe what we both saw last night, realizing the only person somehow capable of releasing that photo would've been Camilla. She'd seen us and now was exposing everything: my guilt, my pain, my love. These thoughts stayed with me through the night, carrying themselves up to the morning as I opened my eyes.

"Hello Mrs. Rivers!" The spritely concierge greeted as I made my way into the living room. "Or should I say, Mrs. Rivera-Marquez?" He tapped his finger on the fresh copy of New York Prestige that sat atop the trays of food. I exchanged a smile to avoid being rude, but hesitated as I read the gut-punching headline.

"You can just call me, Gemma," I replied, wondering if he could see the bags under my eyes as I looked up towards Alejandro's room. I doubted he was still asleep, and the idea that he was waiting on the other side sent me into frenzied anticipation.

I signed the receipt under my own name, the butterflies absent from my stomach as the man left, wheeling the cart into the kitchen to set the table. Amongst the delivery was a sealed manila envelope and a fresh bottle of tequila, *his* tequila. A little ribbon was tied around its neck, embossed with *Congratulations.* I stared at the envelope by the bottle, noticing Lina Castillo's signature.

I wondered what she sent and if she had talked to Parker yet. Had he seen the news; did he even realize that we were in the middle of Times Square? I totally spaced on saying anything, still feeling completely blindsided as I decided to take out my phone and text him. I stopped immediately, hearing Alejandro come down the hall.

"Good morning, *Preciosa*." He entered, clearing the air with surprising contentment.

I turned toward him, relieved at his sight, his body still wet as he wiped off shower water from his freshly shaven cheek.

"Um... good morning."

"Sorry if I kept you waiting," he tightened the loosely held towel along his waist, keeping it flush against his hips. "I'm glad you're up though. We have a busy day ahead of us."

"I know. I still need to take the suit to Ivanna, but I wish we had more time. We didn't even get to do a final fitting, but with everything that happened, I—"

"It will be perfect," he interrupted, cauterizing the end of my concern. "Besides, even if it's a little tight, I think I'd prefer it."

"I just want it to be perfect for you. Maybe I'm overthinking it."

"Well, don't," he asserted kindly. "What's done is done. I'm confident it'll work." He bent over, pressing his lips onto mine, holding a kiss that prevented me from even protesting. Maybe the sentiment was a band-aid to the moment, but the kiss felt more permanent than what I was expecting. With a suck of my lip, I felt temporarily disillusioned, like nothing ever happened. Instinctively, I reached up to trace my nails along the ink of his arm, attempting to wrap the width of my hand around his bicep. I moaned, delighted by the smoothness of his lips.

But he pulled away.

"Are you hungry?" My question stretched across the table.

"Absolutely starved."

"And wet too… I see you were in a rush to get downstairs." I cooled my tea with a breath, blowing as the sun cast perfect shadows along his face.

"So you've noticed."

"It's hard not to."

Alejandro looked me up and down, his cheeks curved into dimples from the sip of his mug. Was he in the mood to flirt? I crossed my legs to see if he would watch, and as he did, he began to tsk.

"I can't help but think you're tempting me on purpose. Don't provoke me, good girl." His hand fell towards the knot of my robe, tugging it but not untying it.

"And why not?" I asked eagerly, feeling embarrassed as he pulled away. My lips fell into a frown before I could stop them.

"If I start now, I won't want to leave."

His otherwise amused expression tittered, though just a moment, slanting to the side. It was in that instance where I could see him—not the man who came down this morning with a smirk—but the one from last night. He was hidden, pretending not to hurt.

"How'd you sleep?"

"Honestly, like a baby," he covered a slice of sourdough with butter. "And you?"

"Mmmmm… I had a hard time, actually, there was a lot on my mind. I couldn't get comfortable."

"Me too," he replied, but then clarified, "about having a lot on my mind that is."

"Was it about us?"

He hesitated, taking a bite of crispy toast. "Actually, no. About my schedule. I've decided to cancel the interview with The Tonight Show."

I scrunched my face.

"But why?" I asked defensively. This interview was the whole point of my employment, the very reason I made his suit. Everything we did was all meant for tonight.

"Do I really need to give you a reason?"

"I think so. You can't just cancel this."

"I can, and I did."

"That doesn't explain why," I confronted but was met with an assertive stare that shut me up.

It was a stupid question. I already knew the reason, I just didn't want to accept the guilt. It was because of me, because of what the whole world saw. He told everyone that I was his girl, the very *same* girl that was just caught kissing another man.

"It didn't feel important," he answered impatiently. "The party is still on though, that's not canceled."

"It is important. We should talk…"

"What is there to really say?" He leaned back, looking away as if bored by it all. "Nothing happened, Gemma."

"A lot has happened. You're pretending it didn't, and I thought we were going to try and be open."

"I'm not pretending anything. Maybe I'm just accepting it."

"That seems unconventional." I narrowed my eyes.

"You shouldn't be surprised. I'm not like most other people."

"No, you certainly aren't," I replied, this time more sarcastic.

He shot me a daring look.

"Whatever. It's me, baby… deal with it."

I physically stopped my jaw from dropping, stunned at the signature catchphrase he used on so many others before. *It's me, baby, deal with it?* Now I knew I wasn't talking to Alejandro, but instead, his counterpart, the well-known Hollywood celebrity. It made my nostrils flare.

"Deal with it? I thought Alex Rivers was dead… but, apparently, he's alive and well."

"Don't act so clever."

"Then don't be so stubborn. You're doing it again." I maintained.

"Doing what?"

"You're running. Just like Alex does. And you're not like that… you're better."

"I'm not running." He restrained himself from leaning in my direction. "I'm moving past this. Let it go."

"That's not going to make us feel better, or at least not for me. I don't usually face my problems head on, but I'm trying to with you. As much as I want us to *move* past it, I know we can do better."

"Better than what? I don't need you to confirm what I already know is true. What happened last night… that photo… it meant nothing. Right?" he asked, partially pleading, his lips pressed into a fine line.

I struggled to express the emotions that had made my week unbearable. Maybe Alejandro was the one, or maybe I was just afraid of losing him now, of losing time to figure out how I felt. "Last night you were so honest, so completely open, and I want that again."

"So, you want truths?" His mug clanked against the table. "I have been speaking my truths, and since you're so eager to tell me—today of all days—what your truth is, then please do so." He refrained from yelling, but he might as well have, his raised voice flustered by the thought of what I could say.

He was right, and maybe this wasn't the time. Was it selfish to think that it was? He pushed me to answer, but my reply was cut short, disrupted as my phone buzzed on top of Alejandro's copy of New York Prestige. His eyes caught the screen, reading the name that popped up.

PARKER

Leaving the Hamptons. If you need more time, I understand. I can stay somewhere else in the city.

My face drained of blood as Alejandro glared at my phone.

"The truth about him?" he asked. "The man who didn't appreciate what he had? Who loves you like friend?"

I flipped my phone around, hiding the screen. How could I say so plainly how all of that was no longer true?

"I just need you to know how it happened," I sighed. "And… how I feel about it."

"You don't need to feel anything. This isn't your fault."

"Alejandro… don't."

"No. It's true. I ran when things got tough and wasn't honest as soon as I could've been. I treated you the same way he did, like you were fragile, not wanting to expose you to my world. If it weren't for that time apart, you wouldn't have gone. This is my fault."

"It's not. It's no one's fault." I reached out, grabbing his hand.

"And what? Now he's ready? Now after all these years he wants you? How does that make sense? How is that fair?"

"It isn't. But—"

"But nothing, Gemma! He saw something new happening inside of you, and now he wants it. Maybe he saw that you cared for me as much as I cared for you and that scared him. And it should because I care more than he ever will. And I was honest about *that* from the beginning. Yes, I have my past; yes, it's ugly, but goddamn it… I have always been honest about how I felt about you!" Alejandro slammed his fist on the table, creating a monstrous thud that echoed through the kitchen, causing me to flinch.

I stared around without moving my head, carefully observing the spilled tea that tipped to its side. Everything became so quiet.

"I'm not sure if that's true. I'm not sure how he feels or how I feel," I answered.

"About him or me?"

"About everything. I don't know how I feel!"

"Well, this is how I feel," he interrupted. "I have put myself out on the line, I made a commitment for the whole world to see. And now, to them, it's a joke. It's just another opportunity to smear my name, the one I barely just got to use. But ask me if I care. Ask me if I give a shit about what they'll say. I won't be ruined by a kiss—a kiss by the way that was so clearly stolen. Fuck, Gemma, let them have the gossip, they can keep it. I just want you, and I need to know that you're still mine… just tell me that," he asked, no longer warning, but begging.

My lip quivered, and before I could crawl into my shell, I spit out a thoughtless answer that satisfied nothing.

"It's complicated," I responded, giving a painful truth that sucked the light out of Alejandro's eyes. He looked over at the cart, focusing on something else. Slowly, he reached for the bottle of tequila that rested on the tray, removing its top to pour a small width of amber gold into an accompanying glass.

"You're right about one thing," he took a quick shot. "It is complicated."

I didn't reply, and all of a sudden, it was me who lacked the courage to say what was needed. After how hurt he was, how distant he became last night, how could I do that to him again?

Alejandro stared at the bottle and the taunting congratulatory ribbon. "I still want to be honest. I'm not running," he finally conceded.

"I want that too."

"But not without its precautions," he said, distracted again by my buzzing phone. Was it Parker? I was determined not to look, allowing it to sit there, to ignore it. Alejandro couldn't. He burned a hole through the phone with a scowl, and if he could, he'd probably reach right through, asserting himself in the most profound way. He was deadly in that sense, powerful beyond what Parker may have even realized. "There is always a cost for fame… I told you this already. What I wanted to share with you could change my whole life… it could change how you see me."

"You can trust me. Don't let this moment ruin what we worked so hard to have." I said as calmly and as sweetly as I could, doing anything in my power to make him feel safe.

He reached for the envelope on the tray, the one with Lina's name on it, then passed it to me, "Gemma… open this up."

"What is this?" I removed a small packet of papers, quickly scanning its header. "You can't be serious," I asked out loud.

"I think it'd be best."

"An NDA?" I questioned, looking back down at the non-disclosure form in my hand. "Why now?"

"I can't chance this. Not with the attention you'll be getting. It was reckless of me to think it could be so simple. You and I… *this* isn't simple."

"But you can trust me… isn't that simple enough?"

"With the headlines about me, with all the backlash, we have to be careful. It protects you as much as it protects me."

"How?" I asked, concerned that this NDA was more of a wall than a door. Was this the new us? A couple shielded by the protection of legal forces. It felt so formal.

"Last night was revealing to say the least. There are a lot of eyes on us now… and after what I saw, I need to know that my secret is safe."

"Safe? As in… from me telling the news?"

"Don't make it sound so nefarious, Gemma. I have to do this. I shouldn't even be out tonight; the whole world is watching me, and Ivanna thinks I should take a step back. But I'm trusting my gut here."

"Because you don't trust me?"

"Because I don't trust them," he growled. "If they ever get anything out of you, even by accident… I need to be protected. Signing this assures that you are legally obligated to deny any rumors you hear about me. Anything you say could be refuted as a lie… one you will be legally obligated to admit."

"But I would never say anything…" I told myself, as Alejandro rolled a pen towards my hand.

"Then you have nothing to worry about." He shot back, wiping his hands free from what little breakfast he ate. "You can think about it, but we can't talk about this now. There's a lot to do, and I'm already rushed as it is. I have to meet Ivanna, collect my itinerary, and be debriefed on the press tour. The NDA can wait, but I do need to know if you've made a decision on L.A." He looked up, pushing for an answer.

"I haven't had a chance to—"

My phone buzzed once more, loud and obnoxious. I finally snatched it off the table to switch off.

It was as if Parker was in the room, somewhere between here and the Hamptons, caught in the middle of this awful conversation. I knew Alejandro didn't want to face how I felt, but the insistent vibrating was luring him to a point of breaking.

"I need to know if you'll be joining me on the press tour," he demanded, twisting his napkin. "I need an answer."

"Well, I need more time," I asserted back.

He poured himself another shot, resting the bottle on the table before taking a long sip, not wincing from the burning tequila.

"I need to know by tonight," he said, his anger more composed, but not well enough. Was this Alex or Alejandro? I hated that I even questioned who he was.

"The kiss…" I interrupted, giving myself the courage to speak my mind. "I was going to tell you on my own, with my words, my feelings. But that was taken away, and now you're taking away my chance to express *my* truth. I need to say it now. Not later like you want."

"There will be a car sent for you tonight, please be ready by nine." He pushed aside the plate of food, ignoring my words. "I'll just meet you at the party."

I sat in silence, my lips curled to the side. The drop of his shoulders was far more telling than what he was willing to say. I had exhausted him, this was all too much for one day, and I knew that. I only wanted to be heard, but maybe he just needed space.

"I want to hear what you have to say," he managed to let out, his hand reaching for any sign of agreement. His fingertips met mine with a delicate graze. "I just need to get through today, and I'm only asking for this moment. Remember, this is *borrowed* time… not stolen. I'll listen. I swear."

As I looked up into his eyes, I could see he was trying, building some fragile bridge for us to cross together on. A single word had the potential to cripple either of us into a series of unchecked emotions, so unanimously, we said nothing. I could give him the day; it was the least I could do.

"You're right. There's time," I nodded.

"But not for the tour, that's something I need to know." He leaned in for a kiss, his lips promising a taste of what our future could be, but pausing before reaching my mouth, kissing my forehead instead. "Whatever decision you make, I know it will be the right one for you," he said, standing up from the table.

I was certain now, that no matter how bad Alejandro wanted Alex Rivers to be gone, that fragments of that celebrity actor remained.

He was pretending, and I knew it, his confidence in my decision making skills laced with doubt, noted by the tequila bottle he sipped from as he begrudgingly left the room.

I loved how rain in New York made me feel, how it sounded against the passenger window where I sat, and despite my resistance to be sentimental, there was something new about the rain; a reminder of Alejandro and the night we saw *The Phantom of the Opera.* Back then it rained as well, and though Parker was supposed to be there, it was Alejandro who showed up.

"Do you believe in fate?" I asked Ivanna, who sat in the back seat of the town car with me.

She checked herself in the tiny reflection of a compact mirror, pushing her lips together into a perfect pout.

"Fate? Maybe curses. Of all the days for it to rain, it had to be today." She shut the mirror in her palm, adjusting the shoulders to her emerald, plunge-neck gown.

"It's not so bad."

"I'm an assistant, babe. I don't like anything I can't control."

"And Alejandro?" I asked, trying to make her smile.

She rolled her eyes. "After L.A., don't even get me started on that man."

I looked back out the window, completely understanding where Ivanna was coming from. Only

Alejandro could be completely maddening and totally endearing at once, like how he managed to force his way into the seat beside me at the Majestic. All I wanted to do was watch the show that night and be alone, or so I thought. I hated how persistent he was at that time, but now, looking back, I adored his resilience.

"I think I like the rain. A lot actually." I finally said out loud.

"Really?" Ivanna's accent jabbed across the seat.

"Yeah. I have good memories from it."

"That's so strange. Truth is, you can't find good eggs in the rain."

"What does that mean?" I laughed.

"It means, visiting Columbia during Easter equals nonstop rain. Do you know what happens to chocolate eggs when they get wet? Christ may have risen, but in Bogotá, the sky is falling in spring. Trust me, no amount of colorful eggs could save the day."

"That's funny, but you do know they go hand in hand, right?"

"Rain and eggs?"

"Yeah, well sorta. Colorful eggs are a symbol of new life, and you can't have new life without rain."

"Is that what you think?" she asked curiously, turning in her seat to face me. "Painting eggs isn't really a thing in Columbia, but try explaining that American tradition to your eighty-year-old *abuelita*. We painted them for a different purpose, to make something beautiful out of something sad—such as us stealing from defenseless hens. It's a one-sided transaction if you ask me. They'd make the eggs, and we'd eat them."

"So that's not a Columbian tradition?" I asked.

"No," she shrugged. "Just a crazy Cortez family one. I guess that's why it felt so special. Meanings always change depending on who you talk to, you know?"

Special? That helped put things in perspective. The truth was, Alejandro and I were also special; that night at the theatre was special, and now the rain was special. And from all these special things, a reminder prevailed that I couldn't ignore; time passes and feelings change.

Meanings change, as Ivanna suggested.

But what hadn't changed, and what had bothered me now for quite some time was the confusion I felt for Alejandro. It was like someone had snapped a piece of myself and molded it into him. I liked that and feared that.

"Clever man," I confessed to myself, as Charles pulled up to the building.

He was always surprising, always symbolic, even the event for New York Prestige had a meaning; its venue a location I could never forget. This was for us.

"I can't believe he picked The Met." Ivanna leaned over me, staring through my window, "So bold, especially after the whole painting scandal."

"What can I say? He himself is bold."

I knew it as soon we turned on Fifth Avenue that he picked this venue on purpose. This wasn't a coincidence, and nothing ever was with him; not this, not for making me his designer, for calling me his *good girl*. Maybe it was fate, but also, maybe fate wasn't done taking me where it needed.

"Be glad we're skipping that. It's a total

nightmare." Ivanna pointed to the distant red carpet outside, its barricade lined with paparazzi and flashing cameras.

"How do we even get in?"

"Right through there," Ivanna motioned towards a fire exit, an otherwise quiet grey door where Alejandro and I once made our great escape from. I looked at it, before looking back at the red carpet.

"This is supposed to be better? Better than being with him, than having our photo taken together?" My thoughts seeped through into a question.

"It's just for now. You know he cares about you… let him take the heat for what's going on, and before you know it, you'll be together at these events, so much so, that you'll begin to hate them."

Ivanna's assurance felt more like an uncomfortable reminder of what had happened. Had the photo of Parker and me not been released, would tonight be different? Would I have been walking alongside Alejandro in my vintage Valentino, his hands gripping tightly on my waist, brushing the fitted folds of black charmeuse down my hips? I wanted to look good for him, to be pulled into his arms for everyone to see. That in itself was a commitment, just like the label he wanted us to have.

"I feel more like a secret going towards the exit." I pressed my hand against my twisted chignon as I stepped out of the car.

"I know it's less grand than the entrance." Ivanna followed behind as I stared toward the concrete steps, half-expecting to see Alejandro standing in his suit. I never felt more distant from him, especially after last night and our conversation this morning.

"I don't mind being in the shadows, but I wish I could be his advocate, to be by his side—"

"*Miss Harrison!*"

The excited call alarmed me, as I turned away from the entrance.

"Shit," Ivanna interrupted, but the person shouted again.

"*Who is the mystery man that you kissed?*"

A pop of light burst toward my face.

"*How did Alejandro react when he saw the news?*"

Another person asked, shooting another series of flashing lights. Cameras appeared, along with questions, all similar to the ones I asked myself, but had no answers for.

I was officially spotted.

"No questions please!" Ivanna held her hand up, her Louboutin clutch a minuscule shield to the photos that everyone began to take. One after another, the paparazzi showed up, their cameras like a dog whistle to others to take more pictures.

"*Has Alejandro forgiven you for cheating? Are you still a couple?*"

"Umm…" I fumbled with my words. *Cheated?* Did I just hear her correctly? Suddenly my vintage Valentino felt cheap.

"Gemma, don't answer them." Ivanna scolded, acting as my makeshift publicist as she shoved our way towards the large steel door.

I struggled to keep up as both men and women

trampled over the train of my dress, marking it up as I finally stepped inside the building. I couldn't just say nothing, having questions thrown at me like stones. No one wanted to listen to me, and after this morning, not even Alejandro had the patience to endure my truth.

"I'm not a cheater!" I shouted my final proclamation as the door slammed shut, and the flashing lights became eclipsed by solid steel.

Ivanna looked at me, disappointed like a corrective older sister.

"What did I just tell you?" She sighed, empathetically kneeling down to fix the bottom of my dress, calmly untangling it. "They just want a quote… and you gave them one."

"Well, at least it's the truth," I answered, overwhelmed and a little tearful. Ivanna stood back up, checking my hair.

"I know, babe, but this is a different world now… it's better to learn now than later."

"It feels like a crash course." I said deflated as she looped her arm around mine.

"Well, you got me at least, and I've already gotten you through a tough crowd before, haven't I? Now let's get you out of here, if today wasn't cursed already, it soon might be." She laughed, saluting a gold sarcophagus as we walked through the Egyptian exhibit.

She couldn't be more right. If curses were a concern for her, then holding my arm was a bad idea. I was positively hexed with attention.

"Don't feel too bad," Ivanna cooed. "You're going to love what you're about to see."

"I always love it here…" I replied, but lost my breath as I entered the lobby of cascading purple lights and flowers. Along the swooping arches and roman pillars hung blooming bouquets of peach carnations and lilies, the room scented like spring with all the iridescent charm of tabletop candles on fresh linen cloths. "She's gorgeous…" I choked out, Ivanna playfully jabbing my arm.

"Not as gorgeous as him," a spritely voice interjected between me and Ivanna.

"Dean?" I shrilled, greeted by the happy-go-lucky grin of Henri's husband. He adjusted the orange, paisley bowtie around his neck, correcting its shape.

"Sweetie, have you seen your man? He's stunning!" Dean pointed with an umbrella, motioning towards a series of large hanging portraits of Alejandro, his body encapsulated in rich black and white tones.

Ivanna shook Dean's hand as they met. "I took that one." She added, pointing to Alejandro harvesting agave in a blazing field, his brawny arms glistened with sweat, cupped by the rolled sleeve of an unbuttoned denim shirt.

"I always assumed he was good with his hands. But now I know it." Henri appeared behind Dean, admiring the same image above. His suit was covered in a black coat, his height extended with the assistance of six-inch heeled designer boots. "Gemma, how are you?" He leaned in for a kiss, as our cheeks greeted each other.

"I'm—"

"Great," Ivanna cut in, stitching a narrative for me. "We had a few bumps along the way, but now we're here." She introduced herself to Henri as I collected my wit.

"It's just… an exciting adjustment," I decided on, taking a moment to realize just how crowded the lobby was. Guests in their finest suits and gowns laughed with indecipherable chatter, their conversations muted with the orchestrated strings that played above on a balcony. My shoulders were still tense until Henri reached over with a comforting hand.

"I saw what happened outside," Dean admitted, collecting a handful of champagne flutes from a passing waiter. "Next time you go out, take an umbrella. It's better for deflecting the shade than giving it."

"Gemma's noticeable right now, and not just because of that dress," Henri nodded, acknowledging my look and scandal.

"Honestly, I'm not sure if I should even be here," I took a long gulp of the crisp champagne. Was everyone else thinking the same thing? This entire event was circled around a man with an alleged murder accusation, and now he was dating a *cheater*? Henri's face tightened as if sensing how uncomfortable I'd become.

"You'll need to be tough for this world…" he advised, clinking the glass in my hand. "Just remember, any publicity is good publicity."

Ivanna shook her head at Henri, but then tried to calm me. "You can relax," she promised. "There are no paparazzi here, besides this is a private event." Ivanna waved around at the crowd, whose darting eyes glanced in my direction.

She was wrong.

I quickly realized how the guests at The Met were no different than the wolves outside. Sure, there were no flashing cameras or screaming questions, but there was something worse, more subtle to the untrained eye.

Whispered gossip.

And to assure myself that I wasn't just paranoid, I reminded myself of the very entity who cohosted this event: *New York Prestige Magazine.*

Of course there'd be gossip, these people thrived off of it, and here I was, a part of the juiciest story they've had all year. As I turned to face Henri, I caught a glimpse of a bright silk dress, vibrant red like blood.

"Shit," I muttered.

"What is it?" Dean followed my eyes, tapping his umbrella.

It was Camilla.

She glared in my direction, making another woman laugh as she whispered into her ear. I tried not to stare as her dark eyes dared me to approach her from across the room. Dean seemed to notice as I turned away.

"Just saw an unhappy face is all…" I replied, trying to play it off.

"Lady in red?" Ivanna questioned.

"Is it obvious?"

"She's giving me sea witch vibes." Dean shivered, but Henri rolled his eyes. "What? That's not a bad thing. It just means Gemma's popular. Anyone worthwhile has haters."

"Gemma has been scandalized, and people are only staring because they're jealous," Ivanna waved.

Camilla viciously stared me down one final time

before disappearing into the crowd, leaving me more intimidated than I already was.

"It's not a reputation I'm proud of," I admitted, toying with the fake jewels hanging from my ear. "I'd rather be known for who I am, not for what happened."

"Well, I'm jealous," Dean shrugged. "Not only did you nab one hunk, but another, as well."

"Elegance, Dean." Henri said, annoyed.

"What? The whole world wants to know who the sexy man is! Gemma is safe to tell us, she knows that!" Dean looked at me, blinking as if Henri was crazy, wanting to grab the one secret that left even New York Prestige in the dark. Ivanna shot a daring look, probably knowing the answer herself, but begging me not to say.

For whatever reason, Camilla hadn't revealed Parker's name. It was me she hated, not Parker, and the fact that she spared him from such scrutiny left me wondering if she still had feelings for him.

"Safe to tell you what?" The question tingled along my bare shoulders, as I turned around.

Everyone gasped, as for once we were greeted by an unusually happy and formally dressed Alejandro.

"Well, hello…" my greeting barely left my lips before Alejandro leaned in for a hard kiss. He pressed into me, his tongue tasting far sweeter than before, layered with velvety spice.

"How are we?" he rasped. I smiled and reached for my lips, feeling the throb that he left. He certainly was more joyous than before, his kiss sweet like oak and chocolate.

"I'm good." I answered, taking note that he'd been drinking. He smelled like *Don Jefe*.

"You certainly are." Henri chimed in, adjusting his glasses, observing Alejandro's new look. He hummed in approval, not hesitating to tug the fabric of Alejandro's jacket. "I'm impressed… it certainly meets my expectations, Gemma."

"She did good, didn't she?" Alejandro ran his arms along the sleeve.

Henri smiled in a way that resolved any doubts I had about my position by his side. Everything was perfect— actually, *perfect*—fitted with both precision and style. Alejandro's broad shoulders sat fitted into a sable black suit, its lapels dotted with matted studs and thin white trim. It was all so complimentary to his black vest and tie. God, he looked like the best kind of trouble.

"It's like she knows me. Inside and out." Alejandro unbuttoned his jacket, propping it open, commanding the respect of the entire floor.

"Marigolds?" Dean asked curiously, admiring the lining.

"Black dahlias." Ivanna looked down, running her fingers along the hand embroidered silk flowers. "Isn't that right, Gemma?"

"The dahlia is the national flower of Mexico." I gleamed, its meaning representing more than just Alejandro's heritage. "The black color is just the right twist, isn't it?"

"I knew she was the right person for the job." Alejandro quirked his head back towards me, giving a meaningful glance that made me smile. It was a moment we shared, a silent but loud admiration for what I'd done for him, for how I saw him. "I knew she could *commit* herself to the task… that there was some *eternal bond* between her and the talent she had."

I turned back to my champagne, horribly downplaying the effects of his words. Of course he knew what black dahlias meant, a symbol for loyalty, for grace, for both intimate and personal feelings shared between two people. He teased me over it, but appreciated the details I carefully picked, because this wasn't just an outfit.

This was *him.*

This was *my* Alejandro.

A suit for the man I knew, both stoic and masculine,

defiant to a scowl with a tenderness that was often concealed inside. He looked down at me with a smolder as Dean continued to clap.

"This is promising," Henri added quietly. "And to think we could be sketching designs such as this, possibly by next week."

"Maybe sooner," Dean interjected. "I just talked to Dana, and she emailed the contract this evening."

Alejandro instantly appeared distant with Dean's words, focusing on the floor over the conversation at hand. If I wasn't so certain that he was happy just a moment ago, I'd assumed he was disappointed, but quickly he relaxed himself right when I caught him.

"As soon as next week for designs?" Alejandro wrapped his hand around my waist, securing me neatly against his body. He began to lean his full weight on me, using my tiny frame for support as he stroked his bottom lip. "I want to talk to you about this campaign. How do you feel about me stealing your star away for a few months, so that she can accompany me on my press tour?"

Steal me away? My heart immediately sank at the request. This was supposed to be my choice. Even though I was hesitant about this project, Alejandro knew it was still important to me.

"Don't be silly," I laughed to save face, resting my palm on his chest. His weight on my body felt heavier now as he leaned a little closer. "Henri, rest assured, I'll be there. Starting tomorrow if you need me." I looked up at Alejandro, "Isn't that, *right?*"

"I'm sure it could wait a few months. Don't you

think it would be fun?" Alejandro looked to Dean and Henri for some approval. Dean buckled in the pressure of Alejandro's chocolate eyes, nodding at both Henri and me. Henri, on the other hand, didn't budge.

"There's a lot of work ahead of us, this is not something we can waste time on." Henri sipped his champagne calmly, shooting me a look that I interpreted as uncertainty.

"Maybe the campaign can be postponed. Gemma hasn't even made up her mind yet. I think she's still considering the position." Alejandro cleared his throat as I pulled away, reaching for my phone as Henri explained the intricacies of a campaign.

Without thought, I opened the newly arrived email from St. La Vie's office, skimming a forty-page contract right to the end. I was determined to settle the question that Alejandro presumed I couldn't answer, and despite his resistance, he needed to hear the truth, one I wasn't sure could wait till the end of the event.

"Done!" I boasted, flipping my phone to the group, showing them the signed e-doc on my screen. "Expect me when you need me, Henri." I turned to Alejandro. "The campaign can't be postponed over us, that's unreasonable to assume." I may have created more tension than I thought as Ivanna stood silently by my side, cringing.

"Oh!" Henri looked at Dean, then back at me surprised. "That's something to drink to!" He tilted his champagne back as Dean clapped once again. An odd atmosphere had morphed over the group as Alejandro glared in my direction. Dean laughed nervously as I looked back down at my phone, which vibrated in my hand.

It was a text from Ivanna, one that left my mouth tacky and dry.

IVANNA

I shouldn't be telling you this, but we already got your plane ticket for tomorrow. I thought you were coming!

Ticket? Ivanna looked over at me as I read the message, her panic shifting between me and the crowd. This was already planned. There was never a choice for me to stay, and I chugged my champagne to keep from shouting.

Tonight was supposed to be special; it was supposed to be about a new Alejandro. Yet everything started to feel backwards, regressing into something I didn't like.

I caught Alejandro spying at my text as I shut my phone off, sticking it back into my clutch. He looked at me with equal parts suspicion and disappointment, as if the text message were the bane of his existence.

"I think that's Lin-Manuel Miranda!" Dean piped up with a nervous laugh, looping his arm around Henri's. "We'll let you two lovebirds be."

"Me, too," Ivanna excused herself. "I'm going to grab us some more drinks." She smiled kindly, stepping away as if to avoid a bomb.

Regrettably, we were alone.

All the attention was still on us, the party practically observing our every move as I turned to Alejandro, faking a smile.

"What the *hell* was that?" I brushed his arms with a pet that appeared to be kind. It wasn't though. I was pissed.

"I could ask you the same. You know these things can be arranged, so why not let this happen?"

"How about you *arrange* your trip around me? How does that sound?"

"Don't be ridiculous, Gemma."

"Ridiculous? You sauntering in with a slur and a big plan is what's ridiculous."

"Forget it. Why do you even want to stay here?"

"Maybe because it's my choice—a choice I thought I had. And why do you want to take me?" I questioned. "Do you really want me to be with you, or are you trying to keep me away from something?"

He didn't even waste a breath before hissing back.

"From *someone*," he possessively pulled me close to his body, my hip digging into his side. "Who just texted you?"

"None of your business. Who I message and who I speak to doesn't concern you." I pitched slightly higher as he turned to the crowd, looking for a reaction. I could have just as easily told him it was Ivanna, that she essentially spoiled his plans to take me away. I didn't bother, wanting to see his true feelings.

"I'm making it my business. I can't have you stay here. I can't have him near you."

"Goddamn you. I knew it. You don't get to decide that. You don't tell me where I go or what I do."

"Maybe not. But you staying says a lot more than you coming with me."

"It says that I can make my own choices. I won't ruin an opportunity just because you're feeling insecure."

"Bullshit," he snapped, for once looking angry at me. "I know better. I've seen it all, and if you stay here, you're asking for trouble."

"Why? Because of Parker?"

"Who else, Gemma? You think this is all some coincidence? You don't think he knew I was leaving soon, and that this was his chance to swoop in? He had an entire lifetime to do what he did, and now you're no longer his to have. You're mine."

"Have you thought to consider that my choice to stay has nothing to do with you or Parker? I take my opportunities seriously. You gave this to me, and now you're taking it back? I don't think so. I'm staying."

"Then you're staying at the penthouse. You can live there; you can be free."

"Free?" I laughed. "Free to do what? To be forced into a new home? That's not freedom, that's control," I argued back, no longer pretending to smile for the people around us. Alejandro was less than considerate, his feverish glare much more pronounced than his signature look.

"That's right. It is control. Something Parker doesn't know anything about. He never took control. He never took charge. I knew the moment I saw you that I needed you, and I've always been clear about that. So no, I won't apologize about being so direct."

"You don't know him, you don't get to judge him like that."

"The fuck I won't. He touched you... *you*... Gemma... and that is a line I cannot forgive. That goes for any man; if anyone ever touches you again—"

"Enough," I snipped. "Don't do that."

"Do what?" He barked, irritated.

"Don't project that onto him. He isn't touching me... he isn't hurting me." I controlled my anger to better soothe Alejandro, keeping myself calm. This wasn't just about Parker; this was about Alejandro's past and how he was stuck in an old desire to fix a problem we didn't have.

"Goddamn it, Gemma. What have I told you about being so stubborn?"

"Why do I care? It's me, baby... deal with it," I spat back just as callously as he did earlier today.

His head dug into my neck, scolding me like he wanted.

"Don't be so frustrating," his nose flared. "I'm not asking you to stay at the penthouse, I'm *demanding* it, and if you don't agree, then tell me I'm wrong. Tell me that I'm not yours, and that he had every right to touch you. Tell me I shouldn't fight for you, that I shouldn't be so fucking pissed that all I want to do is drag you into the dark, push you against the fucking wall, and claim you in the worst ways possible."

Either he wanted to scream at me, or possibly fuck me with punishment. Would he? I imagined so, hidden in the shadows, my Valentino dress ripped as he shoved me along a wall. This was his spell, a promise that trickled between my legs so many times before. I wouldn't fall for it, I couldn't.

"I need a drink, and don't even think about following me," I broke the impenetrable hold he had on my mind and body, not willing to concede or give up everything just because of his powerful effect on me.

He couldn't conceal his grimace.

"I'll be waiting…" he finally let out, lacing his words with a hunger that dug deep into my chest.

Alejandro tugged on the cuff of his suit as I left to lose myself into the crowd. A group of suited men approached his side, distracting him just like I needed in order to get away.

My face was warm with the rush of blood as I leaned against a small corner bar nearby, desperate for anything I could get.

"A glass of merlot," I requested, glancing up at the tall, dirty blonde bartender.

"Right away," he smiled, his hair combed neatly to the side, his green eyes similar to, but not as mesmerizing as Parker's. The irony of this thought didn't escape me, as I was confronted immediately.

"Do you want to take him too?" An annoyed huff bristled to my right.

"Why? Do you have your camera ready?" I turned to face Camilla, who rested her champagne on the bar by my side.

"Hope that didn't cause too much trouble for you. It just hurts to see though, doesn't it?" She pulled her hair behind her ear, mocking a sincerity that irked me.

The guilt I once felt for hurting her was now replaced with the desire to toss another drink in her face. What Parker and I did was terrible, and I could own that, but this reaction, this destructive spread of her leaked photo would have a much longer effect than I could even imagine.

"Whatever masochistic pleasure you got by taking that photo isn't worth the trouble you've caused. Trust me, you've backed yourself into a corner, because Alejandro is dying to rectify what was done. And if New York Prestige insists on having any relationship with Alejandro in the future, you better believe that requests will be made." I threatened her career, flaunting the pull Alejandro had on the magazine. If we wanted her out, we could make it happen, or more so, I could make her life a living hell. But I didn't want any of that, all I wanted was for us to stay away from one another.

"There is always something bigger, Gemma..." she warned, unfazed by my bluff, "and trust me when I say this, I'm a much better journalist than I am a photographer. If you think I can't dig up dirt on either you or Alex, then you have grossly underestimated me." She lifted her champagne, excusing herself from the bar. "I'll be watching you both." She half-smiled before turning to leave, "Enjoy the party."

I only had a moment to process her words, to feel a new wave of concern wash over me, as a glass of merlot crashed along the table.

"Shit!" I hissed, standing up straight, my hands raised to my shoulders. Bloody dark wine and glass poured from the bar and all over my dress.

"Oh my god." The bartender hurried, lifting a clean rag from below the counter. "I am so sorry, I..." he babbled, quickly handing me a bottle of club soda. "Let me," he said unfinished, rushing to my side, dabbing my dress in a fit of panic.

I blinked, still shocked as Camilla looked back, smiling at the ironic scene.

"It's ok," I took an accompanying rag and club soda. "I'll take care of it." I dabbed along my chest, blotting the darkened spots to no avail. The man persisted though, clearly in a haze, kneeling to my side to dab along my hips.

"I-I can't apologize enough..." he stuttered, reaching for my thighs. His efforts were kind, but inappropriate, not fully realizing how his touch felt along my body.

"Thank you, but that's enough." He continued to dab the cloth along my thigh, pressing harder against my skin. "Enough!" I yelled, as his body suddenly lifted from the ground against its own volition.

I screamed from shock, at the sheer speed and strength that warped the bartender into a spinning blur.

"She said *enough!*" Alejandro slammed the man onto the top of the bar, twisting his vest before firmly wrapping his hands around his neck, pushing into it with all his weight.

"Alejandro, stop!" Ivanna ran to our side, reaching for his back but unable to get his attention.

"What don't you fucking understand?" he growled, emitting a misty haze of spit from the sharpness of his question.

I blinked frantically, stuck in a moment; fixated on the sight of his hands, strangling the man's neck. He squeezed and squeezed, until his knuckles dissipated of color, matching my pale and queasy cheeks. The bartender's face went from white to burgundy, his forehead bulging with a pulsing vein, as another bottle of wine fell to the floor. His throat began to collapse on itself.

"Alejandro, let go of him. Gemma, help me." Ivanna looked at me, but I said nothing.

I stumbled back, stroking my neck, calming the rise of fear that clogged the path of air I so desperately needed. Everything echoed as I tried to look away, but couldn't, seeing both Alejandro and a memory that scorched itself up from my head and down to my lungs.

I wish he knew, but he didn't.

No one did.

And regrettably, I was there again, young and scared, awoken with the cold hands that engulfed my little neck. Every sense of awareness, every anxious sound of screaming, of thunder, of terrifying noises hurled this moment to the forefront of my mind, this moment triggering the memory of when my father left and Claire desperately entered my room.

She couldn't stop him from leaving, but she could stop us from feeling the pain of his absence, tricking him with the guilt to stay, to keep us safe. I never understood it, and how could I? And for what? A man? To keep him? And now I carried this secret, the reason why I ran to the dark, why I hid in the closet.

I wasn't the woman in the Valentino dress anymore, instead, I was the little girl in the pink pajamas, screaming for help as my father pulled Claire away with a strong sweeping slap. I tried to fight it back but was unable to resist the single tear that broke loose from my eye.

"Alejandro!" I finally shouted, the entire crowd focused on the scene as the bartender kicked his legs. Alejandro continued, pinning him against the bar, his back crushing shards of broken glass.

"Fuck you…" Alejandro gargled towards the man, whose words began to choke out into desperate gasps of air.

"Stop!" I commanded. "Alejandro, listen to me!" I latched onto his arm, the whites of his eyes bright and full, consuming the stain of his red, tortured face as I viciously pulled him away. The bartender fell to his knees, grasping onto Ivanna for help as she lifted him to his feet. "Look at me!" I begged, his attention switching back and forth as security appeared. "You need to stop!"

"I won't stop!" He silenced me with a shout. "I won't sit here and watch a man hurt you, not him, not Parker!" He slammed his fist onto the bar, displacing the smattering of broken glass against his hand. Everyone stepped back as he began to bleed, but he didn't care, not about the pain, not about the crowd.

"No," I whimpered, stuck in a trance of who we were, of what I saw. "We can't do this anymore. This isn't about Parker, it's about you!"

"Me?" he questioned. "It's not about me. He *fucking* touched you, Gemma. *He* came into our world and tried to steal you away, and if he won't stop, then I won't stop either." Panic filled his eyes, his own past seeping through like boiled ooze, toxic and hurtful, not suitable to be kept inside anymore. A moment passed before

Alejandro whispered, "Tell me it didn't mean anything… tell me, Gemma…"

I looked over at the broken glass, at the judging crowd that watched our moves. The bartender was gone, but his presence remained in my mind, the struggle for his breath, the bulge in his eyes. He was one of the many people who felt the effects of mine and Alejandro's relentless hurt. We hated where we came from, and for some reason that's what drew us together: a volatile, eruptive, resentful couple.

This wasn't an authentic connection, this was an attachment to trauma, an addiction to be rescued, to avoid the fear we carried. Yes, he was the thrill that opposed Parker's predictability, but what was the cost, if not the cancer that plagued our lives and the lives of those around us?

"I have feelings for Parker…" I confessed, spilling out the truth neither of us wanted to know in this moment. "I felt something when he kissed me, and I kissed him back."

"That's not true."

"It is. It has been. No matter how much I like you, I can never give you what you want." I replied in the unbearable silence that followed, feeling the aftershock of his violence. I didn't want to relive that. I didn't want to see it or speak of it, and that's what he begged from me. I stared up at him, my heart shattering at the realization. I had feelings for Alejandro, deep unshakable feelings. But were they healthy? Were they real? "I can't go with you, and I can't be with you."

"No… don't say that." He stared vacantly at me.

"We're done…" I shot him a long and pained look, unable to stay without sobbing.

I turned to leave, but not before he could reach my wrist, the heat of his blood meeting my flesh as he pulled me into his arms, his eyes sobered, imprinting themselves into me.

And then, without question, without resistance, he kissed me, a long and desperate kiss that both soothed and hurt my lips. I couldn't say anything, not that I would try as he pulled away with the most hurtful expression.

"We'll never be done," he asserted with tears in his eyes. "And I swear there will be a day that I kiss you again, that I'll come back for what's mine. These three months are for you… they are borrowed, not stolen. And when I come back, it's to make this right."

"Don't say that," I begged, clutching at my throat, my elbows pressed into my sides; his goodbye wasn't truly a goodbye, but a warning.

"I will," he said quietly. "Because when you think of me at night, of our kiss on the roof, remember that what you felt was real, and that I'll be thinking of it too. This was always bigger than us, we are forever." His last words slipped out as he let me go. "I'm taking you from Parker… and there's not a goddamn thing he can do to stop me." My arms washed over with a chill that soon turned into heat, as not a single word was said, but felt all over my body. He finally allowed me to turn around, to take the first steps of walking away, to make my way through unsuspecting guests who knew nothing about what just happened at the bar, but showed no pity with their high arched brows and elongated whispers.

I didn't owe anyone anything, I only owed myself the life I dreamed of—absent of Claire, of any imperfect memory—to finally have what my heart always desired. Right or wrong, healthy or toxic, I stood up for what I wanted, and I did so with the willing acceptance of the pain it could cause.

This was my choice.

This was my decision.

I pulled out my phone, wiping my tears as I opened a message to Parker, sending three simple words that felt so good.

GEMMA

I'm coming home.

Home. Parker was my home, an honest and true connection that I assured myself was the perfect choice, *my* choice. Things would be different, things would start new, not only with Parker, but with everything in my life. Each step I took confirmed this, turning the wheels in a new direction, as I promised myself that in time, I would forget about Alejandro.

When I walked out into the busy street, I was given a sign. Little drops of rain began to fall upon my skin, covering my body as I looked above, reminding me of the night at The Met so long ago.

Yes.

As I thought before, meanings *do* change, and feelings change as well.

Today was another instance of this, washing away the old, giving space to something new.

And as I hailed a cab, filled with the promise of hope, a looming cloud formed in the back of my mind. An invisible clock began to tick, counting backwards to the words that Alejandro warned me of, that were sealed with his blood that coated my wrist.

He swore it.

He would be back.

He would come for me.

And three months was all I had before those dark eyes would come searching for mine.

Balancing a bag of Mom's leftovers on my knee while holding a case of Gemma's favorite wine was no easy task, especially while fishing out the newspaper that sat wedged in my front door frame. I assumed it was for Gemma, so I tried not to bend it as I walked inside my pitch-black apartment.

"Hamptons treat you well?" the voice in my ear asked, piping through my AirPod as I muscled bags onto the counter.

"About as much as I deserved." I laughed, hiding the obvious shitstorm that was my vacation. What was I supposed to tell Quinn on the other line, the board of directors at Tri-Tech Security? That I confessed my love to the girl of my dreams, and how my then girlfriend essentially threatened revenge. Not something I wanted to mention.

"I figured you'd be celebrating. We're about to close the biggest security acquisition in history. You got the scotch we sent, right?"

"I'll have to check the mail room." I ignored, organizing the bags I brought in, pulling out a fresh bouquet of white tulips. *How do you say sorry?* I asked the florist in the small Montauk cottage before making my way back to the city. She recommended this bouquet, intended more for a friend than a lover. I wouldn't assume anything was happening with Gemma, but I could only hope, pray, beg the universe that someday I'd be giving her roses instead.

"Well, do that quick. It's an expensive bottle." Quinn argued as I pulled out a small vase, filling it with unfiltered Manhattan water.

"What? Is money tight after your multi-billion-dollar deal?"

"Ha. A deal—by the way—that you get all the credit for," Quinn gleamed on the other end of the phone. "Jesus, we're a security company, but not even we could dig up the dirt you found on our competition."

"Things tend to run smoother when you confront someone about their past… insider trading is no exception. Of course their CEO folded over." I arranged the white petals of the tulips without having any idea what I was doing.

"Just accept the credit. This was a manual job, one that only lawyers like you can do, sifting through stacks of documents for paper trails… it all paid off."

"Well, that's my job." I dried my hands, knowing that wasn't completely true. Blackmailing Tri-Tech's competition into selling their company wasn't really my job, but winning was. I didn't like doing it, but it got me closer to my goals, closer to the exchange I wanted.

"I know better, Mr. Jones. You did us a favor… and that's why we're returning it."

My phone chimed with a quiet bell, a reluctant interruption to my important call.

MOM

> Dad and I want to meet you and Gemma
> for dinner next week.

I scrunched my nose, checking the box of wine, worrying that a bottle had cracked as the dry waft of aged grapes hit me from behind. It was leaking all over a pie, its crust a lopsided, red wave.

"Shit," I groaned over the phone.

"Problems?" Quinn asked.

"Everything is a little… chaotic right now," I saw a missed text message from Gemma, sent over twenty minutes ago. She was on her way, and suddenly I became simultaneously nervous and excited.

I replied back to Mom.

PARKER

> I'm not sure if that's possible. What's the
> occasion?

"Sorry, what were you saying?" I removed my denim shirt, feeling already too hot in a plain white tee as I cleaned up the spilt wine. I didn't know when Gemma would be here, or where she was coming from, but I rushed to make things perfect before she got back.

"We looked into Alex Rivers like you requested. Sent a few of our men down to Jalisco to *fix* some security systems that conveniently went down."

"Good timing."

"I agree. It's not as hard as you think when you throw a little cash around. People like to talk."

"Did it cost more than the scotch you sent?"

"Maybe. It sounds bigger in pesos than it does in U.S. dollars."

My phone chimed again as I pulled out a bottle of broken merlot. I let out a muted groan, feeling gut-punched by the random text that appeared.

CAMILLA

Your girlfriend just left the party.

Party? I didn't like how that sounded, especially coming from Camilla. That girl had eyes everywhere, and I didn't want her around Gemma, let alone tracking her.

PARKER

Don't text me about Gemma.

CAMILLA

Sorry! Thought you'd appreciate it... considering that all of New York knows who she is now. Don't you want to keep your precious Butterfly safe?

PARKER

What the fuck does that mean?

I leaned against the cool counter, flipping on the light switch in the living room, half-expecting Mila to be sitting there, giving me the evilest of looks.

"So what did you find out, Quinn?" I stared down at the counter, discovering a small, brown hair tie of Gemma's. A loose strand of auburn hair wrapped around its center, a coiled piece of the woman who I missed so much. I couldn't wait to see her, and what little time apart we had after the Hamptons already felt like an eternity.

"Well, we discovered much more than we ever expected. You wanted us to dig into his family life, but fuck, I never thought we'd actually strike oil."

"Is that so?"

"Mhmm. Turns out Mr. Rivers is very good at keeping secrets, but we found the perfect canary to sing. I got some details that you're going to enjoy."

> **MOM**
>
> We want to go out and celebrate you and Gemma! You're finally a couple!

Really, Mom? I tried not to sigh with Quinn on the phone, Mom's preemptive dinner plans probably stretched all the way to a wedding reception.

"You know, Mr. Jones, we can meet if you want." Quinn's voice hopped over in a glitch, his phone hooking up to his car.

"Name a place."

"How about Campbell? I'm catching a train to Pennsylvania afterwards to meet family."

I received another text while making my way around the counter, tossing my soppy, red rag into the sink. Quinn shouted out his window, complaining about some traffic near The Met.

> **CAMILLA**
>
> Don't tell me you didn't get my gift, Parky? Didn't you see the paper at your door?

A car horn blared on the other end of the line as I went back to the newspaper, reading the headline that I once was so careful not to crease. I thought it was a goddamn joke.

"What the fuck?" I barked out loud, rushing to open a shitty copy of The City Times, my panic evolving into sheer horror as I flipped to a full spread page that featured an overblown photo of the back of my head.

"You there, Park?" Quinn dropped the formality of my name, my non-response an aggressive silence.

"*Rough Waters for Superstar Alejandro Rivera-Marquez,*" read the headline to a photo of Gemma, my face concealed as I leaned down and kissed her. I couldn't believe it, it was us at the Hamptons, our first true kiss, printed in some low-grade ink, like a poorly made family photo.

I scanned the page.

"*Alejandro's latest love interest, Gemma Rose Harrison, has just been spotted in an undisclosed location, getting cozy with the hottest mystery man ever. Photos emerge just a day before Alex had announced his exclusivity with Gemma Harrison, leaving fans wondering what will happen next during this tumultuous time.*"

"Sorry, Quinn… I, uh, cut my finger." I stuttered, re-reading the article, missing some parts, feeling rushed for no good reason. My name wasn't listed anywhere, leaving me to believe that Camilla only wanted to warn me, but punish Gemma. The house was so eerily quiet now, my boots echoing in the kitchen as I paced. I quickly wrote Camilla back.

PARKER

What the fuck did you do?

CAMILLA

Just told the truth… Something you
should have done a long time ago.

PARKER

The truth is, you ever get in Gemma's
way, and you'll answer to me.

CAMILLA

Oh. I like it when you talk like that.
Promise me so I'll know you mean it.

I tried not to throw my phone at the wall as I went back to the paper, its stupid headline like needles to my eyes. *Alejandro Rivera-Marquez?* I hated that he was the center of her even being in this article, that she was just the collateral damage of his bullshit. But most of all, I hated the label he gave them two. *Exclusive?*

"Well, Mr. Jones, like I said, we can meet if you want. This information may be better said in person than over the phone. In fact, I can even arrange for you to go to Jalisco if you'd like, and actually, there is someone there who would like to talk to you."

"Me?" I asked, stopping at the odd mention that anyone from Jalisco would even know who I was.

"Yes. You, specifically. I can get you there, and we'll pretend that you're one of our own."

My phone chimed again.

MOM

Don't blow this Parker... Gemma is like a daughter to me, and you gotta protect what you two have. I've already told you kids before, it's true love.

I scrunched my face as Quinn silently made his way through traffic, re-reading Mom's message.

True love?

God, that was so different than what I heard as a child, encouraged to run towards love, rather than away from it, to protect it, not to be scared of it.

I wanted what my parents had, not what Claire warned me of, and honestly as Mom implied, Gemma was already family. We all loved her, but no one, and I mean no one, could ever love her as much as me.

"How big is this information?" I asked, assessing the power of this potential back up plan to Alex Rivers.

"Let's just say, it changes everything for him. If you want to get rid of Alex Rivers, this will do it."

Just then, the door unlocked behind me, stilling my answer as I looked back and calmed my eyes.

It was my Gemma.

Dressed like a dream, a surreal and delicate goddess, with tears in her eyes and heels in her hand.

And as she looked at me, her expression pouted from the night, I knew that things for us wouldn't be easy, and that there'd be more storms ahead before there would ever be sunshine.

But I didn't care.

I knew my answer to Quinn as Gemma dropped her

heels and rushed into my chest, collapsing herself into my arms for the most desperately needed hug.

I held her, knowing I'd keep her here as long as I could, against the odds; against Camilla; against the press; and most of all, against Alex Rivers, who I'd undoubtedly destroy if he ever found his way back into our lives.

This was for us.

"Count me in," I whispered to Quinn, my face dug into Gemma's hair, "I'll do whatever it takes."

Hang tight, Butterfly,
Mine to Keep series book 3
is on its way...
I promise.

Parker

* * *

LEARN MORE AT

https://www.vivianmae.com/minetokeep

***

Did you enjoy Promise and Punishment? Did you know reviews/ratings help indie authors (like myself) be noticed by more readers?

If you enjoyed this book, please spread the love on your favorite platform with a review! It can be short and sweet, or anything you wish. Thank you for reading.

***

Subscribe to my newsletter for exclusive updates, new releases, reveals, and more: https://www.vivianmae.com/newsletter

Want to discuss your reading? Join my new Facebook reader group: https://www.facebook.com/groups/vivianmaebabes

Bonus Content

Want bonus content from Promise and Punishment?

Please be aware, if you have not read Promise and Punishment *(if you made it here, I'll assume you did)* please know this is your spoiler warning!

Visit the page below for some extra goodies!
https://www.vivianmae.com/PP-bonus

Another book down and I want to thank my ARC team! I love seeing our community continue to grow. You are not just my rock, but the group I can turn to at any point. You care immensely and I couldn't see myself doing this journey without you by my side. It's an honor to grow with you!

I want to make a special thank you to Drita, who is my new admin and has encouraged me to open up my Facebook reader group for my ARC team and for my readers. You've been with me since before Burning Little Secrets came out, you've been such an impactful support to me and I cannot thank you enough for not only being my admin, but being my friend, and being there no matter what. Sincerely, I appreciate and love you!

Is it cheesy that I always want to make sure I thank my husband? Oh well, here goes. Mr. Mae… yes, that's you. Thank you.

That's all!

Kidding… thank you for not just riding this journey, but for practically giving up your social life to be here with me, to stand by my side as we figure out this crazy dream. We went from contemplating writing stories as we took a walk back in 2020, to actually connecting with readers across the world. How amazing is that! There have been readers thanking me for writing my stories, and each time I receive an email from a reader who relates to our character's struggles, I think of you. I think of you, because we're in this together, we have sacrificed a lot of our time and energy together to make something worthwhile, not only for ourselves, but for our readers.

I am proud of us. I love you entirely.

About the Author

Vivian Mae is a Latina indie author, living out of Phoenix, AZ who writes sexy contemporary romance for her naughty readers.

She is married to her best friend, fulfilling her own trope of best friends to lovers.

When she isn't writing, you can find her laughing alongside her husband, binging trashy TV, sneaking chocolates, reading her favorite naughty novels, and dreaming about pizza and wine.

Subscribe to my newsletter for exclusive updates, new releases, reveals, and more: https://www.vivianmae.com/newsletter

Follow me on Facebook, Instagram, Pinterest. Better yet, tag along on my daily Instagram Stories for a peek into my daily shenanigans.